He shone as brightly as any star. Everything about him flashed and shimmered, from the golden streaks in his dark brown hair, the dangerous gleam in his challenging blue eyes, and the lean hard lines of his pugnaciously handsome face to the white flash of his take-no-prisoners grin. Though the men appealed in different ways, Sir Kenneth Sutherland could rival Gregor MacGregor for the title of most handsome man in Scotland, and she suspected he knew it.

Sir Kenneth exuded confidence and brash arrogance. He probably thought she would fall at his feet just like all the other young, starry-eyed ladies seemed to be doing. But she was no longer young, and the stars had been wrenched from her eyes a very long time ago.

Still, she felt an unmistakable thrill shooting through her veins, a spark of excitement that she hadn't felt in a very long time. It was probably her temper. He seemed to bring out a heretofore unknown streak of combativeness in her.

It was the way he looked at her. Confident and arrogant, yes, but also provoking. As if he were daring the world to come at him. As if he were always trying to prove something. He didn't think she could resist him and was daring her to try.

"Running away again, my lady?" he taunted softly. "This time I might have to come after you."

BY MONICA MCCARTY

THE Recruit

A HIGHLAND GUARD NOVEL

MONICA McCARTY

BALLANTINE BOOKS • NEW YORK

A Ballantine Books Mass Market Original

Copyright © 2012 by Monica McCarty

Published in the United States by Ballantine Books, an imprint of The Random House Publishing Group, a division of Random House, Inc., New York.

BALLANTINE and colophon are trademarks of Random House, Inc.

ISBN 978-0-345-52841-4
eISBN 978-0-345-53599-3

Cover illustration: Franco Accornero

Printed in the United States of America

www.ballantinebooks.com

9 8 7 6 5 4 3 2 1

Ballantine mass market edition: November 2012

To my husband, Dave,
who thinks the best wedding gift to ensure a long and
happy marriage is a gag and earplugs (I bet you can guess
which spouse gets to wear which!). With romance like
that, I think my career choice is self-explanatory.
But back to the book . . . Every team needs a utility guy.
After fifteen years in baseball, a good portion of which
was spent in that role, this one's for you!

ACKNOWLEDGMENTS

The fact that you are reading this book about seven months after I finished the first draft is a testament to the incredible team of people I have at Ballantine who crank up the wheels of publishing to warp speed. A huge thanks to my editor, Kate Collins, the copy editors, proofers, and everyone in production for all the hard work in doing so, and to Junessa Viloria for keeping it all on track. To Lynn Andreozzi and the Art Department for outdoing themselves yet again with my favorite—and sexiest—cover to date.

Thanks also to Annelise and Andrea for keeping the business side of everything running smoothly so I can concentrate on the writing.

And finally, to Jami for sharing the highs and lows on a daily basis.

THE HIGHLAND GUARD

Tor "Chief" MacLeod: Team Leader and Expert
   Swordsman
Erik "Hawk" MacSorley: Seafarer and Swimmer
Lachlan "Viper" MacRuairi: Stealth, Infiltration, and
   Extraction
Arthur "Ranger" Campbell: Scouting and Reconnaissance
Gregor "Arrow" MacGregor: Marksman and Archer
Magnus "Saint" MacKay: Survivalist and Weapon Forging
Eoin "Striker" MacLean: Strategist in "Pirate" Warfare
Ewen "Hunter" Lamont: Tracker and Hunter of Men
Robert "Raider" Boyd: Physical Strength and Hand-to-
   Hand Combat
Alex "Dragon" Seton: Dirk and Close Combat

FOREWORD

The year of our lord thirteen hundred and nine. Three years ago, Robert the Bruce's bid for the Scottish throne and the torch for Scotland's independence had been all but extinguished. But against nearly insurmountable odds, with the help of his secret band of elite warriors known as the Highland Guard, Bruce has waged one of the greatest comebacks in history, retaking his kingdom north of the Tay. In March, King Robert holds his first Parliament and enjoys a brief reprieve from battle following a much-needed truce.

But problems with his barons will not keep England's King Edward II occupied forever. The truce is pushed back twice, but eventually the call to muster at Berwick-upon-Tweed and march upon the rebel Scots goes out.

With the English ready to invade and war looming, Bruce's new kingship will face its first big test, and once again he will rely on the extraordinary skills of his Highland Guard to defeat his enemies—both English and Scot. Bruce's kingship may have divided a nation, but he hasn't given up hope of rallying all Scots—even those still loyal to the English—under his banner. But winning their loyalty may prove his biggest challenge yet.

Prologue

September 1306
Ponteland Castle, Northumberland, English Marches

Dear God, who could it be at this hour?

Mary's heart was in her throat as she hurried down the torchlit stairwell, tying the belt of the velvet robe she'd donned over her night-rail. When you were married to one of the most hunted men in Scotland and the man hunting him was the most powerful king in Christendom, being awakened in the middle of the night to the news that someone was at the gate was sure to provoke a certain amount of panic. Panic that proved warranted when Mary entered the Hall, and the person waiting for her turned and tossed back the rain-sodden hood of her dark wool huque.

Her heartbeat slammed to a halt. Though the woman's long, golden hair was hidden beneath the ugliest head covering she'd ever seen and her delicate features were streaked with mud, Mary knew her in an instant.

She stared in horror at the face that so mirrored her own. "Janet, what are you doing here? You shouldn't have come!"

England was no place for a Scot—man or woman—with ties to Robert Bruce. And Janet, like Mary, had too many to count. Their eldest sister had been Robert's first wife; their eldest brother had been married to Robert's sister; their four-year-old nephew, the current Earl of Mar, was being hunted with Robert's queen, and their niece was Robert's only heir. King Edward of England would love nothing more than to get his hands on another daughter of Mar.

Hearing the censure in Mary's voice, her younger-by-two-minutes twin sister flashed her an unrepentant grin and put her hands on her hips. "Well that's a fine welcome after I've sailed around Scotland and ridden nearly ten miles in nonstop rain on the most disagreeable old nag known to man—"

"Janet!" she interrupted impatiently. Though her sister might seem oblivious to the danger, Mary knew she was not. Whereas Mary chose to face reality straight on, however, Janet preferred to run right over it and hope it didn't catch up to her.

Janet pursed her mouth the way she always did when Mary forced her to slow down. "Why I've come to take you home, of course!"

Take her home. Scotland. Mary's heart clenched. God, if only it were so simple.

"Does Walter know you're here?" She couldn't believe their brother would have sanctioned such a dangerous journey. Mary's gaze ran over her sister in the candlelight. "And what in heavens are you wearing?"

Mary should have known better than to ask two questions, as it gave her sister a chance to ignore the one she didn't like. Janet smiled again, pulled back her dark wool cloak, and spread the skirt of the coarse brown wool gown wide, preening as if it were the finest silk, which, given her fashion-loving sister's penchant for wearing exactly that, made her current choice of attire even more remarkable. "Do you like it?"

"Of course, I don't like it—it's horrible." Mary wrinkled her nose, admittedly sharing more than a little of her sister's love for fine things. Were those moth holes? "With that old-fashioned wimple, you look like a nun—and an impoverished one at that."

Apparently that was the right thing to say. Janet's eyes lit up. "Do you think so? I did my best, but I didn't have much to work with—"

"Janet!" Mary stopped her before she could get going again. But God, it was so good to see her! Their eyes met, and her throat started to close. "You shouldn't be h-here."

Her voice broke at the last, and all traces of Janet's feigned good humor fled. A moment later Mary was enfolded in her sister's arms. The tears she'd managed to hold back for the six horrible months since her husband had abandoned her to this nightmare came pouring out.

"You'll be safe here," he'd said offhandedly, his mind already on the fight ahead. John Strathbogie, Earl of Atholl, had decided on his path and nothing would stand in his way. Certainly not her. The child bride he'd never wanted, and the wife he barely noticed.

She'd swallowed what little pride she had left and asked, "Why can't we go with you?"

He'd frowned, the impossibly handsome face that had once captured her young girl's heart turning on her impatiently. "I'm trying to protect you and David." The son who was nearly as much of a stranger to him as his wife. Seeing her expression, he sighed. "I'll come for you when I can. It is safer for you in England. Edward will have no cause to blame you if things go badly."

But never could they have imagined just how badly things would go. He'd left so confident, so certain of the righteousness of his cause and eager for the battle ahead. The Earl of Atholl was a hero, always among the first to lift his sword to answer freedom's call. He'd fought in nearly every major battle in the past ten years over the long war for Scotland's independence. For the cause he'd been imprisoned, forced to fight in Edward's army, had his son held hostage for more than eight years, and had his lands on both sides of the border forfeited (and eventually returned). But none of that had stopped him from answering the call again, this time to take up her former brother-in-law Robert Bruce's bid for the throne.

But after suffering two catastrophic defeats on the battle-field Robert's army was on the run. As one of only three earls who'd witnessed Bruce's coronation and joined the would-be king in his rebellion against Edward of England, her husband was one of Scotland's most hunted men.

But so far Atholl had been right: Edward had not turned his vengeful eye on the wife and son the "traitorous earl" had left behind. The son who'd been taken from her before he was six months old to be raised in an English court and had only been returned earlier this year on the condition that he remain confined to their English lands. But how long could they continue to escape Edward's wrath and the taint of Atholl's treason? Every day she feared looking out the tower window and seeing the king's army surrounding them.

She was so tired of living in fear all the time, trying to be brave. She cried against her sister's shoulder, letting the emotions that she'd fought so valiantly to contain unfurl in hot, choking sobs.

"Of course I had to come," Janet said, murmuring soothing words until her tears abated. Only then did she grab Mary by the shoulders and hold her back to look at her. "What have you done to yourself? You are as thin as a reed. When was the last time you ate?"

She sounded so much like their mother—gone nearly fif-teen years now—that Mary almost smiled. Despite being the younger of the two, Janet had always been the protector. Throughout the disappointment and disillusionment of Mary's marriage, the taking of her son, and the deaths of their parents, sister, and brother, Janet had been the one to dry Mary's tears.

She hadn't realized just how terribly alone she'd felt until the moment she'd seen Janet standing before the fire, soak-ing wet and wearing odd clothes, but *here*.

Without waiting for Mary to answer, Janet took charge, calling for one of the servants to bring them some wine, bread, and cheese. Looking back and forth between the two nearly identical faces, the girl didn't hesitate to follow Janet's bidding. Mary could only smile as she found herself seated beside her sister with a large platter of food in front of her a few minutes later. Janet had divested herself of her wet cloak and hung it by the fire to dry, but had yet to remove the wimple and veil, which, seeing the big wooden cross hanging around her neck, Mary assumed was meant to suggest she was a nun.

She looked at her sister again, the fear returning. "You shouldn't have come, Janet. Duncan will be furious that you have put yourself in danger." She almost hesitated to ask. "How did you manage to travel all the way from Castle Tioram to here without his help?"

Janet's mouth quirked. "I found a more sympathetic set of ears."

Their eyes met. It wasn't hard to guess who she meant. "Lady Christina?"

Their brother Duncan was married to Christina MacRuairi, known as the Lady of the Isles, the only legitimate heir to the Lordship of Garmoran. A powerful force in her own right, Christina wouldn't hesitate to defy their formidable brother if she believed in the cause.

Janet nodded. "It was her idea to dress like this. She provided the men and *birlinn*." Of course, Mary realized. Only Lady Christina's Islanders would have the seafaring skill to slip right under the nose of the English fleet. "We came ashore just north of Newcastle-upon-Tyne. From there I purchased a horse. Twelve pounds for an obstinate nag that must be older than me and isn't worth half that! The man will surely go to hell for taking advantage of a nun."

Janet was so outraged, Mary decided not to point out she wasn't actually a nun.

"It took me a few hours longer than it should have, but

I made it. I passed right by a party of English soldiers and not one of them gave me a second glance."

Mary was glad she was sitting down. Only her sister would talk about sailing hundreds of miles around Scotland through treacherous waters right through the heart of the English fleet, riding ten miles through war-ravaged country-side, and then confronting the enemy as if it were nothing. "Please do not tell me that you rode here alone?"

Janet looked at her as if she were daft. "Of course not. I had Cailin with me."

Mary groaned. Cailin was sixty years old if he was a day. Her father's former stablemaster had been married to their nursemaid, and Janet had had him wrapped around her little finger since they were two. He would protect them both to the death, but he was no warrior.

Janet smirked. "He wasn't too happy to have the top of his head shaved, but he makes a fine monk. I sent him to the kitchens to dry out and get something to eat while you gather your and David's things. We should leave as soon as we can. I brought a gown for you like mine, although I suspect it will be too big." She wrinkled her nose again at Mary's appearance. "Jerusalem's Temples, Mary, you look as pinched and woebegone as a half-starved sparrow." Trust her sister to not hold her tongue for the sake of vanity. Mary knew she'd lost weight, but she hadn't realized how much until she saw her sister's worried expression. "But it will have to do. I just brought a cloak for Davey; he's a bit young to be a monk."

Her son was nine, conceived on her wedding night when she was just fourteen and born while her husband was imprisoned in the Tower of London after his first rebellion. She hadn't seen her husband for nearly two years after they were married. It had been a harbinger of things to come.

She wanted nothing more than to jump at her sister's offer, and if it were just her, she would. She'd do almost anything to return to Scotland—almost. But she had David's future to think about. Atholl's rebellions against Edward had robbed their son of his childhood; she would not let them take his patrimony. Not if there was a chance they could escape this nightmare unscathed.

Mary shook her head, wanting to cry all over again. "I can't. I want to, but I dare not. If we attempt to leave England, Edward will consider us traitors, and David's claim to the earldom will be forfeit. Atholl will come for us when he can."

She had to believe that. Even with all that had happened, she couldn't believe he would leave them to face this alone.

Janet stilled, her big blue eyes growing round and wide. "You haven't heard?"

Something in her sister's voice alerted her; a chill spread over her skin like a thin sheet of ice. "Heard what?"

"Robert has escaped, fleeing to the Isles with the help of our brother and Lady Christina. But the queen's party was taken in Tain over a week ago. The Earl of Ross violated the sanctuary of St. Duthac's and had them arrested." Mary sucked in her breath at the sacrilege. "That is why I came."

The blood drained from Mary's face. "And Atholl?" she said numbly, though she knew the answer.

Janet didn't say anything. She didn't need to. Mary knew her husband would be with the women. He was always with the women. They adored him. He was a hero, after all.

But now it was over. Scotland's hero earl had been captured. Her heart squeezed. After all the disappointments and all the hurt, she still felt the pangs of the girlish love she'd once borne him. Those feelings had been crushed a long time ago, but the thought of her husband in chains resurrected whatever vestiges of those dreams that remained.

Why, John? Why did it have to end like this? She didn't

know whether she was talking about their marriage or his life. Perhaps both.

"I'm sorry," Janet said, putting a hand on hers. She had never liked Mary's husband, but she seemed to understand her feelings. "I thought you knew."

Mary shook her head. "We are alone here. Sir Adam comes when he can. But he was called to court nearly a week ago—" She stopped, realizing the timing was probably not a coincidence. Had he known?

Nay. Mary shook off the thought. Sir Adam Gordon had done everything he could to protect her and David the past six months, even becoming surety for her son's release. He was one of Atholl's closest friends. The two men had fought together for Scotland at Dunbar and Falkirk, and served time together in Edward's army in Flanders when they lost. Although the two friends had taken opposite sides over the issue of Bruce's kingship, with Sir Adam loyal to the deposed King John Balliol and siding with their former English allies against Bruce, she knew Sir Adam would do his best to keep them safe.

"We can't delay," Janet said. "Christina's men are waiting for us. We need to be there before dawn."

Still, Mary hesitated. Atholl's capture hadn't changed anything. Or perhaps it made it even more important that they not do anything rash. But waiting to see whether Edward's wrath would fall on them was a little bit like stepping into a cage with a hungry lion and hoping he didn't notice you.

What should she do? Mary had little experience making important decisions. First her father, and then her husband, had made them for her. She envied her sister's independence in a world ruled by men. Janet had been engaged twice, but both betrothals had ended in death.

Janet must have sensed her uncertainty. She took her by the shoulders and forced Mary to look at her. "You can't stay here, Mary. Edward has lost all reason. There are rumors . . ."

She stopped as if the words were too painful.

"What?" Mary asked.

Tears filled her sister's eyes. "There are rumors that he has ordered our niece Marjory to be hung in a cage atop the Tower of London."

Mary gasped. A cage? She could not believe it, even of Edward Plantagenet, the self-styled "Hammer of the Scots" and the most ruthless king in Christendom. Marjory, Robert's daughter by their deceased sister, was only a girl. "You must be mistaken."

Janet shook her head. "And Mary Bruce and Isabella MacDuff as well."

God in heaven! It was almost too horrible to imagine such barbarity—against women, no less. She swallowed, but a lump of horror had lodged in her throat.

Suddenly, her sister turned to the window. "Did you hear that?"

Mary nodded, and for the second time that night her heart jumped in panic. "It sounds like horses."

Was it too late? Had the soldiers she feared finally arrived? *A cage . . .*

The two women raced to the window of the peel tower, a square-shaped defensive structure that was common in the borders. It was dark and still pouring rain, but Mary could just make out the shadow of three riders approaching. It wasn't until they entered the circle of torchlight below the gate, however, that she saw the familiar arms and her lungs released its vicelike hold on her breath. She heaved a heavy sigh of relief. "It's Sir Adam."

But the relief was short-lived. If Sir Adam was here at this time of night, there was a reason, and given her current circumstances, it probably was not a good one.

Her husband's seneschal admitted him to the Hall a few minutes later. She barely waited for the door to close behind him before she rushed forward. "Is it true? Has Atholl been taken?"

Obviously surprised that she'd heard, he frowned. But noticing her sister behind her at the table, his surprise faded. "Lady Janet," he said with a nod of his head. "What are you doing here?"

Before her sister could answer, Mary asked him again. "Is it true?"

As he nodded, his rough, battle-weary face sagged. Sir Adam was only forty—the same age as Atholl—but the war had aged him. As it had them all, she realized. She was only three and twenty, but sometimes she felt as if she'd lived twice as long.

"Aye, lass, it's true. He's being brought to Kent for trial at Canterbury."

Mary sucked in her breath. In choosing Kent as the place of trial, King Edward was leaving little doubt of the outcome. Like many Scot nobles, Atholl had significant lands in England, including vast estates in Kent. As such he'd been forced to do homage to Edward for those lands. It was as an English subject that the Scottish earl would be tried.

She crumpled, knowing that the charming Earl of Atholl would not escape the noose this time.

She saw the knowledge reflected in Sir Adam's face. But she also saw something else. "What is it?"

His gaze slid to her sister's. "You shouldn't be here, lass. You can't let them see you." He looked back and forth between the sisters. "If I didn't know you so well, I'd have a hard time knowing who was who."

"Can't let *who* see me?" Janet said, echoing Mary's thoughts.

Sir Adam sighed and turned back to Mary. "That's why I came. I rode ahead to prepare you. Edward has sent his men to collect you and David."

Mary froze. She could barely get the words out. "We are being arrested?"

"Nay, nay. I'm sorry, I didn't mean to frighten you. The king merely wishes to see that you and Davey are provided for."

Janet made a loud scoffing sound. "'Provided for'? That's an interesting way of putting it. Is he 'providing for' our niece Marjory as well?"

Sir Adam could not hide his repugnance. "Edward is in a rage right now, but he will reconsider when he has calmed down. I cannot believe he would see a young girl put in a cage." His eyes met Mary's. "The king does not blame you and David for Atholl's actions. He knows you have been a loyal subject to him, and David is like a grandson to him, after the better part of eight years in Prince Edward's household. You and the boy will not be in danger."

"But what if you are wrong?" Janet said. "Would you bet my sister's life on the whim of Edward Plantagenet's temper?" The monarch's apoplectic fits of rage—a legacy of his Angevin ancestors said to be descended from the Devil—were well known. Janet shook her head. "Nay, I've come to take her home."

Sir Adam looked sharply at her. "Is it true, lass? Are you fleeing England?"

But Mary didn't answer his question. She looked up at him, silently begging him to tell her the truth. "Does the king mean to make my son a prisoner in another English household?"

She saw the flicker of uncertainty in his eyes. "I don't know."

Her chest squeezed painfully. Nine years had passed but it might have been yesterday, so sharp were the memories of having her baby ripped from her arms.

Mary made her decision. She would not—*could* not—let her son be taken from her again. The son who was already

more English than he was Scot. She held Sir Adam's gaze.
"Will you help us?"

He hesitated. She didn't blame him. She hated to ask so
much of him when he'd already done so much, but with
Edward's men right behind him, she didn't have a choice.

His moment of hesitation didn't last long. "You are determined to do this?"

She nodded. Atholl wasn't coming for them. It was up to
her now.

He sighed in a way that told her he did not agree but
recognized the futility of argument. "Then I will do what
I can to delay them." He turned to Janet. "You have a
means of transport."

Janet nodded. "I do."

"Then you'd best gather David and be gone. They will
be here any minute."

Mary threw her arms around him. "Thank you," she
said, blinking up at him through watery eyes.

"I will do whatever I must to see you safe," he said
heavily. Mary's heart swelled with gratitude. If only her
husband would have done the same. "I owe Atholl my life."

Though Sir Adam's father had fallen on the battlefield at
Dunbar, her husband's heroics had enabled Sir Adam to
escape. Once she'd been proud of her husband's feats of
bravery and battlefield prowess. But her pride hadn't been
enough for him. Admiring such a man from afar was very
different from being married to one.

She donned the garments Janet had brought for her—
which were indeed too big and hung on her like a
sackcloth—and went to wake her son. If her sister noticed
the wariness in the boy's eyes when he looked at his
mother, Janet didn't say anything. It would take time,
Mary told herself. But after three months, David still
pulled away from her touch. Perhaps if he didn't look so
much like his father it wouldn't hurt so much. But except

for having her light hair, the lad was the image of her handsome husband.

Fortunately, David didn't raise an objection to being woken in the middle of the night, covered in a scratchy wool cloak, and rushed out into the stormy night. Being raised in England as a virtual prisoner—albeit a favored one—had made him very good at keeping his thoughts to himself. *Too* good. Her young son was an enigma to her.

Cailin swept her in a big bear hug when he saw her. She had to bite back a smile. Janet was right; with his round, jovial face and equally hearty belly, he did indeed make a good monk.

Exchanging the horse Janet had purchased for two in her own stables—she would ride with Davey, and Janet would ride with Cailin—they set off toward the eastern seaboard.

It was slow and treacherous going, the road muddy and slippery from all the rain. The rain was too heavy to keep a torch lit, so it was also difficult to see. But far worse was the constant fear, the taut, heightened senses and frazzled nerve endings set on edge, as they sat readied on constant alert for the sounds of pursuit.

Yet with every mile they rode, some of the fear slipped away.

She knew they must be close when Janet confirmed it. "We're almost there. The *birlinn* is hidden in a cove just beyond the bridge."

Mary couldn't believe it. They were going to make it! She was going home. *Scotland!*

But as they crossed the wooden bridge over the River Tyne, she heard a sound in the distance that stopped her cold. It wasn't the pounding of hooves behind her that she'd feared, but a clash of metal ahead of her.

Janet heard it, too. Their eyes met for a fraction of an instant before her sister flicked the reins and jumped forward with a strangled cry.

Mary shouted after her to stop, but Janet, with Cailin behind her, raced ahead. Mary tightened her hold around her son in front of her and surged after her, plunging into the darkness, the sounds of battle growing louder and louder.

"Janet, stop!" she shouted. Her sister was going to get herself killed. Somehow the English must have found the Islesmen, and their sister-in-law's clansmen were fighting for their lives.

Fortunately, if Janet wasn't thinking rationally, Cailin was. He forced their horse to slow, enabling Mary and David to catch up to them.

Janet was trying to wrest the reins from the older man. "Cailin, let me have those." Mary was close enough to see the frantic wildness in her sister's eyes. "I have to go. I have to see."

"You'll not help the men any by getting yourself killed," Cailin said sternly—more sternly than Mary had ever heard him talk to her. "If you get in the way, they'll think about defending you, not themselves."

Janet's eyes filled with tears. "But it's my fault."

"Nay," Mary said fiercely. "It's not your fault, it's mine." And it was. She never should have let it get to this. She should have fled months ago. But when it was clear Bruce's cause was lost, she'd trusted her husband to come for them. Had he spared a thought for what would become of them, when he raced off to glory?

"Who is fighting, Mother?" David asked.

Mary looked into the solemn upturned face of her son. "The men who brought your aunt to us."

"Does that mean we aren't leaving?"

Her heart pinched, hearing the hint of relief in his voice. But could she blame him for not wanting to leave? England was the only home he'd ever known.

God, how they'd failed him!

She didn't answer him directly, but looked at her sister. "We have to go back before we are discovered."

They would never be able to make it to Scotland on their own.

"Don't give up yet, lass," Cailin said. "The MacRuairis know how to fight."

But how long did they dare wait?

The decision was made for them a few moments later when they heard the sound of horses coming toward them. The English were fleeing! But unfortunately, the soldiers were headed for the bridge, and they were right in their path.

"Hurry," Mary said. They raced back toward the bridge before they ended up in the middle of the fleeing Englishmen and the Islesmen, who from the sound of it were pursuing them.

She had just made it to the other side of the bridge when she heard Janet cry out behind her. Mary looked around just in time to see Cailin fall off the horse, landing with a horrible thud on the wood planks.

Everything seemed to happen at once. Janet pulled to a stop, jumping down in the middle of the bridge to help him. Cailin had landed facedown, an arrow protruding from his back. Mary glanced behind her sister, seeing the hillside they'd just escaped now swarming with men. The fierce war cries of the Islesmen pierced the night air. The pursuers had caught up with their prey, and the riverbank had become a battleground.

Mary yelled through the din of swords to her sister. "Leave him! You have to leave him." The English were heading straight for her, trying to evade the Islesmen. Janet was going to be trampled.

Their eyes met, spanning the distance of the forty or so feet that separated them. Mary knew Janet wouldn't leave Cailin. She was trying to lift him under the arms, but struggling under his weight.

Mary turned her horse, intent on forcibly dragging her sister off that bridge if she had to, when she thought she heard a voice shout "no" behind her. But then her horse reared as a terrifying boom shattered the stormy night.

She screamed, clenching David and holding onto the reins for dear life, trying not to slide out of the saddle. She'd nearly gotten the animal under control when a blinding flash of light crashed on the bridge before her. Lightning? And the strangest thunder she'd ever heard.

Oh God, Janet! She looked in horror as the bridge seemed to burst into a ball of flames and her sister disappeared from view. The last thing she remembered was holding her son in front of her as they pitched backward off the horse.

When she woke hours later, warm and dry in her bedchamber, at first she thought it had been a bad dream. But then she realized the nightmare had just begun.

Cailin was dead and her sister had vanished, presumed dead after being swept away in the river when the bridge collapsed. The voice she'd heard had been Sir Adam's. He'd arrived just in time to see her fall. David had been unharmed, but Mary's head had struck a rock, knocking her out cold, and her back was badly bruised.

But her injuries were the least of her problems. If not for Sir Adam their next few weeks would have been precarious indeed.

Protecting Mary from Edward's anger by the lie that she'd been forcibly taken by Bruce's men, Sir Adam made a plea to the king that she be allowed to recover before making her journey to London. Thus, it wasn't until November that she and David were brought before the king. She'd had nearly two full months with her son before he was once again taken from her and imprisoned in the Prince of Wales's household to serve as a yeoman.

She left court, returning to Ponteland (where she'd been ordered to remain) on the fourteenth of November, one week after the Earl of Atholl was hanged from an elevated gallows as befitting his "exalted" status—King Edward's cruel response to her husband's reminder of their kinship. Leaving the city, she was careful not to look up as she passed under the gatehouse of London Bridge, where her husband's head had been impaled on a spike beside those of the other Scottish traitors (or heroes, depending on which side of the border you lived on) William Wallace and Simon Fraser.

The handsome, gallant knight had raised his sword for the last noble cause. Mary had put her love—or was it youthful infatuation?—for Atholl behind her a long time ago, so the depth of her sorrow took her by surprise. But along with her sorrow was anger at what he'd done to them.

She was fortunate, it was said, not to be sent to a convent like the other wives and daughters of traitors. Her "loyalty," the king's fondness for her son, and Sir Adam's surety had saved her. If not for the vows she had made to herself, she would have welcomed the quiet solitude of a nunnery, free from the tumult of a war that had taken her father, brother, and now her husband. But she vowed to see their son restored to his father's earldom, and to never stop searching for the sister who in her heart she refused to believe was dead. The life she knew, however, was gone.

One

July 1309
Newcastle-upon-Tyne, Northumberland, English Marches

Mary handed the merchant the bundle that represented nearly three hundred hours of work and waited patiently as he examined the various purses, ribbons, and coifs with the same painstaking attention to detail he'd given the first time she'd brought him goods to sell nearly three years ago.

When he was finished, the old man crossed his arms and gave her a forbidding frown. "You did all this in four weeks? You had best have a team of faeries helping you at night, milady, because you promised me you were going to slow down this month."

"I shall slow down next month," she assured him. "*After* the harvest fair."

"And what about Michaelmas?" he said, reminding her of the large fair in September.

She smiled at the scowling man. He was doing his best to look imposing, but with his portly physique and kind, grandfatherly face, he wasn't having much success. "After Michaelmas I shall be so slothful I will have to buy an indulgence from Father Andrew or my soul will be in immortal danger."

He tried to hold his scowl, but a bark of laughter escaped. He shook his head as a doting father might at a naughty child. "I should like to see it."

He handed her the bag of coin they'd agreed upon.

She thanked him and tucked it into the purse she wore tied at her waist, enjoying the weight that dragged it down.

One dark, bushy eyebrow peppered with long strands of gray arched speculatively. "You wouldn't need to work so hard if you agreed to take one of the requests I've had for your work. Fine *opus anglicanum* embroidery like this is wasted on these peasants."

He said it with such disgust, Mary tried not to laugh. The customers who frequented his booth were not peasants but the burgeoning merchant class—people like him—who were helping to make Newcastle-upon-Tyne an important town.

The markets and fairs such as the one today were some of the best north of London. And John Bureford's booth, full of fine textiles and accessories, was one of the most popular. In an hour, it would be crowded with eager young women seeking the latest fashions from London and the Continent.

He picked up one of the ribbons, a plush ruby velvet on which she'd embroidered a vine-and-leaf motif in gold thread. "Even on these they notice. The ladies of the town are vying to be the first to secure your talents for a surcote or a wall hanging. Even the hem of a shirt might satisfy them. Let me arrange it; you could name your price."

She stilled, a flash of her old fear returning. Her voice dropped automatically to a whisper. "You did not tell them?"

He looked affronted. "I do not understand your wish for secrecy, milady, but I honor our agreement. No one needs to know it is you. But are you sure you won't consider a few select items?"

Mary shook her head. Preserving her privacy was worth more to her than the extra coin. Three years ago she'd been left on her own, frighteningly ill-prepared to deal with her new circumstances, with no more than a handful of pounds to her name. She could have gone to the king as others in her position were forced to do, but she feared drawing attention to herself. She knew the fastest way to find herself in another political marriage was to put demands on the royal coffers. She might have gone to Sir Adam—indeed, he'd offered to help—but she did not want to be beholden to him for more than she already was.

With the rents from the castle barely earning enough to pay the servants and keep her and her solitary attendant fed, she knew that she had to think of something. *What would Janet do?* She asked herself that often, as she began the daunting prospect of fending for herself.

As a sheltered young noblewoman with little education and few talents, her options were decidedly limited. About the only thing she knew how to do was sew. She and her sister had shared a skill with the needle, and though it held painful memories for her, she began to embroider small items like ribbons, coifs, and eventually purses—things that would not draw attention to the craftswoman.

Unfortunately, that part of her plan had not worked as well as she'd hoped and her "trinkets" had attracted attention. She, however, had not. Edward the son didn't seem to possess the same hatred toward her husband and the "Scot traitors" as his royal sire, and so far the new king had left her alone. She intended to keep it that way.

"I have all that I need," Mary said, surprised to realize that it was true.

It would have been easy to fall apart after losing her sister and husband, having her son taken away again, and finding herself a virtual prisoner in an enemy land. A bittersweet smile played on her mouth. No doubt Janet would have fought against her velvet chains and railed against the injustice every step of the way. But Mary had always been the more pragmatic of the two, coping with the way things were, not the way she wished them to be. She didn't waste time bemoaning things she could not change. The early disappointments of her marriage had prepared her for that.

Although her search for her sister had yielded frustratingly little, and her visits with her son were heartbreakingly few, she'd made a life for herself in England. A quiet, peaceful life, free from the destruction of war.

The constant danger that had been so much a part of her life with Atholl was gone, as was the hurt of being married to a man who barely noticed her. Without them, she felt as if a weight she didn't know she'd been carrying had been lifted off her shoulders. For the first time in her life she didn't have a father or a husband to control her actions, or her sister to protect her, and her confidence in her own decisions had grown. She discovered that independence suited her; she quite liked being on her own.

The days had taken on a predictable rhythm. She tended her duties as the lady of the castle, worked on her embroidery every extra hour she could find, and kept to herself. She'd made the best of her situation and found herself if not happy, at least content. About the only things she could wish for were news of Janet and more time with her son, and she hoped Sir Adam would have good news for her on the latter soon.

She didn't need to draw more attention to herself by taking on the additional work.

The merchant looked at her as if she'd blasphemed. "Need? Who speaks of need? One can never have enough coin. How am I ever to make a tradeswoman out of you if you talk like that?"

His outrage made her laugh.

The old man smiled back at her. "It is good to see you smile, milady. You are too young to hide yourself behind those dark clothes." She was only six and twenty, but she looked ten years older. Or at least she tried to. He grimaced.

"And that veil." He held up one of her ribbons. "You make these beautiful things for others and will not wear them yourself. Tell me this time you will let me find you something colorful to wear—"

Mary stopped him. "Not today, Master Bureford."

The drabness of her clothing, like her working too hard, had become a familiar refrain between them. But as everything else, her appearance was designed to draw little attention. How easily pretty could become plain. Black, shapeless clothing, thick veils and unflattering wimples in dark colors at odds with her coloring, long hours before the candlelight that cut into her sleep, and perhaps most of all the gauntness that pinched and sharpened her normally soft features. *Half-starved sparrow.* She recalled her sister's words with a wistful smile. If Janet were here, she'd put a pile of tarts in front of her and not let her up from the table until she'd gained two stone.

Mary could see the old man wanted to argue, but their difference in rank held him back.

"I should be leaving," she said, suddenly aware of the time. Dawn had given way to morning, and there were already people milling around the booths.

It was going to be another beautiful day. She'd come to quite love the north of England in the summer. The lush verdant countryside wasn't that different from the northeast of Scotland where she'd grown up at Kildrummy Castle. She pushed aside the pang before it could form. She didn't think of her life then. It was easier.

"Wait," he said. "I have something for you."

Before she could object, he ducked into the canvas tent that he'd set up behind the table, leaving her alone to watch his goods. She could hear him muttering as he tossed things around behind her and smiled. How he found anything in all those trunks and crates, she didn't know.

Unconsciously, her gaze scanned the crowds for a golden-blond head attached to a woman of middling height. She wondered whether she would ever be able to go where a crowd was gathered and not look for her sister—and not feel the resulting twinge of disappointment when she didn't find her. Sir Adam begged her to stop. She was only torturing herself, he said. But even if her searches had yielded nothing, Mary couldn't accept that her sister was gone. She would know . . . wouldn't she?

She turned at a sound, seeing that a mother with two small children had come up to examine a tray of colorful ribbons on the opposite side of the table. From their clothing, she could see that they did not possess the wealth of Bureford's typical customers. She guessed the woman to be the wife of one of the farmers. She was clearly exhausted. She held one child in her arms—a babe of about six months—and another by the hand, a little girl of three or four who was staring at the ribbons as if they were a stack of gold. When the child reached for one, her mother pulled her back. "Nay, Beth. Do not touch."

All of a sudden another little girl peeked out from behind her skirts and wrapped her chubby little fist around a handful of the ribbons. Before the mother could stop her, she turned and darted off into the crowd.

The young woman shouted after her in a panic. "Meggie, no!" Seeing Mary standing there and obviously assuming she was the merchant, she shoved the baby in her arms and put the little girl's hand in hers. "I'm sorry. I'll fetch them back for you."

It had happened so fast, it took her a moment to realize she was now holding two children. Mary didn't know who was more shocked, she or the children. Both the baby and the little girl were staring at her with wide eyes, as if they couldn't quite decide whether to cry.

She felt a small twinge in her chest. She remembered so precious little of those few months she'd had with David after he was born, but that look was one of them. It had terrified her. The *baby* had terrified her. She'd been scared of him crying, of every sound he'd made in his sleep, of how to hold him, of whether he was getting enough to eat from the wet nurse.

Of him being taken away from her.

She pushed the memory aside. That was a long time ago. She'd been so young. And now . . .

Now it was in the past.

But the twinge sharpened when she gazed into the baby's soft blue eyes. David was younger than this when he was taken from her, and she didn't think she'd held another baby since. She'd forgotten what it felt like. How they instinctively latched against your chest. The pleasant warmth, and the soft baby smell.

Apparently deciding she wasn't a threat, the baby gave her a big, gummy smile and started to babble at her like a sheep. "Ba, ba . . ."

Mary couldn't help smiling back at him. He—or she, it was impossible to tell at this age—was a cute little devil, with big blue eyes, a velvety cap of short brown hair, and bright, rosy cheeks. Brimming with healthy plumpness, he was quite an armful.

All of a sudden, she felt a tug on her hand. She looked down, having almost forgotten about the little girl. Apparently, she'd decided not to cry either. "He wants his ball."

Mary bit her lip. She thought she was too young to be talking, but the girl possessed a confidence Mary would have envied at her age. "I'm afraid I don't have one." She looked around, not seeing anything that resembled a toy on the table. Recalling the coins the merchant gave her, she dug in her purse and retrieved the small leather bag. "How about this?" Holding it up before the baby, she started to shake it and was rewarded when he flapped his arms and started to laugh. He grabbed for it, and she grinned as he mimicked what she'd done by jingling it up and down, albeit with far more enthusiasm. She hoped the bag was tied tightly.

The little girl—Beth—must have read her mind. "Careful he doesn't open it. He puts everything in his mouth—especially shiny things. He nearly choked on a farthing last week."

Mary frowned, realizing she hadn't thought of that. This little girl knew more about babies than she did.

She was also older than Mary had realized. "How old are you?"

"Fournahalf," she said proudly. Reading Mary's mind again, she added, "Da says I'm small for my age."

Mary noticed her cast another longing glance toward the ribbons. "It's all right," she said. "Would you like to hold one?"

The girl's eyes widened to enormous proportions and she nodded furiously. Not giving Mary a chance to reconsider, she immediately reached for the bright pink one embroidered with silver flowers. She took it between her tiny fingers so reverently Mary couldn't help smiling.

"You have an excellent eye. I think you've picked the prettiest of the bunch."

The child's smile stole her breath. Longing rose up hard inside her before she tamped it firmly down. *In the past* . . .

The mother returned in a flurry of excited breathing and excuses, the wee bandit clamped firmly by the wrist. "I'm so sorry." She placed the purloined ribbons back down on the table and relieved Mary of the baby with her newly free hand.

Mary was surprised by how much she wanted to protest. She felt suddenly . . . bereft.

Forcing the oddly maudlin moment aside, she managed a wry smile. "You seem to have your hands full."

The woman returned the smile, relieved by her understanding. "This is only half. I've three lads helping their da with the livestock." Suddenly, she noticed the bag the baby held in his hand. Her eyes widened like her daughter's had. "Willie! Where did you get that?"

"Don't worry," Mary said, taking it back. "I let him play with it." Anticipating a similar reaction to the ribbon in Beth's hands, she added, "I hope you don't mind. But I should like Beth to have this."

The woman started to protest that it was too much, but Mary insisted. "Please, it is a trifling, and she—" she stopped, her throat suddenly thick. "She reminds me of someone."

It hadn't struck her until now, but the girl bore a distinct resemblance to her and Janet when they were girls. Wispy blond hair, pale skin, big blue eyes, and fair, delicate features.

Seeming to sense the emotion behind the offer, the young woman thanked her and hustled her children away.

"I leave you alone for a few minutes and you are giving the merchandise away for free? That's it, I wash my hands of you. You will never be a tradeswoman."

Mary turned, surprised to see the merchant standing there watching her. Though his words were chastising, his tone was not. From the glimmer of sadness in his eyes, Mary could see that he'd seen more than she wanted him to.

She gathered the frayed ends of her emotions and bundled them back together. That part of her life was over. She'd been both a wife and a mother—even if neither had turned out the way she'd planned. There was no use dwelling on what was past. But the brief exchange sent a ripple of longing across the quiet life she'd built for herself, reminded her of all that she'd lost.

She might never be able to get David's childhood back, but she was determined to have a part in his future. The handful of opportunities she'd had to see him the past few years hadn't brought them any closer, but she hoped that would change. Her son would be leaving the king's household soon to become a squire, and Sir Adam was doing his best to see him placed with one of the barons in the north of England, close to her.

The merchant handed her a small wooden box.

"What is this?" she asked.

"Open it."

She did so and gasped at what she saw. Carefully, she removed the two round pieces of glass framed in horn and connected by a center rivet from the silky bed upon which they rested. "You found them!"

He nodded, inordinately pleased at her reaction. "All the way from Italy."

Mary held them up to her eyes, and like magic the world had suddenly become larger. *Occhiale*, they called them. Eyeglasses. Invented by an Italian monk more than two decades ago, they were still quite rare. She'd mentioned them once when she'd realized how much of a toll the long hours working by candlelight were taking on her eyesight. It was getting harder and harder to see the tiny stitches. "They are magnificent." She carefully placed them in the box and threw her arms around him, giving him a big hug. "Thank you."

He blushed, chortling happily.

Such displays of emotion weren't normal for her—at least not since she was a girl—and she was surprised at the emotion welling in her chest. She realized she felt more affection for the old merchant than she had for her own father.

Just for one moment, her arms tightened as if she would hold onto him for dear life.

Then, suddenly embarrassed, she pulled away. What must he think of her? But her usual reserve seemed to have deserted her. "How much do I owe you?" she asked.

He bristled, waving her off as if she'd offended him. "They are a gift."

She eyed him sharply. "Giving the merchandise away for free? You should be ashamed to call yourself a tradesman."

He chuckled at her attempt to sound like him. "It's an investment in future returns. How can you sew if you cannot see? I intend to make quite a healthy profit off you, milady."

Mary's eyes felt suspiciously damp. "Careful, old man, your reputation as a ruthless negotiator is in jeopardy."

His eyes seemed to be shining a little brighter than normal as well. "I shall deny every word. Now you'd best take yourself away from here, or mine isn't the only secret that will be in jeopardy."

With one more hug, Mary did as he bade.

Though she would have loved nothing better than to enjoy the bright sunshine by wandering around the fair for a while, she knew it was better if she did not. The instinct not to draw attention to herself went deep.

If there was a slight wistfulness in her heart after the exchange with the children and the merchant, she knew it would pass. She had everything she needed. If at times she felt as if she were missing something, she reminded herself to be grateful for what she had.

Finding the groomsman waiting for her where she'd left him, Mary mounted her horse and started on the long ride back to the castle.

With the silver in her purse, the sun shining on her face, and no longer the need to look over her shoulder, she felt a sense of peace that she would have thought impossible three years ago. Against all odds, the frightened, sheltered, overlooked wife of a traitor had built a new life for herself. On her own.

Mary's hard-won contentment turned to barely restrained excitement when she saw who awaited her on her arrival. Sir Adam! Did he bring news of her son? *Please, let him be squired nearby . . .*

She burst into the room. "Sir Adam, what news of—"

But the rest of the question fell abruptly from her lips

when she realized he had not come alone. Her eyes widened. The Bishop of St. Andrews? What was William Lamberton doing here? The former Scottish patriot, who most thought responsible for Robert Bruce's bid for the crown, had been imprisoned by the first Edward for over a year before making peace with the second last year and given partial freedom in the diocese of Durham. In her mind, Lamberton was inextricably connected to the war.

Unease wormed its way through her excitement. She suspected, even before she heard what he had to say, that the day she'd feared had just arrived.

After a quick exchange of greetings, it didn't take the men long to tell her what they wanted. Her legs wobbled. She fell to the bench, which was fortunately behind her, in shock. Just like that, the walls of the life she'd built for herself came crashing down.

Part of her had known this day would come. As the daughter of a Scottish earl and the widow of another—even one hanged for treason—she was too valuable an asset to ignore forever.

But she hadn't expected this. Nay, she couldn't do it.

She stared at Sir Adam, her fingers clenched in the black wool of her gown. "The king wishes me to go to *Scotland*?"

Her old friend nodded. "To Dunstaffnage Castle in Lorn. Bruce"—the Scottish barons who'd sided with the English refused to call him King Robert—"is holding the Highland Games there next month."

Mary knew the former MacDougall castle well. She'd been there once with her husband years ago on a visit to his sister who had married the MacKenzie chief and resided at Eileen Donan Castle, which wasn't too far away.

"You will be part of our truce delegation," the bishop added. Mary couldn't believe the king would grant the recently released prelate—and man so closely tied to Bruce—permission to go to Scotland and negotiate on his behalf.

It was like handing the prisoner the keys and telling him to make sure to lock up after himself. Unlike her, Lamberton didn't have a son in England to ensure his "loyalty."

"The king has granted permission for you to represent the young earl's interests," Sir Adam explained.

Mary eyed him sharply. Surely Edward had to see the futility in sending her to plead on her son's behalf for lands in Scotland? With a few notable exceptions such as the Balliols, Comyns, and MacDougalls, Robert Bruce had taken great care *not* to forfeit the lands of the earls and barons who still stood against him like Davey, in the hopes of eventually bringing them back into the fold and winning their allegiance. But neither would he recognize the claim—and the right to the rents—for those who refused to do him homage. Essentially, they were at a stalemate. Davey was a Scottish earl in name without the lands in Scotland to show for it.

Edward had to realize she would have little hope of success—not while David remained in England. There had to be another reason. "Is that all?"

Sir Adam's mouth thinned, unable to hide his displeasure. "He knows how fond Bruce is of you."

Ah, so that was it! Edward wanted her to spy. Aware that the bishop seemed to be watching her intently, she kept her expression impassive. "How fond he *used* to be of me. I have not seen my former brother-in-law in many years. Even were I inclined," which she was not, "he's hardly likely to confide in me."

"I told him as much," Sir Adam said with a shrug as if to say, *but you know the king*. Fortunately, she didn't, and had done her best to keep it that way. "But Edward is determined that a woman join our group. He thinks a feminine voice would set the right tone for our negotiations, and who better than Bruce's former sister by marriage?"

More like, who could be counted on to return? "So I'm to soften him up to accept Edward's terms, is that it?"

Lamberton couldn't quite bite back his smile at her blunt assessment. "In a manner of speaking, yes."

"I thought you would be pleased," Sir Adam said, studying her with a worried frown on his face. It was an expression she'd grown quite used to over the past few years.

"I am," she said automatically. She knew she should be. Three years ago she'd wanted nothing more than to go home. But she was surprised to realize there was a part of her that didn't want to go. A *large* part of her that didn't want to stir up painful memories.

There was nothing left for her in Scotland. Her brother Duncan had died with Bruce's brothers over two years ago in the failed landing at Loch Ryan when Bruce made his bid to retake his crown. All that remained of her family was her son and her nephew, the five-year-old current Earl of Mar, who had been captured with his mother, Bruce's sister, and the rest of the queen's party at Tain. But both of them were in England. Like her son, the young Earl of Mar was a favored prisoner in Edward's household.

But why now? Why after nearly three years had the king decided to notice her? Just when she'd found some small modicum of peace far from the battlefield of war and politics, he wanted to drag her back in. Resentment she hadn't even realized she had came bursting forward. Hadn't they taken enough from her? Why couldn't they just leave her alone?

Aware that both men were watching her with troubled expressions, and knowing she didn't have the words to explain what she was feeling, she attempted to cover her reaction. "I was merely hoping you'd brought other news."

Sir Adam guessed to what she referred. "The king is quite fond of David. He doesn't seem to be in any hurry to relinquish him. A decision as to which of his barons will have the Earl of Atholl as his squire has not been made. But I think there is a good chance Percy will win the honor."

Her fingers clenched even harder. It was almost too much to hope for. Lord Henry Percy, 1st Baron Percy, had just purchased the Castle of Alnwick in Northumberland. Her son would be so close. "Do you think . . . "

She couldn't bring herself to say the words.

Sir Adam finished for her. "I don't see any reason why you should not be allowed to see him as often as his duties permit. That is—" He stopped.

But she guessed what he was about to say. "That is as long as I do Edward's bidding."

He shrugged apologetically. "Davey—the earl—is most eager for you to go on his behalf."

Her heart leapt with embarrassing eagerness. "Did he say so?"

Sir Adam nodded. "He has not forgotten that it was you who petitioned the king two years ago to return the English lands that had been forfeited upon Atholl's death."

It was the only time she'd ever purposefully brought herself to the English king's attention. With the help of Sir Adam and Sir Alexander Abernethy, who'd raised the coin to pay off de Monthermer, who'd been temporarily given the earldom, her petition had been successful. Her son had half his patrimony—the English half.

If she'd ever had a thought to refuse, she knew she could not. Her son had never asked her for anything before. This was her chance to do something for him. He was nearly ten and three, and still almost a stranger to her. The divide between them would only widen as he approached knighthood. This might be her last chance to bring them closer.

It was time to hold to her vow to see her son restored to the earldom. And perhaps this was a chance to hold to her other vow as well. There was one question that had haunted her the past three years, despite the improbability: Could Janet have somehow made it back to Scotland? It seemed unlikely, and Lady Christina had assured her the men had returned to the Isles alone, but Mary had never asked Robert if he knew anything. Now she could.

Echoing her thoughts, the bishop urged gently, "It is time, lass."

Mary met the prelate's gaze. The years of imprisonment had not been kind to William Lamberton. Like her, he was thin to the point of gaunt. But his eyes were kind, and oddly understanding. His words tugged at her, almost as if he were trying to tell her something.

Resolved, she nodded. "Of course. Of course, I shall go."

Perhaps it wouldn't be as painful as she feared. It could be worse. She'd thought when Edward finally remembered her, it would be to try to marry her off to one of his barons. She shuddered. Being a peace envoy to Scotland was infinitely more palatable than that.

She had no intention of spying for Edward, but she would do her duty and return to her quiet life in England, hopefully with more opportunities to see her son.

Sir Adam looked much relieved. He took her hand, patting it fondly. "This will be good for you, you'll see. You've been too long alone. You're only six and twenty. Far too young to lock yourself away."

Having heard similar words a few hours earlier, Mary bit back a smile. No doubt the proud knight turned respected statesman would be surprised to realize how much he had in common with a merchant. Sir Adam didn't approve of her choice of attire either, but she suspected he'd guessed the reason for it.

"I haven't been to the Games in years," Lamberton said. "As I recall, your husband was quite a competitor." She remembered. It was where his armor had begun to shine.

"It will be fun." Then, apparently forgetting which side he was supposed to be on, he added, "Perhaps one of the competitors will catch your eye."

Mary thought she was more likely—and perhaps more eager—to catch the plague.

Two

🌿

Late August 1309
Dunstaffnage Castle, Lorn, Scotland

Kenneth Sutherland was surrounded as soon as he entered the Great Hall of Dunstaffnage Castle. He was accustomed to a certain amount of feminine attention, but the frenzied atmosphere of the Highland Games took some getting used to. The competitors enjoyed an almost godlike status, with the favorites such as himself having large entourages of followers. Very enthusiastic followers.

Though usually there was nothing he liked more than being the focus of so many beautiful women, tonight he was on a mission. While the king had been here at Dunstaffnage negotiating with the envoys from England, Kenneth had been on a peacekeeping undertaking of his own. He'd just returned from a two-week-long journey north to pacify the Munros, longtime allies of his clan, after a misguided attempt by Donald Munro, his brother's henchman, to kill the king.

Now that Kenneth was back, he was anxious to speak with the king. The Bruce, as the men had taken to calling him, had been putting him off for too long. But as the king seemed to be locked away in the laird's solar with his men, it seemed their conversation would have to wait.

He should be enjoying hearing his deeds on the battle-field recounted minute by minute, but it was out of habit more than true enthusiasm that Kenneth laughed, teased, and accepted the ladies' compliments for a few minutes before taking his seat at one of the trestle tables just below the dais. Normally being the heir to an earldom would warrant a place at the high table, but with the Highland Games about to begin, most of Scotland's nobles—at least those loyal to Bruce—were here.

His sister Helen was seated at the opposite end of the table and rolled her eyes at his "throng of worshipers," as she called them. He responded with a helpless shrug that didn't fool her one bit. If women wanted to throw themselves at him, he sure as hell wasn't going to stop them.

He supposed there were much less pleasant ways of biding his time than being seated between two beautiful young women with a goblet of wine in his hand. But for once, big blue eyes, soft red lips, enticingly low bodices, and platitudes didn't hold his attention. His gaze kept slipping to the solar door.

"Will you be competing in all the events, my lord?"

Kenneth turned to the woman on his left, aware of the gentle pressure of her leg against his. Lady Alice Barclay had been sending him less-than-subtle signals all evening, and it was impossible to miss the invitation in her eyes as she fluttered her lashes up at him. If there was any doubt—which there wasn't—the way she leaned forward to give him a fine view of some rather remarkable cleavage all but shouted "take me."

He smiled. Though she was certainly pretty enough, and those soft, round breasts were generous enough to tempt a monk, this was one invitation he didn't plan on accepting. Lady Alice was the young wife of one of Bruce's most trusted commanders, Sir David Barclay, and therefore forbidden fruit. Kenneth wasn't going to do anything to draw the king's ire. He'd worked hard to prove himself and wasn't about to throw it all away on a woman, no matter how tempting.

But Lady Alice wasn't making it easy. She leaned forward a little more, resting her hand on his thigh under the table and letting one of those plump breasts graze his arm. He felt the hard bead of her nipple through the wool of his tunic, and his body reacted.

A slow smile curved his mouth. At least forbidden fruit until Bruce gave him an answer, and then he might have to reconsider.

"Most of the events, Lady Alice, although I fear I'm not much of a dancer. I will leave the sword dance for those with more nimble feet."

"I think you are being modest. I've heard you are quite nimble, my lord. Especially with your sword." Her hand inched closer to the growing bulge between his legs just in case he'd missed the suggestiveness of her words.

Though he was tempted to see how far she would take it—he'd been a squire the last time a lass had stroked him under the tablecloth in the middle of a feast—he wasn't going to take any chances. With a sigh of regret, he covered her hand with his and eased it off his lap. He smiled, hoping to ease the sting of his rejection. "In the practice yard, perhaps. Alas, that is all I can focus on right now."

Thankfully, the woman on his right decided his attention had been on Lady Alice long enough. "The ladies are already making wagers, my lord. I believe you are favored to win many of the weapon competitions."

He lifted a brow in mock disappointment. "Only the weapons?"

Lady Eleanor, the daughter of Sir William Wiseman, another of Bruce's closest cohorts, blushed, not realizing he was teasing her. "Perhaps the wrestling event as well. But Robbie Boyd still has not said whether he will enter."

As Kenneth was fairly sure Robbie Boyd was a member of Bruce's secret army, he doubted the king was going to let him anywhere near the competition field. Magnus MacKay, Tor MacLeod, Erik MacSorley, and Gregor

MacGregor as well. All past champions of the Games, and all, he suspected, members of Bruce's famed phantom band of warriors. "Famed" because of their almost mythical deeds, and "phantom" because they seemed to slip in and out of the darkness like wraiths, identities unknown. The king wouldn't want to draw attention to their skills, not when the names of the members of his secret army were so sought after.

Rumors of an elite group of warriors—a secret army—had been floating around for years. But it wasn't until Kenneth and his Sutherland clansmen had come over to Bruce's side late last year that Kenneth had figured out that not only was it real, his foster brother had been a part of it. Until he'd been killed in battle, that is. Kenneth intended to take his friend's place among the best warriors in Scotland. If the Highland Games were the recruiting ground for the secret army, he wasn't going to leave any doubt as to his skills.

No matter who he faced.

"I would welcome the challenge," he said truthfully. Wrestling was a bit of a misnomer. Hand-to-hand combat was more accurate. It was an all-out brawl—a melee of two. It was the ultimate contest of strength and fighting ability, matching two opponents with nothing but their fists.

Though Robbie Boyd had never lost in the wrestling event and was considered the strongest man in Scotland, Kenneth never shied from a fight—which admittedly sometimes got him in trouble.

"Are you so sure, Sutherland?" Kenneth stiffened at the familiar voice coming from behind him. "As I recall, last time you did not fare so well."

His shoulders stiffened reflexively, but when Kenneth turned to look at the man who'd taken a seat beside his sister while his attention had been fixed on the solar door, there was no sign he'd heard the taunt.

He didn't *usually* shy from a fight, he amended his earlier thought. Until now. *Sangfroid*, he told himself. Kenneth was going to be on his best behavior, even if it bloody well killed him. And not just with the women. He was determined to keep his temper in check and not let his bastard of a soon-to-be brother-in-law get to him, even if MacKay seemed to be making it his personal mission in life to rile his temper and prove him unworthy for Bruce's secret army.

He wasn't rash—or a hothead—damn it!

Magnus MacKay had been his enemy, nemesis, and all-around thorn in his arse since Kenneth had been old enough to hold a sword. MacKay had bested him on the field when they were youths more times than he wanted to remember. But he did remember, every one of them. No more. Kenneth was done coming in second. He'd spent the better part of the past three years honing his skills in battle, becoming one of the best warriors in the Highlands. He was determined to prove it by winning a place in Bruce's army. If MacKay didn't stand in his way, that is.

He smiled at the man his sister planned to marry at the conclusion of the Games. "As I recall, neither did you." Magnus's face darkened. He didn't like losing any better than Kenneth did, and they'd both lost at the hands of Robbie Boyd that year. "But that was four years ago. Perhaps we've both improved?" And because he never could resist taunting the bastard back, he added to the women around him, "Although I'm afraid you won't get to see MacKay fight. He is still nursing an arm injury."

The women immediately expressed their disappointment and well-wishes for his swift recovery, while Kenneth grinned at the glowering Highlander. He knew full well that MacKay's arm was fine, but Bruce had prohibited him from entering the competition. He also knew just how much the warrior who prided himself on toughness would bristle at the idea of "nursing" anything. He would feel the same.

"I'm not—" MacKay stopped so suddenly and with such an "oof" of air that Kenneth suspected his sister's elbow had just connected rather firmly with his ribs. After looking down at Helen, who smiled angelically back up at him, MacKay's anger fizzled. "Fortunately, I have a very talented healer to nurse me back to health."

It was Kenneth's turn to glower. Although no one else at the table had picked up on the sensual innuendo of MacKay's words, he sure as hell had. The idea of MacKay marrying his little sister was bad enough, but the bastard had better damn well keep his hands off her until *after* the wedding. Noticing the heat rising to his sister's cheeks, however, Kenneth suspected it was too late.

He was reconsidering his vow not to fight with MacKay, when the door to the solar opened and men began to emerge from the room. Intent on reaching the king before he left, he quickly excused himself and crossed the twenty or so feet to the solar. The guardsman standing at the door would have refused him entry if the king hadn't glanced over and waved him in.

"Just the man I wanted to see. Come in, Sutherland, come in," Bruce said.

As the king had seemed to be avoiding him, Kenneth was surprised by his words. "You wished to see me, Sire?"

Bruce motioned him forward toward a seat opposite him at the council table. Only a few men remained in the room. Kenneth recognized the famed swordsman and trainer Tor MacLeod on his left, Sir Neil Campbell on his right, and to his surprise, William Lamberton, the Bishop of St. Andrews, next to him. He'd heard the bishop was part of Edward's truce delegation, but why was he here now?

After greetings were exchanged, Bruce said, "Have you given any more thought to our last discussion?"

It took Kenneth a moment to realize to what he was referring. Then he remembered. The last conversation he'd had with the king was after Kenneth's brother William, Earl of Sutherland, had announced his plans to marry their clan's healer, Muriel, rather than the king's sister Christina when she was released from English captivity. The king wanted an alliance with the Sutherlands, and now that duty would fall to him, as William had named him his heir. Kenneth didn't know the details, but Muriel apparently was barren. At some point—he hoped many years from now—the earldom would fall to Kenneth or his son.

But finding a wife hadn't been foremost on his mind. It wasn't that he didn't want one; it simply didn't matter to him who he wed. As long as she was noble with the right connections and could bear him a few sons, one woman was as good as another. He supposed he'd prefer if the lass was attractive, as it would make the begetting of those heirs easier, but he had enough experience to call on memories if he needed a little help.

It wasn't as if a wife would have any effect on his day-to-day life. He'd go on as he had before. His sister and brother might feel differently, but Kenneth was not moved by emotion. For men like him, marriage was a duty. He'd loved lots of women; he didn't need to love his wife.

"Aye," he lied. "I have. Did you have someone in mind?"

Kenneth was expecting the king to put forth his sister Christina, as he had to his brother Will. The former Countess of Mar was still being held in England, as was her young son, the current Earl of Mar. Kenneth knew how important it was to Bruce to unite all the Scottish earls under his banner, and the countess's next husband might help influence that decision.

But it was a different widowed countess that Bruce spoke of—Atholl. "I'm not sure whether you are aware, but my former sister-in-law, Mary, is a part of Edward's delegation." Suddenly, the bishop's presence made a little more sense. He vaguely recalled seeing Atholl's wife once years ago when he was still a squire with the Earl of Ross. She'd been quite pretty, he thought, and much younger than her husband. He also knew she'd been kept a virtual prisoner these past few years in England after her husband's execution.

He nodded, and Bruce continued, "The lass is dear to me, she was still a child when I married her sister, and I thought if she could be persuaded to remarry one of my men . . . "

He didn't need to say the rest. As with Christina Bruce, Mary of Mar had a young son and earl in England. The right husband might be able to persuade her and her son to join Bruce. Of course, there was one major obstacle. "I doubt Edward would approve of the match."

Bruce smiled wryly. "You're right, with the way things stand now. But there are ways we might be able to get around that. There is, however, a bigger problem."

"What's that?"

It was the bishop who answered. "The lass has no interest in remarrying." He paused. "She's had a difficult time of it the past few years."

Understandable, given the circumstances. He resisted the urge to rub his neck, thinking of the traitor's death that had befallen Atholl.

"Where does her allegiance lie?"

The king and the bishop exchanged looks, but it was Bruce who spoke. "To her son, but beyond that I am not sure. She holds no love for the English king, but whether she would convince her son to rebel against him and join us, I don't know." He smiled. "My former sister-in-law is far more obstinate than I remembered—and far more politic in her answers. I doubt anything will come of it. All I ask is that you meet her, and see if you would suit. If not, I have other women for you to consider."

They spent some time discussing a few of the other possibilities, but it was hard for Kenneth to feign enthusiasm when he had something else far more important on his mind. He finally had his opportunity when the meeting dissolved.

"Sire, there is something I should like to discuss with you if you can spare a few more minutes."

The king nodded. Kenneth suspected he knew what it was about when Bruce dismissed Campbell and the bishop but had MacLeod remain.

He could feel the fierce Island chief's scrutiny, but addressed his words to Bruce. "I want in. I want to be a part of your secret army." He considered it a good sign when neither man protested with a "what secret army?" He continued, "I think I've proved my loyalty to you these past few months."

Kenneth had been part of the king's retinue on his royal progress across the Highlands. He'd helped save the king's life a couple of weeks ago when his brother's henchman and a secret killing team of Saracen-style "assassins" had made attempts on it.

"You have," the king agreed.

He shouldn't have to prove himself, damn it. "If you doubt my battle skills, I will cross swords with any man—"

MacLeod arched his brow in challenge, but it was the king who interrupted. "Your skills are not at issue."

"I am not as adept as Gordon was with the black powder, but I have some knowledge."

His friend and foster brother, William Gordon, had been a part of Bruce's secret army and had died last year in an explosion. Kenneth suspected the unusual knowledge of the Saracen black powder was part of the reason he'd been on the team.

MacLeod and the king exchanged another look, but neither said anything.

Despite his intentions, Kenneth felt his temper prick. "This is about MacKay, isn't it?"

"He has expressed some concern," the king admitted.

"He says you are rash, have a hot temper, and lack discipline," MacLeod said bluntly.

Kenneth swallowed his anger. As he suspected, Bruce
wanted him on the team, but he wouldn't invite him to
join unless MacKay went along with it. "If he means fierce,
aggressive, and fearless, I won't argue that. If you wanted
discipline, I would think you'd be at a tournament of
knights, not at the Highland Games. Highlanders aren't
disciplined. We fight to win." He paused, seeing the hint of
a smile play Bruce's mouth. "If MacKay agrees, will you
consider it?"

After a moment, the king nodded.

Kenneth turned to go have a frank discussion with his
future brother-in-law, when MacLeod stopped him. "But
you'll have to prove yourself to me."

The way he said it suggested he wasn't going to like
whatever MacLeod had in mind. But proving himself
wasn't anything new; Kenneth had been doing it since the
day he was born—even in that he'd come in second.

Kenneth waited for his sister to leave the Hall before
confronting the man only God knew why she intended to
marry. He stepped in front of MacKay as he exited the
tower on his way to the barracks, blocking his path. "I
thought we had a deal."

MacKay smiled. "What deal?"

He gritted his teeth, fighting for patience. "I wouldn't
stand in your way of marrying my sister, and you don't
stand in the way of me joining the secret army."

"I recall a conversation on the subject, but I don't remember ever agreeing to anything. And if you think you could
stop Helen from marrying me, I'd like to see you try."

Kenneth's jaw locked, knowing he was right. His sister
had made it clear that his opinion on her marriage didn't
matter. God save him from a modern "independent"
woman! Sweet and biddable suited him just fine.

The truth was, if he weren't so used to hating MacKay, he might actually like the arse. His Sutherland ancestors were probably rolling in their graves at the sacrilege. The MacKays and Sutherlands had been enemies for as long as he could remember. MacKay might be a stubborn bastard, but he was also one of the best warriors Kenneth had ever fought beside. "Perhaps not, but I don't think you want to be the cause of discord between Helen and me. She may love you, but she also loves me."

MacKay frowned, as if he didn't like being reminded of it. "What do you want? If you think I'm going to sing your praises to Bruce—"

"I don't need you to sing my praises. I can do that on my own—on the field. I just need you to stay out of my way."

His old enemy and longtime competitor eyed him carefully. "I'll admit, you're not bad. But 'not bad' is far from the best. You aren't fighting with the English anymore," he said sarcastically, referring to the Sutherlands' recent shift in allegiance to Bruce. "Are you sure you can compete with the most elite warriors in Scotland?"

"Not only compete, but win." He paused. "Look, I know you need someone to take Gordon's place."

"No one can take Gordon's place," MacKay snapped.

Their eyes met. He better than anyone understood that. Gordon had been his foster brother, but he'd been MacKay's partner. A friend to them both—ironic, given their enmity. "You're right. But I'm the next best man for the job, and you know it."

MacKay's jaw clenched, and his silence seemed a tacit agreement of sorts.

Sensing an opening, Kenneth went in for the kill. "Bruce has recruited men from the Games before. I'd wager that's what brought you to his attention four years ago." More silence. "Let these Games be no different. If I win the overall championship, you'll agree not to interfere."

It was a bold offer. The overall champion was the competitor who had the highest ranking across all the events. Given that he was no dancer and only a decent swimmer, he'd have to do extremely well in all the other events.

McKay shook his head. "Not good enough. Many of the best competitors won't be competing."

He meant himself, as well as the other members of the secret army.

Kenneth tried to rein in his temper, but MacKay made it bloody difficult. He was a provoking bastard. "Then what do you suggest?"

"Win them all, and I'll welcome you in myself."

He couldn't be serious. "All?"

"Only the weapon events," MacKay clarified, as if it were the most reasonable thing in the world.

"No one has ever done that." Kenneth was so outraged, he feared he was sputtering.

MacKay shrugged, not bothering to hide his smile.

Kenneth cursed his own arrogance under his breath. MacKay had turned it against him. "You know I'm not very good with a bow. Neither are you, if I recall. Gregor MacGregor might not be competing, but his young brother John is, and he's reputed to be nearly as good."

"Fine. No archery, but you'll have to win the wrestling competition instead."

Kenneth gritted his teeth. *Sangfroid*, damn it. But he could feel the heat rising. MacKay had backed him into a damned corner and knew it. "Fine. It's a deal."

He stepped aside to let MacKay pass by—or swagger by, the smug bastard.

"Good luck, Sutherland. You're going to need it."

Kenneth wouldn't give him the satisfaction of showing his anger. He didn't care what it took; he was going to win.

If there was anything Kenneth knew how to do, it was fight. He'd been doing it practically since the day he was born. Nothing had ever come easily for him. But he didn't mind. It had only made him stronger and more determined to win.

He was about to return to the Hall to find a nice big tankard of ale to cool his anger, when a group of women approached and he thought of a better way to soothe his temper.

He supposed there was one thing that had always come easily for him.

Three

❧

Having just made her third mistake in the last ten minutes, Mary put down her embroidery. She had to do something. She was so restless. Stretch her legs, perhaps? Despite the lateness of the hour, she decided to go for a walk.

The journey, the return home after so many years, simply *being* in Scotland again had affected her more than she'd expected. Though her immediate family was gone, seeing Lady Christina, Lady Margaret (Atholl's sister who was now wed to the MacKenzie chief), and even Robert had been nearly as overwhelming.

All the memories that she'd kept so carefully bottled up inside were threatening to explode. She didn't want to remember. Didn't want to miss them. Didn't want to think of Scotland as home when her life must be in England.

She'd been here only a week, yet she felt the pull so strongly it threatened to destroy the contentment she'd fought so hard to achieve. It was as if she'd taken a piece of slate and wiped it clean, only to discover later that the lines had been etched into the stone, not made from chalk.

Worse, her mission had been a failure. The negotiations for peace had stalled, as they always did over the issue of Bruce's kingship. Robert refused to sign a peace treaty that did not recognize his sovereignty and Edward refused to sign one that did. No woman's voice could change that.

As she expected, Robert was sympathetic and understanding toward her son's plight—and had no intention of forfeiting his lands—but he also would not recognize David as Earl of Atholl until he did fealty for those lands. Something that was impossible as long as her son was in Edward's power.

The stalemate continued.

Moreover, also as she expected, Robert was hardly inclined to share his secrets with her. Her mouth twitched with a wry grin. Especially after she'd told him outright that Edward wished her to spy on him, so if he had any dark secrets, to make sure he made them easy for her to discover.

After a moment of shock, Robert had burst out laughing and told her she sounded just like her sister. Isabel, he'd meant. The bold, speak-her-mind sister he'd fallen in love with and married when he'd been a lad of eighteen, and who'd died a few years later in childbirth. Mary hadn't realized how much she'd changed, but he was right.

Of Janet's presumed death, his sorrow had been nearly as great as Lady Christina's. And like her brother's widow, he claimed to know nothing of what had become of her.

The peace envoys had managed one small success, however, in extending the truce until November.

Mary could hear the sounds of merriment coming from the Hall as she hurried down the stairwell from the tower chamber she shared with some of the other ladies and the two attendants Edward had provided for her—probably to keep an eye on her.

Highlanders could dance until dawn, and from the sounds of it, the feast was still going strong. *Perhaps I should have . . .*

She stopped herself. She was right to have begged off the feast tonight. She couldn't allow herself to be drawn in.

She'd been doing her best to keep to herself, but it was getting harder and harder to stay away from the festivities.

Harder and harder not to get caught up in the excitement. In the *fun.*

God, how long had it been since she'd had fun? She'd almost forgotten what it was.

But being here made her remember. Being here made her remember a lot of things.

One more week. That was all she needed to make it through. They were leaving at the end of the Games, and then she could return to her life in England.

But the sounds around her seemed to challenge that characterization. Music. Voices. Laughter. Those were the sounds of life.

No. She pushed it aside. Quiet. Peace. Solitude. Independence. That was what she wanted.

Finding those things at a castle in the midst of the Highland Games, however, was all but impossible. She hurried down the corridor and out into the *barmkin*, heading for the postern gate, which exited toward the beach.

It would be peaceful there, gazing up at the moonlit sky. The stars were different in the Highlands. Bigger, brighter, closer. Her mother had told her it was because the "high" lands were so near to heaven. Mary could almost believe her.

The stars in England were—

She stopped herself again. She couldn't let herself keep comparing; it would only make leaving that much more difficult.

Don't dwell on what you can't have.

She was about to pass by the stables when she heard a strange sound that stopped her. It sounded like a pained moan. Glancing around, not seeing anyone, and thinking that it was odd not to have a stable lad at the entry, she was about to walk away when she heard it again. Louder this time, and followed by a hard grunt.

Was one of the horses in distress?

She rushed inside, following the beam of light from the

torches, barely noticing the pungent smells of animal and hay that hit her the moment she entered. It was pleasantly warm and sultry, the animals providing a natural, radiating heat.

Two torches had been fixed on the posts at the entrance, spilling off a wide enough pool of light to see that nothing appeared out of the ordinary. Well, except for the apparent absence of anyone to watch over the animals. The horses were in their stalls, and—

She stopped, hearing it again. Then, as if following their own direction, her feet started moving toward the sound, which seemed to be coming from one of the stalls at the far corner of the building. More moans and cries. Not animal, she realized, but . . .

She felt a prickle of something tingle down her spine, a premonition, right before they came into view.

Human.

She came to an abrupt stop, as if she'd slammed into a wall. She sucked in her breath, her body frozen in shock. The sight that met her eyes was unlike anything she'd ever seen. She felt as if she'd been plunged into a den of sin, an orgy of sensation, a sensual banquet for the eyes.

A man—an extremely muscular and powerfully built man—stripped to the waist, with his braies loosened and hanging onto his buttocks by the barest of margins, was on his knees in the hay, gripping the hips of a woman who was on her hands and knees before him. He was plunging in and out of her from behind. Mary's eyes widened. *From behind!*

Her first reaction was one of concern. Was he hurting her? But although the scene was in profile, from the half-lidded eyes and fierce sounds of pleasure the woman was making no effort to contain, she was enjoying it. Enjoying it rather a lot.

Mary knew she should go, but her feet seemed incapable of movement. She was transfixed by the look of rapture on the woman's face. She didn't recognize her, but she was young, probably about nineteen or twenty, and very pretty. Her long blond hair was loose and tumbling around her shoulders in soft waves. She was well curved, with wide hips, full breasts, and softly rounded limbs. Although technically the woman was clothed, her gown was loose to the point of falling off at her bodice and the hem was tossed up around her waist, leaving little of her body that was not exposed.

"Oh, yes!" the woman cried. "God, it feels so good. You're so big." She was arching her back, rocking her hips against him eagerly.

The man's movements, by contrast, were almost lazy. He reached forward to fondle one of her sizable breasts, and the woman's moans and cries took on a frantic edge.

Mary couldn't look away from his hands. Darkly tanned against the pale softness of the woman's skin, they were big, well formed, and as strong-looking as the rest of him. He was a lean, perfectly honed weapon of war. Atholl had been a muscular man, but this man defied comparison.

A blacksmith could have forged the broad shield of his chest, and not an ounce of fat marred the steely slabs and ridges of muscle that narrowed to a V at his slim waist and hips. Tight ropes of muscle lined his stomach like a ladder carved into the sheer granite face of a cliffside. Even the curved flanks of his backside looked hard and tautly muscled. And his arms . . . his arms were like battering rams, thick and powerful, rippling and flexing with every movement.

Muscles like that could only be earned on the battlefield.

The sheer masculine perfection of his body might have given her the illusion of a Greek god but for the numerous scars that gave proof of his humanity. Still, it was a thing of beauty, something to be admired—hard and chiseled as any statue, but bronzed and radiating warmth.

Or maybe that was her. Looking at him made her feel all hot and tingly.

"Do you like that, my sweet?" he purred.

Mary jolted at the sound of his voice. Sweet heaven! It was dark, deep, and mesmerizing, brimming with sensual allure. It was the voice of sin, and it blanketed her body with heat.

"Tell me what you want," he murmured, weaving his sensual web around them both. It was as if he were talking to her.

Mary wanted to look at his face but couldn't seem to take her eyes off his hands. He was rolling the woman's nipple between his fingers as if massaging it to a point, and then squeezing gently. Seeing those big, blunt-edged fingers work so deftly . . .

Her own breasts felt heavy, her nipples peaking under the thick wool of her gown.

The woman seemed incapable of speech. Her eyes were closed, her lips parted, her expression one of total rapture.

A rush of memories hit her hard, memories that had been buried a long time ago. Feelings and sensations that had confused her at fifteen and been blunted at eighteen now returned, clearer, sharper, and stronger. Much stronger.

Passion, Mary realized. In that one look she saw the realization of something she'd never known but had instinctively longed for. How she envied the woman!

"Please," the woman begged.

She wanted something and seemed increasingly urgent to find it. The man's strong hands started to roam her body, touching her in ways that seemed to increase the woman's agony. Or pleasure; the two had seemed to have become one. He was teasing her, each caress of his hands calculated to stoke the flames of her desire.

His hips moved at a steady beat, slow and easy, in long, deep strokes. Not the frantic, hurry-up-and-get-it-over way Mary remembered.

He was drawing out the woman's pleasure.

My God, he *cared* about her pleasure. All his efforts seemed to be focused on the woman. He was moving as if he had all the time in the world.

But the woman had had enough. "Please . . . "

Mary took such pity on her, she almost told him to put the poor creature out of her misery.

But she wasn't miserable at all. The woman was in heaven.

He slid his hand down between the woman's legs and his fingers dipped between them in the place . . .

Mary gasped, feeling a rush of heat between her legs, almost as if he were touching her there. She shifted, feeling hot and uncomfortable. The warm air of the stables felt sultry, the small area too intimate.

She couldn't breathe, poised on the precipice of what would happen next.

The man leaned forward, pulling the woman up against him, and put his mouth on the nape of her neck, nuzzling, nipping, almost as if he were a stallion.

He *was* a stallion, Mary realized. A prized stallion. Sleek, lean, and hard, exuding a raw, unharnessed strength. A creature of magnificence to look upon.

Even in profile she could tell he must be handsome. He had dark, wavy hair, just a shade too long to be reputable, a nose that appeared to have been broken more than once but was still nicely proportioned and reasonably straight, high cheekbones, a wide mouth, and a strong, square jaw.

She had no doubt he was a lord. Even if she hadn't seen the jeweled handle of the sword resting against a stool beside his leather surcote, the aura of arrogance and authority was eerily familiar.

He was undeniably attractive, but it was what he was doing to the woman that made it impossible to turn away, that made Mary's skin flush, her breath catch, and her breasts heavy.

That made her want him to do that to her.

Mary couldn't seem to turn away as the woman stilled, and then cried out, her body shuddering with the release of something incredible. For a moment her face was filled with such rapture it seemed divine. Oh . . . it was amazing!

When she was finished, the woman went completely limp, as if her limbs had lost their bones. All that was holding her up seemed to be his hands.

Mary looked at those big hands, the thick, powerful fingers, and followed them up, over a stomach clenched with tight bands of muscle, past the incredible chest, to the equally incredible face that was now turned toward her.

My God, he was looking at her! She jolted, riveted to the floor by piercing blue, feeling the shock not just at being caught, but also of awareness.

Attractive was an understatement. He was one of the most handsome men she'd ever seen. Deep-set brilliant blue eyes in startling contrast to the darkness of his hair, a bold, aggressively sensual mouth, a nose that had been broken (as she'd anticipated), but the crook only seemed to enhance the pugnacious, masculine appeal. None of his features was perfect, but together . . .

She almost heaved a dreamy sigh. Together they were incredible. Hard, physical, brutally male. It was a face to stir even a heart that should know better.

But it was the way he was looking at her that sent her heart slamming to her toes.

His warrior's heightened senses had alerted Kenneth to the woman's presence well before he heard her startled gasp. He wouldn't have lasted very long in this war if someone could sneak up on him—even while engaged in the more sensual pursuits.

Although "engaged" was probably putting it strongly. Engaged implied interest, which he was fighting hard to maintain. He'd been silently wishing for the woman to come already before they'd been interrupted.

It was hardly uncommon in a crowded castle to come upon two people giving way to their baser needs. It wasn't common, however, to stand there and watch.

Rather than run off in shocked embarrassment as he'd expected—as she should have done—the woman had seemed transfixed. At first, when he'd seen all that black and the wimple, he'd thought her a nun. All she was missing was the natural wool scapular over her gown.

Amused, given her prim, officious attire, and not wanting to frighten her off, he hadn't looked at her directly but watched her out of the corner of his eye.

Not that she'd seemed likely to catch his gaze, as her attention wasn't focused on him but on the face of the woman beneath him.

Lady Moira had seemed the wisest of the options presented him tonight. Choosing a bedmate was becoming something of running the gauntlet, trying to avoid any connections to the king or his important lords that might land him in trouble. As the widowed attendant of Lady Elizabeth Lindsay, Lady Moira seemed unlikely to give him any problems.

She was also young, uncomplicated, eager to please, and lusty. A perfect combination, to his mind.

Except he hadn't been able to muster much enthusiasm for the task. Such interludes, which had suited him well in the past, had started to feel rote. Stale. Interchangeable.

He'd attributed it to his focus on the task ahead of him, but maybe it was something else. Maybe he needed a little excitement.

The wee interloper seemed to have provided it.

God knew why, as there was hardly much to her. His first impression was of a ghostlike, colorless creature hidden behind the ugliest, most shapeless clothes he'd ever seen on a woman who wasn't old enough to be his grand-mother or living in a convent.

She wasn't either. The slight, pinched face, half hidden behind a pair of what he assumed were glasses, was smooth of lines, and the rings she wore on her fingers, along with the brooch pinned to her gown, suggested she was a lady of some position. Perhaps, like Lady Moira, an attendant to one of the noblewomen.

When he'd first glanced at her, he thought there was something familiar about her. But if he'd met her before he could not place her.

Not surprising, as she seemed perfectly forgettable. Almost *too* perfectly forgettable. There was something fine in her delicate features that seemed obscured. An echo of beauty that could not be completely erased.

He wished he could see her eyes better. And her hair. Though from the light golden brown of her softly arched brows, he suspected it was blond.

There was no reason in Hades why this slight, bland woman who looked about the farthest thing from wicked could be inspiring him.

He'd wanted to shock her. See a flush rise to those pale cheeks. Rattle the prim and serious from her laced-up-tight exterior. Give her a performance to remember.

She seemed entranced by Lady Moira's pleasure, as if she'd never seen anything like it. Realizing she probably hadn't, he'd set out to instruct her. He always saw to his bedmates' pleasure, but he extended it, drew it out, purposefully touched Lady Moira in places that were sure to shock.

And they did. But to his surprise, they also aroused.

Both of them. When the little voyeur's breath sharpened and started to quicken, he felt his body respond. Everything felt a little hotter, and a hell of a lot harder.

He couldn't believe it—the wee drab wren was turning him on.

Hell, if he'd known how much fun it would be to have

someone watching him, he would have done this a long time ago.

Anticipation built inside him. He was tempted to drag it out longer, but he couldn't wait to see how she reacted to what he was going to do next. She was going to like this. Nearly as much as Lady Moira did.

He buried himself full hilt, reached down between Lady Moira's legs, and stroked her until she started to come. She cried out her pleasure in a soft, keening wail.

But he kept his gaze on the wicked, wee interloper the entire time. He watched her face soften, her lips part, and her eyes fill with such naked longing he would have given anything at that moment to be the one to give her the pleasure she craved.

Jesus. His stomach muscles clenched, fighting against the jolt of lust. He hadn't expected this. Hadn't expected it to affect him so much. But watching the sensual awakening on her face, the combination of shock and desire— unwilling desire—was one of the most erotic things he'd ever beheld.

He was no longer in doubt that he would be able to come.

Who would have ever thought that beneath such a dull, listless exterior lay the dormant passion of a wanton?

The lass was completely unaware of what she was doing to him. But he wanted her to know. He wanted her to look at him.

Finally, she did.

At first he'd been annoyed by Lady Moira's request to take off his shirt, feeling a little bit like a stallion at market. But he was glad for it now. Glad he could see the open admiration and innocent hunger as the woman's gaze roamed every inch of his bare skin.

Aye, she wanted him. But what surprised him was that he also wanted her. How he wished it was her that he was buried deep inside of right now.

When their eyes met, he let her see exactly what he was

thinking. Her eyes looked huge behind the two pieces of glass, and they widened even farther when she felt the force of his lust. It wrapped around them, coiling, tightening, drawing them together as if there were no one else in the world.

His blood was pounding hard now. He could feel the sensations gathering at the base of his spine and knew he wasn't going to be able to last much longer.

Without thinking about what he was doing, but knowing that he didn't want anything—or anyone—between them, he pulled out of the woman beneath him and fisted his hand around himself. Holding the other woman's gaze, he started to stroke himself. He imagined it was her gripping him. Her tight, wet heat pulling him over the edge. The eager expression on her face made it easy.

He groaned, his hand quickening the pace. Every muscle in his body clenched with anticipation. He could feel it. Almost . . .

Her eyes hadn't left his, but he knew she'd guessed what he was doing because her mouth opened in shock. A perfect little O.

Her breath hitched in a shocked gasp, and the erotic sound sent him over. His arse clenched. He let out a deep groan, jerking his pleasure in deep pulsing streams.

When he was done, their eyes met in one long, hot moment of primal awareness. He could almost feel the frantic beat of her heart against his and hear the quickening of her breath in his ear. He would have given nearly everything at that moment to touch her. To slide his hand between her thighs and feel the warmth and dampness that he knew he would find there. How many strokes would it take to push her over?

But the spell was broken by Lady Moira. "That was amazing. I'm glad to say this is one time the rumors were not exaggerated. You're every bit as spectacular as they say with that long sword of yours."

Kenneth felt a prick of annoyance that was no doubt unwarranted. He didn't expect more from her than swiving, so why would he expect a more interesting comment than a reference to the size of his cock?

Lady Moira had collapsed in a well-sated heap on the hay-strewn floor when he'd released her, but she'd revived enough to put herself in a slightly more elegant position on her back.

He'd forgotten all about her. Apparently, as had their interloper. He just caught the edge of her horror-stricken expression before she turned and fled out of the barn, the Devil nipping at her heels.

He let her go. But part of him actually wanted to go after her.

Lady Moira sat up. "Did you hear something?"

He shook his head and reached for his shirt, wondering what the hell was the matter with him. "It was one of the horses. You'd better fix your clothes. The lads will be returning soon."

The lady babbled platitudes for another quarter hour while he helped her with her hair and gown before he could finally escort her out of the stables. His mind was on the other woman. Who was she? And more incredibly, why the hell did he care?

He'd never done anything like that before in his life, and he wasn't quite sure what had provoked him to such wickedness. He didn't usually find himself turned on by prim little wrens. But something about her reaction—the innocent arousal and not-so-innocent hunger—had fired his blood in a way that defied explanation, turning something that should have been forgettable into something . . . different. Memorable.

What had started out as a taunting game had taken an unexpected turn, leaving him vaguely unsettled. He'd gone too far, and he knew it. But he hadn't forced her to stand there and watch. And he sure as hell hadn't expected either of them to enjoy it so much.

The lass intrigued him. But all his focus right now was on earning a place in Bruce's secret army. A lass, no matter how intriguing, wasn't going to distract him.

Four

❧

"I'm glad to see you have recovered, Lady Mary."

The king paused before her seat on the way to take his own in the stands that had been set up to watch the competition. Modeled on the ancient Roman amphitheater, a circular field had been set off by a wooden fence surrounded by tiers of wooden benches. The king's party, however, watched from a special viewing platform erected especially for the Games. As it was a warm day, she was glad for the addition of a canvas tent overhead.

Mary was seated at the far end near the stairs, with her former sister-in-law, the MacKenzie chief, and their three young daughters. Their two sons were competing in some of the events. She returned the king's smile, hoping he mistook her pink cheeks for warmth and not embarrassment. "Much better, Sire."

For four days since that horrible night, she'd feigned illness to avoid the possibility of coming face to face with *him*. Aye, she was hiding like a coward and had no shame in admitting it to herself.

"I was worried you'd miss all the fun. It's been an exciting Games so far. One of my knights is creating quite a stir. He's won nearly every competition he's entered and is on his way to being named champion. He's the Earl of Sutherland's brother and heir, Sir Kenneth. Do you know of him?"

She shook her head, wondering why this felt like more

than polite conversation. "It's been many years since I've been to court, my lord."

Robert's face shadowed. "Aye, lass, I know. I would that it had been different. You've been missed. I hope you will return soon." He paused and gave her an innocent smile. "Perhaps next time you will bring your son?"

Mary's mouth quirked with amusement. Robert Bruce had never been subtle about what he wanted. It had taken a bold man to attempt to wrest a crown from Edward Plantagenet's iron fist. Robert had made no secret of his wish to have her son under his banner. But secreting her son out from under the English king's nose would be a risky proposition, and for what? What was there for her in Scotland but politics, intrigue, and men who would control her future? Things from which she'd been blissfully free in England. Besides, she remembered what had happened the last time she'd tried to leave.

"I should like that, Sire," she said noncommittally.

"I would like you to meet him." At her confusion, he added, "Our soon-to-be champion. Perhaps you will sit with us at the feast tonight?"

Something about the way he said it set off alarm bells clanging in her head. If the king wished her to meet a man, it wasn't hard to guess why. But she was just as eager for a Scottish husband as she was an English one. "It would be an honor, Sire. I do hope I shall feel up to it."

But alas, she suspected her illness was going to return in full force.

The king moved off to have some words with the MacKenzie chief, and Mary settled back in her seat to watch the contestants who had just begun to gather in the field.

She could feel the excitement growing around her; it was impossible not to get caught up in it. Even in self-imposed exile in her room she hadn't been immune. She'd watched from the tower window, too far to be a part of it, but not far enough away not to want to be.

She hadn't been able to stay away. She told herself it was because people were starting to worry about her health—not just her former sister-in-law, Lady Christina and Margaret, but also the lady of the castle, Lady Anna Campbell. But she didn't think she could listen to one more evening of the ladies she shared a chamber with reliving every minute of the day's events without seeing it for herself. The only time she'd been to the Games, she'd been so enthralled with her husband that she didn't remember much else.

All of a sudden she heard a large roar go up in the crowd. She turned to Margaret. "What is that for?"

Margaret grinned, pointing to a man who'd just entered the field. "Him."

Mary followed the direction she'd indicated and froze. Oh God, it was *him*! Though he wore a steel helm that masked his face, something about that arrogant set of his shoulders made every muscle, every nerve ending, every inch of her body tense with instant recognition. Or perhaps it was that the very breadth of those shoulders, the bulk of his arms, and every muscle of that imposing chest had been emblazoned on her consciousness.

Her gaze dipped before she could stop herself. It wasn't until she'd returned to her room that she realized she still had her glasses on—she'd tied them around her head with a ribbon so they wouldn't keep falling off while she was sewing. That must be why he'd looked so . . . *large*.

So much for the hope to never see him again, to bury what had happened in the deepest, darkest corner of her memory and pretend it had never occurred. Seeing him brought it all back again.

Heat crawled up her face. What could she have been thinking? Why hadn't she run away? She *should* have run away. She still couldn't believe she'd stood there and watched as first he'd pleasured the woman and then as he'd . . .

As he'd pleasured himself.

She'd never seen a man take himself in his own hand before. Surely it was a wicked thing to do? She just hadn't realized wicked could be so arousing.

She couldn't think about it without feeling the heat of shame wash over her (at least she told herself the blast of warmth that shot over her skin was from shame). Sweet heaven, she'd never felt anything like that before in her life. For a moment, when he'd looked into her eyes as he'd found release, she'd actually let herself believe that she'd done that to him. That all that intensity, all that heat, all that raw masculine energy as he'd taken his pleasure had been for her.

The way he'd looked at her . . .

No man had ever looked at her like that. As if she were desirable. Even when she'd been young and pretty, her husband hadn't seemed to notice. Not when he had so many beautiful women falling at his feet.

Listen to her, what a fool she was! After all these years she still thought she could inspire a man's lust. She hadn't been able to keep her husband's interest when she was at her best; how could she think to attract a man now, when she'd purposefully made herself look as unattractive as possible?

Worse, she knew he'd seen her arousal and guessed how much she wanted what he was giving that woman. The passion and pleasure she'd only glimpsed but had never experienced.

How pathetically ironic that the most sensual moment of her life had occurred when she wasn't even a participant!

Mary didn't know whether she was more horrified at him or at herself. Him for his wickedness or her for enjoying it. Mostly, she was just embarrassed. He was probably still laughing at her. The silly little mortal who'd thought a god could actually be interested in her—even for a moment.

But she couldn't help asking, "Who is he?"

"Impressive, isn't he?" Margaret said with a mischievous twinkle in her eye.

Obviously, Mary had given something away in her expression. She shrugged indifferently, but it didn't fool either of them.

"It's the man the king mentioned," Margaret said. "Sir Kenneth Sutherland of Moray. He's been something of a surprise. No one expected him to do this well. His brother was a champion a few years ago, but Sir Kenneth has never won anything before."

Mary's heart lurched for one silly beat before she tamped it back down to reality. It was only natural to experience a flicker of girlish delight at the prospect of an alliance to such a handsome man, she told herself. But she wasn't a young girl anymore. She was a woman who knew better than to let herself get carried away by illusions. She'd married one arrogant, handsome knight, and it had led to enough misery for a lifetime.

"It would be quite a coup, you know," her former sister-in-law said.

Mary's brows gathered across her nose in question. "A coup?"

"To bring him to the altar. There isn't a young, unmarried woman here who wouldn't like to do that. Especially since his brother the earl named him heir."

Margaret appeared to have picked up on the king's intent, as had she.

"But surely that is only temporary, until the earl has sons of his own?"

Margaret shook her head. "The rumor is that the earl will have no sons. One day Kenneth Sutherland or his son will be earl. If his handsome face wasn't enough of a temptation, a future earldom has made him one of the most sought-after men in Scotland. And it seems the king is offering him to you like a stuffed bird on a gold-encrusted platter."

Mary's mouth quirked in spite of herself, the image was so ridiculous. She'd had her fill of overstuffed peacocks. "If that is what Robert intends, then I'm afraid he will be disappointed."

Mary could feel Margaret studying her face and kept her expression impassive. "You can't tell me you aren't the slightest bit tempted."

She was tempted, but not for marriage. The sinful thought popped in her mind before she could stop it.

Good God, what was wrong with her?

She sighed, knowing full well what was wrong with her. She'd seen exactly what was wrong with her. She shook her head firmly. "I've no wish to marry again."

Margaret gave her a sympathetic look. She had witnessed the heartbreak and disappointment of Mary's marriage firsthand. "Wishing has very little to do with marriage for women in our position though, does it?"

It was the harsh truth. But Mary would rather enter a nunnery than be forced to marry again. At least then she would be in control of her own destiny.

"Not all men are like my brother, Mary." Margaret frowned, watching as Kenneth Sutherland took the field to square off against his first opponent in the hammer event. "But perhaps you are right not to be tempted by him. I fear Kenneth Sutherland has left a trail of broken hearts behind him every bit as long as my brother's."

Hearing her suspicions confirmed was oddly disappointing. But the comparison, once made, was hard to dislodge. As the competition got underway, it only became more solidified in her mind.

She might have been eighteen again, sitting in the stands watching her husband for the first time and witnessing a hero in the making. Atholl, too, had been magnificent. She'd never forget how excited she'd been. How she'd sat in her seat, heart in her throat, and watched the man she'd been married to for three years but who was still essentially a stranger to her compete in the various events.

Separated from her by imprisonment during the first year of their marriage, and forced to fight for Edward in Flanders during the second, Atholl had only been permitted to return to Scotland a few months prior. He'd joined her at Blair Castle for only a few weeks before leaving to attend his duties at court. She'd been so looking forward to the Games, not simply because it was the first time she'd been allowed to attend, but also because she would finally be spending time with the handsome man to whom she was married. The unpleasantness of the first coupling on their wedding night had given way to a slightly more pleasurable experience on his return over two years later, and she had a very unmaidenly interest in learning more.

At first it had felt like a faerie tale, with him cast as the handsome knight in shining armor and her as the pretty maiden for whose favor he fought. She'd never forget when he'd won the spear event and he'd turned and bowed to her in the stands. The crowd had gone wild at the romantic gesture. She'd thought her heart would burst with pride and happiness.

But the faerie tale hadn't lasted long. Atholl always knew how to play to the crowd. The gesture had been for them, not for her. A few nights later she'd learned the truth. Her husband did not come to her bed because he'd found another. Indeed, if the conversation she'd overheard the following morning was accurate, he'd found many to choose from.

When she'd tearfully confronted him, he hadn't bothered to deny it. Instead, he'd been angry at her for interfering in matters that did not concern her. Yet even after that horrible conversation, she had refused to accept the truth. She'd thought that if she could make him fall in love with her, he would forget about the other women. But her attempts only seemed to make it worse. The harder she tried to hold on to him, the more he distanced himself from her.

She was his wife. The mother of his son. His occasional bedmate, when he was reminded of his duty. But one woman would never be enough for a man like him. There were some men that craved—nay, thrived on—the admiration of many. Atholl was one of them. It had taken her years of disappointment, jealousy, and heartbreak, however, to understand it.

It had partially been her fault, she knew. She'd idolized him, placing him on such a high pedestal that the only place he could go was down. She'd learned there were no such things as heroes, only men. Time had given her perspective. It had been foolish to pin dreams on him that he could never hope to fulfill. Theirs had been a political marriage. Had she not been so young and filled with unrealistic dreams, perhaps it would have turned out differently.

From the way Kenneth Sutherland incited the crowd, she suspected he was cut from a similar cloth as Atholl's. He seemed to thrive on the cheers as one by one he defeated every man who took the field against him. Nevertheless, she found herself applauding along with the rest when he managed a particularly quick or otherwise impressive victory.

It was a brutal event, quick and dirty. The two combatants squared off in the makeshift arena, exchanging blow after blow of the bone-crushing hammer until one man was knocked to the ground. With Sir Kenneth it didn't take long. His attacks were fast and fierce. He wielded the weapon as if it were a child's toy, making his opponents look like, well, children.

Only his final two opponents gave him much of a contest. When Fergal MacKinnon, a great beast of a man, managed to get a solid blow into his left side, Mary held her breath along with the rest of the crowd as they waited to see whether he would fall. He didn't. The blow only seemed to galvanize him, making him stronger and more determined. He mounted a no-holds-barred attack on the hulking warrior, taking him down with a series of powerful, merciless swings of the hammer.

Mary gripped the wooden plank of her seat more than once during the final competition, but never did she doubt that he would win. There was something driving him, a powerful force behind him that she along with the rest of the crowd seemed to sense. The Graham warrior gave him a battle, but in the end it wasn't enough.

Kenneth Sutherland was hailed as victor of the hammer event to the enthusiastic cheers of the crowd. And for one moment, when he ripped off his helm and the sunlight caught him in its golden embrace, Mary's breath stopped. He was truly magnificent. A man to be admired. As the flock of women who suddenly surrounded him seemed to agree.

Unaccountably disappointed, Mary started to turn away. But something made her glance back. She gasped, feeling the force of his gaze connect with hers like a lightning rod. For a moment she froze, pinned to the ground by the piercing intensity of his gaze. Her heart pounded in her chest as his head dipped in a nod. It was just like all those years ago with Atholl. And God help her, just like then she felt a silly, giddy bubble of maidenly pleasure rise inside her before reality interceded. She quickly looked away, ducking behind a man who'd stood in front of her.

It was impossible, wasn't it? There were too many people around; he couldn't have picked her out of a crowd. She looked around, thinking he might have been looking at someone else. But when she peeked again, her heart stopped cold.

Dear God, he was heading right for her!

Kenneth was in his element, enjoying every minute of his moment in the sun. He'd been born for this. Fighting. Competing. Winning. Aye, most of all winning.

It had taken him years of hard work, determination, and pulling himself out of the mud more times than he wanted to remember, but he was on the cusp of achieving what he'd wanted: to be the best.

One more event to go and a place in Bruce's secret army would be his. He was going to do this; he could feel it. He exulted in the cheers of the crowd, knowing they could feel it, too. Fate and destiny had joined forces behind him, and nothing was going to stand in his way. For the first time, there would be no one in front of him. Tomorrow, after the wrestling event, he would be named champion.

He'd already achieved something no man had ever done before, winning all five weapon events. In one more sign that fate was with him, he'd won the archery contest. It had taken the shot of his life to defeat John MacGregor, but he'd done so by less than a quarter of an inch.

He wished he could have seen MacKay's face. After tomorrow there would be no doubt that he deserved to take his place among the best warriors in Scotland in Bruce's secret army, and his former rival wasn't going to be able to do a damned thing to stop it.

Kenneth glanced up to the king's pavilion, pleased to see Bruce clapping along with the rest.

That was when he saw her. His wee voyeur.

He'd found himself looking for her more than once over the past few days—four, he realized—and had begun to wonder whether he'd imagined her. But nay, there she was, sitting serenely and inauspiciously at the end of the king's platform with Alexander MacKenzie and his wife. Was she one of Lady Margaret's attendants, then?

Shedding some light on the mystery should have been enough to put the matter behind him. Right now he should be thinking of only one thing: tomorrow's contest. He shouldn't be wondering what it would be like to be the one to cut those too-tight laces of hers and release some of the passion she had bottled up tightly beneath that austere facade.

Hell, he knew there were men who fantasized about debauching a nun; he just hadn't thought he was one of them. But he couldn't deny the fierce hum that ran through his veins when he thought about ripping off that shapeless black gown that she donned like armor to reveal the wanton he'd glimpsed hiding beneath that fade-into-the-background facade.

He wanted to make her gasp. Wanted to see her lips part and color flood to her cheeks when he touched her. He wanted to be the one to make her shatter for the first time.

To his surprise, when he caught her gaze, he found himself nodding to her. Acknowledging in some way that he hadn't forgotten her. He'd never singled out a woman so publicly—or done anything that could be construed as romantic—and the gesture took him aback.

Although he doubted anyone else had noticed, she did. He could have seen her eyes widen from halfway across Scotland, let alone the fifty or so paces that separated them. He was more amused than surprised when she immediately ducked behind the man in front of her. But if she thought she could escape him so easily, she was mistaken.

He amended his earlier decision. Hell, he'd worked hard. He could afford to relax and enjoy a little previctory celebration. He wanted her, and waiting no longer seemed necessary.

He started toward her, but he'd barely exited the arena before he found his path blocked by the first of many well-wishers. He heard some form of "Sir Kenneth, you were magnificent" from the female contingent, and "Bloody impressive fighting, Sutherland" from the male.

After working so hard to get here, he should have been savoring every minute of this; it was what he'd always wanted. Yet instead he found himself impatiently scanning the platform and stairs where he'd last seen the lass. But the crowd was too thick and the lass too small for him to pick her out.

He finally managed to extract himself. Threading his way to the base of the stairs, he caught a glimpse of black in the sea of colorful silk moving away from him. He smiled, thinking it ironic that her plain clothing, which he suspected was meant to hide her, was what identified her.

He would have gone after her, but Lady Moira caught him first. "Congratulations, my lord, on yet another victory. Were you by chance looking for someone?" She batted her eyelashes so aggressively he was tempted to ask whether she had something in her eye. Normally, such coquetry amused him, but right now he found it annoying.

His mouth tightened impatiently as he saw his prey slipping away.

Moira stood with Lady Elizabeth Lindsay, who seemed amused by her companion's efforts. Lady Elizabeth was reputedly devoted to her husband and nothing Kenneth had seen suggested the contrary. She was friendly and polite, but nothing more. Which suited him just fine. Although she was a beautiful woman, she was shrewd, stubborn, and opinionated. He didn't envy Lindsay the headache. Challenges were for the battlefield, not the bedchamber.

"We are all trying to figure it out," Lady Elizabeth said.

"Figure what out?" he asked, glancing over her shoulder, trying to keep his eye on his prey.

"Who the nod was for," Lady Elizabeth said.

He looked at her, barely hiding his surprise. "Nod?"

"Aye, it created quite a stir. The ladies seated around me were all quite sure you were nodding to them," Lady Elizabeth said with a smile.

Ah hell, he guessed it had been more noticeable than he realized. Kenneth hid his reaction behind a wicked smile. "I was," he said.

Lady Moira nearly yelped with pleasure, clapping her hands together. "I knew it. To whom?"

"I'll leave that to you to figure out," he said with a playful wink. "Now, if you'll excuse me. I see my sister, and I need to have her patch me up so I'll be ready for tomorrow's competition."

It was only partially a lie. The blow he'd taken across the ribs was starting to throb beneath his habergeon. The shirt of mail offered scant protection against the impact of steel on bone, and he suspected he had a fairly nasty bruise brewing. He would see Helen to get it fixed up, but *after* he caught up with his little nun, who was weaving her way through the crowd at nearly a run in her effort to avoid him.

She was only running from the inevitable. Almost as certain as he was that he would win tomorrow, Kenneth was certain that before the night was out, he would have her under him. Or perhaps on top of him.

He felt a pleasant tightening in his groin just thinking about it.

She'd just passed through the gate into the castle when he saw her stop and turn.

"Mary, wait!" he heard someone—a woman—say. He turned, recognizing the speaker as Lady Margaret MacKenzie. "Where are you going in such a rush?"

Mary. He should have guessed. A common, unremarkable name that would draw no attention—just like the rest of her. He was only a few feet away, but she hadn't seen him yet. "I think the sun—"

She stopped suddenly, her eyes widening and mouth caught in an O of surprise as she saw him. On such a severe countenance, it shouldn't be so sensual. But it was the same expression that had thrown him over the edge in the barn.

In the sunlight, without the glasses hiding half her face, he got his first really good look at her. Her hair was still hidden beneath an ugly black veil and wimple, her gown was still boxy and shapeless, her skin was still pale, her features were still too sharp—especially her cheekbones, which stuck out prominently over sunken cheeks—and there was still an overall gray, ghostlike quality to her, but on closer scrutiny he knew his instincts had been right. The hint of prettiness and intentional obscuring of beauty was even more obvious in the stark light of day.

There was no hiding her eyes, and they were spectacular. Round and overlarge in her hollow-cheeked face, they were a remarkable greenish-blue, and framed by thick, long lashes that seemed incongruously soft on such an otherwise brittle exterior. Her mouth, too, was soft and full, with a sensual dip that made him think of a bow on a package he wanted to unwrap. Preferably with his tongue.

As soon as their eyes met, she instinctively dropped her gaze as if hiding her eyes from his view.

Hiding. That was exactly what she was doing. The question was why, and from what.

"Lady Mary, Lady Margaret," he said, approaching the two women with a bow.

Lady Margaret turned to him with a gasp. She gaped at him, and then at Mary. "You've met?"

He grinned, seeing the blush rise to Mary's cheeks.

"Briefly," she said tightly.

The lass really needed to relax. She was pulled as tight as a bowstring.

"Not *too* briefly," he corrected, unable to stop himself from teasing her. He liked seeing the color in her cheeks. "I'm looking forward to furthering our acquaintance. I hope you are not bored with the Games already? Perhaps they are not *exciting* enough for you?"

He knew he was being horrible, but he couldn't help teasing her.

She wasn't shy, though. Her eyes met his full force, flashing at him in outrage.

"Oh, it was exciting, wasn't it, Mary?" Lady Margaret interposed.

He thought she nodded, but her jaw was clenched so tight it was hard to tell. "I'm sure Sir Kenneth has heard enough accolades for the day, Margaret. He doesn't need to hear them from us."

She gave him a smile that made him frown. She had a way of making it sound unflattering. He was used to reading a certain amount of feminine admiration in a woman's gaze, but with her there was only cool challenge. He didn't think he liked it.

"There is still the sword dance to be held this afternoon. If Lady Margaret doesn't object, I would be happy to escort you."

Lady Margaret looked at him in surprise. "Why would I object?"

"No!" Mary said over her. Her blush deepened as she realized she'd spoken too harshly. "I mean, I regret that I must return to the castle. I'm feeling unwell."

Lady Margaret became immediately concerned. She put her hand on Mary's arm. "Is that why you rushed off?" She laid the back of her hand across Mary's forehead. "You do look flushed."

Mary nodded, not looking in his direction. Probably to avoid his provoking grin. "I think the sun was too much for me."

Lady Margaret turned to him. "Mary has just recovered from an illness. This was the first time she's had a chance to see the Games all week."

"Is that so?" he drawled.

She couldn't avoid looking at him any longer. He could see a flash of anger in her blue-green eyes that reminded him of sun glinting on the sea. He hadn't expected so much spirit from such a quiet exterior, and his intrigue grew.

"Aye, I've been very unwell."

He swore he could see her chin stiffen, challenging him to disagree with her.

"My sister is a healer. If you like, I could send her to you."

Her mouth thinned, hearing his challenge. "That is very kind of you, but I'm sure that will not be necessary. I think I just need to lie down."

"Lying down sounds like a wonderful idea."

Though there was nothing suggestive in his voice, he knew she'd understood when he heard her sharp intake of breath.

She was outraged, as no doubt she should be. But he could also see by the delicate flutter of her pulse below a surprisingly velvety-soft-looking cheek that she was more intrigued than she wanted to let on.

The devil! The man had no shame. He was propositioning her right in front of Margaret, fixing her with that taunting look in his eyes—as if he knew a naughty secret. And blast him, he did!

There was such a heavy undercurrent of suggestiveness running between them, Mary was certain Margaret must feel it. Not wanting to guess what he would say next, she was glad when one of Margaret's daughters came up and distracted her with a plea to go with her friends to the sword dance.

Realizing he was no doubt trying to get to her, she schooled her features into a polite mask and bowed her head. "My lord."

She turned away to head for the nearest tower, but he grabbed her arm. "Wait."

She flinched at the contact. The heat of his hand on her arm was like a brand, startling in its intensity. She could feel the imprint of every one of those thick, blunt-edged fingers pressing into her. Talented, deft fingers that could bring so much pleasure.

Heat washed over her. *Don't think of it.*

But all she could do was think of it.

Standing so close to him was hard enough. Her pulse had taken a sudden erratic lurch and her skin felt strange— as if a thousand bees were buzzing all over her—the moment he drew near. She felt like very dry kindling hovering over a roaring fire. When he touched her, her body flooded with a warm, drenching heat that told her exactly what she was feeling: desire.

Instinctively sensing the danger, she wrenched away.

Surprisingly, he let her go. His hand released her almost as quickly as she'd tried to remove it. When she gazed up at him, there was a slight frown between his brows, almost as if he'd felt it, too. *Ridiculous*.

Once again she nearly had to blink from the brightness. When she'd first glanced over and seen him standing there, she felt as if she were looking right into the sun—or rather, right at the Sun god himself.

It was only his mail sparkling in the sun like a shimmering star, she told herself. But with the layer of dirt from battle covering him, she knew it wasn't just that. It was he. He shone as brightly as any star. Everything about him flashed and shimmered, from the golden streaks in his dark brown hair, the dangerous gleam in his challenging blue eyes, and the lean hard lines of his pugnaciously handsome face to the white flash of his take-no-prisoners grin. Though the men appealed in different ways, Sir Kenneth Sutherland could rival Gregor MacGregor for the title of most handsome man in Scotland, and she suspected he knew it.

Sir Kenneth exuded confidence and brash arrogance. He probably thought she would fall at his feet just like all the other young, starry-eyed ladies seemed to be doing. But she was no longer young, and the stars had been wrenched from her eyes a very long time ago.

Still, she felt an unmistakable thrill shooting through her veins, a spark of excitement that she hadn't felt in a very

long time. It was probably her temper. He seemed to bring out a heretofore unknown streak of combativeness in her.

It was the way he looked at her. Confident and arrogant, yes, but also provoking. As if he were daring the world to come at him. As if he were always trying to prove something. He didn't think she could resist him and was daring her to try.

"Running away again, my lady?" he taunted softly. "This time I might have to come after you."

She kept her voice steady, but her heart was fluttering like the wings of a butterfly trapped under glass. "I told you, I'm not feeling well. I need to rest."

But he was right. She *was* running away, and she didn't like him pointing it out.

She turned to face him and looked into his eyes. It was a mistake. She could feel it again. That piercing, riveting hold. And the heat that pulsed through her body.

"You don't need to be embarrassed." His voice spread over her skin like a seductive, warm caress.

"I'm not embarrassed," she protested. But the heat that rose to her cheeks told a far different story.

"It's much more fun doing than watching, you know."

Mary blinked at him in shock, not quite sure that she'd heard him right. But she had. She looked around to make sure no one had overheard him. Fortunately, Margaret was still speaking with her daughter. There were a few curious stares from passersby, but no one seemed to be listening.

He didn't give her a chance to reply. "Meet me tonight. After the feast." Mary stared at him in something between outrage at his sinful suggestion and awe at the bold straightforwardness with which it had been made. He was truly something. "Once you are done with your duties," he finished.

A small frown gathered between her brows. "My duties?"

"To your lady," he said, motioning to Lady Margaret. "You are one of her attendants?"

My God, he didn't know who she was! Mary was about to correct him when something stopped her. She wondered what he would do when he realized he'd just propositioned the woman the king wanted him to marry?

"You certainly don't waste any time," she said wryly. She didn't know why she was surprised; she'd seen his aggressiveness on the battlefield.

"I don't believe in playing games. We both know what we want."

He wanted her? But why, when he had a flock of women following him around like a retinue? Given the efforts she'd taken to dull her appearance, she was oddly flattered. And more surprisingly, she found herself oddly charmed by this too-handsome, too-arrogant, outrageous warrior with his cocky, provoking smile who knew what he wanted and went right for it.

She tilted her head, looking at that gleaming smile flash in the sun. "Does anyone ever refuse you?"

His mouth quirked. "Not very often. If you recall, I have much to recommend me."

She remembered. She remembered exactly what he looked like under all that mail. Remembered the body that was every bit as steely and hard. Mary was more tempted than she wanted to admit—the man was a walking platter of confection. A sultan of sin. But she had no interest in joining another harem.

"Alas, I'm afraid I will have to disappoint you."

He didn't seem to have taken her refusal to heart. "Are you married?"

She shook her head. "Widowed."

He nodded as if he'd anticipated her answer. "Then there is nothing to prevent you."

"Prevent you from what?" Margaret asked.

"Joining me for a dance after the feast," he answered

without missing a beat. "With your permission, of course, my lady."

"My permission?" Margaret said. "Why would—?"

"Lady Margaret is very accommodating to all her attendants," Mary interrupted.

Margaret was looking at her as if she had two heads, but Sir Kenneth didn't appear to notice.

He bowed to Margaret, and then herself, with far more flourish than the situation warranted. "Then I shall look forward to seeing you both after the feast."

The look he sent her gave her no doubt of what he intended. He really was wicked. And a suddenly wicked part of her thought it would be fun to knock this champion-in-the-making down a few pegs. Mary felt a smile turn her lips. Perhaps she would attend the feast after all. She was going to enjoy seeing his face when he realized his mistake.

Five

Mary managed to avoid an immediate interrogation by Margaret, who was dragged off to the sword dance by her daughter after Sir Kenneth took his leave, but a few hours later she came bursting into the chamber Mary shared with her attendants and a few of the other ladies.

"It was you!" she said excitedly.

Looking around at the curious gazes of the other women, who were already starting to ready themselves for the feast, and realizing this was something she probably wouldn't want everyone to hear, Mary put down her embroidery and steered Margaret over to the mural chamber inset into the thick stone wall. It wasn't as much a chamber as a large stone bench with a cushion, and a heavy velvet curtain for privacy.

After settling on the bench, she folded her hands in her lap and asked calmly, "*What* was me?"

"He was nodding to you, wasn't he? Oh, everyone is talking about it, trying to figure out whom Sir Kenneth nodded to after his victory. Lady Moira and Lady Alice both insist it was they, but I know it was you!" Margaret was grinning like a young girl with a naughty secret. "It's so romantic!"

Mary made a face. She knew exactly how much store to put in romantic gestures. She shifted her gaze. "It could have been anyone."

But Margaret wasn't fooled. "It wasn't anyone, it was

you. Why else would he have come right up to you afterward? I saw the way he was looking at you. Why didn't you tell me you'd met before?" Suddenly, her brow furrowed. "But why did you let him think you were one of my attendants?"

Mary bit her lip, feeling the shame heat her cheeks. She met the kind eyes of her former sister-in-law and weighed what she should say. It had been so many years since she'd felt the urge to confide in someone—or had anyone to confide in, for that matter. Not since Janet. But Margaret had always been kind to her, perhaps pitying the young girl her brother had married. She, too, had been a young bride, although her marriage seemed to have turned out well enough.

"I hadn't met him," Mary answered. "Not really." She took a deep breath and gave a very short explanation of what had happened. Margaret's eyes widened and her mouth dropped with every word. Mary didn't know what the other woman had expected to hear, but it certainly wasn't this. Shock was written on every inch of her pretty face. Although Margaret had to be nearing her fortieth saint's day, like her brother, her classical features gave her a timeless beauty.

"So you see," Mary finished, "it's merely a game to him. He thinks that because of what I witnessed, I'm an easy mark, and that I am only too eager to be the next woman in line to jump in his bed."

Although Mary had skipped over the more salacious details, such as the position she'd found him in, the manner of his release, and the embarrassing extent of her reaction, from the way Margaret was looking at her, she must have guessed. "And are you?"

Mary thought about lying, but instead she let out an exasperated sigh. "More than I would like to admit." The heat in her cheeks intensified. She wasn't used to talking so openly. "I know it's wrong, and I would never do something so sinful. I've probably shocked you with my wickedness, but he was quite . . . impressive." She made a face. "As he is well aware. The man is too arrogant and cocky by half."

A mischievous smile curved up Margaret's mouth. "I've heard quite *cocky*." She lowered her voice to a whisper. "He's reputed to be quite, um, *generously* formed in a certain male appendage."

It took Mary a moment to realize what she meant. Her eyes went huge with shock. "Margaret!"

Long sword, Lady Moira had said. Now she understood. Apparently, it hadn't been her glasses.

Margaret gave an unrepentant shrug. "Ladies talk. It's hardly a secret, although I admit it isn't one for polite conversation. But after a long feast and a few goblets of wine, some of the ladies can be every bit as ribald as the men."

Mary had been more sheltered than she realized. It seemed there was an entire world she was missing.

"He's the perfect man, you know, for a night of sin. Were you ever to contemplate it."

For once Mary did not ask herself what her sister would do. She feared the answer. "But that's the problem, isn't it? A night isn't an option for women like us. And I could never marry such a man. He only sought me out because he doesn't know who I am. Seducing a widowed attendant is quite different from a countess the king wishes him to marry." She smiled. "I admit, I'm looking forward to his surprise when he finds out his mistake."

Margaret returned her smile. "I am, too. Sir Kenneth is a charming scoundrel, but his behavior has been outrageous. Perhaps it will teach him a lesson." She paused. "But you could always tell him after. Why shouldn't you not have a night, if you wish it, Mary? If anyone deserves a bit of sin, you do, after all you have been through. You're a widow, not beholden to any man. Surely you know it is not uncommon?"

Hardly. Atholl had taught her that. "It doesn't make it any less wrong," she said softly.

Margaret smiled and patted her hand. "Of course, you are right. Now who is the wicked one?" She laughed and gave her a mischievous wink. "But don't forget, if you change your mind, you can always repent for your sins later. I should think he would be worth at least a few dozen Hail Marys."

More like a few hundred. Mary fought back the smile, but in the end laughed along with her former sister-in-law. Who knew it could be so much fun to be a little wicked?

The torches had already been lit for the coming night when Kenneth finally dragged himself from the soothing hot waters of the bath his sister had arranged for him. Helen didn't think any of his ribs were broken, but you wouldn't know it from the ghastly-looking mass of purple, black, and red that covered a large portion of his left side. And you sure as hell wouldn't know it from the pain. It hurt like the bloody devil.

He'd made a mistake. Become too aggressive. Assured of his victory, he'd tried to end it too soon and in the process had given MacKinnon an opening. The other warrior had taken full advantage of it with a blow that could have put a swift end to all Kenneth's plans. He knew better, damn it. He sure as hell wasn't going to let it happen again.

There was nothing his sister could do for it beyond providing a tight binding tomorrow, having him soak in a hot bath tonight, and giving him a draught of nasty-tasting brew for the pain. It relaxed him. Perhaps a little too much. He could have fallen asleep in the warm water and been happy to skip the feast entirely.

He'd avoided most of the long meals and celebrations during the week, preferring a Spartan routine while he competed. But the king had specifically requested his presence tonight to meet Atholl's widow, who was leaving soon, and MacKay had told him in no uncertain terms, when he'd come to collect Helen earlier, that he'd better be there. With the result tomorrow all but assured—as Kenneth had anticipated, Robbie Boyd had not entered— he could afford to relax his guard for a few hours.

Besides, he had other plans he didn't want to miss.

He was surprised just how eager he was to see Lady Mary again. He didn't let her prior refusal deter him. He was confident in his persuasive abilities. She'd been shocked and outraged, but she'd also been tempted. He'd seen it in those brilliant eyes of hers before they'd started flashing at him.

He didn't know what it was about the lass that provoked him to such wickedness. But there was something about the way she looked at him that made him feel as if she were still wearing those glasses of hers—as if she were seeing him too clearly and judging him too harshly—and he couldn't resist.

He frowned. There was more to her than the laced-too-tightly repressed wanton in a nun's habit than he'd antici-pated. He'd expected a shy, passive lass who would be flattered by his attention.

She wasn't either.

His frown deepened. He didn't know why he was both-ering with the lass at all. She wasn't like his usual bed-mates. She was older, plainer, and far from the "throng of worshipers" his sister teased him about.

He wasn't usually forced to make such an effort. Women came to him. Hell, he couldn't remember the last time he'd had to go to this much trouble for a lass.

He supposed it was the novelty that was drawing him. But he was surprisingly eager for the second part of his night to begin. He couldn't wait to see whether the glimpse of raw sensuality was as hot as it appeared.

He'd blocked out the simpering and giggling of the maidservant who'd been given the task of bathing him, but heard it now as she began to help him into his braies. He didn't encourage her obvious interest, however, and quickly donned his breeches, tunic, and plaid, wincing when he had to lift his hands over his shoulders. He allowed her to help him pull on his boots to avoid bending over, but buckled the dirk that he was never without around his waist himself.

His hair was still damp as he made his way across the courtyard from the makeshift bathhouse in a small corner of the kitchens, where the fire had not only kept him warm but had proved efficient at heating the water as well.

There weren't many people milling about as the feast had already gotten underway, but he greeted a few of the guardsmen who were posted around the *barmkin*. Even before he climbed the stairs and entered the East Range of the castle, he could hear the raucous sounds of celebrating coming from the open windows of the Great Hall. He was glad to see that he wasn't the last to arrive, as the corridor to his left was still filled with people making their way into the celebration. Before he could follow them, MacKay blocked his path.

"You're late," he snapped.

Kenneth's jaw locked in what had become almost a reflex when it came to his interactions with his future brother-in-law. "You have the fine makings of a nursemaid if you ever get tired of warfare. I didn't realize my comings and goings were so important to you."

MacKay returned his glare. "They aren't. The king sent me to see what was taking you so long."

"I had something to attend to."

MacKay smiled. "Helen told me you were injured. I hope it isn't serious." He shook his head in mock disappointment. "It would be a shame if you lost tomorrow."

"Helen exaggerates. I'll be fine to fight tomorrow, and just like all the other events, I'll win. I hope you are ready for a new partner."

MacKay's eyes flared. "If you win tomorrow, you'll deserve to be my partner. But I wouldn't count my victories too soon; it's not over yet."

Kenneth wasn't listening; he barely registered MacKay's half-smile before turning away. Out of the corner of his eye, something had caught his attention. Or should he say *someone* had caught his attention?

"You're fortunate Lady Mary hasn't arrived yet," MacKay said.

Another Mary. Kenneth had forgotten Atholl's widow's given name was Mary. His mind was on the Mary at the other end of the corridor, near the donjon. At least he thought it was her. He couldn't see her face, but the clothes were dark and plain enough to stand out.

Except this woman seemed to be *laughing*. She was looking up at the man opposite her—

Kenneth stopped. *Bloody hell.*

Without realizing it, his fists clenched at his sides and his mouth fell in a hard line.

Why was she talking to Gregor MacGregor?

He started toward them.

"Where in Hades are you going?" MacKay called after him. "The king is waiting for you."

But Kenneth was too angry to heed him. "I'll just be a few minutes."

He heard MacKay mumble something along the lines of "it better be important" behind him, but he was already striding—stalking was probably more accurate—down the corridor.

As he drew nearer, his instincts were confirmed. It was his nun. She'd changed for the feast into a gown of deep emerald silk and a matching veil, albeit without the ghastly wimple. He could actually see her neck. It was a pretty one, long and slender, with creamy-smooth, milky-white skin. His eyes narrowed. What else was she hiding? The cut of the gown was still shapeless and the embellishments still plain, but he supposed green was a marginal improvement over black. The color, however, was too dark and harsh against her fair skin—

He stopped himself. Bloody hell, he sounded like a lady's maid. He couldn't recall ever noticing a lady's attire before—except perhaps to figure out how to get it off.

His steps fell a little harder and his mouth grew a little flatter as he drew closer. He didn't know why he was so irritated. But when she put her hand on MacGregor's arm, looked up at him, and smiled, Kenneth felt a spike of something hotter and edgier than mere irritation.

MacGregor saw him first and nodded. "Sutherland."

Kenneth could tell by the tone in his voice that he'd sensed something was wrong, though damned if he knew what it was any better than MacGregor did.

Lady Mary turned on hearing his name. The smile immediately slipped from her face. Why that reaction bothered him, he didn't know, but it damn well did.

His jaw clenched. "The feast has started," he bit out.

The lady ignored him. "Thank you, my lord," she said to MacGregor. "I fear I would have been looking for hours without your help."

MacGregor explained. "Lady Elizabeth lost her kitten."

"Lady Margaret's youngest daughter," Mary clarified when it was clear he didn't know to whom they were referring. "I was able to recruit Sir Gregor in our search." The smile on her lips and flush on her cheeks when she looked up at the other man made Kenneth's fists and jaw clench even harder. She didn't look dull and colorless at all.

"Fortunate, indeed," he said, unable to completely mask the dryness of his tone. Sir Gregor wasn't a "Sir" at all; MacGregor wasn't a knight.

He and MacGregor exchanged glances over her head. *Back off*, he told McGregor wordlessly. "I will escort Lady Mary to the Hall."

MacGregor looked more puzzled than put out, but he

conceded without argument. Kenneth was too angry to wonder about that.

"My lady," MacGregor said with a bow, and then to him, "Sutherland."

Kenneth hadn't realized how tense he'd been, until his muscles started to relax as the man reputed to be the most handsome in Scotland walked away.

Lady Mary was watching him with furrowed brows. "What was that about?"

He didn't know himself, damn it, and suddenly he felt as if he'd revealed something he shouldn't have. He buried his anger behind a mask of feigned concern. It was his duty as a knight to warn her off, he told himself. "You should watch yourself with him. MacGregor has made more than one woman forget herself."

She had the gall to burst out laughing. "This, from you? Isn't your warning a bit ironic considering our first meeting?" Their eyes held, and he felt the strange urge to shift his feet. If he believed it possible, he would have thought he was embarrassed. "Nor did he invite me to his bed the first time we spoke." She allowed her gaze to follow the other man's disappearing form. "Pity," she said under her breath.

But he heard it. His blood spiked hot. That edgy irritation returned full force. His muscles flared and his mouth fell in a hard, uncompromising line. He took her arm and forced her gaze back to him. "Stay away from him."

She should be terrified. He never spoke to women like this. He was in full, fierce warrior mode. But her eyes only narrowed at his tone, and then on his hand when it became apparent that she wasn't going to be able to shrug him off so easily this time. "What right do you have to speak to me like this? You have no claim on me."

He told himself to cool down, but there was something in her gaze that snapped the precarious hold he had on his temper like a dry twig. She might not have meant it as

a challenge, but he'd taken it as one. Young, uncomplicated, eager to please, and lusty. She might be the last,
but he was already regretting not sticking to his typical
sort of bedmate.

Seeing a door behind her, he opened it and pulled her
inside. It probably had been a storage room at some time,
though judging from the shelves of books and folios, the
thickly cushioned bench and chairs, and the brazier, it had
been turned into a library. But he was only vaguely aware
of his surroundings. He closed the door behind him, spun
her around, and pinned her against it with the hard slam
of his body.

She gasped—in surprise at the suddenness of his movements or at the sensation of contact, he didn't know.

Damn. He'd forgotten about his ribs. Yet pressed against
her, it wasn't pain he was feeling but awareness. She was
more slight than he'd realized, slim and delicate. He had
to be careful not to crush her. He could feel the bones of
her hips, but also, he noticed, the small, soft curves of her
breasts. For unremarkably sized breasts they seemed to be
eliciting quite a reaction. His body crackled with a frantic, unfamiliar energy. It was lust, but lust unlike any he'd
ever felt before.

It didn't make any sense, but he was too angry to wonder how a too-skinny widow past her prime, doing her
best to look unattractive, was making him feel like a squire
about to tup his first maid.

He intended to show her exactly what kind of claim he
had. He'd seen her first, damn it. If anyone was going to
cut those too-tight laces of hers and watch her explode, it
was going to be him.

Planting his hands on either side of her face, he leaned in
closer. She smelled good. Not with the overwhelming,
cloying scent of strong perfumes, but a faint whiff of flowers, as if she'd bathed in rose petals.

Her breath did an enticing little hitch as his face lowered. In the dim light of the fire he saw her lips part in innocent invitation, but it was the flutter of her pulse below her jaw that sent a pool of heat rushing straight to his groin.

Aye, she wanted him. He could almost taste the desire on her lips, and it shot through him with a surprisingly powerful surge.

"I'm making one," he said, staring in her eyes and daring her to deny him.

He could see her eyes widen as she took in his meaning. "I don't—"

He cut off her protest with a kiss. He'd only meant to make his point, to stake his claim with a possessive, irrefutable press of his mouth. But the first touch of his lips on hers changed his mind.

He suddenly understood the poetical allusions of bards. The ground did indeed feel like it had shifted as he was hit with an overwhelming blast of sensation. Passion exploded between them on contact. The kind of raw, primal passion that reached down, grabbed him by the bollocks, and wouldn't let go. Aye, his bollocks could feel it—as did his cock.

His bodily reaction to her was fierce. Primal. The strange attraction vibrating between them tightened, and the connection once made could not be undone. It had happened to him before—an unexpectedly powerful reaction to a woman on an elemental level—but never to this extent.

Hell, he wouldn't need the recipe for black powder if he could bottle this.

He hadn't expected this at all. It was a surprise. A pleasant one, but a surprise nonetheless. Who would have thought he'd be so turned on by a colorless little wren? The fierce attraction didn't make sense, but it was undeniable.

Christ, her lips were so soft they didn't feel real. He groaned, sinking a little deeper in the kiss. And so sweet.

He couldn't believe how sweet. He'd had honeysuckle once, and that was what he thought of now. Blooming in the warm sun.

He moved his lips over hers. Slowly at first, urging her response. She wasn't fighting him, seeming to be in almost a stunned daze, but it was equally clear she didn't know what to do.

He showed her. With slow, gentle strokes, he told her with each lingering drag of his lips on hers exactly what he wanted from her.

She mimicked his movements tentatively at first, and then with growing confidence as the kiss intensified.

A shudder of sensation rippled through him. His chest buckled. It felt incredible. He had to fight the urge to sink in deeper, to bend her to him and take everything he wanted from her all at once.

He felt strange—drugged with desire. It was coming over him too fast and hard. He was hot and hard—and getting harder by the minute. And she was practically melting against him. The press of his hips against hers had become a sweet grind, as the gentle friction of their kiss intensified.

Christ.

He groaned, needing to taste her deeper. His hand was on her cheek, caressing the velvety-soft skin, his fingers urging her to open her mouth. When she did, he wanted to let out a roar of pure masculine pleasure. He wanted to plunder her mouth with his tongue, claim every inch of her surrender.

But instead he forced himself to slow. Swallowing her gasp of surprise, he swept his tongue inside, letting her get used to the sensation.

But slow wasn't working. Not when she responded. At the first slide of her tongue against his, he felt his control slip. With every stroke, every taste, he was descending deeper and deeper into a mindless haze. The smooth seduction was becoming a conflagration of urgent groans and frantic movements.

His body was responding to her with an urgency he couldn't recall. He couldn't seem to get enough.

The roar of lust in his ears grew louder, drowning out everything else. It was pounding through his veins in a rush of hot molten lava. All he could think about was the tiny woman against him. The feel of her slight body pressing against his. The feel of her mouth sliding under his. How much he wanted to hitch her up against the door, wrap her legs around him, and sink inside her.

He couldn't remember the last time he'd gotten this hot from a kiss. The awakening of her desire was egging him on.

He dug his fingers through the hair concealed by the veil, groaning at its silky softness. Cradling the back of her head, he brought her mouth closer to his. The kiss grew harder, hotter, more carnal. She was dissolving against him like warm sugar and he couldn't seem to devour her fast enough.

The sensations firing inside him were too strong. His desire was too intense. His heart was beating too hard, his blood rushing too fast, his skin feeling too hot. He felt himself sinking deeper into the kiss, sinking deeper into her. Moving closer to the point of no return.

From a damned kiss.

He had to stop.

He tore his mouth away with an oath and had to stop himself from stumbling back. It felt as if he'd been caught up in a whirlpool, and then suddenly tossed out.

He stepped back to put distance between them, trying to clear his damned head. He felt light-headed, as if he were moving in a haze.

What the hell was wrong with him? The tincture his sister made him take must have been more potent than he realized.

It couldn't just be from a kiss.

But one glance at her equally dazed eyes and he had to wonder.

Looking at her was a mistake. His groin tugged hard. Painfully hard. He was no longer in doubt about his fantasy. She was the very embodiment of the wanton nun, and when he looked at her swollen mouth, her half-lidded eyes, and her flushed cheeks he wanted to rip those clothes off her and debauch her thoroughly.

"Meet me after the feast." He could barely get the words out, his heart was beating so fast.

She blinked up at him—apparently, like him, trying to clear the haze from her head. Their eyes met in the soft glow of firelight. She didn't say a word; only the heaviness of their breathing and the occasional snap and crackle from the fire in the brazier broke the long silence. She was staring at him, looking for something deep in his eyes while she waged some kind of internal battle.

After what seemed an interminable pause, she finally answered. "I can't." He would have pulled her in his arms again and tried to change her mind, but she stopped him with a hand to the chest. For something so small, it proved surprisingly potent. "It has to be now."

He stilled. "Now? Why?"

She shook her head. "It just does. I can't explain."

"But the feast." Damn it, Bruce was expecting him. He would be furious if he missed the meeting he'd arranged with the countess. "Surely, a few hours won't make a difference?"

He made a move toward her, but she spun away from him and shook her head. "Now or never—it's up to you."

He frowned, hearing something in her voice that made him think she meant it. He didn't like ultimatums, but he also heard something else. She thought he would refuse.

He *should* go straight to the feast and forget about her. But one glance at those still-pink cheeks and swollen lips

and he wasn't sure that was possible. The lass was definitely a distraction he didn't need, though a damned enticing one.

What the hell. What was a half-hour? The king and the
countess could wait a little longer.

He smiled, calling her bluff. "Then now it is."

Mary blinked. "What?"

He wasn't supposed to say yes.

He smiled that slow half-smile of his that seemed to
reach down to her toes and yank all the good sense right
out of her.

He moved closer, the heat of his body engulfing her. It
was like standing next to a raging fire. He was so hot she
couldn't think straight.

Why couldn't she find herself attracted to a man of non-
threatening proportions just once? She inched back away
from him, instinctively looking for somewhere to go. But
he seemed to take up all the space. Tall and broad-
shouldered, his powerful form dominated the small room,
radiating a volatile energy.

He'd even stolen the air. Every breath was filled with
the subtle scent of his soap. She'd never known a man
could smell so good. Clean and warm, with the faint
trace of sandalwood.

She was too aware of him. Aware of every inch of that
hard, muscular physique that had been plastered against
her. She'd never felt so many muscles, and every one—
every bulge, every band, every solid slab—was burned into
her memory.

As was that kiss. My God, she'd never felt anything like
it! Her body still shook from the aftereffects. She'd been
consumed by sensations unlike anything she'd ever imagined. He'd robbed her of her breath, her mind, and even
her bones, turning her into a melting pool of desire. All she
could think about was the pressure of his mouth, the

warmth of his tongue licking into her, the hardness of his body, the feel of his arms around her, and the exquisite sensations building frantically inside her.

She hadn't wanted it to ever stop.

It had been a glimpse—a powerful, wonderful glimpse—of everything that she'd been missing. And he was offering her a chance for more. This time, it wasn't Eve holding out the apple of temptation but Adam. And one taste of sin wasn't nearly enough.

But look what had happened to Adam and Eve.

She stopped suddenly when the back of her legs met the edge of what felt like a table. She hadn't gotten much of a view of the room before he'd blocked it with his body.

Her heart pounded in her chest, trying to keep up with her racing pulse. Could she really do this?

"I—I thought you were anxious to go to the feast." She sounded as nervous as she felt.

He stepped toward her, in one stride erasing the distance she'd put between them. All six foot three—four?—inches of pure masculine temptation. His mouth curved in that slow, provoking smile that dared her to try to resist him, revealing a flash of perfectly straight white teeth. His too-long hair slumped forward across his brow roguishly, and she had to stop herself from reaching out to tuck it back. She'd like to say she wasn't shallow enough to be affected by a handsome face, but the beat of her heart betrayed her.

"The feast can wait."

His eyes ran down the length of her body. She wasn't long, but the slow slide of his hot gaze made her feel that way. He lingered at her breasts, as if he could see right through the thick wool of her gown to the nipples peaking below. The flare of hunger in his eyes made her knees turn to jelly. She wished it was from fear, but the coinciding flutter in her belly felt like anticipation.

One night . . .

Temptation beckoned, but she tried to resist. "Isn't the king expecting you?"

She hadn't thought he would accept her offer. Or had she? Had it been some kind of test to see how badly he wanted this? Did he want it as badly as she did?

Apparently, he did. She had no idea why he wanted her with so many young, beautiful women hanging at his feet, but he did.

Don't read anything into it.

"It will wait."

She could wait, in other words. Mary might have been annoyed by his obvious disinterest and lack of regard for the woman the king had chosen to be his wife, but then he reached down and swept his hand along the curve of her cheek. She sucked in her breath. The feel of those warm, callused fingers on her skin made every nerve ending crackle. But it was the gentleness of the gesture that completely disarmed her. She felt a stab of longing so fierce it stole her breath. For one silly heartbeat she wanted to snuggle into the caress.

No! She wasn't a romantic girl anymore. This was passion, nothing else. She needed to remember that. But Kenneth Sutherland was far more dangerous than she'd realized. Not only did his kiss make her burn with passion, his gentle touch roused far more dangerous emotions.

And this too-handsome-for-his-own-good, arrogant warrior with the face and muscular physique of a Greek god was built for a fantasy, nothing else.

"You've no reason to be nervous, little one. I'll be gentle."

But gentle wasn't what she wanted from him. She wanted a fierce storm of passion. Lust, not tenderness. She wanted to feel what the woman in the barn had felt. Just once.

He looked into her eyes. The sensual curve of his mouth tantalizingly close, lips that had touched hers only inches away. She could still taste him on her tongue. She had never imagined sin could taste so good. Dark and spicy, with a hint of clove.

"You want this, Mary. I know you do. Just say yes."

She stared at him helplessly, paralyzed by the sin of her desire, unable to say the words that would set aside a lifetime of morality.

It wasn't right.

But was it really so wrong?

Neither of them was married. They wouldn't be hurting anyone. She was six and twenty. A widow for three years, an overlooked and neglected wife before that. This might be the last chance to experience what she'd once dreamed about before her young girl's illusions were shattered by a husband who hadn't wanted her and had never given her remotely what she'd seen in the barn.

This man wanted her and could give it to her. With no conditions. No bonds that could not be dissolved. A man on her own terms.

It would only be one time. One night of passion. One night of sin. Was that too much to ask for?

He seemed to sense her struggle. Reaching behind her, he removed a flagon of wine that must have been on the table. "Here," he said, holding it out to her. "Drink this. It will relax you."

She did as he bade, nearly choking when she realized it wasn't wine but whisky. He laughed, urging her to take another drink. She steeled herself, taking a long sip of the fiery brew.

When she was done, she handed it back to him. She wondered if maybe he wasn't quite as confident as he appeared when he took a long, hard sip of the flagon as well—emptying it.

His eyes seemed a little hotter when he leaned over her again, putting his hands on either side of her hips as she rested against the table. "Tell me, Mary," he repeated, the lilting huskiness of his voice adding a new level of temptation. She'd descended from purgatory straight to hell.

She shuddered. Powerful arms and the broad shield of his chest surrounded her like a steel cage. She couldn't escape if she wanted to.

But she didn't want to. She'd learned to make her own decisions, hadn't she? She was going to do this.

That is, if her heart would stop racing long enough for her to take a breath.

But breathing became an afterthought when his mouth found the tender spot next to her ear. The heat of his breath against the damp skin sent a hot bellow of desire rushing through her. His mouth trailed along her jaw and then dipped to her neck, finding all the sensitive places along the way. She shuddered and moaned, defenseless against the powerful onslaught of sensation. He pressed a kiss on the frantic beat of her pulse.

"Say yes, Mary," he whispered.

"Yes. Please, yes."

Six

The moment the word was out of her mouth, he fell on her with a fierce growl of possession that sent a thrill right down to her toes. The chains of his passion had been released, and there was no holding him back. It was magnificent. Physical proof of his desire for her.

The slow, seductive caress of his lips on her throat and neck turned ravishing. He devoured whatever inch of bare skin he could find with his lips and tongue. Kissing. Sucking. Sliding and flicking his tongue over her fevered skin until she thought she would die from sheer pleasure. And then his lips were on hers again, and she was certain of it.

His tongue licked into her mouth, filling her with the exquisite taste of him.

For such a powerfully built man, his lips were surprisingly soft. And warm. Deliciously warm. She wanted to sink into him and never come up. She returned his kiss with all the newly wrought passion surging through her veins.

His kiss devastated, destroying whatever lingering doubt she had with each fierce stroke. Her chest squeezed with longing. She wanted this. Wanted it desperately. Wanted it more than she'd ever dreamed possible. He was making her feel things she'd never felt before. Her body tingled and burned with a restless energy. Feelings long dormant had come to life. She felt alive in a way she hadn't felt in a long time. She savored it. Welcomed it. Let it crash over her in wave after thrilling wave. He was a hot, drenching storm to her parched desert.

Her heart beat wildly in her chest on an impatient race toward the unknown. She clutched at him, her fingers digging into the granite of his shoulders, as his tongue claimed every inch of her mouth. And she let him take it, surrendering to the plunder with fierce abandon.

Her breasts were crushed to his chest. She moaned at the contact, reveling in the sensation of the solid weight of him over her. There was something deeply arousing about the feel of all those muscles pressed up against her. Something primal in the bodily proof of his masculinity and her femininity. He was big and strong; if there was ever a man built to protect, it was he.

Although she no longer looked to a man to protect her, she did like the way all those muscles felt against her. It seemed strange that something so hard and unyielding could make her want to curl against him and never let go.

But it wasn't just their chests that touched. He dipped his hips toward hers, and she gasped.

Goodness! It was one thing to take note of his size out of the corner of her eye, it was another to have the blatant evidence burning into her stomach. Thick and hard, she could feel every sinful inch of him throbbing against her.

But instead of fear, the proof of his arousal sent a frisson of excitement pulsing between her legs. She felt the strangest urge to move. To rub up and down against that hardness.

As if reading her mind, he slid his hand down to cup her bottom and lifted her more firmly against him. With a groan, he started to rock his hips.

Mary saw stars. A burst of sensation exploded inside her. Heat poured through her limbs, gathering in a damp, anxious pool between her legs.

She no longer thought about moving, she *had* to move. Her hips rocked back, grinding against the hard thickness that was both the source of her frenzy and the only thing that could ease the strange restlessness.

She wanted to feel him inside her. To feel him filling her. To feel him thrusting, possessing, bringing her all the pleasure she'd witnessed on the face of that woman.

Feelings, responses, urges that she'd experienced as a young bride but had buried beneath the shame of an indifferent husband burst free.

She held nothing back, straining toward him. Plastering every inch of her body to his. But still it wasn't close enough. She felt the passion reverberating through him in muscles flexing under her fingertips. He was straining, too. Straining against something he wanted just as badly as she did. It was like unharnessing a bolt of lightning. A clap of thunder. Raw, volatile energy ready to be unleashed.

She could feel the pounding of his chest, hear the heaviness of his breath. She wanted to go faster. To have him give her everything she could feel building between them. The hot promise of sensation clenched low in her belly.

He was kissing her so hard, pressing his hips against her so firmly, it seemed nothing could come between them. They were melded together. Not even the barest whisper of air could pass between them. Only heat. Impossible heat.

Suddenly, he tore his mouth away with an oath. "Bloody hell, wait!"

Whether he was talking to himself or her, she didn't know.

She blinked at him dazedly, shocked from the swift curtailment of pleasure. She felt like a child who'd been gorging herself on stolen sweets and then had the plate removed—guilty and unsatisfied. The only consolation was that she was still in his arms. But then those, too, were gone.

She barely stopped herself from sounding the whine that rose to her lips. Swollen lips. Lips that a moment ago had been crushed to his.

He looked at her fiercely, as if blaming something on her. "We're going to do this right."

"That wasn't right?" She blushed, realizing she'd spoken aloud.

His mouth twisted in a wry grin. "I see your point. Perhaps I should have said that table doesn't look very comfortable. Nor does it look very strong. I wouldn't want to break it."

She read the wicked glint in his eye and felt a rush of heat—and not just to her face—when she thought of the force that it would take to break it. The hard, powerful thrusts—

She stopped herself, pushing away the naughty images. Sweet heaven, one taste of passion, and he'd turned her into a wanton!

Almost as if he could read her thoughts, she saw the flare of heat leap into his eyes. The piercing blue darkened to almost black.

He made a sound under his breath that might have been another oath and turned away. If she were still a silly, starry-eyed girl, she would think this paragon of masculine virility was struggling to control himself.

He'd changed from his earlier warrior's garb to a plaid and a fine dark-blue embroidered tunic for the feast. He unfastened the jeweled pin that held the plaid from around his shoulders, and then laid it out on the stone floor. Sinking to his knees, he held out his hand. "It's not as comfortable as hay, but it will have to do."

She bit her lip, trying not to smile. He really was wicked to tease her so. She looked down at his outstretched hand. Now was the time she should be having second thoughts. God save her for being a horrible sinner, but she didn't have a single thought to stop him. Not a one. She put her hand in his and allowed him to help her down, telling herself there was nothing at all romantic about this. He wasn't *her* gallant knight, he was a fantasy.

But when he captured her in his arms, eased her down on the plaid beneath him, and looked into her eyes, her heart was pounding and skipping all over the place.

The warmth was back. He was holding her again, and stretched out against him on the floor, she felt strangely vulnerable. It was intimate, this. Lying with him, they might have been in bed together as husband and wife.

It didn't feel illicit. It didn't feel wicked. It felt . . . right.

No! She felt a stab of fear, wishing she could tell him to go back to the table. Wishing he'd never stopped. Wishing he'd just let the passion explode between them and be done with it.

He pressed a soft kiss on her mouth, still looking into her eyes.

His gaze hypnotized. He was entrancing her, putting her under some kind of spell, making her think, making her believe, that this was somehow special.

One night.

His finger traced her cheek and dipped down to behind her ear. "Your veil," he said huskily. "Can you put it back on by yourself?"

She nodded. "Why?"

She had her answer when he started to pull the pins from her hair. A moment later her veil was tossed to the side.

He drew in his breath.

Her gaze shot to his, and what she saw there made her turn away, shying from the unexpected pleasure. Her hair had been her one vanity. But it had been hidden for so long, she'd wondered if a man would still find it pretty. If his expression was any indication, the answer was yes.

She could feel the weight of his scrutiny as his fingers ran through the long waves.

"It's a sin to cover something so beautiful." His voice was almost reverent. After a moment, he cupped her chin, turning her gaze to his. "What else are you hiding, my Mary?"

She shook her head wordlessly, something in his voice causing her to panic. This was a man who could uncover secrets. Who could dig up emotions buried a long time ago. *My Mary* . . . "Nothing," she managed in a gasp.

He didn't believe her. "We shall see."

And then he kissed her, turning that gasp of panic into one of pleasure.

She could taste his intent. He kissed her like a man with a purpose. This wasn't a kiss meant to seduce but one that was already certain of the end. Bold. Fierce. Carnal. He was taking what he wanted, yet giving her everything in return. He kissed her as if he couldn't get enough of her, as if he was never going to let her go.

Her body responded as if there had never been an interruption. All the passion he'd roused in her returned full force. She slid her hand around his neck, bringing more of his weight down on top of her.

His erection was pressing against her thigh, but he shifted, nudging it closer to the place she wanted it.

She must have cried out. He growled in response, his movements quickening, becoming more frenzied. He slid his hand along the curve of her hips and she arched against him like a cat.

Who was this woman? What had he done to her?

His kiss slid from her mouth, down her chin and to her throat. "You're so sweet." His voice sounded tight, strained.

She could hear the sounds of her breathing in her ears but was too overcome to care. She couldn't seem to do anything but writhe in restless anticipation as his mouth burned a trail down her throat and his hands singed an equally hot path over her body. He knew exactly where to touch her. His hands were on her hips, her stomach, the curve at her waist, and then—finally then—her breast.

He cupped her, squeezed, molded her into his hand, and she moaned at the absolute wonder of it.

His mouth had descended as far down her bodice as the

modest gown would allow him to go. "God, I wish we had more time," he murmured. "I want you naked." A memory of his bare chest flashed before her eyes. She shuddered at the thought of all that hot, tanned skin against her. He lifted his head to look into her eyes. "I want to see these pretty nipples before I take them in my mouth."

He placed his mouth right on the spot he was talking about. She gasped, feeling the damp heat right through the silk and linen.

She arched into his mouth, and she heard him swear again as he sucked. Sucked hard. Sucked so she could feel the sweet tightness around her nipple and shimmery needles of pleasure shot to her toes. She started to moan, soft, urgent sounds that she'd never made before.

He made a harsh sound and pulled away. "God, you're killing me," he said, before returning his mouth to hers for a fierce kiss.

He was moving faster now, with none of the smooth finesse he'd exhibited before. His movements were harsh and stiff, almost clumsy. He was showing none of the detached control she'd witnessed in the barn. Could she really be doing this to him?

He loosened his tunic, fumbled with the ties of his breeches and braies, and worked the edge of her gown up over her hips.

Breaking the kiss, he leaned over her. A slump of dark hair hung forward across his brow, and she fought the urge to tuck it back. His eyes were dark and burning with the same emotion she'd seen in them when he'd taken himself to release with his hand: lust.

For me.

"I need to be inside you."

His hand dipped between her legs, and she gasped. The gentle brush of his finger against the sensitive, quivering flesh sent a thousand shivers racing up her spine.

"You're so hot," he groaned.

Whatever embarrassment she might have felt at his words was erased when his finger slipped inside her. She jolted at the exquisite stroke.

"I knew you'd be like this." He groaned again. "You're made for this, little one."

She didn't know what he was talking about, but the finger stroking inside her felt too good for her to care. Something strange was happening. The needs of her body had taken over. The quivering intensified to a pulse, and then to an insistent throbbing. She felt as if she were climbing, reaching for something she couldn't see.

"That's it," he said encouragingly. "Let it come, love. Let it come."

The soft endearment broke through the haze of her pleasure, but she pushed it away. *It doesn't mean anything.*

But she hadn't expected this bold, wicked warrior to be so . . . tender.

His finger was plunging in and out. Her hips rose on their own to meet the heel of his hand. He pressed against her, murmuring words in her ear. "That's it, love. Fly."

Looking into his eyes, she froze, startled by the intensity of sensation that gripped her. Their eyes held for one long heartbeat before they closed as the sensation exploded inside her in a hot, pulsing spasm. She *was* flying. Soaring in a dreamy world of sensation. The pleasure was indescribable. So much more than she'd imagined. But she couldn't hold on to it. All too soon it was fading away.

She opened her eyes, seeing him leaning over her. His gaze was hot with an emotion she couldn't read.

"You're beautiful," he said fiercely.

She smothered the flare of feminine pleasure. It didn't mean anything. He probably said that to all the women.

Except she couldn't recall him saying it to the woman in the barn.

He moved over her, leveraging his chest over hers. She

fought the urge to glance down, filled with very unmaidenly curiosity.

She sucked in her breath, feeling the blunt tip of his manhood probing her entrance.

She steeled herself for the pain.

"Relax," he said. "I told you I'd be gentle."

She blushed. How could *that* be gentle? Long sword indeed. A *steel* long sword!

But after a moment she believed him. He rubbed the tip of himself against her until she started to relax.

The quivering started again. Her breath began to quicken. She watched his face in the semidarkness. The aggressive masculine jaw clenched and determined, the sensual mouth tight, the sharp blue eyes piercing, the strain that tensed his muscles.

It was killing him to go slow. But he was doing it for her.

The gentleness confused her. It wasn't what she expected from him. It wasn't what she wanted from him. "Now," she told him.

If he was surprised by her demand, his body was too eager to argue with her. Slowly, he started to push inside, using the dampness of her body to ease his way.

Her eyes widened as her body stretched to accommodate him.

She thought it would hurt. It *should* hurt. But instead she realized it felt . . . amazing. He filled her in a way she'd never been filled before. Every incredible inch was a possession. A claiming. A fist of heat pulsing inside her.

Oh God, yes. This was it! This was what she'd been waiting for. Mary couldn't wait to feel him move, to feel him thrusting inside her. All that lust. All that raw passion she'd witnessed in the barn.

Except he wasn't doing that at all. He was holding perfectly still—achingly still—staring at her with a look on his face that made her heart tug. It was a strange mix of surprise and confusion. And he seemed to be looking deep into her eyes for the answer.

Something sharp and poignant passed between them. Something beautiful and impossible. Something that had no place in a fantasy of sin.

Instinctively she wanted to turn from it. But she couldn't seem to break the connection.

Finally, when she thought she couldn't bear the intensity another moment, he started to move. The first thrust sent a shock wave of sensation exploding up her spine. She gasped at the wonder of it. At the all-encompassing pleasure that swept over her with each exquisite stroke.

He groaned, closing his eyes and tipping back his head as if the pleasure had overwhelmed him as well. "God, you feel good," he said with another groan, as his hips lifted and sank again, the slow, circular motion reverberating through her.

She gripped him harder, fighting to hold on as wave after powerful wave of sensation threatened to drag her under. She wanted to close her eyes and give over to the pleasure.

But he wouldn't let her. His gaze held hers in its intimate embrace, not letting go. The intensity of it stole her breath. She felt her heart squeezing.

No! This wasn't what she wanted. This was all wrong. She didn't want emotion. Her chest wasn't supposed to squeeze. It was too intimate. Too gentle. Too sweet.

He was supposed to be a fantasy, but this felt too real, tapping emotions she'd buried long ago.

If only he would stop looking at her.

She had to do something. Focus on something else. She almost wished she was on her hands and knees like the woman in the barn. She wasn't that bold, but she had another thought and blurted, "Will you take off your tunic?"

Kenneth felt as if he'd entered another world. A world that was entirely new. A world where all his previous experience counted for shite. He was sailing blind and without an anchor. It was unsettling and exhilarating at the same time.

He liked swiving. Liked it a lot. Hell, even when it wasn't great it was still damned good. And when it was good there was nothing like it.

But this . . .

This was unlike anything he'd experienced. Something about it resonated. Hell, *everything* about it resonated. From the moment he'd entered her it had felt different. The pleasure had been acute. The pure mind-numbing bliss of sinking into all that warm, soft flesh and feeling her body grip him like a glove. A very wet, very tight, very hot glove. He'd felt a powerful bolt of sensation right to the tip of his cock.

That he understood. What he didn't understand was the rest. The fierce, primal wave of possessiveness that made every instinct in his body scream "mine," followed by the strange feeling of rightness, and an equally fierce wave of protectiveness.

He'd promised her he'd be gentle, and he wanted to be. He wanted to make it good for her.

He'd watched her face as he entered her, saw her cheeks flush, heard the sharp intake of breath as he forged deeper and deeper, filling her.

And when it had happened, when they'd been joined completely . . .

A fierce wave of emotion had reached up and grabbed him by the throat. He'd never felt lust like that before. Lust that settled in his chest and squeezed.

He should be going fast. The king was waiting for him. But it felt so damned good, he didn't want it to end. Buried deep inside her, the tight, wet fist of her body gripping him, he thought he just might be content to stay here forever.

He took it slow. Dragging out every last inch of his thrusts, sliding nearly all the way out before sinking into her again. But still it wasn't deep enough. Wasn't close enough.

It was bloody strange. He couldn't seem to stop looking at her. Hell, he couldn't ever recall holding a woman's gaze for so long. But with her hair tumbling around her face, her cheeks pink, her lips swollen, her eyes hazy with passion, he couldn't look away. The lass had come alive in his arms.

Christ, he realized. *She's beautiful.*

He seemed to stop breathing. Something hot and tight was lodged in his chest. It made him want to hold her gaze. To cup her cheek in his hand and bring his lips to hers in a soft kiss.

The oddity of his reaction made her request all the more jarring.

He stilled. "What?"

She dropped her gaze from his, biting her lip. A blush rose to her cheeks. "I-I . . . " She stammered, peeking up at him from under her lashes. "I was just remembering, and thought it would be nice . . . "

She couldn't seem to finish.

"You thought it would be nice if I took off my tunic?" he said blandly.

She nodded, clearly mortified. "Aye."

There was no reason he should be bothered by the request. Perhaps he should even be pleased. Obviously, she'd admired what she'd seen in the barn and wanted to see it again. A woman admiring his body was nothing new. Hell, he wanted her admiration. But something about the request made him feel like a stallion at market, and given his oddly tender feelings of a few moments ago, it stung.

Bloody hell, what was wrong with him? He sounded like a woman, overly sensitive and overanalyzing every little nuance. Why should he care if she wanted to admire his body? Hadn't he told her the same thing? He wanted to see her naked, and if it wasn't for the difficulty in re-dressing her, he would have torn that bloody gown right off her shoulders.

A tunic, however, was easy enough to put back on. And it would be nice to have her hands on him.

With that thought in his mind, he grabbed the hem off his tunic that was already bunched at his waist and jerked it over his head, tossing it to the side. "As you wish, my lady," he said with a cocky grin.

She gasped, her eyes wide with concern. "You're hurt!" She reached out as if to touch him, but then pulled back as if she were afraid to cause him pain.

He glanced down at the mottled skin, having forgotten about his injury. The pleasure she was giving him was far better medicine than the vile-tasting brew his sister had made him consume, or the long drink of whisky he'd had a few moments ago.

"It's nothing."

She started to argue, but he forced her mind back on what was happening with a little push.

She startled, unthinkingly grabbing for him. Which was exactly what he'd intended. The warm softness of her palms on his skin sent a fresh wave of heat pulsing to his groin. Very nice.

He thrust again. Harder this time. And deeper.

She gripped him harder, her tiny fingers digging into the muscles flaring off the back of his arms.

Aye, that was good. He held himself there, strangely content to just savor the moment of connection. "Any more requests, my lady?" he said huskily, teasingly.

She lifted her gaze from his chest long enough to look into his eyes. He'd meant it as a joke, but she looked oddly serious—worried even. "Faster, please. Just make it faster."

He frowned. Obviously, the lady wasn't as content as he was to make it last. He felt a flicker of temper.

His jaw clenched, tightening his mouth. Well, never let it be said he didn't give the ladies what they wanted.

"Wrap your legs around me," he instructed. Giving her a long, hot look, he added, "And hold on tight."

She was in for the ride of her life.

He surged inside her, and she cried out at the possessive force of it. Her eyes shot to his. "Like that, do you?" he taunted.

She nodded dazedly.

A surge of satisfaction shot through his veins. Holding her gaze, he surged again. Over and over. Faster and faster. Giving her exactly what she wanted, the soft echoes of her gasps egging him on.

He groaned as the familiar pressure started to build in his loins and gather at the back of his spine.

Damn, it felt good.

He could feel her heels digging into his buttocks, her hands sliding from his arms to roam wildly over his hot, slickening back. He was working hard and his body was beginning to show it. His muscles were straining, his arms were sore from propping himself up, and his breath was coming fast from the exertion of thrusting and pounding.

It was hot and hard, lust in its most raw and primal form. But it was also something more. Something deeper. Something that stirred him in the darkest reaches of his soul every time he looked into the fathomless blue of her eyes.

Beautiful.

He could feel it coming. Sensation was building to a frantic beat. His body clenched tighter in anticipation. He gritted his teeth against the urge to come, fighting for control.

He didn't want to do this alone.

He had no reason to hold back. He'd made her come. He'd done his duty. Kept his side of the unspoken bargain in liaisons such as this. He'd give her pleasure and she'd give him pleasure in return.

But nothing about this felt like a duty. Nothing about this felt like his usual liaisons. Something about this felt important, and he knew it wasn't going to feel right unless they came together.

He didn't know why—hell, he didn't even want to think about it—he just knew it was the way it was.

But God, he wanted to come. His arse clenched against the pull of sensation as her body gripped him, milking, fighting to hang on to each hard stroke.

He wasn't going to have long to wait. Her breath was coming faster now. Harder and more insistent. She was undulating beneath him, arching her back and lifting her hips to meet the frantic rhythm of his thrusts. Her eyes were half-lidded, her lips parted, her head rolling back—

"Look at me," he ordered, his voice tight with the pressure.

She didn't want to look. He could see her reluctance as her eyes opened and moved slowly to his. A bolt of shock shot down his spine. Something passed between them. Something hot and intense. Something that sent them both over the edge.

She gasped.

His entire body clenched.

She let out a sharp cry of pleasure that tore through the last strands of his restraint. The pressure he'd been holding in check exploded in a blinding blaze of passion. He couldn't have pulled out if he'd wanted. He drove hard and deep, as his body broke apart. As the most powerful release he'd ever found shuddered over him in wave after powerful wave.

Jesus.

It was the most intelligent thought he could muster. His mind was gone. All that was left was pleasure. The most incredible pleasure he'd ever experienced.

When the last spasms of release had ebbed from his

body, he collapsed on top of her, every muscle, every ounce of his body spent. Even his bones felt like jelly.

After a minute, the heavy sounds of their breathing began to quiet. Realizing he was probably crushing her, he found the strength to roll to the side.

He couldn't ever remembering feeling so weak. It was a damned good thing the contest wasn't today. He'd barely be able to stand, let alone defeat whoever would stand against him tomorrow.

He didn't know quite what to make of what had just happened. He was having a hard time ordering his thoughts. But the lass had surprised him. The sweetness of her passion went far beyond the sensual promise he'd noticed in the barn. He couldn't remember the last time he'd enjoyed a liaison more. Hell, he doubted he'd *ever* enjoyed a liaison more. He frowned, remembering another oddity. Even when he was a lad, he'd always withdrawn before spilling his seed. But he was too bloody sated and contented to give it more than a passing thought. All he knew was that the strange ennui that had been dogging him was apparently gone, and he wasn't ready to let go of her. Not yet.

What had she done?

Mary's heart pounded in her chest as she stared at the ceiling. It was made of stone. The small library had been built into the thick walls like the vaulted storerooms below.

But it was gray and colorless, with little to distract her, so her thoughts returned to what had happened. To the cataclysmic event that had devastated her just as harshly and ruthlessly as a raging wildfire, leaving only ashes in its wake. It had been amazing. Wonderful. More beautiful than anything she could have imagined. And that was the problem. How was she ever to put this behind her? How was she to go on with her life in England and forget about the passion she'd found in his arms?

How was she going to forget about him?

He wasn't supposed to be like this. She'd wanted a too-handsome, too-arrogant man built for sin. She'd wanted lust, nothing more.

He rolled to his side, leaning up on one elbow to look at her. She felt his eyes rake her face and held her breath as his hand reached out and brushed aside a few strands of hair that she hadn't even noticed were tangled in her lashes. The touch was so intimate—so sweet—her chest squeezed with longing.

His fingers lingered on the side of her face, turning her gaze to his. "You're full of surprises, aren't you, little one?"

The way he was looking at her made her chest ache. She stared up at him wordlessly, not knowing what to say. She felt exposed. Raw. Vulnerable. What had just happened had stripped the last years of hard-wrought independence from her as if it were no more substantial than a thin chemise, revealing the lonely, heartbroken girl underneath who'd so much wanted her husband to love her. And Kenneth Sutherland, the soon-to-be champion, the handsome knight, the hero with an adoring throng of admirers, was cut from the same cloth.

At least she thought he was. Had she been unfair? Was there perhaps more to him than she'd thought?

It surprised her how much she wanted to be wrong.

Her heart slammed against her ribs when he leaned down and kissed her. It was a soft, lazy kiss. A tender kiss. Everything she shouldn't want, yet craved like a greedy child.

Lifting his mouth from hers, he smiled. "When can I see you again?"

Her heart stopped. *One night.* "I-I'm leaving soon," she hedged.

His eyes narrowed. "I hope not *too* soon. You'll stay at least until after the Games? My sister is getting married on Saturday. There will be a few days of celebration."

Did he want her to go to his sister's wedding? She tried to hold back her racing heart but it was sprinting away from her. "I don't know."

"Of course—it depends on Lady Margaret. Would it help if I talked to her for you?" He slid the back of his finger down her cheek, down her throat, and over the firm slope of her breasts, drawing a feathery circle around the tip. "I'm not done with you yet," he said in that dark, husky voice of his that seeped right through her good sense. "I don't think I'm going to be done with you for quite a while."

Her skin prickled. Her nipples beaded. Her breath quickened. Her entire body responded to the sensual promise in his words. Was it just words, or did it mean something? She had to find out. "Lady Margaret told me you are to be betrothed."

He frowned, as if he were surprised she'd heard about that. "What does that have to do with us?"

She looked away so he wouldn't see the stone of disappointment he'd just cast carelessly at her heart. He said it with such honest befuddlement she couldn't even be angry with him. She was angry with herself. "Nothing," she said softly. "It has nothing to do with us."

Why should he think there was anything wrong with making love to another woman while his betrothed or his wife waited for him at whatever castle he put her in? There was nothing wrong with it. It was the accepted—expected—thing for noblemen in a political marriage. She was the one who had unrealistic expectations, not he.

One night was all she'd wanted, so why was she disappointed that it was all she was going to have? His response had just ensured it.

"Good," he said, rolling back over and tucking her against him. She rested her cheek against his chest, listening to the beat of his heart and trying not to cry.

"We should go," he said, though his voice gave no indication of any hurry. "But I'm just so damned tired. I can't seem to make myself get up."

His voice trailed off. She wasn't surprised when a few minutes later she heard the even sounds of his breathing. He'd drifted off.

Grateful for the reprieve, she was careful not to wake him as she slid away from the warmth of his body, stood, and straightened her clothes. All she could think about was getting out of there. She didn't want to face him again. Not here, and not at the feast.

This had been a mistake.

Kenneth Sutherland wasn't like her husband at all. He was far more dangerous. Atholl had never bothered to try to seduce her. Kenneth Sutherland seduced with every long look, every gentle touch, and every heart-pounding kiss.

Would she ever learn?

She needed to leave. Not just this room, but Scotland. Before she forgot how to be content with what she had and yearned for things that would only make her miserable. Again.

Seven

❧

Kenneth woke slowly, trying to clear the fog from his mind. But his head felt as if someone had sheared a sheep inside it. Opening his eyes, he shot upright, startled by his surroundings. By the shards of light streaming through the planks of the door.

He winced at the knife of pain in his side.

Hell. Covering the offending area with his hand, he braced himself as he stood. Whatever dulling effects last night had worked on his pain, they were gone.

Last night. He realized three things at once: it was morning, he'd missed the feast, and he was alone.

He swore, not knowing what angered him the most.

What the hell had happened to him? It felt as though he'd been knocked out. The moment he'd closed his eyes, he'd slipped into a deep sleep. He hadn't slept that solidly in years.

His mouth fell in a grim line when he reached down to pick up his tunic and saw a swatch of dark green silk. He knew what had happened to him. *She* had happened to him.

Why in Hades had she run off without waking him?

In many cases he would be relieved to wake up and find himself alone after a night of lovemaking, but damn it, this wasn't one of them. He vowed to go back to uncomplicated and eager-to-please just as soon as he was done with her.

He jerked on his tunic, wrapped the plaid back around

his shoulders—the fire in the brazier had gone out hours ago, and it was bloody cold in here—and picked up the offending veil.

He and Lady Mary were going to have a nice long talk about what he was going to expect from her—a little common courtesy, for one thing. And she wasn't going to run off like that again. *He* would decide when it was time to leave, damn it.

He stalked out of the library, slamming the door behind him, and headed toward the Hall to look for her. But it seemed the morning meal had ended some time ago. There were only a few people milling about, and none was the one he wanted to see.

Just what the hell time was it?

He swore again. The morning was quickly going from bad to worse. If the morning meal was over, that meant he didn't have much time until the wrestling competition got under way. One of the most important days of his life, and he'd nearly slept through it. His anger at his wee nun was growing. She'd distracted him. And had done a bloody efficient job of it, damn it.

He grabbed a piece of bread and cheese from a tray as one of the servants passed by and washed it down with a swig of wine. As he exited the Hall, he winced, shrinking back from the head-piercing rays of sunlight that blasted him. Damn, his head felt like he'd drunk far more than a tankard of whisky. Squinting, he scanned the courtyard, and then winced again. It wasn't because of the sun this time, but who he saw striding toward him.

"Where the hell have you been?" MacKay demanded. "I hope you have a good explanation for disappearing last night. The king was furious."

Kenneth ignored MacKay and greeted his sister, who had come up next to him.

"Are you all right, Kenneth? You don't look well," Helen said.

His side hurt like hell, but he wasn't going to tell her that with MacKay standing there. "What did you give me?" he asked. "I fell asleep and just woke up."

"Nothing that should have—" She stopped, biting her lip. "Did you drink any wine or whisky last night by chance?"

"I drink wine or whisky every night. What difference does that make?"

She looked up at him guiltily. "I must have forgotten to mention that mixing the draught with wine or whisky might make you a tad sleepy."

Kenneth's mouth tightened. "Aye, you seem to have forgotten that part."

Well, at least he knew why he'd slept so hard. Although he suspected there was another cause that had affected him as much as the whisky. He'd slept the dead sleep of a man who'd been well satisfied. *Too* well satisfied. Instead of worrying about what had happened to his wee wanton, he should be preparing for the Games.

"I will explain what happened to the king after the competition," he said to MacKay, who was still glaring at him from Helen's side. "And apologize to Lady Mary."

McKay gave him a hard look. "Aye, well in that you were fortunate. Lady Mary sent word late that she was not feeling well."

Kenneth frowned, thinking it fortunate indeed. Almost too fortunate. A prickle of unease teased his consciousness.

"What's that?" MacKay said, pointing to the veil.

Damn. "Nothing," he said, scrunching the silk in his hand and tucking it more firmly against his side.

But MacKay wasn't having it. His eyes narrowed on the swathe of fabric at his side. The very feminine swathe of fabric. "Don't tell me you ignored the king's invitation for a woman? What were you thinking? It seems you have as much discipline over your co—" He stopped, giving Helen an apologetic look. "Over your desire as you do over your temper." He shook his head. "I bloody well hope she was worth it."

Kenneth's teeth clenched. Surprisingly, he realized, she was, but he wasn't about to explain himself to MacKay. And he sure as hell didn't like being scolded as if he were a wet-behind-the-ears squire.

Damn it, he was tired of this. He was tired of his boyhood nemesis lauding it over him as if he were his superior. He wasn't. And today Kenneth was going to prove it.

"I need to get ready," he said, refusing to let MacKay bait him. He needed to have his sister wrap his ribs. "Helen, if you would meet me in the barracks—"

"There you are," Gregor MacGregor said, walking toward them from the loch. From the damp hair and drying cloth wrapped around his neck, Kenneth assumed he'd been bathing. Half the castle's population—the female half—was probably still at the beach right now. "I thought you said you were going to escort Lady Mary to the feast?" His eyes were laughing. "I bet the king is wondering what happened to you both. I thought she wasn't interested in a betrothal. But maybe you convinced her?"

Kenneth froze. The blood drained from his face. "Who?"

MacGregor's brow creased with his confusion. "Lady Mary. I assumed after you saw us in the corridor that—"

"Mary of Mar," Kenneth said tonelessly, feeling as if a stone had just dropped in his gut. She'd deceived him. The wee nun wasn't a lady's attendant at all, she was the widowed Countess of Atholl. The woman the king had picked out for him as a bride.

Why hadn't she told him?

His mouth fell in a hard line, anticipating that he wasn't going to like the explanation.

"You didn't," MacKay said under his breath, looking at the veil.

Kenneth stiffened. The tic in his cheek jumped. He glared at him, daring him to say a bloody word.

But like him, MacKay never backed down from a challenge. That was probably one of the reasons they were always at one another's throats.

The bastard laughed. "My God, you didn't even know who she was! I knew you'd find a way to screw this up. When the king finds out, your being champion isn't going to matter."

Kenneth clenched his fists, the laughter grating like nails under his skin. Worse, he knew MacKay was right. The king wasn't going to take kindly to him seducing his former sister-in-law. So much for avoiding the gauntlet of dangerous women! He couldn't have picked a more inappropriate bedmate if he'd tried.

MacGregor wasn't any better. He let out a low whistle. "I doubt that was what the king had in mind to convince her."

"There will be no reason for the king to find out," he warned them.

Neither man disagreed, but neither did they agree.

Helen gazed up at him with a worried look on her face. She knew how much this meant to him and feared he might have just done something he could not undo. "You'd better do something to make it right," she said. "And I'd do it quickly. Lady Anna told me Lady Mary is leaving soon."

His blood spiked. Lady Mary wasn't going anywhere, damn it. Kenneth turned on his heel and stormed toward the donjon, rage surging through his veins. He couldn't ever remember feeling this much anger toward a woman. Women were easy. They didn't give him trouble. He had no reason to get angry with them. But it seemed Lady Mary possessed a singular ability to elicit any number of strange reactions from him.

"Don't take too long," McKay taunted. "The Games are

about to begin. You wouldn't want to be late and forfeit your place in the competition."

Kenneth shot him a black look. "Don't worry. This won't take long."

He and his soon-to-be betrothed were going to have a very short conversation.

The flurry of activity going on around them didn't stop Margaret from trying to question her.

"But why must you go now? I thought you planned to stay until after the feast tomorrow. There will be a great celebration to close the Games."

Mary turned to give instructions to one of the maid-servants on in which trunk to place the limited jewels she had left, before answering. "As I said, King Edward has given the bishop leave to stay in Scotland for a few more months to try to effect a truce, but he is eager for a report, and the bishop thought it best if I give it to him person-ally." At her suggestion, of course.

Margaret didn't look convinced. "Are you sure that is all? You never did say what happened to you last night. I sent one of your ladies to see what was wrong, but she didn't find you in the room." Margaret paused meaning-fully. "It's strange. I noticed Sir Kenneth was missing as well. The king was quite vexed by his absence."

Mary hid her blush by turning to give another instruc-tion. Margaret suspected what had happened, but for some reason Mary couldn't bring herself to confide in her. She didn't want to talk about it. She didn't want to think about it. Being wicked no longer seemed like something she wanted to laugh about.

By the time she finished speaking with the servant, she'd managed to compose herself. "It was probably when I was at the beach. I needed some fresh air." She knew she needed to give her sister-in-law more, so she added, "David will be at Alnwick Castle soon, and I should like to be there when he arrives. It's been nearly a year since I've seen him."

The longing in her voice left no doubt of the truth of that, and Margaret was instantly contrite. "Of course you do! I'm sorry, I can see why you are anxious to go. I can't imagine what it would be like to have one of my babies taken away from me." She shivered as if the mere thought had sent a chill through her blood.

How could Mary tell her it was so much worse than that? You couldn't imagine the pain until you experienced it. It was one of the worst things any mother could ever go through.

"You are still young, Mary. Have you ever thought about having another child?"

The dull ache in her chest turned into a hard stab. A merciless stab. Even if she let herself admit that she yearned for another child, the price of having one was too high. Independence. Control over her own fate. "I believe you need a husband for that," she said wryly.

Her words were punctuated by a crash, as the door slammed open.

A half-dozen faces turned as Sir Kenneth Sutherland strode into the room like some conquering barbarian.

Mary froze, feeling the blood drain from her face. He was looking right at her. Nay, "looking" was too benign for the fierce, all-consuming black glare that seemed to reach across the room and capture her in a steely grip.

Instinctively, she took a few steps back.

Despite the fury emanating from him, he cocked a lazy brow. "Going somewhere, *Lady Mary*?" The emphasis he put on her name sent chills racing up and down her spine. "I hope you weren't planning to leave without saying goodbye."

Mary wasn't fooled by his pleasant banter. He was looking at her as if he'd like to throttle her. Every word was a threat, a challenge. An invitation to do battle.

His gaze skidded over the piles of clothing and open trunks. "There's something we need to talk about before you finish packing."

Her heart drummed frantically in her throat. This was how a deer must feel when it turned and found itself in the hunter's sights, an arrow pointed at its heart. Trapped. Cornered. With nowhere to run.

She managed to find her voice. "You can't come barging in here like—"

"Leave," he ordered the other women in the room. "Your mistress and I have something to discuss in private."

To Mary's horror, they scatted like terrified mice. Only Margaret paused. But even she recognized his authority.

He had no authority, blast it! This was exactly what she sought to avoid.

Her sister-in-law gave her a worried look. "Will you be all right?"

Mary was tempted to say no, but she read the determination in every inch of his furious, combative face. From the clenched jaw, to the tight lips, to the piercing blue gaze locked on her, she knew that he was going to say his peace—with or without Margaret in the room.

She nodded. Margaret gave her a long, searching look and left.

The shock of his arrival had dissipated, and the brief pause while the others left was long enough to restore her courage. She straightened her back and turned to face him coolly. "What right do you have—"

She stopped, eyes widening when he tossed something on the bed. The dark green billowed in a silken cloud before landing in a pool on the ivory bedsheets, a stark, damning reminder of what she'd done.

"You forgot something before you ran off last night, *Lady Mary*." There it was again, that hard emphasis on her name. "Or should I say, *Countess*."

Mary cringed inwardly at the confirmation of her sus-

picions. He'd learned her identity. She'd known he
wouldn't be pleased when he discovered the truth. But
she hadn't expected this kind of extreme reaction to a
little tweak of pride.

He closed the distance between them in a few steps, but
she stood her ground, refusing to back away even though
every instinct in her body urged her to run. Her heart
slammed in her chest. Well over six feet of hard, angry
warrior looming over her wasn't exactly unintimidating.

But he wouldn't hurt her. Somehow she knew that. For
all his fire and quickness of temper, she sensed an undercurrent of control.

"Why didn't you tell me? Why did you lie to me and let
me believe you were one of Lady Margaret's attendants?"

She gave a far more careless shrug than she felt. "It was
your assumption. I saw no reason to change it."

His eyes narrowed. She could tell he didn't like her attitude. What had he expected? That she would get down
on her hands and knees and beg his forgiveness? Probably.
It was no doubt what most women of his acquaintance
would do. Women who were eager to please him. Well,
she wasn't one of those women.

She had nothing to apologize for. It was he who'd started
this with his wickedness in the stable, and then by taunting her with the feelings he'd aroused in her. He'd gotten
no more than he'd given—and exactly what he'd asked for.

"Not even when you knew what the king intended? That
he has proposed a betrothal between us?"

Her back stiffened. She looked down her nose at him.
Unfortunately, as she had a rather small nose it lost some
of its dismissive effect, although from the way his fists
clenched it was enough. "Especially then. I am not in the
market for a husband."

His eyes flashed like a lightning storm. The fury of his
temper was truly something to behold, and she wondered
if she'd been too quick to assume she was in no danger.

"But you are in the market for something else?"

She executed a perfect Gallic shrug of indifference that made a muscle jump in his jaw. She knew she was pressing against the limits of that control, but she couldn't seem to stop herself. Something about this man brought out every instinct in her to fight. "Why are you acting the aggrieved party? You made an offer, I accepted. It's something I've no doubt you have done *many* times in the past."

He grabbed her arm before she could turn away, hauling her up against him. The heat of his body engulfed her. "What is that supposed to mean?"

She tried to wrench away, but his grip was like a manacle. Did he have to smell so good? It was confusing her. Reminding her of last night. "It means I'm sure it's not the first time you've enjoyed a meaningless liaison with a woman whose name you do not know or can't remember."

A hard, angry flush had risen to his cheeks. "So you wanted a tumble in the hay, is that it?"

Mary felt her cheeks heat at the crassness of his language, even if it was the truth. "Is that not what you wanted?"

His clenched mouth came closer to hers, and she couldn't stop the reflexive shudder that ran through her. Her body didn't seem to care if he was angry; all it recognized was hot, fiercely aggressive masculinity. "What I wanted? I prefer to be made aware that the woman I'm taking to my bed is going to be my wife."

Mary stiffened. Perhaps if the word had been uttered with any hint of softness it might have been different. But it wasn't, and she bristled at both his tone and his assumption. She met his glare with one that was every bit as fierce as his own. It seemed she had a temper as well. "You presume much, my lord. I believe it is still the custom to ask for a lady's hand before assuming a betrothal."

His eyes flared at the challenge. "And I believe I did all my asking last night." He pressed his hard body to hers, reminding her of exactly what he meant. She jolted at the intimate contact. "And you answered. A most enthusiastic 'yes, please yes' if I recall correctly."

His voice was low and mesmerizing, sending a blast of melting dampness to the place that remembered him the most. She shuddered, seeing from the wicked smile that curved his mouth that he knew what he was doing to her.

Big and possessive, his hand slid down her back and over her hip to cup her bottom, bringing her more firmly against him. "Should I ask again, Mary?" he whispered, his mouth only a hair's breadth from hers.

For one treacherous instant she wanted to say yes. She wanted to lift her lips up to his and take the pleasure he offered. Her body vibrated—pulsed—with a restless energy.

But it wasn't only pleasure. It was far more. Succumbing to him would mean giving up everything she'd achieved the past few years and losing herself all over again.

She hated how weak she felt. How much she wanted to say yes. How easily he could make her forget herself.

Kenneth Sutherland wielded a power over her that was far more dangerous than the girlish infatuation she'd felt for her husband. The desire she felt for him was that of a woman, a woman who had learned exactly what he could do to her, and how it felt to experience the pleasure of passion.

But no matter how badly she wanted him, she would not let this control her. She would not let *him* control her. This too-handsome, too-arrogant warrior who didn't think she could resist him. Who couldn't even trouble himself to ask her to marry him but just assumed she would jump at the chance. Why wouldn't she? Look at her. An unexpected blast of heat pricked her eyes.

For once she didn't have to think about what her sister

would do. She pushed back. "Let go of me!" Surprisingly, he released her. "How dare you manhandle me like that! I will not be bullied by you or anyone else into a marriage I do not want. I told you before I don't want a husband, and as difficult as it is for you to understand, that includes you. Especially you."

A glint of steel sparked in his eyes. "What is that supposed to mean?"

"It means that *if* I were ever to marry again, which I certainly have no intention of doing, it wouldn't be to a profligate with a penchant for taking women in stables or storerooms."

Though his expression betrayed nothing, she could feel the fury radiating from him in hot, pulsing waves. "I think you mean libraries."

She flushed. "Be that as it may, we wouldn't suit."

"On the contrary, I think we suit quite well."

The heat of his gaze left no doubt as to what he meant. He was right. Even now, the attraction snapped and crackled between them like wildfire.

But it wasn't enough. "As you pointed out last night, what does that have to do with marriage?"

She forced herself not to wither under the intensity of his gaze. His voice when he spoke was deceptively calm, but she sensed he was one hair's breadth away from snapping. "Are you saying you would be my mistress but not my wife?"

She lifted her chin, forcing herself to meet his gaze. "I'm saying I will be neither. I'm returning to England, and that is the end of it."

She turned away, but not before seeing the dangerous white lines tightening around his mouth. He was struggling to control his temper, and she knew her dismissiveness was testing the limits of that control. She suspected it had been a very long time since someone had refused

Kenneth Sutherland anything, and coming from a pinched sparrow of a woman past her youth, she wagered it stung. But she knew it was better this way. He was a fighter, and showing any weakness or vulnerability would give him a place to attack.

"And the king?" he said. "Have you informed Bruce of your intentions?"

"Robert understands my position. He knows I have no wish to marry anyone—Scot or English. Nothing has changed that." When he looked as if he might challenge that point, she added, "He will not learn of anything else from me, and even were he to discover what happened, such interludes are hardly uncommon."

His teeth clenched so tightly, she could almost hear them grinding. "Aye, I believe you've pointed that out."

Something in his voice made her uneasy. If she weren't certain it was his pride speaking, she might think her refusal had genuinely hurt him.

She picked up the veil that was lying on her bed like an albatross and carefully folded it. "Now, if you will excuse me. I need to finish packing." She peeked out at him from under the edge of her lashes. From the way his muscles were bunched up at his shoulders and his fists were clenching and reclenching, she thought he might argue with her. Her heart raced; she needed a way to be rid of him. "Don't you have a competition to win?" She glanced out the window at the stands, which even now were beginning to fill. "It looks like they will be starting soon."

He took a step toward her, and she held her breath when he reached out as if to take her arm again. But he glanced out the tower window behind her and let it drop.

For a long moment he stared at her as if he wanted to say something. Say quite a lot of something, actually. But then, he seemed to think better of it. He gave her a mocking bow. "My lady."

And in one hard tug of a heartbeat, he was gone.

She thought she should feel relieved, but standing there alone, the room suddenly empty, she felt a loss that didn't make sense. Nor could she escape the feeling that she'd just made a terrible mistake.

Eight

❧

Kenneth tried to keep his mind clear, but all he could see was red. His temper was running loose, and the heat of battle was only making it run hotter. He grabbed the fist that was heading for his face and twisted it behind his opponent's back, hearing a satisfying pop.

Not in the market for a husband, damn it!

With a cut of his foot behind the heel of the man now howling in pain from a dislocated arm, Kenneth knocked the other warrior to the ground, pinned him with his foot (which wasn't necessary, as he wasn't intending to get up), and claimed his victory—the third of the long morning.

All she'd wanted was a quick tumble in the hay. He didn't know why it was angering him so much, but he kept seeing those big eyes looking at him wide and unflinchingly. *Knowingly.*

Profligate? Bloody hell!

The sun beat down on him as he jerked the helm off his head and stormed out of the arena, barely acknowledging the cheers of the crowd. For a man one win away from being declared champion and fulfilling his bargain with MacKay, thereby earning a place in Bruce's secret army, he sure as hell wasn't enjoying himself. All he could think about was the earlier exchange he'd had with Lady Mary. *Mary of Mar,* damn it to hell.

His blood still surged and his pulse still spiked just thinking about it. In fact, he was spending more time thinking about her than he was about his opponents. He knew he'd been lucky so far. None of the men he'd faced had given him much of a battle. But he needed to get himself under control for the final challenge.

He'd retired to the barracks between rounds to rest and have Helen rewrap his ribs, but his squire, Willy, had told him a new contestant had entered the ring and was creating quite a stir. It was probably just the mystery. The man had refused to give his identity. Nothing like a mystery to rile the crowd's excitement. Hell, had he thought of it, Kenneth might have done it himself.

But Willy said the warrior was a skilled competitor, and nearly as strong as Robbie Boyd. Kenneth knew it had to be an exaggeration—he would have heard of such a man before.

He wasn't worried, but he thought he'd see for himself.

He sat on a bench just on the other side of the gate reserved for the competitors and allowed Willy to wipe the blood and sweat from his brow and fetch him some ale thinned with water as he waited for the next competitors to take the field.

If anything stung more than his pride right now, it was the throbbing in his side. But his ribs were holding up well enough, and the pain wasn't anything he couldn't manage. He'd protected his side without being obvious, not wanting to give his opponents a target. Fortunately, the thin shirt and *cotun* the contestants wore as armor hid the bindings. Often the wrestling event was conducted naked to the chest, but Bruce followed the more modern, "civilized" approach of light armor. Usually, Kenneth found it an impediment, but right now he was grateful for it.

His eyes kept straying to the king's platform, although he knew she wouldn't be there. Had she gone already, he wondered? It was embarrassing how tempted he was to go after her and stop her. Though why and how, he didn't know. She'd already made her feelings clear. Damned clear.

She'd *refused* him. He still couldn't believe it.

His mouth tightened and his temper boiled anew. She'd used him. If it weren't so bloody humiliating, it would be almost humorous. He conveniently ignored the fact that he was the one that had given her the opportunity, and had started this whole mess, by taunting her in the stable.

What was important was that she'd tricked him. Used him, even though she'd known full well that the king wished for an alliance between them. She'd suspected that he wouldn't have taken her to his bed if he knew her identity and had purposefully kept the truth from him to take her pleasure.

Why was it bothering him so much? It wasn't anything that hadn't happened before. He knew there were other women who'd wanted no more from him than she did—a good tumble—but damn it, hearing it from her had been different.

Because it wasn't what he wanted from her. That was the problem. He was angry at himself because he'd felt something, and she hadn't.

He didn't know why, but for the first time in his life he'd felt what could only be described as tenderness for a woman, and his tentative attempts to show it had been rebuffed. He'd told himself the little things he'd noticed when they were making love had been his imagination. The turning from his gaze. The request for him to take off his shirt. Wanting him to go faster.

But it hadn't been his imagination, damn it.

He took another swig of ale and tried to calm the pounding in his blood. The sense of restless energy. The urge to slam his fist over and over again into a wall.

He needed to calm down, to get himself under control

and forget about it. Hell, he should be thanking her. He had enough strife in his life; he didn't need it from a woman.

He glanced over to the castle, but the yard was still deserted. Had he missed her, then?

Suddenly, a hush fell over the crowd.

"There he is, my lord," Willy whispered.

Kenneth's eyes narrowed on the man entering the arena. He wore a steel helm that covered his face, but even on first glance, Kenneth could see that Willy was right. He was nearly as big and strong-looking as—

Bloody hell.

The blood slid from his face for one frozen moment in time before surging hotter and harder than before. His mouth fell in a flat line and his fists clenched into balls of steel at his side.

Kenneth recognized the man even if the crowd didn't. Magnus MacKay, the bloody bastard! Apparently, there was nothing he wouldn't do to see that Kenneth didn't win. Even take to the field against what Kenneth suspected were the direct orders of the king.

Kenneth watched in icy fury as MacKay played to the crowd, whipping them into a frenzy. MacKay could have defeated the last opponent between him and the final round in a matter of minutes, but drew out the battle with the skill of a born showman. Yet it was more than that, and Kenneth knew it. MacKay was good. One of the best he'd ever seen. But Kenneth was better. And he was going to do what he'd been doing since the day he was born: prove it.

He was a man to be taken seriously, even if his wee wanton in a nun's habit didn't think so. Part of him wished she were here to see it. But he wasn't going to think about her anymore. He was in for the battle of his life, and he couldn't afford to let anything distract him.

Sangfroid, damn it. He'd better remember it.

* * *

"Surprised to see me, Sutherland?" MacKay taunted as they squared off in the arena a short while later.

They circled one another, each one waiting for the other to make the first move.

"I'd wager I'm not the only one," Kenneth replied. "Did you tell the king what you had planned, or did you come up with this little disguise all on your own?"

He could see the other man's eyes harden through the steel slits in the helm. "I told you you'd have to get past me first."

"Beating you will only make victory that much sweeter."

"You sound confident for a man who's already suffered a few blows today."

MacKay feigned a step toward him as if he meant to attack, but Kenneth wasn't fooled into taking the opening as MacKay quickly retreated.

"What are you talking about?" He'd won all his contests so far.

"Why, Lady Mary, of course. I assume that since she's still leaving, you did not convince her to marry you. The king will not be pleased."

Kenneth didn't need to see his face to know that MacKay was grinning. He could hear it in his damned voice. He wanted to lunge at him, but forced himself to get a rein on his temper and stay back. *Be patient*, he told himself. *Don't let him get to you.* But MacKay was a provoking bastard. "You let me worry about the king."

"It won't be necessary." MacKay made the first move. It was a good one. He stabbed a hard punch with his right and then threw a low uppercut with his left. When Kenneth moved to block it, he attempted to get a lock on him by twisting his body and locking him in a stranglehold. But Kenneth read the move and rallied with one of his own, hearing the satisfying crunch of MacKay's jaw as his fist connected with his chin under the helm to snap his head back.

MacKay swore, and that was the last recognizable sound they made for a while as the two men launched into a fierce battle. Nothing was off limits. They pounded with their fists, kicked with their feet, pummeled with their bodies. They took turns at wrapping one another in deadly holds and fighting to break free.

They were evenly matched. Too evenly matched in both strength and stubbornness. Neither of them would give up.

And they both knew how to fight dirty. MacKay lost no opportunity in targeting Kenneth's bad side, landing whatever punches he could on his bruised ribs. "How are those ribs feeling, Sutherland?" he managed to taunt through deep breaths. "I hope nothing is broken."

If they hadn't been, they were now. But Kenneth didn't care. All he could think about was seeing that bastard on the ground, and finally putting the matter of who was best behind them.

And he was close, damn it. He could feel it. One mistake, that was all he needed. One little opening and he'd have him.

"The ribs are fine," he managed, his breath just as short as MacKay's. "How's your jaw?" Kenneth feigned with his right and landed another satisfying uppercut with his left to MacKay's jaw. "Helen isn't going to be too happy if it's broken for your wedding."

Something flashed in the other man's eyes.

Guilt? Kenneth shook his head. "She doesn't know about this, does she?" He laughed. "Maybe there won't be a wedding to worry about."

MacKay swore and launched himself at Kenneth, pummeling and swinging with a violent ferocity that took every ounce of his skill to defend against.

MacKay had to tire eventually. Kenneth just had to be patient awhile longer.

Finally, they broke apart, both bending over heaving great gulps of air as they fought to breathe.

Unconsciously, Kenneth glanced toward the castle and stiffened. A handful of guardsmen were gathered in the yard, and a small figure had just emerged from the donjon and was making her way down the tower stairs.

He looked away quickly, but it hadn't been quick enough. He'd made a mistake. MacKay had caught the movement and recognized what was happening. "If you want to go after her, I'll wait," he taunted.

Kenneth bit out something foul, telling him he could go do something that was physically impossible.

"Hit a nerve, did I?" MacKay added. "Don't tell me you actually *wanted* to marry the lass."

Kenneth felt his blood spike but tamped it down. *Stay cool.* But his fists clenched at his sides with the urge to re-taliate. It wasn't in his nature not to fight back—or to be patient, for that matter.

MacKay let out a low whistle. "I never thought I'd see the day. I guess the lady wasn't impressed?"

"Shut the hell up, MacKay."

"Or what?"

Kenneth held himself still, refusing to be baited. But the urge to wipe that taunting grin off the face behind the helm was nearly overpowering.

"Or maybe that was all she wanted? Is that it, Sutherland? Tell me, do you get paid a fee like a prized steed? Aye, a stud fee." He laughed.

That was it. The last thread Kenneth held on his temper snapped. He lunged toward MacKay, not thinking about anything other than shutting him up.

He lost control, and with it, the battle. MacKay took full advantage of his anger, lulling him into a false sense of victory before snatching it back at the last minute. MacKay feigned submission, bending over and letting Kenneth pound on him until he was exhausted. Then he rose from the apparent dead and attacked, striking blows against Kenneth's weak side until he collapsed on the ground.

He must have passed out. Either that or he was deaf to the cheers of the crowd, because he never heard the call for MacKay's victory.

He'd lost. *Lost!*

He stayed on the ground, not wanting or having the strength to get up.

MacKay stood over him, looking down on him with that superior smirk of his. "Your temper, Sutherland. It will get you every time. Until you can learn to control it, you'll never be one of the best."

The worst part was that he was right. Kenneth had let his temper get to him. Had let *her* get to him.

He picked himself off the ground and struggled to his feet, as he'd done many times before. Too many times. The knowledge burned in his gut. He'd been so close . . .

But this wasn't over. He wasn't going to give up. He'd find a way into Bruce's army, if it killed him.

And heaven help Mary of Mar if their paths ever crossed again. He would teach the wanton little siren in nun's clothing a lesson she would never forget.

Nine

❧

Kenneth was going to be the last man standing if it killed him. And it seemed the others were determined to do just that. Perdition? That was putting it mildly. He'd rather spend an eternity of punishment in the fiery pits of hell than another two weeks of Tor MacLeod's "training" in the wintry bowels of the Cuillin mountain range.

They'd been climbing up the icy, desolate mountainside for hours at a pace that might as well be called a run. He couldn't ever remember being this cold and tired. Every muscle, every bone in his body hurt—even his teeth. Although that was probably because he'd been grinding them so hard trying to keep a rein on his temper. *Sangfroid!* It was so damned cold he should have ice in his veins, let alone "cold blood."

But unfortunately, his blood was still running hot. It wasn't just MacKay testing him now; he had ten of the fiercest, most highly prized warriors in Christendom doing everything they could to get to him. To make him quit. But no matter how unpleasant or harassing the task, how difficult the ordeal, or how many irritating names they called him, he was determined to grit his teeth and bear it. He'd been given one more chance, and nothing was going to stop him from earning a place in Bruce's secret army.

Of the handful of potential recruits who'd started with him over three months ago, only two remained in the war of attrition that was MacLeod's training. One had quit the first week; the other two had lasted the first few months of training, only to fall in the first few days of Perdition once training had resumed after an all-too-short break for Christmastide, the twelve days from Christmas Eve to Epiphany.

Apparently MacLeod was human after all; he'd wanted to spend the holidays with his expectant wife and young daughter. Otherwise it was sometimes hard to tell. Over the past few months of training, MacLeod had pushed Kenneth and the other recruits to the edge of their physical and emotional limits. Kenneth might have come to despise him if "Chief," as he was known among the men (to protect their identities, the members of the secret army used war names), hadn't done every task he'd asked of them right beside them—usually better than all of them. Even now, when most of the men appeared ready to collapse, Chief barely seemed winded. Kenneth respected the hell out of him.

MacLeod's endurance nearly matched MacKay's. After living side-by-side for nearly three months, MacKay, too, had Kenneth's grudging respect. The skills that had brought each team member to Bruce's attention had become apparent, and his brother-in-law's (the wedding had gone on, although Helen had been nearly as furious as Bruce, which had resulted in Kenneth being given another chance) ability to navigate the Highlands, his physical endurance, and his toughness were extraordinary. It was MacKay's place as the best all-around warrior on the team that Kenneth intended to challenge.

His efforts to perfect the recipe for black powder had not progressed much beyond unstable, inconsistent, and dangerous. He could manage to put together something that would cause damage, but he was hardly at the level

Gordon had been. Unfortunately, his friend hadn't thought to leave any notes behind.

Finally, MacLeod called a halt to the march. "We'll stop here for the night."

Kenneth wasn't the only one to heave a sigh of relief. He shrugged off the heavy pack he wore strapped to his back—the terrain was too steep and rocky for goats or deer, let alone horses—and collapsed on the nearest rock. A quick glance at the other weather-beaten faces, mostly hidden by various forms of wool and fur, told him the rest of the men were doing the same.

Even Erik MacSorley, known as Hawk, was quiet—a rarity, indeed. Some of the men were still a mystery to him, but Hawk wasn't one of them. The gregarious, quick-with-a-jest seafarer could always be counted on to lighten the mood. He was an easy man to like. Much like Gordon, he thought sadly.

Kenneth bent over, leaning his forearms on his thighs and willing his body to recover. If he'd learned anything in the past few months, it was that when he was at his weakest point—when he most needed a rest—he was sure not to get it.

He had all of five minutes to recover before MacKay proved his point. Kenneth didn't need to glance up—the large, looming presence had become instantly recognizable. A bit like the shadow of the grim reaper.

"Rest time is over, Recruit. You're on watch tonight," MacKay said. "Unless you're too tired?"

Admitting that would give the whoreson too much bloody satisfaction. Kenneth clenched his jaw and used what little strength he had left to drag himself to his feet. "Not to do my duty."

Kenneth couldn't bring himself to use MacKay's war name of "Saint." The appellation couldn't be farther from the truth. "Satan's spawn" suited him much better. Kenneth's longtime nemesis might have been forced by Bruce and

Helen to let Kenneth join the men who would battle for a position on the team, but that didn't mean he had to like it—or that he would make Kenneth's path an easy one.

But as much as Kenneth would like to claim otherwise, MacKay didn't single him out for extra torture. Nay, the torture was spread around evenly and thickly. Even when he was a squire he hadn't been forced to do so many menial tasks. He'd never dug so many cesspits, fetched so much wood or peat for a fire, cleaned armor until his fingers were raw, and even washed soiled linens. Yet ironically, the tasks that he looked down upon as beneath him a few months ago had become his moments of peace and relative relaxation.

"Good," MacKay replied. "You, too, Recruit," he addressed the only other man unfortunate enough to still be around to answer to that name. Kenneth had come not to mind it. It was a hell of a lot better than some of the other names they called him.

The first time Hawk had seen him taking a piss, he'd taken to calling him The Steed. Kenneth was used to the jests about the size of his manhood, and normally he would have shrugged it off, if Steed hadn't transformed into Stud thanks to MacKay. Though his brother by marriage hadn't shared the origin of the name, the private jest was enough to set his teeth on edge every time he heard it. It was also a constant reminder of exactly who was to blame for his current predicament.

He was sure that was why he thought of her so often. Even more than four months later, Lady Mary's easy dismissal of him as a potential husband stung. His own reaction to her, he tried not to think about. He was sure it hadn't been nearly as incredible as he remembered. Surely he'd had better, even if he couldn't remember a specific instance. He would prove it, just as soon as he finished his training. Profligate? More like monk, of late.

But just because he chose to accept a few of the offers

thrown his way didn't make him a profligate. He was glad
she'd refused him. The last thing he needed was a wife who
didn't understand a man's needs. But why had it seemed to
bother her so much?

"You need to see to the evening meal," MacKay was saying to the other recruit, "starting with a fire. Then you can
find us something to eat. I think we could all do with some
fresh meat tonight."

Although he knew everything about him as a warrior,
Kenneth knew little personal information about his fellow
recruit other than that he spoke and dressed as if he were
from the Isles. He was certainly large and fair enough to
have some Viking blood in him. His brother-in-hell was
unable to stifle a groan. Kenneth didn't blame him; finding
something to eat in these stark, frozen mountaintops was
going to be a Herculean—if not Promethean—task.

Watch suddenly seemed like a pleasure jaunt by comparison. Kenneth pulled a few things from his pack, and as
he started away to take his position on the outskirt of
camp, he wondered at MacKay's unusual generosity.

But the voice that was anything but saintlike stopped
him. "Where do you think you're going, Recruit?" Kenneth
turned around slowly, dread seeping through every inch of
his aching limbs. "You'll watch from up there."

Kenneth followed the direction of his hand to the peak of
the mountain above them, still a good two hundred feet up.
Straight up. It wasn't the distance as much as the steep,
sheer facade that made dread settle in his gut like a stone.
To reach the place MacKay indicated, Kenneth was going to
have to scale the rocky peak with his hands and feet, a task
that would be difficult even were he well rested and able to
feel his fingertips. Pulling his body up with his already
weary limbs was going to be next to impossible.

For the past few weeks, he'd swum until he thought his
lungs would give out, been pushed over varying terrains at
a pace that would kill most men, fought with every kind of

weapon imaginable, and had even been buried to his waist and had to defend himself with just a shield as spears were tossed at his head by a circle of warriors. He hadn't balked at any of it, no matter how impossible it seemed. But this was too much.

The two men faced off in the near darkness. Though it was only a few hours past noon, daylight was already slipping away. Kenneth could feel the scrutiny of the ten other men as they waited in silence for his response, but none of them would intervene. This contest was between MacKay and him alone.

Every instinct in Kenneth's body urged him to tell McKay to bugger off. To refuse.

To quit.

Going up there right now would be a suicide mission. One slip on the icy rocks and Kenneth would fall to his death. MacKay knew it as well as he did. Kenneth could see the challenge in the other man's gaze, not daring him to refuse as much as daring him to accept.

How far will you go? he seemed to be asking.

To the death. That was what was required of them. Chief had told them many times before. If you want on this team, you have to be willing to sacrifice your life for the good of the team. Did Kenneth want it that badly?

He thought he did, but it wasn't until that moment that he knew it for a certainty. He wanted to be the best. He wanted to be part of something that was not just important but also historic. He'd been working for this moment his entire life, and he wasn't going to turn back now.

"Aye, you're right," he said equitably. "I'll be able to see much better from there."

Something flashed in the other man's eyes. Respect? Kenneth didn't know. Truth be told, he no longer cared. He wasn't proving anything to MacKay, he was proving it to himself. He turned and started toward the peak. Almost impossible wasn't impossible. He would do this, damn it.

He'd reached the base of the area from where he would start his ascent when he heard the sound of footsteps behind him. It was bloody disconcerting how he knew who it was. Apparently, he didn't even need a shadow to recognize his old nemesis.

"Have you learned nothing in three months?"

Kenneth turned slowly to face his brother-in-law. He bit back a few choice replies, and simply stared at him. For once he didn't feel like fighting, even with MacKay—he was too bloody tired.

MacKay gave him a long look. "If you're going to get yourself killed, don't do it without your partner."

"Aye, well you sent my partner on a fool's mission for fresh meat."

He couldn't bite back all the sarcasm, and MacKay shook his head. "You had me worried for a minute. I've grown so used to seeing that belligerent, 'I dare you to try' look on your face, and I thought we'd actually beaten it out of you. Hell, without the prickly attitude I could actually learn to *like* you." He gave a dramatic shudder from behind the long wool scarf wrapped around his neck and lower face. Like the rest of them, he hadn't shaved in nearly two weeks and tiny droplets of ice clung to his face. They had all begun to look and smell like wild beasts. "And you never know, the recruit might find something. You just have to know where to look."

Belligerent? What was he talking about?

MacKay had retrieved a rope from his pack and had started to tie it around his waist. He handed him the other end.

"*You're* going to be my partner?" Kenneth couldn't keep the incredulity from his voice.

A flash of pain crossed the other man's face, and Kenneth knew he was thinking about his first partner, the man who'd been a friend to them both: William Gordon.

Rather than lash out as he usually did, however, MacKay

merely shrugged. "Aye, well, the rest of them are too exhausted. Besides, your sister would have my hide if I let you crack your pretty head open on those rocks. She's still mad about my taking advantage of your injury at the wrestling event." He shook his head. "I must admit, you've surprised me these past few months. I didn't think you had it in you. But you've shown more control than I thought possible. Hell, even *I* lost my temper a few times with Hawk's needling."

Kenneth couldn't believe it. He stared in shock at the man who'd been his enemy since the day he was born. "Does that mean you won't stand in the way of my joining the Guard?"

The Highland Guard was how they referred to the team.

MacKay gave him a long look. "It isn't over yet, but if you make it through training and the rest of it, I won't object."

Kenneth wondered at "the rest of it," but he knew he had to focus on one thing first: getting himself up this damned mountain. Whatever they threw at him these next few days—what remained of Perdition—he was going to be the last man standing. After that, "the rest" was going to be easy by comparison.

Alnwick Castle, Northumberland, English Marches

Mary sat before the looking glass in the tower chamber that had been provided for her and her attendants, as the serving girl put the finishing touches on her hair. It had been brushed to a shimmery veil of gold, twisted, and then braided around her head with a cerulean silk ribbon that matched her gown and—not coincidentally—her eyes. The back had been left loose to tumble around her shoulders in the manner of a young girl. She actually felt like a young girl. The intricate hairstyle was said to be popular on the Continent, and she had to admit it was flattering.

After years of hiding and fading into the background, it felt strange to have her hair so visible. Strange, but also freeing. Slowly and cautiously, in the months since Mary had returned from Scotland, she had cast aside the dour armor that she'd used to protect herself. Armor that had kept her safe and hidden but had also prevented her from living a full life. A life of not just contentment, but passion and happiness. She was done hiding.

She forced herself not to think about the man responsible for her transformation. The man who'd brought passion and so much more into her life. She'd thought of that night—thought of *him*—far more often than she wanted to admit, even to herself.

The feeling that she might have made a mistake had not waned. She'd panicked, beset by a cacophony of feelings she hadn't expected. She regretted the cold manner of her dismissal of his suit and wondered if she'd misjudged him. Admittedly, she barely knew him. But he'd reminded her so much of her husband and so much of her painful past that she'd felt her heart breaking all over again.

She had given him a chance, she reminded herself. When she'd asked him about his betrothal, he'd made his views on fidelity in marriage perfectly clear: *What does that have to do with us?*

If she'd hoped running away would make her forget, however, she'd erred.

But it was too late now. Her life was here in England, and she had even more reason than the rational or irrational fear of another unwise emotional entanglement for never wanting to set eyes on Sir Kenneth Sutherland again. Still, she would thank him for what he'd given her for the rest of her life. She closed her eyes for a moment as the bubble of joy rose inside her, impossible to tamp down.

As the serving girl stepped back, Mary took one last look in the glass and nodded her approval. There was very little that remained of the pale, gaunt woman in plain clothing who'd gone to Scotland to negotiate on her son's behalf and had been awakened like a butterfly shedding its cocoon. Her face was fuller, her eyes brighter, her lips redder, and her skin a more healthy pink. Her gown, although not like the extravagant, height-of-fashion concoctions she'd been partial to in her youth, was pretty and befitting a lady of her stature—a far cry from the shapeless black, gray, and brown gowns she'd hidden behind for three years.

The old merchant would be ecstatic, she thought with a smile. She might not be in the first flower of her youth, but the bloom was not completely off the rose. And more important, she was happy. Happier than she'd been in a long time. And it showed.

With a word of thanks to the serving girl, Mary made her way down to the Great Hall of Alnwick Castle with her attendants, Lady Eleanor and Lady Katherine, the same two women who'd accompanied her to Scotland. She found pleasure in their company now. Once she relaxed her guard, she realized how much she'd missed female companionship. Perhaps it had been Margaret who'd made her remember.

The trip to Scotland had brought back many memories, and though she knew it was best not to dwell on them, she missed her old friends and her former home. Maybe someday . . .

She stopped the thought before it could form. Her life was here now; she would make do with what she had.

The Hall was already crowded and boisterous when Mary and her ladies entered. The Great Hall of Alnwick Castle was something to behold, even without the colorfully dressed noblemen and women gathered for the midday meal. The castle itself was one of the largest and most imposing she'd ever seen, with its seven semicircular towers, square keep, and massive curtain wall. The Great Hall was its jewel. The massive, vaulted room looked like a small cathedral, except that the crown of rafters was of wood and not of stone. The plaster walls were painted a bright yellow and lined with wooden panels and decorated with tapestries. Colorful silk cloths with embroidery every bit as fine as hers covered the long tables and fine silver platters, candelabra, and pitchers sparkled from every corner of the room. Huge circular iron chandeliers hung from the rafters, and despite the midday hour were set ablaze with scores of candles.

Lord Henry Percy had become one of Edward's most important magnates, and his new castle certainly showed it. He had plans, he'd confided in her, to make it even more formidable, with more towers and improvements to the curtain wall and barbican. Those Scot barbarians (he immediately apologized—excluding her, of course) wouldn't dare attempt an attack.

Sir Adam was already seated at the dais, but he rose and came forward to greet her as she approached. She returned his smile, grateful as always for the presence of her old friend.

"You look beautiful, my dear," he said, leading her to her seat.

She blushed, still not used to compliments.

Another man rose and gave her a gallant bow. "I couldn't agree more," he said. The way his gaze slid over her brought another rush of heat to her cheeks.

Sir John Felton was Percy's best knight, and much to Mary's surprise, since her arrival a few weeks ago he'd shown a marked interest toward her. As the mother of a young earl—who was presumably subject to influence— she was as much a marriage prize to the English as she was to the Scots. But his interest seemed to go beyond that, and she had to admit, she was flattered by it.

At thirty years of age, Sir John was in the prime of his manhood. He was close to six feet tall (not as tall as Sir Kenneth, she thought, before she could push away the comparison), with a thick, muscular build that gave credence to his reputed invincibility on the battlefield. He was also reputed to be the most handsome of all Percy's knights, and nothing Mary could see disproved that. With his thick, golden-blond hair, deep green eyes, and finely wrought features, he could give Gregor MacGregor a challenge—or Sir Kenneth, she thought again, this time unable to prevent the pang.

Why was she doing this? What hold did this man have on her? For goodness' sake, it had only been one night.

But oh, what a night! Even as the memories flooded her, she pushed them away. She had to stop this pointless fixation on a man who could never be hers. Her future was here. But maybe some day, if she let herself, she might find a man with whom to share it.

The idea of marriage, of giving up her independence, which had once been anathema to her, no longer felt out of the realm of possibility. With the right man, under the right circumstances, perhaps she could be persuaded. The peace and solitude she'd once craved were now tinged with loneliness. She'd caught a glimpse of a life she'd been missing and had opened her eyes to the possibility.

It wouldn't be with Sir John. There were too many . . . complications. But perhaps it could be with someone else when she returned from France late in the summer—yet one more thing she had to thank Sir Adam for. He'd arranged for her to accompany him on his journey to the French court in the late spring.

Had he guessed the truth? At times, she wondered. Something about their relationship had changed, although she couldn't quite put her finger on it. He didn't seem pleased by Sir John's courtship.

Unlike her son.

Her mouth quirked with a smile, thinking of Davey, as she murmured her thanks and took the proffered seat between the two men on the bench. He would be vastly disappointed. Her son idolized Sir John in the way of a young squire who looked up to a great knight. He'd been shocked by his hero's interest in his mother.

Actually, it was probably Davey's reaction just as much as Sir Kenneth that was responsible for Mary's transformation. The first time her son had complimented her on her appearance, she'd realized it pleased him to see her looking well. She wanted to make him proud of her. Had she unwittingly embarrassed him by her former drab appearance? She cringed, hoping not.

She knew preciously little about young boys, but since Davey had joined Percy's household a few months ago, she'd begun to feel as if she was beginning to understand her son a little more. He was at an impressionable age, but also an age when he was trying to assert his manhood. As Sir Adam had suggested, the king had been pleased by her efforts on his behalf—even if it had yielded little—and had permitted her to see Davey as often as her duties allowed. Sir Adam had brought him to see her at Ponteland every other Sunday, but it wasn't until the invitation came to Alnwick that they'd been able to spend any extended amount of time together.

The polite reserve that had characterized their relationship had relaxed enough to make her think she glimpsed the occasional sign of genuine affection. Sir John was partially responsible for that, she knew. She peeked out from under her lashes at the formidable knight beside her. If he approved of her, she followed her son's thinking, she couldn't be all that bad.

Mary was trying not to press Davey on their relationship, but her normal patience seemed to have deserted her. She longed to be closer to him and feared her eagerness showed along with her pride every time she looked at him. He was a favorite of the king and was on his way to becoming the same with Lord Percy. Having recently

turned thirteen, her son was already exhibiting hints of
his father's prowess on the battlefield. He was a well-
formed lad, tall and boyishly handsome. Though quiet
and more reserved than his father had been, he was also
more thoughtful—and more deliberate. Cautious, she
realized. Like she. She had every right to be proud of
him, and she was.

"I hope you don't mind," Sir John said from her side.
"But I arranged for David and a few of his friends to join
us at the dais tonight."

"Mind?" Mary turned to him in surprise, just in time
to see her son enter the hall and look toward her. Tears of
joy pricked behind her eyes. It wasn't just at Sir John's
thoughtfulness—it must have taken some persuading to
allow squires to sit at the dais—but also at what her son
was wearing. Beneath his velvet surcote, she could see the
edge of his shirt. A shirt she'd embroidered for him. She'd
given him things before, but this was the first time she
could recall seeing him wear one. "Thank you," she said
to Sir John, her eyes damp.

He took her hand and bowed over it as he stood to make
way for the youths. "You're welcome," he said with a
smile that hovered just on the edge of intimacy. "I hope I
shall have many more opportunities to bring a smile to
your face."

She lowered her eyes, feeling the blast of heat to her
cheeks. She knew she should stop him, that it wasn't fair of
her to encourage him, but it had been so long since a man
had shown an interest in her. Appropriate interest, she
amended, thinking once again of the man about whom
she'd vowed not to think.

But she couldn't stop seeing Sir Kenneth's face. Hard and
intent in the semidarkness as he'd held himself over her—

She pushed the image away. It hadn't meant anything.
He probably looked at every woman he'd made love to like

that. Except she knew for a fact he hadn't—at least he hadn't with the woman in the stable.

She had to stop this. But that one night had given her far more than she'd bargained for, in more ways that one.

If Sir John noticed her momentary distraction, he didn't show it. "I hope you have decided to accept Lord Percy's invitation and travel with Sir Adam to Berwick for Gaveston's arrival?"

Mary nodded. She could hardly refuse. Piers Gaveston, the recently created Earl of Cornwall and King Edward's much despised favorite, had been recalled from exile in Ireland (where Edward had been forced to send him when Gaveston had riled the anger of many important nobles) and been ordered to Berwick to ready for the planned campaign against Scotland when the truce expired in March. The king would follow in late spring. The barons had been called to rally at Berwick, including Sir Adam and Lord Percy—which meant Davey as well. Despite the call to war, her son's presence guaranteed her eager acceptance.

"Good," he said, a decidedly anticipatory glint in his eye. "I want you to know, Lady Mary, you can rely on me for anything."

Mary didn't know what to say. The last thing she wanted to do was rely on a man again, but she heard the heartfelt honesty in his words, and the tiniest part of her—the girl-who'd-longed-for-a-handsome-knight part of her—responded.

Would he feel the same way when she returned from France? It seemed unlikely. There were some things no man would be expected to overlook. Although she had a plan, she knew there would be whispers.

She was saved from having to reply, however, by her son's arrival with his friends. Sir John had made room for him to sit beside her, and when Davey sat down on the bench, all her thoughts turned to her son.

"You're wearing your shirt," she said, unable to hide her eagerness.

His face heated and his gaze flickered to his friends. She could see the relief when it was clear they hadn't heard. "It's very . . . fine."

Mary couldn't tell whether that was good or not. Should she not have mentioned it? She bit her lip.

"Thank you," he added, looking uncomfortable but not ungrateful.

"You're welcome," she answered softly, letting his attention return to his friends.

It was clear he was in awe of being seated at the high table but was doing his best not to show it in front of the other lads. Though she longed to pepper him with questions and learn everything she could about his new duties, Mary took a cue from her son and forced aside her exuberance, acting with an equanimity she did not feel. Even if she still thought of him as the babe torn from her arms, he wasn't that child anymore. He didn't need her to wipe his nose when he sneezed, cut his meat when he ate, or dry his tears when he fell.

What did he need her for?

She didn't know but was determined to find out.

It soon became apparent that as eager as she was to learn about him, the boys were eager to hear from Sir John. So rather than ask questions, Mary contented herself with basking in her son's happiness as Sir John regaled them with war stories. Though many times Mary wanted to object to the more gory details, she kept her mouth firmly closed. Davey and the boys were spellbound.

She had her reward at the end of the night. Davey was about to race off with the rest of his friends, when he turned over his shoulder and said with all the careless, nonchalance of youth, "Thank you, Mother. That was the best meal ever."

He didn't realize the gift he'd given her or the swell of happiness he'd put in her chest.

This was going to work.

Mary was being given another chance at motherhood, and she would do whatever she had to do to hold on to it. Nothing and no one would take it away again.

Ten

❧

Late January 1310
Dunstaffnage Castle, Lorn, Scotland

"I hear congratulations are in order," the king said, looking up from the stack of parchments waiting for his signature before him.

One week after Kenneth had finished his training on the frozen peak of the Black Cuillins by successfully avoiding capture from the other ten members of the Highland Guard for nearly two days (one day longer than the other recruit), he stood in the laird's private solar of Dunstaffnage Castle before Robert the Bruce and most of his new Highland Guard brethren. Only Boyd and Seton were absent, having been sent south to join Edward Bruce in the borders as soon as they'd finished training on Skye.

Kenneth indeed had been the last man standing, and the satisfaction of his victory had not waned one bit. He'd done it. He'd earned his place in Bruce's secret army, even if not in the outright way he'd planned.

"Thank you, Sire," he said.

"You are to be commended," Bruce added. "From what I hear of Chief's Perdition, surviving at all is an accomplishment, but he said you distinguished yourself." Bruce shot a glance toward MacKay, who was standing in the back corner of the solar. "Even managed to quiet Saint's objections, I see."

Not completely, Kenneth thought. Enough for MacKay to not stand in the way of Kenneth joining the team perhaps, but not enough to take him as a partner. MacKay had made it clear their partnership on the mountain had been temporary. Kenneth shouldn't give a shite what his onetime enemy thought, but surprisingly, he did. His brother-by-marriage still didn't completely trust him, and it bothered him. But as much as it pricked, Kenneth could not completely blame him. His temper had gotten the better of him more than once with MacKay around to witness it—including a time last year when he'd gone after MacKay and very nearly taken his sister Helen's head off instead. But he vowed to earn that trust. They were brothers now. In more ways than one.

Though MacKay would never say it, Kenneth knew there was something else he was thinking about—that they were all probably thinking about. He might have earned his way onto the team, but he had yet to establish his place among the best warriors in Christendom. Men whose skills were obvious. Men who'd been fighting together for years and had formed a tight bond. He was the new man. The recruit. Unproven, and despite his accomplishments at the Games and in training, he knew they still had questions about him. He would answer them in time, but until then, he knew they would be watching him. Seeing what he could do. Evaluating and deciding where he could best be used.

His strength—his skill—lay in his versatility. Bruce and MacLeod would see that they could use him anywhere. Whether paired with MacSorley and MacRuairi on the seas, with MacKay, Campbell, and MacGregor in the Highlands, or with Seton, Boyd, MacLean, and Lamont in the Borders, he could be inserted in any mission wherever they had need of him.

Right now, he was also the best replacement they had for Gordon. But it remained to be seen whether his abilities with black powder would prove reliable enough to depend on. If only he had those old notes of Gordon's grandfather. The old warrior fancied himself something of an alchemist and had written copious notes about his experiments with the Saracen thunder and flying fire while on crusade with Kenneth's grandfather. It was in Outremer where the bond between the two clans had been formed. But unfortunately, the journal had burned in one of Kenneth and Gordon's less successful experiments while they'd both been fostered with the Earl of Ross.

It seemed no matter what Kenneth did, he somehow still ended up having to prove himself. It might have been different had he bested MacKay at the Highland Games. But he hadn't. He'd been so close . . .

His jaw tightened reflexively, as once again his wanton little nun's face flashed before him. Not for the first time, he longed for their paths to cross again. He couldn't help feeling that somehow she'd gotten the better of him. Next time—if there was a next time—she wouldn't be so fortunate.

But he suspected it would be quite some time before he saw Mary of Mar again. The war might be under a truce, but the fighting had not ended. There were still skirmishes, especially along the Borders. And the truce would be coming to an end soon. It was originally supposed to end in November, but had been pushed back twice: first to January, and now until March.

Although Ewen Lamont and Eoin MacLean would be leaving for the Borders soon to help Boyd and Seton keep pressure on Edward, pressure that it was hoped would lead to a permanent truce, Kenneth assumed that he'd stay in Lorn with Campbell, MacGregor, MacKay, and Helen (Kenneth still couldn't believe MacKay had agreed to her serving as the Guard's de facto physician), while MacSorley, MacRuairi, and MacLeod kept watch on the west. In addition to keeping the trade routes open, the biggest threat right now came from the western seaboard. John of Lorn, the heir to the chiefdom of Clan MacDougall, was active again.

Mary of Mar would have to wait.

When neither he nor MacKay responded, the king apparently decided not to press. Instead, he asked, "Your sister mentioned that you were close friends with Henry Percy?"

Kenneth was taken aback by the question and immediately tensed, trying to clamp down on the defensiveness that sprang instinctively from any mention of his recent shift of alliance. It was only a little over a year ago that he'd been fighting with the English against Bruce. "We were," he said carefully. "But that friendship ended when I gave my allegiance to you, Sire."

Bruce must have realized the question was an awkward one. "No one questions your loyalty. I only wonder if you think it possible that this friendship could be rekindled?"

Kenneth frowned, wondering what the Bruce was getting at. "I doubt he was very happy with what he would perceive as my defection to the enemy camp. He is proud and arrogant in the manner of most Englishmen and unforgiving when personally slighted." But theirs had been a friendship of mutual admiration for skills on the battlefield. "In the right circumstances, aye, I think we could be friends again." A wry smile lifted one corner of his mouth. "But I should warn you, Sire, if you are thinking to find a sympathetic ear in Percy, you will be fighting a war you cannot win. He is English to the bone, and though he and Edward might not see eye-to-eye on the matter of Gaveston, he is loyal to the English crown." His lands and fortune depended on it.

Bruce smiled. "It's not Percy's loyalty I was thinking of, but yours." Kenneth stiffened, but the king waved him off. "A temporary shift, that's all. I want you to go to England, renew your friendship with Percy, and see what you can find out about Edward's plans. Percy has campaigned in Scotland before; Edward will rely on his experience."

"You think war is finally coming, then? There will not be any more delays from the trouble with his barons?"

Bruce shook his head. "I think the election of the Lord Ordainers will force Edward's attention north. He'll fight a war in Scotland to avoid the supervision of his barons." In large part because of Gaveston, King Edward had been forced to agree to reform of the royal household and the appointment of "Ordainers" who would carry out the mandate. "Aye, war is coming," Bruce said. "This will be our first test against the English since Loudoun Hill over two and a half years ago, and I intend to be ready for it. We assume they will use Edinburgh Castle as their base, but see what you can find out. We want to know where he is going and hit him hard."

Kenneth did not question the importance of the mission, just his role in it. He'd never spied before, and frankly, deception didn't sit well with him. He was a Highlander, but he was also a knight. MacRuairi had warned him that if he wanted to fight with the Highland Guard he was going to get dirty, and he suspected this was his first test. He just hadn't anticipated that his first test would be alone. He wasn't going to break through the tight bond these men had forged from England.

Part of him couldn't help wondering whether there was another reason he was chosen. Was this a test of another kind? Was his loyalty still in question?

The acid of bitterness rose to the back of his throat, but he tamped it back down.

"They will be suspicious," Kenneth said. He'd be fortunate if the English didn't throw him in the closest dungeon.

"Perhaps at first," the king agreed. "But your past should work in our favor. Your change of allegiance was both recent and reluctant."

Kenneth's jaw hardened, wanting to argue but knowing he spoke the truth. "At first, perhaps."

"They don't know that," MacLeod pointed out.

"You aren't exactly known for your even temperament," MacKay added. "That hot temper of yours just might work in our favor. A falling-out with your brother the earl and Bruce won't seem out of character."

Kenneth bit back the angry retort, forcing himself to stay cool, though he wanted to point out that a hot temper didn't equate to disloyalty. Instead, he addressed the king. "Percy will still be suspicious."

The king smiled. "Well, then, you will just have to prove it to him."

Any reluctance Kenneth might have felt was dismissed when he heard Bruce's plan. It wasn't without danger, but it should work to prove his "loyalty."

Being sent to England on his first mission might not be his first choice, but he supposed there was one side benefit. He smiled. Lady Mary was in England. He just might have his chance to rekindle their "friendship" and exact a little retribution sooner than he'd anticipated.

Eleven

✣

One Week Later, Candlemas, February 2, 1310
Berwick Castle, Berwick-upon-Tweed, Northumberland,
  English Marches

Kenneth would never have guessed how quickly he would come to appreciate his training. But being tossed in a dank, pitch-black hole all night—Berwick's pit prison—seemed luxurious compared to some of the "accommodations" he'd had on Skye. He'd actually slept quite comfortably once his nose desensitized to the lingering scent of shite and piss from the last occupant.

The first part of his plan hadn't gone quite as smoothly as he'd hoped. His arrival and request to speak to Percy had caused a stir. He'd expected that. He just hadn't expected that the first person he'd see would be Sir John Felton. It had definitely been a spot of bad luck to come face-to-face with Percy's champion.

There had been tension between the two men from the first. Felton hadn't liked the friendship that had sprung up between him and Percy. Nor had he liked it when Kenneth came close to besting him on the practice field with the sword one day—an act that he'd perceived as a challenge to his place as Percy's greatest knight.

Upon seeing him and hearing that Kenneth was changing his allegiance once again, Felton had tossed him in the pit prison until he could find Percy. As it had taken him all night, Kenneth suspected he hadn't been looking very hard.

The frosty reception from Percy hadn't been much better, though the chill had warmed considerably when he'd heard what Kenneth had to say. Percy had barely blinked when Kenneth claimed to have had a falling-out with his brother after a heated argument over the recent attempt on Bruce's life by his henchman (with whom Kenneth feigned sympathy). Shifting alliances were all too common in the long war, and Kenneth's maneuverings to be in a position to claim his brother's estates should Bruce lose might be opportunistic, but that also made it understandable. Kenneth also knew his well-known temper—damn MacKay for saying so!—was as much to blame for the ready acceptance of his story.

Perhaps he should be offended by how easily they'd believed him—except for Felton, who'd stormed out a short while ago in a huff—but he was just pleased that his stay in the pit prison would not be an extended one.

His new brethren wouldn't have to come rescue him. At least not yet. He was being given a chance to prove himself. Kenneth was going to prove his loyalty to the English by betraying Bruce. At least that was how it would look.

He looked around the small solar at the decidedly more friendly faces. With Felton gone, there was only Percy, a handful of his most trusted knights, and Sir Adam Gordon.

Kenneth had been genuinely glad to see the older warrior. Sir Adam had been William Gordon's uncle and head of the family. He'd been good to Kenneth when they were young, and when William had decided to fight with Bruce, they'd shared the disappointment.

When Kenneth had fought with the English, Sir Adam had looked after him, doing what he could to advance him in Edward's army with choice words in the right ears. If there was anyone he looked forward to betraying less than Percy, it was Sir Adam.

"We will leave at sunrise," Percy announced. "That should give us plenty of time to reach Ettrick Forest and intercept the supply carts before darkness falls. You are sure the attack is set for tomorrow night?"

Although English garrisons still held most of the important border and lowland castles in Scotland, including Edinburgh, Sterling, Bothwell, Roxburgh, and Perth among others, keeping them provisioned—especially those not accessible by the sea—proved a challenge. If the English controlled the strongholds, Bruce controlled the countryside, and the cart trains were often attacked by "the rebels." Advance knowledge of one of these attacks was a difficult lure to resist. Adding Bruce's phantom army made it impossible.

Kenneth wasn't surprised that Percy had decided to go himself. The chance to capture members of Bruce's secret army would tempt any Englishman with ambition or pretensions toward greatness. The reward from the king would be considerable, but being known as the man who'd finally caught the phantom band . . . that would make him a legend.

He nodded. "Bruce's men like to attack at night in isolated areas. This pass in the forest right before the junction in the road to turn east toward Roxburgh," he pointed to the spot on the map near the Aln River and the small village of Ashkirk, "was chosen for exactly that."

"Furtive tactics," Percy said with distaste.

"Aye," Kenneth pretended to agree. "Bruce's pirate warfare might work to capture supply carts, but it merely proves how ill-equipped he is to meet Edward's army like knights on the battlefield."

The coming war had been another reason given for Kenneth's change of allegiance. But he understood what these men did not: that Bruce had no intention of taking the field against Edward until he was ready.

Percy stood and gave him an assessing gaze. "I hope you are right about this. It will go very badly for you if you are wrong. Now I have a feast to attend and a delay to explain to Gaves—" he stopped and corrected himself—"Cornwall. He may have some questions for you. After you change." His gaze slid over Kenneth with a shudder. "It seems Felton was a bit overzealous in his greeting. He should have let me know of your arrival immediately."

Kenneth tipped his head, acknowledging the semi-apology.

"You have some men with you?" Percy asked.

"Just a few of my household men," he said. "I dared not attempt to leave with more. They are waiting for me in the forest." His mouth turned. "I was unsure of my reception."

Percy smiled for the first time. "Your caution was understandable in the circumstances."

"I will send some of my men to fetch them," Sir Adam said. "Sutherland can stay with me in my chamber."

Under guard. Neither Percy nor Sir Adam said it, but Kenneth heard it nonetheless. He wasn't surprised. They would keep a close watch on him for a while.

Kenneth was escorted a short while later by two of Sir Adam's men to the Constable Tower, where a bath had been arranged while his horse and the bag holding the few items he'd brought with him was tracked down. Exchanging the mail shirt he'd been captured in for a surcote, he left one of his men to clean it while he was escorted to the Hall. The Earl of Cornwall did indeed have some questions for him.

Unfortunately, as he hadn't eaten in nearly twenty-four hours, the tables had already been moved for the dancing and music. He was able to snatch a few pieces of cheese, however, from a passing serving girl who was removing the remaining trays.

The music had already begun and the revelers had formed the circle carol dance. He gave the dancers no more than a passing glance, weaving his way through the crowd to the dais at the back of the room.

Sir Adam leaned over and murmured something to the man at his side. Though Kenneth had never met him, his pretty face, fine ermine-lined mantle, and heavy gold chain with one of the biggest sapphires Kenneth had ever seen hanging from his neck identified him as the king's favorite. Hell, he looked like the king himself.

The earl frowned, watching him with interest as Kenneth came forward at Sir Adam's motion.

"Sutherland," he said. "I hear you have had a change of heart."

"Aye, my lord."

The gaze that held his was more intense than he'd expected. For all the hate and condemnation he inspired, Kenneth could see right away that Sir Piers Gaveston was not a man to dismiss. He hadn't gotten where he was by being a fool—not a complete one, anyway. "I will hear more about it after the feast."

The brief interview concluded, at least for now, Kenneth and Sir Adam took their leave.

They'd just stepped off the dais when he felt a prickle on the back of his neck. Out of the corner of his eye he saw a flash of golden-blond hair swinging in a cloud of shimmering silk.

He stilled, a buzz of awareness shooting up his spine, every nerve ending in his body coming alive.

He turned, looking at the woman who'd caught his eye. She had her back to him, and by any objective measure, there was nothing about her that should be familiar. She was laughing, for one thing. Dancing, for another. Her hair was tumbling loose about her shoulders for all the bloody world to see, not hidden behind some hideous veil. She was not skinny as a starved bird who looked like he could blow her over with one breath, but healthy-looking with gentle curves—nay, *substantial* curves, he corrected, looking at her shapely round bottom.

There was no way in hell he should have recognized her. But he did.

It was only when he saw the man's hand linger on her waist that he glanced over at her partner. At the man who was making her laugh.

Kenneth stiffened again, this time with rage. Every possessive bone in his body—bones he hadn't even known he had—flared to life.

Felton. What the hell was she doing with Felton?

His mouth thinned, the reason for Felton's early departure from the meeting suddenly clear.

"Is something wrong?" Sir Adam asked.

Kenneth forced his fists to relax, not realizing they'd instinctively clenched. He shook his head, not trusting himself to speak without the venom spewing through his blood.

The dance came to an end, and Felton started to lead her off the floor toward them. She was only a few feet away when she finally looked in his direction.

His breath caught, feeling as if he'd been poleaxed across the chest. The beauty that he'd glimpsed behind the nunnish facade was revealed in its full glory. Her face was fuller, softening the features that had seemed too sharp. Her skin was luminous, a flawless ivory, pinkened with the flush of her dance. Her eyes were a bright and sparkling blue, her lips red and smiling. She even had a small dimple just to the left of her curving mouth.

His mouth, by contrast, fell in a hard line.

She didn't see him right away, noticing Sir Adam first. But almost as if she sensed him, too, her gaze shifted to his.

He had the satisfaction—and right now, it was bloody well satisfying—of seeing her eyes widen, and every drop of the blush Felton had put in her cheeks drain from her face in shock.

Their eyes held, and all the emotions that he'd felt that morning five months ago, the stinging anger that had led to his loss of control and defeat, came rushing back. He stared at her like a hunter who'd just caught a prey that had been eluding him. Nay, a prey that had run away from him.

But now she was his.

His mouth curved in a slow, anticipatory smile. "Hello, Lady Mary. It seems we meet again."

And his voice left no doubt that this time there would be no escape.

Mary had felt something odd swirling in the air all day. She'd arrived at Berwick Castle the night before, but she'd seen little of the men all day. Sir John had been late to escort her to the feast for the Purification of the Blessed Virgin Mary, or Candlemas as it was also called. Sir Adam had arrived even later with Lord Percy and had given her an apologetic smile as he'd taken a seat on the bench near Gaveston—or rather, the Earl of Cornwall.

The earl was known as being extremely sensitive to any lack of regard for his position. Even referring to him by the name Gaveston rather than Cornwall could be cause for disfavor. But when he wasn't within hearing, many of the nobles refused to call him by the name of the earldom that had always been reserved for members of the royal family. The more titles and riches Edward lavished on his favorite, the more the other barons hated him.

Though Lord Percy had answered the king's call to muster—one of the few English barons who had done so—the acrimony between him and Sir Piers was well known. Yet the men had been locked in discussion for most of the meal.

Something was commanding their attention. She wondered what it was.

Barely had the question formed when she felt a prickle of

awareness. Nay, a prickle of danger. It was the feeling of being watched. She felt a twitch, like that of a mouse under the predatory gaze of the hawk.

She turned in the direction of the oppressing weight and froze. The bottom fell out of her stomach. Her legs swayed as if she might swoon.

It wasn't possible. But it was . . .

Dear God, it was *him*. Sir Kenneth Sutherland in all of his aggressively masculine perfection. He was even more handsome than she remembered—and she would have sworn she remembered *everything* about him. But his eyes were an even deeper blue than her imagination would allow, his jaw harder and more challenging, his face leaner and with a few more nicks, his shoulders broader, and his arms even thicker with muscle. She'd forgotten how it felt to stand so close to him. How tall he was. How powerfully built. How stomach-knottingly handsome.

But most of all, she'd forgotten how it felt to be caught in that magnetic gaze. *Caught*. That was exactly how she felt.

Panic surged through her. "Why are you here?" she blurted, as if he might have discovered the truth.

But he couldn't have, she reminded herself. *He couldn't know.*

"You've met?"

Sir John's question startled her from her trance of panic—and fear, she realized. Deep-seated fear.

He didn't sound pleased.

Suddenly the reason for his question hit her. She stared at Sir Kenneth in mute horror, unsure what to say. Had she given him away? Did they know he was with Bruce?

But apparently it wasn't a secret. "Aye," Sir Kenneth said. "In Scotland at the Highland Games last fall."

From the glares shooting back and forth, it was obvious these two men didn't like one another.

"Aye, that was it," she said as if the matter were beneath her regard. "I'd almost forgotten."

She caught the spark in Sir Kenneth's eyes and knew he hadn't mistaken her implication.

"Of course," Sir John said, giving her a smile that was both too indulgent and too proprietary. "You attended the Games while on your peacekeeping mission for the king. You would have occasion to meet many of the rebels." He gave a small sneer of distaste.

Sir Adam finally took pity on her bewilderment. "Young Sutherland has declared his allegiance for Edward."

Mary couldn't hide her shock. Her gaze flickered to Sir Kenneth's. "You have?"

A muscle tightened in his jaw, as if sensing her disapproval. "Aye."

"When?"

"Only last night," Sir John said, a hint of snideness in his tone. "How fortunate for us that Sir Kenneth has once again decided to switch sides."

She could tell by the tiny white lines that appeared around Sir Kenneth's mouth and the sudden glint in his eye that he hadn't missed the disparagement, but he did not rise to defend himself. Which, from what she knew of him, was strange. He definitely didn't seem the type to let a slight go by. Rather the opposite. She'd gotten the impression he was usually raring for a fight.

Though it was hardly uncommon to jump from one side of the border to the other, Mary was unaccountably disappointed to hear that he'd left Bruce's army. Over the past months, she'd wondered if she'd somehow been wrong about him. But this show of loyalty—or rather, disloyalty—seemed proof that she wasn't.

She wanted to ask him why, but dared not prolong the conversation that had already gone on too long. So instead, she merely agreed, "Fortunate indeed." Going on as if the matter meant nothing to her, which indeed it shouldn't, she added to Sir Adam, "I'm feeling rather tired. I think I shall return to my chamber."

"I will see you back—" Sir John started, but she cut him off. The last thing she wanted to deal with right now was an insistent suitor. "That won't be necessary. Lady Eleanor and Lady Katherine are waiting for me. I will see you on the morrow."

"Unfortunately, it seems I must delay the ride I promised you," Sir John said.

"Oh?" She couldn't completely hide her disappointment. He'd promised to take her for a ride tomorrow and bring Davey along. Of course, he'd left that part out. Clearly, he was trying to stake some kind of claim, as if he'd sensed something between her and Sir Kenneth.

But there was nothing between them. There couldn't be.

"Something has come up," he explained. "I will be away from the castle for a day or two, but I promise we shall go as soon as I return."

She didn't need to look at Sir Kenneth to see him tense. She could feel the anger radiating from him in hot, powerful waves. She was beginning to feel like a meaty bone being fought over by two snarling hounds, and she'd had enough of it. Neither man had a claim on her.

But a tiny voice in the back of her head told her that wasn't completely true. And the longer she stayed here, the more danger she was in of Kenneth discovering the truth. She had to leave. But where could she go? And what of Davey? They'd only just begun to get to know one another again.

Feeling as if her world was being ripped apart all over again, Mary fought the urge to run and started slowly away. But she'd taken only a few steps when his voice reached out to snake around her.

"Lady Mary."

She gave a cautious turn over her shoulder.

He smiled. A smile that twisted through her chest and

coiled low in her belly. "I look forward to renewing our *acquaintance*."

She felt the gasp rise in her throat and only barely managed to prevent it from escaping. She could only hope her expression gave no hint of the panic surging in her chest. She nodded, as if it had merely been a polite comment, as innocuous as it sounded.

But it wasn't polite or innocuous. His meaning rang clear to her. The moment she passed through the entry of the Great Hall, she started to run. Only later, when she'd reached the safety of her chamber, did she remember her attendants.

Twelve

🌿

By the time they neared the place in the royal Ettrick Forest where they would "surprise" Bruce's men who were lying in wait to attack the supply cart from Carlisle, it was taking everything Kenneth had not to give Felton the fight for which he was so obviously clamoring. During the long ride west from Berwick Castle, Percy's champion knight took every opportunity to insult, discredit, and argue with him about every facet of the mission.

Kenneth knew he should be used to it. Hell, he'd heard far worse from MacKay over the years. And after the past few months of nonstop prodding by the other members of the Highland Guard, he'd thought he had a steel rein on his temper and ice in his veins.

He did. Except, it seemed, when it came to one subject. Each time Felton mentioned Lady Mary—which seemed to be in every other sentence—Kenneth could feel that steel rein start to slip between his fingers. The muscles in his shoulders were so knotted with tension, he'd developed a damned crick in his neck.

If Felton was to be believed, they were as good as betrothed. And if Felton's relationship with the young earl was any indication, it was probably true.

David Strathbogie, Earl of Atholl, had come along as one of Percy's squires. At dawn, when they'd gathered in the courtyard to depart, Kenneth had taken one look at Lady Mary's young son and had argued against it.

"It's too dangerous for the lad," he'd said to Percy. "He would be a valuable prisoner if something were to go wrong and Bruce's men were to get hold of him."

It was the truth. Hell, Bruce would love to get his hands on the young Earl of Atholl. So why was he trying to prevent it?

Percy had seemed about to agree when Felton interrupted. "If Sutherland is telling the truth, the danger should be minimal." His voice left no doubt as to his thoughts on the matter. "If he isn't, I will watch out for the lad. He won't come to any harm under my command. He'll stay in the rear, well protected and well away from any danger. Besides, the lad is ready to see action beyond the practice yard, aren't you, David."

The solemn lad with his mother's startling blue-green eyes had looked uncertain, but at Felton's praise he puffed up considerably. "Aye, my lord," he said to Percy. To Kenneth, he cast an unfriendly glare. "I'm ready, and I should like to be there to see the usurper's phantoms captured."

The lad sounded so bloody English, it was hard to believe his father had died for that "usurper."

Kenneth hadn't known the previous Earl of Atholl well, but from the way he was spoken of amongst Bruce and the Guard, Lady Mary's former husband had been a fierce patriot, gallant knight, and skilled warrior. An honest-to-God hero, Kenneth thought, not knowing why his jaw was clenched so tight.

In any event, Felton's recommendation and the boy's eagerness proved enough for Percy. " 'Twill be good experience for the lad. I was his age when I served as squire in my first battle. Just keep a good eye on him, Felton."

Felton nodded as Percy rode forward and cast a smug look of victory at Kenneth.

It was to David that Felton spoke of Lady Mary during the long day of riding, but Kenneth knew it was more for his benefit than the lad's. Felton was making his claim loud and clear. The boy seemed thrilled by the prospect of a union between his mother and the lauded knight.

Kenneth, however, felt his blood growing hotter and hotter by the minute. His teeth had been clenched for so long his jaw had start to hurt. If he didn't know better, he would have thought he was jealous.

Of a woman. How bloody ridiculous! He had his pick of just about any woman he wanted; he didn't need to trouble himself with *one*. Even one who made his blood rush hot just standing next to her.

The changes in her appearance should have made him happy. God knows it helped explain his strange attraction to the lass. But he wasn't happy about it at all. He wanted her back the way she was, when he had been the only one to see the passion beneath the colorless facade.

Suddenly, an image of her softly rounded bottom sprang to mind. Well, perhaps he wouldn't take back *all* the changes. The curves could stay.

He wasn't jealous. The only reason Felton's taunts were grating on him was that he intended to teach Lady Mary a lesson and didn't want anyone interfering.

Kenneth hadn't forgotten how she left him, or how it cost him the battle with MacKay. Her ready dismissal of him still grated. Both at Dunstaffnage and the day before. *"I'd almost forgotten."*

To a man whose first instinct was to fight, those words were like a gauntlet tossed at his feet. A challenge he couldn't resist. And this was a battle he had no intention of losing. For a man who preferred to keep his challenges confined to the battlefield, he was surprised by how much he was looking forward to it.

Aye, he was going to make her pay for all the trouble she'd caused him. First with that delectable little body of hers, and then with her heart. By the time he was done with her, she'd be looking at him like he hung the damned moon. His mouth curled with annoyance, glancing at the riders behind him. Not unlike the way her son was looking at Felton.

"How much farther?" Felton bit out, coming up beside him. "It will be dark soon, and if this attack of yours is real, we should be getting into position. If this is some kind of trick, I'll see you hung by your—"

"Relax," Kenneth said, as if he were pacifying an over-eager bairn. "We're almost there. If this is a trick, you'll know soon enough."

Felton flushed angrily. "Is that supposed to convince me?"

Kenneth gave him a hard look, letting some of the rage he'd been bottling inside show. "I'm not trying to convince you of anything. I don't give a shite what you think, Felton. Hell, I've heard you boast countless times what would happen to Bruce's phantoms if you ever came face-to-face with one. Well, here's your chance. If you're worried that you and half a bloody garrison of men aren't enough to defeat a few rebels—"

Felton's stiff English control cracked. "I'm not worried, damn it."

"Good," Kenneth said curtly. Ignoring the blustering knight, he turned to Percy. "The pass I mentioned is just ahead. You'll want to have your men in position and hidden well before Bruce's men arrive, in case they send a scout ahead to watch for the supply train."

Percy's plan was to hide a short distance away from where Bruce's men intended to launch their "surprise" attack. The carts and armed soldiers from Carlisle would proceed as originally planned, but when Bruce's men attacked, the soldiers would be ready for them. Once the two sides were engaged in battle, Percy and the rest of his men would circle around them, catching them in an impenetrable net.

But "impenetrable" wasn't enough to hold the Highland Guard.

Kenneth might have been worried about the number of men Percy had brought with him—fifty in addition to the soldiers from Carlisle guarding the carts (he wasn't taking any chances in letting the illustrious phantom warriors slip through his fingers)—but he'd seen the Highland Guard in action. He doubted a hundred men would be enough to hold them. Moreover, Striker—Eoin MacLean—had planned the "attack" with a second route of escape if it proved necessary.

Percy turned to Felton. "Your men are ready? I will be counting on you to make sure they cannot break through. I don't care what it takes, do not let them escape!"

Felton appeared unconcerned. "If Sutherland is telling the truth, my men will be ready. The place on the road they've chosen leaves them little room to maneuver." He knelt down to draw a crude map in the dirt. "It is dense forestland with a steep rise on one side and the Aln River on the other. We will circle around from all directions once they have launched their attack. As long as the soldiers protecting the cart can hold them off while we get in position, we will have them."

Percy looked at the ground for a long moment, studying every possible escape route. If he considered the cliff, he quickly discounted it. Who would jump over twenty feet into a narrow river in the darkness? "Good," he said with a curt nod of the head.

When he'd moved off, Kenneth turned to Felton. "Don't forget about the lad," he said, indicating the young Earl of Atholl. "I don't think his mother would appreciate if you got him captured."

Even in the fading daylight, Kenneth could see the angry flush flood Felton's face. "The boy is none of your concern, and neither is his mother."

Kenneth was being warned off, and if he were wise he

would have walked away. But Felton had driven one too many stakes in his claim.

He smiled. "Are you so sure about that?"

Felton's fists clenched, and for a moment, Kenneth thought—hell, hoped—he was going to strike him. But instead, he looked Kenneth over with a coldly assessing stare and returned his smile. "It wouldn't be the first time we've competed for something. And like all the other times, I'm sure the result will be the same."

Outwardly, Kenneth showed no reaction to the taunt, but inside was a different matter. He would love nothing more than to prove to Felton just how wrong he was, but Bruce had warned him to keep a low profile. To do nothing to bring attention to himself or his skills. Besting Percy's champion would sure as hell do that.

Kenneth had newfound sympathy for MacKay, who'd been forced to do much the same thing in the face of Kenneth's taunts last year.

All he could do was grit his teeth once again. "Just be ready."

They didn't have long to wait. Kenneth's Highland Guard brethren—or the majority of them at least; MacLeod, MacRuairi, and MacSorley had stayed with the king—arrived about an hour after dusk to take their positions. Campbell and MacGregor had passed within a few dozen feet of the English position, as they'd ridden south to supposedly scout the arrival of the provision train. Kenneth knew they'd been spotted, although the two warriors gave no indication of it. Campbell was too good to miss them. The clear night and full moon provided enough light to see the signs on the landscape left by fifty men.

Not long after Campbell and MacGregor passed by, they heard the clomp of horses and the clatter of carts being pulled along a bumpy road. Felton motioned to one of the soldiers in the carts as they passed, alerting them that the place was near, but taking care that he could not be seen from the road ahead.

The air was thick with tension now as the train rumbled by them. They would not be able to see the attack, but they would be able to hear it.

The minutes tolled slowly. Kenneth could see the anxiousness on the faces of the men around him as they waited for the first sounds. The familiar battle scent of fear laced with anticipation hung in the air.

Finally, a fierce battle cry tore through the night, and a moment later, there was the answering clash of steel. Felton sprang from his position on the opposite side of Percy and began barking commands. His men took off in all directions, fanning around the attack to cut off all means of escape.

Kenneth, Percy, and Felton approached slowly, taking care not to alert Bruce's man of their presence.

Percy's men were good, he'd give them that. For Englishmen they were doing a damned find job of imitating Bruce's "furtive" methods. If this had been a real attack, the Highland Guard might have been in trouble.

But his friends knew what was coming, and they'd be ready.

Finally, Kenneth and the English reached a turn in the road where they could see the battle. About a hundred feet ahead of them, pandemonium reigned. Swords, pikes, axes, hammers—a symphony of weaponry flashed like a lightning storm in the night air before them. If he hadn't known better, the sight of Bruce's "phantoms" would have taken him aback as well. Wrapped in dark plaids, with their blackened faces, helms, mail coifs, and *cotuns*, the Highland Guard did indeed look like wraiths, flying through the night air in a whirl of death and destruction. He noticed more than one man startle beside him.

"They're only men," Percy reminded them softly, but there might have been a hint of uncertainty in his voice. Then he stood, brandishing his sword about his head. "For England!" he shouted, leading the charge.

Only Kenneth hesitated. He looked around to where Felton had instructed the young earl to remain, protected by a half-dozen soldiers who would prevent the Guard from escaping to the south. "Remember," he warned the lad. "Stay back, and out of the way."

Wide-eyed, transfixed by his first glimpse of battle, David nodded.

Kenneth raced forward, taking his position on the east flank where Percy was shouting out his commands. The Highland Guard had already fought their way through the first line of defense—the soldiers protecting the cart—and Percy was ordering the outer line forward, tightening the noose.

The plan was for the Highland Guard to create a hole in the defense and slip through before the English were in position. It should have been simple enough. With Percy's remaining men spread all around, the eight guardsmen could easily defeat the dozen or so closest men and slip into the cover of darkness.

But something was wrong. The Guard was taking too long.

It took Kenneth a minute to realize that one of the Guard had been injured—Seton, maybe?—it was too dark to tell. The guardsman nearest him—this one he had no problem recognizing, Boyd's powerful form being impossible to mistake—was locked in battle with three of Felton's men and couldn't break free of them. MacKay was trying to make his way over to help them, but Felton had seen what was happening and ordered a handful of his men to stop him.

Unfortunately, Seton—he was sure it was he now—

Boyd, and MacKay were on the opposite side of the road from the rest of the Guard, and the time for creating that hole was quickly disappearing. The noose was tightening and would become harder and harder to break through.

Timing was everything, and they were losing it. Kenneth was trying to think of a way to help without making it obvious, but his own position on the outer line beside Percy hampered him.

Then things went from bad to worse. Improvising, the Guard decided to make two holes. MacGregor, Campbell, MacLean, and Lamont broke through the line in the northwest and escaped along the planned route through the high pass. MacKay, Boyd, and Seton would take the backup route along the river. Splitting up made sense. That wasn't the problem. The problem was that between the three guardsmen and escape was the young Earl of Atholl.

Would they be able to tell in the darkness it was only a lad? The boy was tall already, and with his mail and helm . . .

Ah hell.

"Get back!" Kenneth shouted, but the boy was too far away and the din of battle too loud for him to hear the warning.

Realizing the danger, Felton had moved his men around to protect the boy. The added men were making it harder for the three guardsmen to break through and giving Percy the delay he needed.

"Don't let them escape!" Percy shouted, ordering the rest of his men to circle around from behind.

MacKay, Boyd, and the wounded Seton were fighting their way forward, but they needed to hurry up. The rest of the army was closing in fast. They only had a handful of seconds to get away.

One by one, they cut through the men standing before

the boy. The earl was trying to back up, but he wasn't moving away fast enough. Felton was doing his best to fend off MacKay, but the others were no match for Boyd, and even an injured Seton.

Finally, they had their hole. Seton and Boyd slipped through and headed for the edge of the hillside.

"Stop them, Felton!" Percy shouted. "They're getting away!"

Percy's champion was good, but MacKay was better. He feigned a swing of his sword from the right, but at the last minute dropped his hands, spun, and delivered a blow from the opposite side, sending Felton careening to the ground on his arse.

Kenneth didn't have time to enjoy the moment, however. MacKay was past Felton and headed for the others when he saw the lad—except he didn't know it was a lad. He thought he was just one more soldier in his way.

Kenneth was almost there.

MacKay lifted his sword.

"Nayyyy!" Kenneth shouted, leaping through the air, his own sword raised to block the blow meant for David.

His gaze met MacKay's shocked one as their swords clashed right before the terrified boy's face. Unfortunately, due to the angle and the fact that Kenneth was flying through the air, the swords did not meet squarely, and the blade of MacKay's two-handed long sword skidded sharply off the blade and into Kenneth's arm.

The shot of pain and hot pulse of blood told him the powerful slice of MacKay's blade had found a narrow gap between the sleeve of his habergeon and gauntlet and penetrated the padding underneath to find flesh. Quite a bit of flesh, he suspected, feeling the amount of blood seeping through as he tried to staunch it with his gauntleted hand.

Kenneth hoped he was the only one to hear his brother-in-law swear and mutter a hasty apology in Gaelic before disappearing into the darkness.

Moments later, Kenneth heard a splash below and knew his friends were safe.

Not surprisingly, not one of the Englishmen attempted to jump off the cliff to go after them.

Thirteen

For the better part of two days, Mary had plenty of time to consider what she should do. With Sir Adam in constant attendance to the Earl of Cornwall and Davey having accompanied Lord Percy, Sir John, and—to her surprise—Sir Kenneth on some last-minute journey to Roxburgh (at least she thought it was Roxburgh, though Sir Adam had been unusually vague), she'd been left largely to herself.

Although she was certainly eager to avoid Sir Kenneth, and truth be told Sir John as well, she wanted to tell Sir Adam and Davey of her plans to return to Ponteland as soon as possible.

Her chest squeezed at the thought of leaving so soon after arriving. It wasn't fair. She'd just begun to make inroads with her son, just started to get to know him, and *he* had to show up and ruin everything.

Mary's first instinct had been to toss a few items in a bag that night and find the nearest ship to take her to France. But once the initial shock of seeing Kenneth Sutherland in all his too-handsome glory in *England* had passed, she'd calmed down. Well, at least enough not to run to the stables and jump on the first horse.

There was no reason to be scared, she told herself. No reason to overreact or do anything rash. Perhaps he did not mean to stay long?

But Mary knew that even a few days was too much to risk. She would return to Ponteland on the pretext of attending to a matter with the estate and return to Berwick and Davey as soon as she was able. As soon as he was gone.

After that . . .

Her chest squeezed again.

After that, she would see.

Her hands instinctively went to her stomach. She would do whatever she had to do to protect her unborn child.

The child she hadn't planned for.

The child she'd never allowed herself to think was possible.

The child that for one moment she hadn't wanted. What would she do? She wasn't married. The babe would be branded a bastard and she a whore.

But those few moments of fear had faded quickly and joy had set in. Joy that permeated every bone, every fiber of her being. Joy at the miracle she'd been given. A baby. A second chance to be a mother. In the face of such a gift, no matter how illicitly given, everything else had seemed secondary.

Mary may not have been able to prevent them from taking her first child, but this one would be different.

She did not delude herself that it would be easy, nor did she minimize the difficulties that needed to be overcome, but she was determined to do whatever was needed to keep her child.

It would not be the first time a woman had given birth out of the bonds of wedlock. As long as she was careful, as long as there was a pretext to believe in, they might whisper and wonder, but what else could they do?

France was to be her pretext. It was somewhere she could retire beyond the eyes of Edward's court. The child would be a foundling she'd brought back to England with her.

Some might suspect the truth, but Lady Mary of Mar, the widowed Countess of Atholl, in the far, war-torn north—far away from London—was hardly likely to provoke much gossip. She'd been ostracized before when it had been no fault of her own, so she could withstand anything for her child.

There was an added benefit to her plan. As a foundling, the child would be beneath the scrutiny of any king, English or Scot. The babe would be hers. No one could take it away.

Except for one person.

The chill that hadn't left her bones since the moment she'd seen him standing in the Hall made her shiver. If Sir Kenneth discovered the truth, he could threaten everything. Perhaps he wouldn't care—God knows he might have fathered hundreds of bastards, given his reputation—but something warned her differently. There was more to her "perfect man for sin" than she'd initially thought.

She'd never considered telling him. With him in Scotland loyal to Bruce, what was the point? But now that he was here . . .

Nay. She shook off the thought. It was too late. The child didn't change anything. *"What does that have to do with us?"* She couldn't go through that again. Sir Kenneth was still too much like her husband, and—she thought of the silly pang that had tightened in her chest when she'd seen him—she was still too much the girl who would let him break her heart.

But it was going to be hard to leave Davey. She'd also hoped to have a chance to extend the search for her sister to Berwick-upon-Tweed. She consoled herself that it would not be for long. Davey would be too busy with his duties to Lord Percy to miss her, and Janet . . .

Her sister could be anywhere. Even in France.

Mary was walking back to her chamber after breaking her fast when she learned that Percy and the others had returned. But when she asked one of the other squires where she could find Davey, the lad said that he'd gone to Sir Adam's chamber with the doctor. In a burst of panic,

Mary raced across the courtyard to the Constable's Tower, which housed many of the higher-ranking noblemen.

Although a royal castle, Berwick was primarily used as an administration center and garrison. But with the call to arms, the important border castle that had already seen more than its share of war could hold only a small portion of the three thousand knights, men-at-arms, and servants who were expected to heed the king's call to muster. It was, she suspected, an indication of Sir Adam's favor that she had been given a room in the massive donjon tower with her attendants and a few of the other ladies.

By the time she'd climbed the three levels of stairs to Sir Adam's chamber, she was gasping for breath. Not bothering to knock, she opened the door. "Davey, are you all—"

She froze. Three faces turned toward her. Davey, an older man who she assumed was the doctor, and the very last man she wanted to see: Sir Kenneth Sutherland.

—*right?* she finished the thought. But it was clear Davey was fine. He was standing to the side as the doctor finished wrapping a piece of cloth around Sir Kenneth's forearm. *He* was the one who was injured, not her son.

Realizing they were all still staring at her, heat rose to her cheeks. "I'm sorry. I heard a physician had been sent for, and I thought it was for Davey."

"I'm fine, Mother," her son said, embarrassed.

She smiled at him tenderly. "I can see that."

Her gaze turned to Sir Kenneth, although she was careful not to let it linger as he wasn't wearing a shirt. Memories of that tanned, muscular chest haunted her, and she feared her face would show every one of her sinful dreams. Good God, he was even more powerfully muscled than before! What had he been doing, lifting rocks the whole time?

She quickly shifted her gaze, her mouth dry. "I hope it is not serious?"

"As I was assuring your son, I'm fine. Isn't that right, Welford?"

The older man frowned, two darts of blue narrowing under bushy white brows. "As long as it does not fester. The barber seems to have been adept with his iron." The disdain in his voice gave the impression that this was not always the case. "It has stopped the bleeding at least for now. But it was a wide, deep gash, and I may need to seal it again."

Mary shuddered, thinking of the pain of a hot iron seared across an open wound.

Kenneth waved him off and shrugged a linen shirt over his head, enabling Mary to breathe again. "It will be fine."

The physician had obviously dealt with stubborn, too-tough warriors before. He gathered his belongings and started toward the door. "If it hurts, there is a medicine I can—" He stopped, shaking his head. "I know, I know, it will not hurt." He muttered something under his breath as he left, shutting the door behind him.

Mary was tempted to go after him, but not without her son. What was he doing in here, anyway? And how had Sir Kenneth been injured? "Davey, perhaps we should leave Sir Kenneth to see to his injury. I'm anxious to hear about your journey to Roxburgh."

He gave her an odd look. "We didn't go to Roxburgh. We went to the Ettrick Forest to catch Bruce's phantoms."

For the second time that morning, the color drained from Mary's face. "You *what*?"

Not realizing the state of panic he'd thrown her in, Davey went on. "Hell's gates, it was something! We almost had them, thanks to Sir Kenneth." He shook his head in boyish amazement. "I've never seen men fight like that. At least I think they were men. It was difficult to tell, until the one got close enough when he came at me with his sword."

Mary was grateful that the edge of the bed was so near, because her legs suddenly didn't feel strong enough to hold her. She sank onto the soft mattress, grabbing one of the four wooden posts to steady herself.

Davey was oblivious and opened his mouth to continue, but Sir Kenneth cut him off. "You're frightening your mother, lad. Perhaps you might share your stories with your fellow squires instead?"

The boy's eyes lit up with excitement. It was obvious that the prospect of telling battle stories to an appreciative audience was too tempting to resist. "If you are sure you don't need anything?" It was Mary's turn to frown. Why was Davey being so attentive to Sir Kenneth? "Do you need help with your armor?" he asked.

"I don't think I will be wearing armor for a while, but I'm sure your mother can get me anything I need." Mary shot him a glare, not mistaking the innuendo. "Go," he said to Davey. "I'll see you in the yard in a few minutes."

Davey raced by her but she stopped him. "Wait," she said, catching him by the arm. She reached out and gently smoothed his hair back from his face. She gave him a tender smile. "You have a smudge on your brow." She tried to wipe it away with her thumb.

For a moment, he seemed to sink into the caress, enjoying the motherly contact. But then he startled and twisted his head away. "Don't!" He cast a mortified glance to Kenneth. "It's nothing."

Before she could think how to respond, he darted out of the room.

The rejection, though understandable, stung. Thirteen-year-old boys didn't need their faces wiped by their mother. No matter how desperately she longed to go back to recapture his lost childhood, she could not.

Not with Davey at least.

"When I was his age, everything my parents did was embarrassing to me—especially my mother. Now I'd give anything to have her fussing over me."

Mary stiffened, not realizing how carefully he'd been watching her—or how much her expression must have given away. Embarrassed and yet strangely moved by his effort to soothe her. "She died?"

He nodded. "Some years back."

Not liking the moment of connection—or perhaps liking it too much—she changed the subject to the one that had been bothering her. "Why are you here in Sir Adam's chambers, and why was Davey with you?"

He reached for a black leather surcote that had been tossed on the back of the wooden chair and started the somewhat tricky proposition of putting it on with a bandaged arm. She resisted the urge to offer to help, knowing she shouldn't get too close to him.

She thought he might be avoiding her question, but finally he said, "I'm staying with Sir Adam and the boy offered to help." He arched a brow speculatively. "I could ask the same of you."

She blushed, knowing he had a point. She shouldn't have come to Sir Adam's chamber alone. "Sir Adam is an old friend of my husband's—and of mine."

"Then it seems we have something in common. Sir Adam's father fought with my grandfather in the last crusade. I've known him since I was a lad. I fostered with his nephew."

He winced when the bandaged part of his arm tried to pass through the sleeve.

She bit her lip, but kept her feet planted. "Your arm, will it be all right?"

He gave her a mocking smile, finally shrugging the surcote onto his shoulders. "I didn't think you cared, Lady Mary."

She glared at him impatiently.

His mouth quirked. "I might not be able to lift my sword for a few days, but there should be no lasting damage. Nor should it affect other body parts, if that's what you are worried about."

She flushed, despite knowing that he was just trying to

embarrass her. Apparently the man was outrageous on both sides of the border. "I'm sure England's eager young widows and their attendants will be greatly relieved."

The dry observation only seemed to amuse him. She knew she should go. But something stopped her. Something about what Davey had said. Something she didn't want to believe.

What did Davey mean, *"Thanks to Sir Kenneth?"* She worked it out as she spoke. "This journey to Ettrick was because of you. You told them where Bruce's men would be." She stopped and looked at him, aghast. "You betrayed them."

Although there was no outward sign that her accusation bothered him—his expression remained perfectly impassive—she had the feeling that it had. His perfect, dare-you-to-resist-me mouth tightened almost imperceptibly. "I think that's a rather dramatic way of looking at it. I had knowledge, and I used it. This is war, my lady. 'Betrayal' is part of the game."

"Is that what this is to you, a game? Pieces on a chessboard to move around? Ebony or ivory, you choose whatever side will put you in a better position?" The tic in his jaw was the only sign that she'd pricked his mocking facade. "What of honor? What of loyalty?"

He threw the challenge back at her with a taunting smile. "We all make our choices. What of you, Lady Mary? You are a Scot in England, the same as I. What of *your* honor? What of *your* loyalty?"

She flushed and said starchily, "My honor and loyalty are to my son."

His gaze bored into her, almost as if he were trying to see inside. Trying to read her secrets. "Why do you care, Mary? Why does my appearance here seem to have caused you so much distress?"

Some of the heat drained from her face as fear sent a chill racing through her veins. Suddenly, she was very conscious of the fact that they were in a room alone together, and she was sitting on a big bed. She sprang up. "It doesn't. It hasn't. I was merely surprised. Last time I saw you, Robert was lauding your many talents and getting ready to throw a celebration in your honor."

Something glinted in his eyes. "Aye, well, things change." His gaze drifted over her. The glance had been brief. Cool. Impassive. There was nothing in it that should have made her stomach knot and her skin flush with heat. But she felt as if he had taken store of every change, every detail, every slight difference in her appearance. His words bore her out. "Like you, for instance. I see you aren't hiding anymore."

She stiffened, not sure why his words made her feel so uneasy. It was almost as if he didn't like the changes. "I wasn't hiding."

"Weren't you? Then I take it you have reconsidered a life in a convent?" A knowing smile curved his mouth. Though he hadn't moved from his place across the room, she inched closer to the door. His gaze darkened with heat. "Maybe I had something to do with that?"

Mary told herself it was anger that made her feel so hot, not the memories that husky tone evoked.

She forced herself not to react to his teasing, instead effecting a smile of bored disdain. "Some things haven't changed. You are as arrogant in England as you were in Scotland."

"So there is another reason I find you looking as beautiful and fresh as a May queen, and not buried beneath the drab habit of a nun?"

Mary hated the way her heart skipped at "beautiful." He thought she was beautiful? It shouldn't give her so much pleasure.

Embarrassed by how close he'd come to the truth, and at her own weakness, she shot back at him angrily, "What makes you think I've given you a second thought since leaving Dunstaffnage?"

"Because I can think of nothing else."

The curt, matter-of-fact admission took her aback. She blinked at him in shock, waiting for him to take it back with a mocking smile or turn it into a sensual ploy with a heated glance. But he did neither. He just stared at her, a challenge in that steady blue gaze.

Was it true? Had he been thinking of her?

She felt a strange lurch in her chest but forced it back. Why was he doing this? What game was he playing?

Perhaps that was it. Lust, like war, was a game to him. She'd refused him, and like any born competitor he wanted to win.

She forced a laugh. "You expect me to believe that? What is it, my lord knight, were there not enough admirers tossing flowers at your victory parade? Did you need one more? The only reason you are talking like this is because I did not drop willingly at your feet like all the others. Perhaps I should just tell you how wonderful you are and then you can forget it as I have. Is that why you surround yourself with all those starry-eyed young girls? Girls who don't think beyond a pretty face and impressive display of muscle? Maybe they would hold your attention longer if they had something more interesting to talk about!"

For a minute she wondered if she'd gone too far. Instinctively, she glanced toward the door, ready to make an escape. But in three long strides he'd crossed the distance between them and blocked her.

How had he moved so fast? For such a big man, he moved like a cat. A very big, very strong cat.

They were standing close now. Too close. She could feel his heat, feel the shadow of his big, muscular body looming over her. He should smell horrible. The sweat of battle and of his long ride should be overpowering her. But instead, the heady scent of leather and wind made her want to inhale. Desire flooded her. Memories flooded her. Hot damp skin. The faint taste of salt on her tongue.

"There was no victory parade."

The words shocked her from her sensory stupor. "What? When I left, you were—"

"When you left, I was facing my final competition. I lost."

There was something in his voice that bothered her. Her brows gathered together. "It was just one event. You won many others."

He shrugged.

"You were still named champion?"

"Aye."

She didn't understand why one loss was so important to him, but she sensed that it was. Very important. "It was just a game."

He gave her a long look. "Not to me."

"Why is winning so important to you?"

"Because I know what it's like to lose."

It was almost as if he were somehow blaming her. "Well, I'm sorry, but as I had nothing to do with it—"

She tried to sweep by him, but he took her by the arm. "Didn't you? You left before we finished." Her heart was fluttering wildly. *It's fear*, she told herself. "I could almost think you were running away. Just like you are now. If you don't care, what are you scared of?"

She froze. "Nothing."

His eyes held hers. "I don't believe you."

He leaned closer, and Mary felt a burst of panic. "We were—are—finished, whether you choose to accept it or not. Believe it or not, you are not the only man in the kingdom, my lord."

His eyes flared. She didn't know what provoked her to challenge him, but she couldn't seem to help herself.

"You can't be talking about Felton?"

Something about his attitude infuriated her. Did he think the handsome knight could not be interested in her?

She arched a brow. "Just because I did not wish to marry you does not mean I could not be persuaded to marry someone else. Why not the most handsome man at Berwick?"

She was doing it again. Challenging a man who couldn't resist a challenge. Who was volatile. Raring for a fight. It was like throwing confections to a bairn and daring him not to eat them.

He leaned closer, and for a moment she feared he would kiss her. The pounding in her chest was because she didn't want him to. She didn't want to feel the heat of those warm, soft lips on hers.

His gaze pinned her. "I think you'd better reconsider."

Her breath was so tight she barely managed, "Why?"

He smiled. "Because I don't think Felton would like having his wife in my bed, and that's where you are going to be."

Mary gasped. But he didn't let her reply. He opened the door and left her standing alone in the room, gaping.

Fourteen

"When will you go?" Sir Adam asked.

Mary hadn't missed the slight frown between his dark brows. It had taken most of the day, but she had finally managed to pull Sir Adam aside for a few minutes to speak with him privately. Knowing how much she enjoyed watching Davey, he suggested they sit near a window in the Great Hall that overlooked the practice yard.

The warriors weren't yet in position, but Mary's eyes kept straying outside. How she would miss this! Her chest pinched again at the unfairness. But it could not be avoided. Her last conversation with Sir Kenneth was proof enough. And if there was one thing Mary had learned, it was that when she sensed danger, she should run and not wait around for someone else to help her.

In his bed? Her stomach dropped. *Dear God.*

"As soon as transportation can be arranged," she answered. "Tomorrow, if possible."

The frown on those familiar craggy features deepened. His face was so known to her, she did not often take the time to look at him. He must be three and forty now, she realized. Still a handsome man. If only she could think of him that way. Her mind went to another man who she did think of that way, but dearly wished she didn't.

Irony. Not funny at all sometimes.

"Does Davey know?"

She nodded. "I told him before the midday meal."

"When will you return?"

Something in his gaze caused her to turn away. "As soon as I am able."

There was a long silence, and Mary's gaze slid to the window. She started to smile, catching sight of Davey. But then she noticed the knight he was speaking to: Sir Kenneth. Mary didn't understand why her son had suddenly attached himself to the rebel knight. It was as if he'd transferred the adulation he'd had for Sir John to Sir Kenneth. Actually, she'd seen very little of Sir John today. His greeting on seeing her at the midday meal earlier had been stiff and reserved, almost as if he were embarrassed about something.

But it was Sir Kenneth who concerned her. Was he trying to get to her through her son?

"It's him, isn't it?"

Mary turned back to Sir Adam in confusion. "What do you mean?"

"Sutherland. He's the man you met in Scotland. He's the father of your child."

Mary's heart stopped. Her eyes widened in astonishment, and perhaps also in fear.

Sir Adam must have seen it. "You've nothing to fear, Mary. Your secret is safe with me. I will do whatever I can to help you. Why do you think I volunteered to go to France and asked you to accompany me?"

Mary continued to stare at him in shock. "You knew?"

A wry smile crossed his hard features. "My wife had ten pregnancies. Even though you've put very little weight on—weight that you needed—I know the signs." He held her gaze, and said softly, "And I know you."

Mary bit her lip and dropped her eyes, feeling the heat rise to her cheeks. *He loves me*, she realized with a pang of sadness. How could she not have guessed how he felt all these years? She could see it so clearly now.

She lifted her gaze back to his. "I'm sorry."

He seemed to know what she meant. She loved him, but not in the way he wanted.

He cleared his throat and looked away to the window. "Does he know? Is that why he has come to England?"

Panic replaced the moment of awkwardness. She shook her head frantically. "Nay, and I have no wish for him to find out. His arrival here has nothing to do with me."

She could tell Sir Adam didn't approve. "I've known Sutherland for a long time. You need not fear that he will not do right by you."

"I have no wish for him to do right by me." A wave of emotion rose in her throat and pricked her eyes. "I can't do it again. I could never marry another man like Atholl."

Sir Adam held her gaze; the compassion she read there nearly undid her. But she could also see the anger. "I loved your husband as a brother, but he had all the sensitivity of an ox. He had no idea how to treat a young bride. I told him so, many times, but . . . " He shrugged. "He was stubborn and used to doing what he wanted. He said you would adjust."

"I was very young and naive."

He grimaced. "That's no excuse. But are you so sure Sutherland will be the same?" He shook his head. "Lord knows I spent half my time pulling him out of fights when he was young, and he has always been quick to take offense and quicker to use his fists, but the lad always struck me as sensitive."

Mary tried not to choke. *Sensitive?* "Are we speaking of the same man? Sir Kenneth Sutherland is too arrogant, too bold, and too popular with the ladies by half." *What does that have to do with us?* Those were not the words of a sensitive man. "He would probably take the child from me out of spite for refusing him."

Sir Adam lifted a brow. "So he did ask you to marry him? I was surprised to think he hadn't. The lad always had a fierce streak of honor in him."

Mary refrained from commenting on "the lad." It wasn't honor that had precipitated his offer—or rather, non-offer—but Robert the Bruce. Now that he was no longer Bruce's man, pleasing Bruce would not force his hand. "Please," she said, putting her hand on his arm. "Please promise me you will say nothing."

His gaze fell to her hand. Mary felt her cheeks fire at the unconscious gesture, not realizing how it would seem. She moved it away as inconspicuously as she could.

"It is your secret, Mary. I will not interfere. Not unless you want me to. There are other choices, if you do not wish to marry him. I will protect you any way I can."

She knew what he was offering, and was deeply touched by it, but she would not do that to him. She would not take advantage of his feelings for her and marry him just to give her child a name. She cared about him too much to hurt him, as her feelings—or lack of them—were bound to do. "I know," she said softly. "And I thank you for it, but I can do this on my own."

He nodded as if he'd expected her to say as much. "Then we will go to France in the spring as planned."

Despite the fact that she had to leave Berwick, Mary felt a surge of relief knowing not all her plans had gone awry. And it was comforting to have someone share her secret.

Sir Adam stood. "I will have my men escort you to Ponteland tomorrow."

"Thank you," she said. He started to turn away, but she stopped him. She couldn't believe she'd almost forgotten to ask. She took out two silver coins from the bag she wore at her girdle. "I was planning to send a man around to the local churches. Would you do it for me, and give him this for his troubles?"

Mary did not have to explain, and he didn't have to ask why. Sending men to the local churches to inquire about her sister was a common request. He took the coins reluctantly but did not comment. He didn't need to. She knew how he felt: that this was a waste of time and money, and that her inability to put her sister's death behind her was preventing her from moving past it.

The subject of her sister had always been a difficult one between them. Ever since that night, he'd been uncomfortable speaking of Janet. Almost as if he, too, felt some of the blame for what had happened. But he'd had nothing to do with it. If it was anyone's fault, it was hers.

She glanced out the window again and frowned. This time, it wasn't just Sir Kenneth and her son, but Sir John as well. They seemed to be having some kind of argument, but after a moment, Davey left without the eager bounce in his step.

"Is something wrong?" he asked.

"I don't know. It seems Davey has taken a liking to Sir Kenneth, and I admit, it makes me uneasy."

Sir Adam's brow furrowed. "You mean you do not know?"

"Know what?"

"It's the talk of the castle. Sutherland saved the boy's life."

By saving the young earl's life, Kenneth had become an instant hero among the English ranks and, in the process, had made a bitter enemy. If Felton hadn't liked him before, he despised him now. Not only had the heralded knight been bested by one of the rebels and suffered the indignity of being set on his arse, he'd also nearly been responsible for the death of the young Earl of Atholl. That Kenneth had been the one to save him, he seemed to take as a personal insult. The fact that the young earl seemed to have transferred his idolatry only made it worse.

Kenneth had just learned from the lad that his mother was once again intending to flee, when Felton interrupted and sent the boy on some fool's errand. "Stay away from my squire, Sutherland. I do not wish the lad to pick up any bad habits, and you are keeping him from his duties."

Kenneth quirked a brow. "*Your* squire? I thought David squired for Percy."

Felton flushed angrily. "As his champion and the best knight in his retinue, Lord Percy has entrusted me with the earl's training."

Kenneth wanted to ask him whether that included falling on his arse, but he knew it was wise not to antagonize the knight any further. He was already out for blood as it was, and Kenneth knew Felton would be watching him closely. He needed to keep his temper in check.

But Felton made it damned hard to turn the other cheek. The knight leaned closer so his words would not be overheard, his eyes narrow and hard. "I know why you're doing this. But it won't work. Winning over the boy won't win over his mother."

The mention of Lady Mary was enough to loosen Kenneth's tongue. "And getting him killed will?"

Felton exploded in fury. "How dare you suggest I had anything to do with what happened! No one could have anticipated they would attempt to escape by jumping over a cliff. The earl was well protected."

"Then how the hell did he nearly die, and I end up with this?" Kenneth lifted his injured arm, which was stinging like the devil. "I warned you it was too dangerous to take the lad. Next time don't let your attempt to impress a lady affect your judgment."

"By God, if you weren't injured right now you would pay for your arrogance. I am still the best knight around here, and I won't have a disloyal, opportunistic Highland traitor question my decisions. Winning a few barbarian games doesn't make you a champion. Here, you are nothing until you prove otherwise."

The smug bastard had managed to strike a nerve—a rather raw nerve. Anger ran hot through Kenneth's veins and being wise was forgotten. "I don't know, perhaps you could use a little Highland instruction. The 'barbarians' seemed to have put you on your arse easily enough."

The look of raw hatred in the other man's eyes almost made Kenneth regret his words. Almost.

"I'll see you pay for that, you traitorous bastard."

"You can sure as hell try."

They might have come to blows—injured arm or not—if Kenneth hadn't glanced over to the gate and seen something that made his blood run cold and his anger at Felton fizzle like water on hot rocks.

Jesus. Christ. God damn it to hell. A string of more oaths and blasphemes followed—silently, thank God. But it took every scrap of his training not to react. Keeping his expression carefully blank, Kenneth looked away from the group of women entering the castle gate, but fear prickled on his skin like a sheet of ice.

Before Felton could reply or notice his distraction, he added, "I will look forward to it." And walked away, heading toward the practice yard where the women had gone.

It wasn't unusual for women from the village to watch the soldiers practicing. Nor was it unusual for the soldiers to find the evening's entertainment from amongst the spectators. Every camp had its followers, and a castle was no different. By the time he'd made his way over to the far side of the yard near the barracks, the women were already mingling with the soldiers who'd finished their duties for the day—including the beautiful red-haired woman who'd caught his attention.

Long auburn hair tumbled down her back in a veil of loose waves. Her rough, homespun kirtle was low on her chest, revealing far more of her bosom than he cared to see, but which left no doubt of her plans to attract a companion for the night.

She was flirting with one of the older men-at-arms as he approached. A relatively safe choice, but it didn't temper his anger any.

When she saw him, her eyes widened in feigned excitement and a slow, seductive smile curved on her mouth, as sensual and promising as any wanton's. "My lord," she said in a husky gasp. "Where have you been? It's been so long since I've seen you, I thought you'd forgotten all about me."

The man-at-arms turned to him, disappointment keen on his face when he recognized Kenneth. "Sir Kenneth," he bowed. "I did not realize mistress Helen was yours."

"She's not," Kenneth said, looking into the twinkling eyes of his sister. Damn it, she was MacKay's responsibility now. What the hell was the bastard thinking? He managed to control his anger long enough to play his part. "We met the last time I was in Berwick." He took her hand and placed a gallant kiss on it. "Though I am looking forward to renewing our acquaintance."

Seeing that another had claimed his entertainment for the evening, the man-at-arms made his graceful retreat.

For the next few minutes they made a very public show of "renewing" that acquaintance. Helen sidled up next to him, flirting, batting her lashes, and flaunting her heretofore-unknown ample wares for all to see. If he were MacKay, he'd toss her over his knee for acting like such a jade. Hell, he was glad for his sister's sake that the fierce Highlander wasn't around to see the appreciative English glances at her breasts, which were practically falling out of her gown. As her brother, he had to stop himself from pulling the useless scrap of wool up to her neck and putting his fist through a few sets of teeth.

She ran her fingers up his arm. "You're hurt!" Her eyes flashed naughtily. "Perhaps there is something I can do to make it feel better?"

It wasn't easy to pretend seduction with his little sister—especially when he'd like nothing more than to throttle her—but Kenneth played along. "Why don't we go someplace where you can examine it in private?"

He slid his arm around her waist and pulled her against him, turning around to address one of the men who was standing nearby. Percy was still keeping a close eye on him. "Tell Percy I'll be back in time for the evening meal. The lady is going to *tend* my wounds."

"Aye, I'm going to make you feel all better," she said with a lecherous wink.

Before the soldier could object, Kenneth started to pull her toward the nearest storeroom but changed direction when he heard her mutter "stables" under her breath.

"Give us a few minutes, lads," he said to the stable boys. "This won't take too long."

The boys snickered and moved outside.

The moment the door was closed, Kenneth turned to her in fury. "What in God's name do you think you are doing here? And why the hell did Saint let you come alone!"

"He didn't," MacKay said, jumping down from the rafters above where bales of hay were stored. He was dressed as a peasant, and Kenneth detected the strong whiff of fish. "And keep your voice down, Ice, unless you want half the English army to come investigate." He glanced angrily toward his wife. Though he'd called Kenneth by one of the "ironic" names MacSorley had coined to prod him about his hot temper, MacKay seemed to have forgotten his own. "And pull up your damned gown!"

Helen ignored the directive, put her hands on her hips, and looked at them both angrily. "If you two would just relax—"

It was the wrong thing to say. Both Kenneth and MacKay exploded, expressing the depths of their very *un*relaxed anger at seeing her acting the jade in a yard full of Englishmen. Apparently, MacKay had caught quite a bit of her performance.

Helen let them have their say, but she clearly paid it no heed. "If you are both finished acting like overprotective nursemaids, perhaps I can see to what we came for?"

Before Kenneth could bark out another "why the hell are you here?," MacKay explained, "She insisted on seeing to your arm herself."

"And you let her?"

MacKay shot him a deadly glare. "I'd like to see you stop her. She said you were part of this now, and it was her *duty*." He spat the last word, mumbling under his breath that he must have been crazy to let her do this—a point to which they were in agreement. "That it was my fault you were hurt in the first place, and if you lost your arm, she would blame me."

Kenneth turned to his sister, eyes narrowed. "You've been hanging around Viper too long." She was learning to fight dirty.

Helen lifted her chin. "It worked, didn't it? Now, let me see it."

MacKay handed Helen a leather bag, and she removed a few things as Kenneth shrugged off his surcote and unwrapped the linen bandage that the doctor had used to bind the cut. She gave a soft cry when she saw the ugly-looking mass of bloody, singed flesh, but went immediately to work on it.

MacKay distracted him from the pain of her examination by asking him about what had happened. Kenneth gave a quick explanation, hearing MacKay's muttered oath when he learned the identity of the soldier he'd almost killed.

"It was too dark to see his arms."

Kenneth nodded. "I figured as much. It was just bad luck that your blade found a gap between my mail shirt and gauntlet."

He winced as Helen poked and prodded the wound, then applied a salve. "Ouch," he said, pulling his arm away. "That burns."

"You think nothing of putting yourself in the line of a blade, but whinge about a little medicine? By God, you men are all alike. I don't know why I don't wash my hands of the lot of you."

He could see her blinking away tears and realized how worried she'd been about him. He took her in his arms and kissed the top of her head. "I'm fine, Angel." He used the war name the Highland Guard had taken to calling her as the team's healer. "Thank you."

She blinked up at him, nodded, and then proceeded to give him a long list of instructions on how to care for the wound and what to look for, and extracted his promise to send for her if it festered. MacKay gave him the name of a friendly barkeep in town who could be trusted with a message, though they'd previously devised other ways of communicating should the need arise.

Kenneth took the opportunity to apprise MacKay of what he'd learned from the English warriors. So far, it wasn't much—which bothered him. "I would have expected more activity by now. More supplies going north to bolster the English-held castles for the additional men."

"There is still plenty of time."

"Aye." It was true. He frowned.

"What?"

"I don't know. I guess I would have expected Clifford to be more involved. He and Percy are close, and with his interests in the Borders"—Sir Robert Clifford had vast holdings in the North of England and had been given James Douglas's lands in Scotland by Edward—"I would have expected him to stick close to Percy. But he seems to be coming and going from Carlisle Castle quite a bit. I was thinking of volunteering on his next—"

"Let us worry about Clifford. Your job is to stay close to Percy. Stay on task, Sutherland. You don't want to screw this up."

Kenneth's jaw clenched, hearing the warning he didn't need: he was on probation. He nodded. Message received loud and clear.

Realizing the stable lads wouldn't stay away for long, Kenneth said, "You need to get out of here. I assume you have a plan?"

"I will go out the way I came in," Helen said.

"Striker and Hunter are waiting outside," MacKay said before Kenneth could object. "I came in up the postern gate from one of the fishing boats." That explained the smell. "I left a very pungent bag of salmon near the kitchens to retrieve for my descent." He smiled. "The stench should be enough to prevent too many questions."

While Helen packed up her bag, MacKay asked in a soft voice, "Everything else is all right? They do not suspect anything?"

Kenneth shook his head. "The ruse worked. How is Dragon?"

MacKay frowned. "Angry, bitter, and short-tempered as usual, but he'll mend."

Kenneth had been surprised that the Yorkshireman was part of the Guard. From what he'd seen, the disgruntled, England-born, Scotland-bred Alex Seton was often at odds with the other members of the Guard—especially his partner, Robbie Boyd.

Kenneth thought about mentioning Lady Mary's presence at the castle, but something held him back. He supposed he knew MacKay would warn him off, and he didn't want to hear it. *"Bàs roimh Gèill,"* he said. Death before surrender.

MacKay repeated the favored parting words of the Highland Guard and gave his wife a too-long-for-Kenneth's-mind kiss before retreating to his hiding place.

Kenneth was about to put on his surcote, when Helen told him, "Leave it." She reached over and untied his shirt, pulling it loose from his breeches. "There, you look more rumpled."

He reached down and picked up a handful of hay, tossing it over her head, laughing as she waved her hands in protest. Then he reached over, snatching a piece of hay from her hair, and grinned. "So do you."

She shook her head in mock chagrin. "Lord knows you probably have far too much practice at this. I assume the English lasses are as silly and adoring as the Scottish?"

She was right about the practice, he thought with a wry turn of his mouth, his mind going back to the last time he'd been caught in the stable. But his grin fell at the mention of "silly and adoring." Helen's words were all too close to the accusations Mary had made. She was wrong. He didn't surround himself only with women who flattered him. He was sure he'd had countless conversations on other subjects, though damned if he could think of any that hadn't been with his sister—or Mary. But she held his attention more than any woman before, and he didn't like half of what she said.

It also reminded him of what he'd learned before his sister's arrival. But if Mary of Mar thought she was going to escape from him again, she was in for a surprise.

Arm in arm, they exited the stable, looking to all who might see like very contented lovers. Kenneth wasn't surprised to see the men who Percy had watching him standing nearby, nor was he surprised when they followed him to the gate.

He pushed her out with a playful pat on the bottom. She giggled and turned around, reaching up to place a kiss on his cheek, whispering for him to be safe, before scattering through the gate in the fading darkness.

Kenneth turned and started walking back toward the Hall. He'd taken only a few steps when he felt the unmistakable weight of someone's gaze on him. He looked across the courtyard and saw a woman rushing down the stairs and across the courtyard toward the donjon. *Lady Mary.* He knew it was her, just as he knew she'd seen him.

He swore, wondering how much she'd seen.

If her pace was any indication, it was enough.

He hoped to hell she hadn't recognized Helen. At the same time, he realized what she would think if she hadn't. His mouth fell in a grim line. He had nothing to feel guilty about. He had every right to be with another woman. It was she who had made clear exactly what she thought of him: a good tumble. He was just playing to profligate form.

But he still wished she hadn't seen him.

He let her go. For now. But this wasn't over. Not by any measure.

It doesn't matter. Unshed tears blurred her eyes, and all Mary could see was dark green as she pulled another gown from the ambry and tossed it on the bed. The dresses that had been hung only a few days ago were going right back into her trunks. The maidservant scrambled to keep up with her.

"Are you sure everything is all right?" Lady Eleanor asked with obvious concern.

Mary nodded, forcing herself to smile though her throat was tight and her eyes prickled. "I'm just tired, that's all," she said, feigning chirpiness to cover the high emotion in her voice.

What did she care if he was with a woman? It didn't matter that her chest had felt like a boulder landed on it when she'd seen Sir Kenneth exit the stables with the red-haired creature on his arm.

The stables. She knew only too well what he did in the stables. It shouldn't have hurt so much. She knew the kind of man he was. It should simply prove that he wasn't for her. But the burning in her chest, the crushing weight of disappointment, didn't seem to want to understand.

They were nothing to one another. Just because they'd shared a night of passion, just because she'd felt something more, just because he'd asked her to marry him, just because there hadn't been a night that passed that she hadn't thought of him, just because she was carrying his child, and just because her heart had jumped to all kinds of silly conclusions when she'd seen him here didn't mean anything. The one night that had meant so much to her probably meant nothing to him. Despite what he'd said, he probably hadn't given her a thought until he saw her dancing with Sir John.

When she'd heard what he'd done for Davey, she'd been so overwhelmed with gratitude, she might have confessed everything to him and been ready to believe anything he said. Thank God she hadn't. Heroic feats on the battlefield wouldn't make him a good husband. In fact, in her experience it was just the opposite. She was grateful, but it had nothing to do with them.

"You're sure you do not wish to go to the meal?" Lady Katherine said.

Mary shook her head, a wave of nausea that had nothing to do with her pregnancy and everything to do with the prospect of seeing him rumpled and satisfied having risen inside her. "Beth can bring me something to eat if I get hungry."

The girl nodded eagerly. "Aye, my lady. I will have a platter sent up from the kitchens."

And a big pitcher of wine, she wanted to add.

"See," Mary assured the two women who were looking at her with troubled expressions on their faces. Apparently her acting ability wasn't as strong as she'd thought. "I shall be fine. Beth will take care of me. Go to the meal. I believe the earl has arranged for some minstrels tonight. I will probably fall asleep right after I finish packing."

The ladies hesitated, but eventually she was able to push them out of the room. By the time she and Beth had managed to finish packing her trunks and bags, she was indeed ready to retire. Beth helped her remove her gown and gave her a plush velvet robe to put on while she sat by the brazier to finish her embroidery.

As soon as the girl left to fetch her something to eat, Mary took out the tiny piece of linen. Her chest tightened. It was a cap she was working on in secret for the baby. Sometimes the need—the desperation—for this child rose up so hard inside her she couldn't breathe. All the love she'd wanted to give to her husband and son.

She perched the glasses on her nose and went to work, trying to put what she'd seen out of her mind and focus on the baby.

No matter what else had happened, she could not regret what she'd done. Her one night of sin with Sir Kenneth had given her this child.

But it didn't lessen the hurt any. She was a fool. What had she expected? She was nothing to him, and he should be nothing to her. She gnawed on her bottom lip. If only the woman hadn't been so young and pretty. Even from a distance she could detect the fine features and gorgeous red hair. She was vaguely familiar, but Mary figured that she'd probably seen her around the Hall before.

Her hands seemed incapable of managing the tiny stitches, so she removed the glasses from her nose, put the embroidery aside, and closed her eyes for a moment.

When the knock came, assuming it was Beth, she bid her to enter. She heard the door shut, and when the girl didn't say anything she opened her eyes to tell her just to leave the tray. Instead she jumped to her feet in shock.

She stared at the man who'd invaded her chamber— who'd invaded her sanity. Sir Kenneth Sutherland stood— lazed, actually—with his back against the door and his arms crossed against his chest, watching her. The relaxed pose didn't fool her. She could feel the danger emanating from him.

Dread sank to the bottom of her stomach like a stone. "What are you doing here? Get out!" She hoped she didn't sound as scared as she felt.

He smiled, glancing toward the trunks. "Running away

from me again, Mary?" His gaze slid down her ready-for-bed-clad form, and she hastily clenched the edges of her robe tighter even though she knew he could not see anything. He let his arms fall to his sides and made a tisking sound. "For someone who purports not to care or have a thought about what happened, you seem to be very anxious to get away from me."

He took a few steps closer to her. Why had she never noticed how small the room was? And who had lit the fire so high? The temperature seemed to have gone up twenty degrees. But the blast of heat wasn't coming from the brazier. The pounding in her heart told her exactly who was the source of the heat.

"I have to ask myself why," he said idly. He took another step, and she almost yelped like a frightened pup. He smiled as if he'd sensed it. A big, lazy, knowing smile that set alarm bells ringing up and down her spine. "You know what I think? I think you're scared about how I make you feel. I think you're scared not because it meant nothing to you but because it meant a lot. I think that if you didn't care as much as you say you don't care, you would be sitting down for the evening meal right now, not hiding up in your room." He held her gaze. "I think you want me."

Mary gasped with outrage. He was arrogant, overbearing, and so cocksure of himself. It didn't make it any better that he was also right. Not that she would ever let him know that. "I'm not hiding, I'm packing. Not that it's any business of yours, but I am not leaving to avoid you. There is a pressing estate matter to which I must attend."

He laughed. "Very pressing, I'm sure." She looked up, terrified to realize how close he was standing to her. No more than a foot separated them. "Is that why your pulse is fluttering, your cheeks are flushed, and your heart is beating so hard I can hear it?"

Her eyes widened in alarm. That wasn't possible, was it? But he only smiled, her reaction giving her away.

She started to retreat, backing away from the chair she'd been gripping like a lifeline. Only then did she remember the baby cap. She sucked in her breath. It lay in the middle of the chair with her glasses like a beacon. All he had to do was look down. If he hadn't heard her heart pounding before, he surely heard it now. She prayed . . .

Too late. "What are you doing?"

He reached for it, but she snatched it and the glasses from him before he could pick it up. "Careful! You'll break the glasses." Praying her cheeks weren't as hot as they felt, she added, "It's a piece of embroidery I'm working on." She tucked it in the basket she used before he could look at it closer.

His eyes narrowed at her odd behavior, and for a minute she feared he might reach in after it. "For whom?"

She said the first thing that popped into her head. "I sell them at the market in Newcastle."

He arched a brow, and she felt her defenses prick. "It is a perfectly acceptable way of earning money. How else should I have provided for myself when my husband was executed and my dower lands confiscated?"

He gave her a long appraising look. "I wasn't judging you. I'm merely surprised, that's all."

Having avoided disaster, she just wanted him to leave. "Why are you here? Why are you doing this? Why does it matter to you what I do, when you have so many other women to choose from? Was your tumble in the stables this afternoon not enough for you?"

He showed no shame at what she'd seen. Nor did he deny it. Had she really hoped he would?

Instead, he merely arched a dark brow wickedly—good God, even his brow was sensual! Was there any part of him that was not? "Jealous, little one?"

"No!"

But her protest was too strong and too quick. He closed the gap between them in one stride. She tried to step back, but all she could feel was the hard press of stone. He'd backed her against the wall, and there was nowhere for her to go.

"You don't care?" he challenged, his eyes locking on hers.

Everything inside her was racing. Her heart, her pulse, her blood. "I don't."

He leaned down, his face inches from hers. Their bodies weren't touching, but she could feel the heat, feel the weight of him pressing down on her.

Mary couldn't breathe, conscious of the soft swell of her stomach between them. Despite the fact that the bump was still barely noticeable—fortunately, the weight she'd gained had been distributed fairly evenly so far—she was so certain that he would somehow sense it. That he would know the moment he touched her. Every inch of his body was so engrained on her memory, she assumed he would notice the changes.

But he didn't. His hand slid around her waist, and he pulled her up against him. Even though he had the use of only one arm, she would have been hard pressed to escape if she'd tried.

"Then prove it. Kiss me." His lips hovered just above hers. "Kiss me, Mary," he groaned, right before his mouth fell on hers.

Her heart slammed into her chest at the contact. She dissolved into the heat. Melting against the hard granite of his body and the warm, velvety softness of his lips.

She descended—nay, plummeted—into a vortex of pleasure. Hot, mindless pleasure that pulled her into a molten whirlpool of madness. The fierceness of the passion that exploded between them claimed them both. She kissed him back. Clutching. Her fingers digging into the hard muscles of his arms as she fought to get even closer.

She moaned as his tongue licked into her mouth, as he

bent her to him and plundered the deepest reaches of her soul, leaving no part of her unclaimed. Untasted.

Her heart beat wildly in her chest. Blood pounded in her ears. She was hot and weak and needy, her body clenching and quivering in anticipation.

He groaned, a deep guttural sound that made her heart flip, and dug his fingers through her hair to grip the back of her head, shifting the angle to kiss her even deeper.

She could feel the hardness of his manhood pressing against her insistently. He started to circle his hips to hers, and she made a sound of pure pleasure at the sweet friction. Heat clenched between her legs. She could feel her body softening, weakening, opening for him.

The memories of passion were visceral and immediate. She wanted him inside her, right here, right now. She wanted him to lift her skirt, press her up against the wall, and surge deep inside. She wanted to feel him moving, thrusting, slamming harder and harder. She wanted to feel the sweet crest of passion, feel her body spasming around him. And she wanted to hear him cry out. To see him stiffen. To see his face tense with the force of his passion.

And he wanted it, too. His hand was on her hips, her bottom, sliding up over her stomach to cup her breasts, her—

Stomach. Her mind caught up a fraction of a second too late to stop him.

He stilled.

For one long heartbeat nothing happened. She waited. In a moment of desperate self-delusion, she wondered if perhaps he hadn't noticed.

But the calm was only a harbinger of the strength of the storm to come. When he lifted his gaze and his eyes fell on hers, the wrath was upon her.

Fifteen

At first when Kenneth's hand slid over the slight round-ness, it didn't penetrate. He was so half out of his mind with lust that he couldn't completely process what he was feeling.

She was so soft and sweet. She felt so good in his arms. The urgent little sounds she was making were driving him wild. All he could think about was getting inside her. He wanted to possess her. Claim her. Force her to acknowl-edge the strange connection between them.

He'd never felt anything like this before, and damn it, he needed to know she felt it, too.

But slowly the vague prickle at the back of his conscious-ness grew. Eventually understanding slid through the fiery haze of his passion like a blade, splitting it apart from end to end, leaving nothing but cold rage.

He didn't want to believe it. Couldn't believe it. But the truth swelled under his hand.

Suddenly the changes he'd noticed in her took on a very different meaning—as did her anxiousness to leave.

He jerked his hand away and stepped back from her as if scalded. Hell, he had been. Burned and betrayed.

"You are with child." His voice was every bit as harsh and cold as he felt.

This time the fear in her eyes was warranted. Emotion crackled and fired dangerously inside him as he struggled for control. But the battle had already been lost. His hands clenched at his sides, every muscle in his body tensed and flared.

She didn't say anything, his anger seeming to have rendered her mute. She just stared up at him with big blue eyes, looking so damned vulnerable, so ridiculously innocent. But she was neither.

"How long?" His voice cracked like the whip flailing inside him. He grabbed her by the arm and jerked her up against him. "How long?" he repeated, not caring that he was scaring her. "And don't think about lying to me."

"I, I—" Her eyes skittered away, for once unchallenging. But he was too furious to enjoy it.

"It's mine," he said flatly. He'd known it from the first moment his hand swept over the soft swell. He didn't need her to confirm it, but damn it, she would. "Tell me, damn it."

Maybe if she'd begged for understanding. Maybe if she'd continued her moment of feminine meekness and contriteness, he might have reacted differently. But the defiance and cool challenge that had pricked him from the first returned.

He was angrier than he could ever recall, and she didn't care. He'd seen fierce warriors quake in their boots when he lost his temper, but she stood toe-to-toe with him, utterly oblivious to the danger. Apparently, she knew just as well as he did that there wasn't any. No matter how angry, how furious, he would never hurt her. He wasn't used to fighting without the advantage of physical strength, and it was bloody disconcerting.

"It's mine!" she shouted, twisting her arm out of his hold. "Yours may have been the seed that took root, but the child is mine. I want nothing from you, as I'm sure you'll be glad to hear."

Kenneth flinched as if she'd slapped him. She couldn't have made her opinion of him—her disdain—more clear. She'd wanted only one thing from him.

Suddenly, another thought struck him cold. It was bad enough to not be taken seriously, to be thought of as nothing more than a ready cock, but what if passion wasn't all she'd wanted from him? His jaw was clenched so tight he could barely spit out the words. "Nothing but my seed. Is that it, Mary? By God, did you plan this?"

She drew back in shock. "Of course not!"

He stared at her, searching for any sign of deception or guilt. There was none, but he knew better than to be deceived by her air of innocence.

She must have sensed his hesitancy. "It was not I who pursued you, if you'll recall. This was as much a surprise to me as it is to you. It was an accident. I was married for over ten years with one son. I never dreamed this would happen."

Unconsciously, her hands had gone to her stomach and a soft expression swept over her features. She looked so lovely and happy, so different from the drab, half-starved nun he remembered. His heart did an odd little start.

He ached to touch her again, to finish what they'd started, but she'd deceived him. "Yet you are pleased that it did."

It wasn't a question, though she took it as one. She met his gaze full on. "Aye. My son was taken from me before he was six months old. Can you imagine what that was like? I was only fourteen. I never had a chance to be a mother to him, but this baby—" She stopped, her voice tightening with emotion. "This baby will be different."

He was aware of the general circumstances of her past, but didn't realize that her son had been taken from her when he was so young. He remembered his own mother. How she'd doted on him and his brother and sister. How tenderhearted and loving she'd been, so different from most noblewomen. Mary was the same, he realized.

But he didn't want to feel sorry for her. He didn't want to think about how she had suffered. Intentionally or not, she'd taken something from him and then tried to hide it.

She gazed at him with her hand over her stomach protectively—as if he would somehow harm them. The gesture infuriated him. She'd cast him in the role of enemy, and he wanted to know why.

"You should have told me."

She glared at him, not heeding the warning in his voice. "What difference would it have made? You were in Scotland and I was here. We were on different sides of the war."

"And now that we are not?"

A faint blush pinkened her cheeks, and her gaze dropped. "I didn't think you'd care. As prolific as you are in your . . . uh, relationships, I assumed this was not an infrequent occurrence. I thought you'd thank me for not telling you."

Kenneth felt his temper spike hot again. She knew nothing about him. "Oh, I care, and your assumptions are dead wrong. I may have had my share of bed partners—which is nothing that I need to apologize for—but I've never had an 'accident,' as you put it."

He'd also never allowed himself to take his release inside a woman before, but for some reason he didn't want to tell her that.

She bit her lip contritely and also, he noticed to his extreme irritation, adorably. She blinked up at him. "You haven't?"

He ignored the urge to take that lip between his. Anger and desire were a potent mix that was proving hard to resist. "Nay, not a bastard to be found, I'm afraid, and I have no intention of allowing my firstborn son to be the first."

"Son? Why would you assume the child is a boy?"

He gritted his teeth. "Because if I'm going to be forced to marry you to give this child a name, you will bloody well give me an heir."

She paled. "Married? You misunderstand. I have no intention of marrying you. It isn't necessary. I've already made arrangements—"

"I don't give a shite what kind of arrangements you've

made." She startled at the crudeness of his language, her face growing a little paler. "It is you who misunderstand. You don't have a choice. You will marry me."

Mary's heart dropped. "No," she choked out in a strangled gasp. She shook her head. "No."

His smile was merciless. "I'm not asking. You'll marry me if you want to know this child."

Mary looked up at him in horror, at the hard, ruthless warrior who radiated icy rage and left her no doubt that he meant what he said. Worse, he had the power to carry out the threat. He had all the power. She might be the one carrying the child, but in the eyes of the law, she had no rights. She was a woman in a man's world. Whatever independence she'd carved out for herself was illusory. She hated him for making her see it.

She'd underestimated him. Misjudged him. Thought that he was as feckless and uncaring as her husband.

But she'd made a mistake. A horrible one. Too late, she saw what her first impression of a handsome hero with an adoring throng had missed: the core of steel and the iron will forged by years of fighting. The man who hated to lose, and the perseverance that had made him a champion. He wouldn't give up until he achieved what he wanted. The baby. Her. It didn't matter.

Her stomach rolled. This couldn't be happening. Her darkest fears had come to life. To save another child from being taken from her, she would have to submit to the will of another man who didn't care about her. She would lose the power to make her own decisions, lose the ability to control her life, and give it to him to do with as he wished.

Moreover, it wasn't only her hard-won independence at stake, but her heart as well. Even standing here in this room with him furious with her, a part of her wondered if it could be different. He made her feel things she didn't want to feel. She'd tried to protect herself against it by running away, but how could she do that if they were married?

Was she doomed to another loveless marriage? To watch another husband adored and fawned over by a bevy of willing admirers?

Her stomach knifed. She couldn't bear it. After what she'd been through, she would not—*could* not—slip back into the role of the adoring, trusting, and subservient wife. She couldn't pretend it didn't hurt when he left her bed for another's. And it would hurt. If what she'd felt today was any indication, it would hurt quite a lot.

But what choice did she have? Her heart squeezed. Her baby . . .

He didn't bother waiting for her to respond. For the second time, he hadn't bothered to ask her to marry him. A silent sob buried itself in her chest. He'd left her no choice, and they both knew it. "I will speak to Sir Adam and leave for London at dawn."

"London?"

"Edward will be furious if we wed without his permission. Fortunately, the new king is more of a romantic than his sire, and I think I can convince him to agree to the necessity for a quick and quiet ceremony. We'll have to hurry, with Lent approaching."

Despair weighed down on her. She was being dragged along already, no matter her wishes.

"Why are you doing this?" she whispered. "Why are you forcing me to marry you, when you know I have no wish to do so?"

"I told you, my son will have a name."

"And after that? What happens after you have your heir, what then? Will that be enough?"

He stilled. "What do you mean?"

She lifted her chin and met his gaze unflinchingly. "I should like to know what more will be required of me."

His eyes narrowed, the white lines around his mouth

nearly making her want to take a few steps back. "This will not be a marriage in name only, if that is what you are thinking. I will not be barred from my wife's bed."

"Even if I don't want you there?"

He gave her a long knowing look, and for a moment she feared he would prove her wrong. "Are you so sure of that, Mary?"

His voice was low and husky. Entrancing. Seducing. A temptation impossible to resist. Her heart squeezed. She wasn't sure at all. Just the way he was looking at her made her stomach knot and skin prickle with heat.

But she couldn't allow herself to be deluded. "So I shall be expected to breed your children, what else?"

Apparently, he didn't like her cold, matter-of-fact tone. He took her by the shoulders and forced her to look at him. "Why are you acting like this, damn it?"

Her heart clenched. Because she wasn't a foolish girl anymore. Because the only way to protect herself was to not have any illusions or unrealistic expectations. She wouldn't go into this marriage like she had the first—blind and full of silly romantic dreams. This was an alliance born of necessity—a business arrangement—and she would treat it as such. "I am simply trying to be clear on what shall be expected of me. I've never been forced into marriage before."

Clearly, he didn't appreciate her sarcasm. His hands fisted. "Your duty and fidelity, damn it. Just like in any other marriage."

Fidelity. How easily his arrow found its mark without even aiming. "And is the same required of you?"

She meant it to come off as sarcastic, but the way his eyes held hers, she feared he saw too much. "Do you wish it to be?"

She covered her embarrassment with a sharp laugh. As if such a thing were even possible. "You forget I've seen you at work, so to speak. I've also been married before. I know how an alliance between nobles works. I will turn a blind eye to your dalliances, and once I have done my duty in bearing your children, you will do the same. I merely meant, what am I to get in return for doing my duty in bearing your children?"

His mouth hardened, and his eyes glinted with a dangerous spark of steel. "You will have my name, my protection, and preside as chatelaine over any land the king returns to me. One day the child you are carrying will be the Earl of Sutherland." He leaned closer. She could see the dark shadow of his beard along the hard lines of his jaw and remembered how it had felt rubbing over her skin. "And every time I take you in my bed, you will come. That is what you will get, my lady." She flinched at his blunt crudity, ignoring the flicker of awareness that surged through her. "But know this—I don't know what your experience may have been before, but I will never be blind."

She flushed, not mistaking his meaning. Fidelity went in only one direction. He expected her to be faithful but made no promise in return.

Open eyes, she told herself. *No illusions*.

She hardened her heart. It was an alliance, nothing more. He'd made that clear. She had to remember it. "You will, of course, seek my son's wardship and marriage?"

His brow furrowed for a moment, as if he hadn't thought of it. "Aye."

As her husband, it was only natural that he would seek control over the young Earl of Atholl. He might have switched kings, but the power and influence he would garner by marrying her had not changed. Indeed, she knew that had been the attraction for Sir John as well.

Sir John. She bit her lip. He would not be pleased. But it could not be helped. She could only hope he would understand.

Mary knew she was trapped. She had no choice. She

would steel her heart and hold Sir Kenneth to his word. "You will protect me and my children?"

He eyed her warily. "Aye."

"And do nothing that will put us in danger without consulting me?"

His expression shuttered, his face utterly still. For a moment she thought she saw something flash in his eyes, but when his mouth fell in a hard line she realized it must have been anger. "We are at war, Mary. But you have my promise that I will do all in my power to keep you safe."

"That is not good enough. I need your word that you will not make decisions that will affect us without telling me. I won't have another marriage like the first."

His mouth thinned. She could tell he didn't like being pushed into a corner. Well, too bad. She didn't either. And that was what he was doing by forcing her to marry him.

"I will do my best," he agreed.

Their eyes held for one long pause. She sensed there was something more that he wanted to say, but she also sensed that he was telling the truth. What could she do but trust him? She just prayed he was more worthy of that trust than Atholl. Her life and that of her children's she put in his hands. She nodded. It was enough. "Then I will await your return from London."

She turned away. He hesitated for a moment as if he would say something, but then moved to the door. He was about to close it behind him when something made her stop him. "Sir Kenneth."

He looked back over his shoulder. "Aye, my lady?"

Their eyes held again. *Be careful.* "Godspeed," she whispered.

One corner of his mouth lifted in a boyish half-smile, and he nodded.

Her heart stabbed with a longing so strong it took her breath away. When he looked at her like that she could almost believe in faerie tales again, of handsome, gallant knights who made a young girl's heart dream.

Dear God, how could she protect herself against that?

What was she going to do?

What she always did. Make the best of it. But when the door closed softly behind him, Mary sank onto the chair, covered her face with her hands, and cried.

Sixteen

❧

Coldingham Priory Church, Berwickshire

One week later, Kenneth was standing under the chancel arch of Coldingham Priory beside Sir Adam and the Bishop of St. Andrews, who'd recently returned from Scotland, waiting for his bride.

The journey to London had been easier than he could ever have expected. He knew it was due in large part to one of the men standing beside him. Sir Adam had smoothed the way, first with Cornwall and Percy in enabling Kenneth to leave Berwick, and then, when he'd offered to accompany him, with King Edward.

Thanks to his old friend, he and Mary not only had their permission, but also a tale to explain the surprise announcement of their marriage. A chance encounter in Scotland of enemies, a secret betrothal, and a love so strong as to compel him to change allegiance. Ironically, their marriage would serve not only to legitimize their child, but also his motives for being in England.

If their story were true, they would actually already be married. A betrothal promise to wed coupled with consummation created a marital bond. But as the church frowned on clandestine marriages, they would have a ceremony—albeit a private one. As there had not been time to read the banns, at the king's bequest, the Bishop of Durham—who had authority over both Coldingham

Priory and the Scottish Bishop of St. Andrews while he was being kept in England—had granted them a dispensation to wed without them. Perhaps thinking of Mary and their recent trip, Sir Adam had suggested Lamberton as the officiant. Since Kenneth suspected the good bishop was still in league with Bruce, he knew he had better apprise the king of his marriage soon. A task he wasn't looking forward to discharging.

About the only thing that could have made the journey a greater success was if Kenneth had been able to uncover any information that would help his mission. But the single nighttime foray into the king's chambers that he'd managed under the watchful eye of Sir Adam and his men had yielded nothing of value. Indeed, so far Kenneth had done nothing more than corroborate what they already knew: the English were mustering at Berwick, and the king would follow in the spring. All he'd gained on this mission so far was an injured arm and, in a few minutes, a wife. Neither of which was likely to impress the king or his fellow guardsmen with his abilities. He might be on the team, but until he proved himself he was going to feel like a recruit.

When one of the monks approached the bishop to tell him that the lady had arrived, Sir Adam pulled him over to one side. "Are you sure you wish to go through with this? If you are having any second thoughts—"

"No second thoughts," Kenneth insisted adamantly. It was true. Although he was still angry at Mary for trying to keep his child from him, and he still had every intention of teaching her a lesson, he was thinking more rationally now. He regretted the threat he'd used to force her to agree. He'd lost his temper and wished he hadn't put it quite that way. He wouldn't have taken the child from her—he wasn't a monster—but all he was thinking about was getting her to agree. That was all that had mattered. Which didn't make sense. Whom he married—as long as she was acceptable—wasn't supposed to matter to him. He'd like to think it was about the baby, but he knew it wasn't just that. Part of him *wanted* to marry her.

God knew why. She gave him more trouble than any woman ever had before and didn't seem to waste any opportunity to challenge him. She didn't fit any of his prerequisites. Well, except for lusty.

With the considerably more pleasant thought of the wedding night to look forward to, he added, "I know what I'm doing."

Not for the first time, he saw something in the other man's face that gave him pause. The older knight had gone to a great deal of trouble for them, and though Kenneth was grateful, he'd also begun to suspect why. It wasn't Sir Adam's friendship with Kenneth or Atholl driving him, but his feelings for Mary.

"The lass has already suffered so much. The loss of her parents, both brothers and sisters—including her twin." He hadn't realized she was a twin. "Having her son taken from her when she was so young, and then Atholl . . ." Sir Adam's voice dropped off as if he were struggling to find the right words. "Atholl broke her heart well before he embroiled her in his rebellion. Not even she knows how close she came to imprisonment."

Kenneth felt an uncomfortable stab. He wasn't sure whether it was the mention of a husband she'd obviously loved or his own guilt about his plans to do the same. Perhaps both. The promise she'd managed to extract from him didn't sit well. He regretted the need to deceive her about his true purpose here, but even were he tempted to confide in her—which he sure as hell wasn't—it was safer for her if she were in the dark in case anything went wrong.

She'd made her choice when she gave herself to him in the library that night. They would both have to live with the consequences.

How Bruce would react to the marriage, he wasn't sure.

Certainly, it complicated Kenneth's mission, and he knew the king wouldn't want her to be in any danger, but he also knew that if Mary could be persuaded to convince her son to change sides, Bruce would be thrilled to have the young earl back in the Scottish fold. Thrilled enough, hopefully, to overlook the fact that Kenneth had seduced his "dear" sister-in-law and managed to get her with child.

It wasn't just stung pride driving him now, but his mission. He had every intention of making sure that when the time came, she was eager to go with him. Damned eager. Over-the-moon-in-love eager. But Mary was proving difficult. Normally women came to him. He had little experience in the pursuit. He'd never wooed a woman before, but how hard could it be?

She wasn't as indifferent to him as she wanted to think. *Godspeed.* Her parting words had surprised him. She'd been worried about him. Aye, perhaps this wouldn't be too hard after all.

For some reason the subject of Atholl bothered him. It seemed once again that he was coming in second, this time as a husband. But it was a chance to learn more about her. "What happened?"

Sir Adam hesitated again, his loyalty to Atholl obviously making him weigh his words carefully. "Mary was only a girl when they were married, and Atholl . . . well, he was in his prime. He was one of the best knights at court. Handsome. Charming. Everyone loved him. Including his young bride. But he was too busy lifting his sword for glory, and half the skirts of the women at court, to worry about a young girl's feelings. He found the task of bedding 'a child,' as he'd called her, distasteful, but did his duty. After that, I don't think he ever really saw her as any older. He had his pick of any of the ladies at court, and didn't see the need to hide them from his wife. I'll never forget her face when she learned the truth." There was a far-off look in the older man's eyes that couldn't help but rouse Kenneth's sympathy. But then Sir Adam turned and gave him a sharp look. "I hope you will have more care."

Kenneth looked away, almost regretting having asked. He'd wanted insight, and he'd gotten it. *Profligate*. He understood now the source of her disdain and wariness.

But that didn't mean he was going to bind himself to one woman for eternity. He would have laughed if he didn't feel so much like frowning. Mary of Mar had certainly occupied his thoughts—hell, his dreams—for five months more than any woman before, but it wasn't likely to continue much longer.

Still, he wasn't a completely unfeeling arse—most of the time. He would take care not to flaunt his liaisons. "I will."

Kenneth could see that his answer hadn't pleased Sir Adam. He looked as though he wanted to say something else, but at that moment Mary entered the priory and all eyes turned to her.

He forgot to breathe. The burning that had made his chest feel so tight a few moments ago intensified. She looked . . . *beautiful*. A fey creature. Something not of this world. A ray of sunlight caught her hair in its golden glow, casting a shimmering light around her. Her gown was of such pale, iridescent blue silk it almost seemed to be silver. It, too, shimmered with each step she took as she made her way down the wide aisle toward him.

He barely noticed David walking beside her. All he could see were big blue eyes gazing at him with wariness, and the paleness of her translucent milky-white skin. She loomed so large in his mind, he forgot how small she was. But in the massive church with its high cathedral-worthy ceilings, she looked very tiny and very vulnerable.

She was scared, damn it. And no matter how angry he was with her, it didn't sit well with him. He strode down the aisle, crossing the distance in a few long steps. He held out his hand, offering for hers. "My lady."

Her eyes widened a little more at his gallantry, but after a few moments of hesitation she placed her tiny fingers in his. Christ, they were soft—and cold. Tucking them firmly in the crook of his arm, he escorted her the rest of the way down the aisle to where Sir Adam and the bishop waited for them.

Wooing his bride, he suspected, wasn't going to be as much of a hardship as it should be.

Mary had been more anxious than she could have imagined for word of a marriage that had been forced upon her. Would King Edward be angry? Would he agree? It wasn't that she was worried about *him*.

At least that's what she told herself. But when the note came last night for her to meet Sir Kenneth at the priory, and then when she'd seen him across the church, standing there . . .

The tug in her chest told a different story.

He looked so big and strong. So handsome. It didn't seem possible that in a few minutes he would be her husband.

What was she going to do? How would she harden her heart against this surge of emotion every time she saw him?

No matter how open her eyes were, she feared her heart would always be blind.

His consideration only made it worse. When he came forward to offer her his hand—to offer her reassurance—she almost wished for Atholl's indifference. It was far easier to fight against than kindness.

But she had to admit that the strength of the arm under her hand throughout the short ceremony was like a lifeline. Something solid to hold onto in the daze that threatened to overwhelm her. She might be going into this with her eyes opened, but it seemed to make no difference in the bundle of nerves twisting inside her.

She was doing it again. Putting her life in the hands of a

man. Every instinct seemed to clamor not to go through with it. But what could she do?

It seemed to happen so fast. One moment they were discussing the terms of the agreement that had been worked out with the King—Edward had agreed to return some of her dower properties in Kent, which had been forfeit upon Atholl's treason—the next they were outside the church door, going through the formality of reciting their vows in public (though no one but monks were around to object), and then he was sealing those vows with a chaste kiss.

At least it was supposed to be a chaste kiss. But the moment his lips brushed hers, a surge of desire sent a hot rush through her blood that was distinctly *un*chaste. One might even call it *carnal*. He must have felt it, too. His fingers lingered for a moment, softly brushing the curve of her chin.

When he finally lifted his head, their eyes met in the soft haze of morning sunlight. They might have been the only two people in the world. Everything around her seemed to slip away. She couldn't put a name on what passed between them, except that it felt significant.

Still dazed—this time from the kiss—Mary was surprised to realize the wedding was over. Since she was a widow, there would be no blessing and mass by the priest in the church after the recitation of vows. Nor, given the circumstances, would there be a feast to celebrate.

Just like that, she was a wife, and their child was legitimate, no matter how "early" the birth.

She accepted the subdued congratulations of Sir Adam and the far more enthusiastic ones from the bishop, before turning to her son. If anyone was more stunned by the haste of this wedding than her, it was Davey. She was too embarrassed to tell him the truth. She would. She bit her lip. At some point.

"I know this has come as a surprise to you" she said. "I hope you are not disappointed."

She knew Davey had thought—hoped—she might marry Sir John. But her son's expression was impossible to read. His unusual ability to hide his thoughts made her chest squeeze with the reminder of how he'd learned such a skill. She cursed Atholl, the war, and the fates for her son's stolen childhood.

"It's your life, Mother. I hope Sir Kenneth will make you happy."

Happy was too much to hope for. Mary would settle for not completely miserable. "I want you to be happy, too." He seemed puzzled by the thought, and another stab of guilt struck her. She reached for his hand and took it in hers, saying earnestly, "You are an important part of my life. You always have been, even when we weren't together. Not one day passed that I did not think of you."

He looked at her, and for a moment his too-solemn expression cracked. She caught a glimpse of the longing that so mirrored her own. It struck her then that she and her son were more alike than she realized—they were both treading new ground and didn't know how to reach out to the other.

"I thought of you, too."

A hot wave of tears pressed against the back of her eyes, and she smiled with happiness at the gift he'd given her.

Sir Kenneth—her husband—had been speaking with Sir Adam and the bishop, but he turned back to her. "If you are ready, we should be on our way."

Mary swallowed a hard lump in her throat. It struck her with cold reality that she didn't even know where she was going. He could send her where he willed, and she would have no say in the matter.

Once again his perception surprised her. "I'm afraid I must return to the castle immediately. I assumed that you would accompany me, but if you should like me to make other arrangements—"

"No," she said. "The castle will be fine." She'd feared he

meant to send her away, and she wanted to be near Davey for as long as possible.

"Very well. I will leave instructions to have your things moved to my chamber. Sir Adam has graciously offered to give us the use of his."

Mary paled. Sweet heaven, they would be sharing a room! Why hadn't she thought of that? Suddenly, the prospect of being sent away didn't sound so horrible. Her gaze went to her son. The desire to be with Davey warred with her fear of all that would come with sharing a room with her husband.

I will not be barred from my wife's bed . . .

Suddenly the night ahead loomed very large. Unlike her first wedding, it wasn't because she didn't know what to expect; rather she knew exactly what to expect. The knot low in her belly tightened. *It's not anticipation, it's not . . . fool!*

"My lady?" He held out his hand again, the taunting lift of his brow suggesting he'd guessed the source of her struggle.

With one last helpless look at Davey, she tamped down the surge of apprehension rising in her chest like a tidal wave and slid her hand into his. The sudden warmth that enfolded her proved oddly reassuring. At least for a while. But as the sun made its determined march across the horizon, and the day slipped into night, her apprehension returned tenfold. The night to come was all she could think about.

Mary gazed out the tower window into the courtyard, but she could see little in the torchlit darkness. The apprehension that had been her constant companion as she waited for her new husband to join her had begun to wane as the night darkened. It had grown so late, she'd started to wonder whether he would come at all.

She'd seen him ride out earlier with a large troop of

men, but had yet to see him return. Of course, she hadn't been watching for him. She stared out of tower windows all the time.

Although not usually in the middle of the night.

She'd dismissed her attendants hours ago; it had to be near midnight by now. Had something happened? Had he reconsidered?

She smoothed her hand over her stomach, sizing the swell beneath her palm. She didn't feel overlarge, but she was definitely changed from the last time he'd seen her. Had she become too round? Perhaps he did not relish the idea of bedding a woman heavy with child?

She hadn't thought much about her figure until now. What if he no longer found her attractive?

She would be glad of it, of course. Not being forced to do her wifely duty would certainly make it easier to keep herself—and her heart—at a safe distance. But relief wasn't what she was feeling at all. The hollowness in her chest felt more like disappointment.

Resigned to their marriage, resigned to the fact that he intended to take her to his bed, she knew it was too much to think that she could control her desire, so she'd resigned herself to the passion as well. How had he said it? *Come.* Her cheeks burned, remembering his crude boast. As long as she kept it crude—kept it about the passion—her heart would be safe.

As always, she was determined to make the best of the situation. What else could she do?

With a sigh, she trod back over to the chair where she'd left her needlework. The bed loomed to her right, but she did her best to ignore it. Though it had been a long day of getting settled, answering questions, and avoiding others as the news of their marriage spread throughout the castle like wildfire, she knew if she tried to go to sleep she would lie there in the darkness wide awake. She might as well be productive. Besides, she had almost finished the linen cap for the baby. She'd put hours into the small piece, and it was one of her finest.

Retrieving her glasses, she slid them on her nose and began to work. She had lost track of time when the door suddenly opened.

She startled, her pulse jumping to her throat. It was her husband. Apparently, he'd decided to make an appearance after all.

A blast of heat washed over her as he strode into the room. Awareness, nervousness, and anticipation all rolled into one jumbled mess. Though he had every right to be there, it felt like an invasion. He dominated the small room, taking it over with his mere presence. Given how physically imposing he was, it was strange that she'd never felt intimidated by him. Aggressively large, his muscles honed to a blade's edge of raw power, he looked like a man who was born to fight in an arena. A gladiator of old. With all the fierce, primitive masculinity and barely restrained fire to go along with it. But it wasn't fear that was making her stomach knot, heart flutter, and skin tingle.

He was so effortlessly handsome. His dark hair was damp and curling in loose waves around his face. Wherever he'd been, he'd taken the time to bathe. But he hadn't shaved, and the dark shadow of his beard outlined a jaw that was already too rugged and masculine. He'd removed the armor that she'd seen him in earlier, and wore a plaid over a plain linen shirt and breeches.

Looking at him made her heart ache. If only she were the type of woman who was immune to a handsome face. It would make this so much easier.

"You're still awake? I thought you might have gone to bed by now."

"I was just about to," she lied. "Where were you?"

Atholl had always hated when she'd questioned him

about his absences, but Kenneth seemed unbothered. "I rode out with Percy to near Kelso Abbey. There were reports of rebels in the area. There were, but they were long gone by time we arrived."

"I'm surprised that you are back so soon. Kelso is quite a distance away."

"Most of the men stayed. But I was rather anxious to return."

His smile sent a shiver of awareness racing down her spine. Suddenly, she was very conscious of two things: they were alone, and they were married.

Surprisingly, he didn't press the matter. He moved over to the table where a pitcher of wine had been set out, poured himself a cup, and dropped down on a chair opposite her. She tried not to notice the muscled legs stretched out before her. But good gracious, the black leather stretched over the powerful muscles of his thighs like a second skin! He looked exhausted—she could see the dark circles under his eyes and the lines of weariness etched around his mouth—yet he clearly wasn't in any hurry.

She glanced to the small fireplace on her left between them, but it didn't seem to be burning any hotter. It was he. Or she. Or maybe both of them. If only her heart and stomach would stop fluttering. She couldn't think.

Growing more nervous as the silence dragged on, she said, "I'm surprised they let you roam about so freely."

One corner of his mouth lifted in a wry half-smile. "Noticed my watchdogs, did you? Aye, well, they've relaxed a little. Our marriage helped. Percy is almost convinced of my loyalty."

"Sir Adam informed me of the king's embellishment to our tale. They must not know you very well if they think you would change allegiance for the love of a woman."

He lifted a brow. "And you do?"

Their eyes met, and she felt the heat rise to her cheeks.

He was right. She didn't know him; she was making assumptions. It made it easier to push him away.

"Actually, I think it has more to do with David's wardship. Why would I do anything to jeopardize a chance at that? My interests, you see, are in England."

She felt an unexpected stab of disappointment. "And is that what matters to you?"

"We all do what we have to do, Mary. Isn't that what keeps you in England? Your and David's interests are here. Or is it Bruce that you are opposed to?"

"Of course not," she said automatically. Then, realizing how treasonous her words could have sounded, she added, "Robert was my brother-in-law twice over—he was married to my sister and my brother was married to his sister. I hold a great deal of affection for him."

He considered her for a moment, but then changed the subject. "It's for the baby, isn't it?" he asked, pointing to the cap that had fallen to her lap when he entered.

Belatedly, she recalled the glasses still perched on her nose and slid them off as unself-consciously as she could manage. She nodded.

"May I see it?"

She handed it to him, waiting with a surprisingly anxious heartbeat as he scrutinized it with a thoroughness that would have made Master Bureford proud. "It's magnificent," he announced finally.

Mary told herself that she shouldn't be so pleased. But she couldn't stop the burst of pleasure and pride that swelled inside her.

"Thank you," she managed, embarrassed by her own reaction.

"Did you really sell these?"

She stiffened, anticipating his disapproval. "Aye." And she would continue to do so. But uncertain how he would react to that, she decided to keep that to herself for now.

"I'm impressed. It couldn't have been easy for you."

Empathy? That was the last thing she expected from him—and the last thing she wanted. Being so attracted she couldn't think straight was bad enough. She didn't want to like him, too. "It wasn't. But that was a long time ago, and a time I would rather not remember."

If he noticed the wall she'd erected around the subject of her past, he didn't show it. He handed the cap back to her. "Perhaps you wouldn't mind stitching something for me one day?"

Mary flinched. It felt as if she'd been kicked in the chest. He couldn't have surprised her more than if he'd actually done so. Pained memories came back to her of the countless hours she'd spent on the special surcote she'd made for Atholl, only to have him toss it away with barely a glance when she'd given it to him. She'd poured all her love into that garment, and he'd rejected it as if it had been nothing. To him, it had been.

Now Kenneth asked her to make him something? For the first time, she noticed not the similarities, but the differences between the two men. Though part of her wished she hadn't.

"Perhaps," she managed evasively.

He studied her over the rim of his cup, as if he'd sensed somehow that he'd struck a nerve and was trying to determine the source.

She went back to work so she wouldn't have to meet his eyes, but kept pricking herself with the needle under the weight of his scrutiny.

As the moment of silence stretched, her heartbeat seemed to quicken. Her hands dampened. Her throat grew dry. The bundle of nerves knotting in her stomach returned, as did the butterflies fluttering in her chest.

He, too, appeared increasingly edgy. He stood to replenish his cup, muttering something about whisky. Out of the corner of her eye, she saw him toss back the cup and take a long drink of wine before slamming it down on the table.

"Are you going to do that all night?" he snapped.

She put down her embroidery slowly, realization dawning. *My God, he's nervous!* It seemed inconceivable that this arrogant, cocky warrior with his own retinue of female admirers could be nervous. It was charming—and rather sweet. Two words she'd never thought to use to describe him.

"I can put it aside now, if you'd like."

All of a sudden his demeanor changed. He swore and dragged his hands through his still damp hair. "Hell, I'm sorry." He gave her another one of those boyishly wry smiles that landed in her chest with a thump. "I've never done this before." She lifted her brow, and he laughed. "Had a wedding night," he clarified.

She had, but nothing about that night reminded her of tonight. Then she'd been a frightened girl, ignorant of what was to come, and in awe of her much older husband. She'd been so shy and intimidated, she'd barely said a word to him. She remembered disappointment, pain, and shame.

Now she was a woman, only a few years younger than he, scarred by the past, perhaps, but also stronger. Bolder. Wiser. She was no longer in awe of a handsome knight, knowing there were no heroes, only men. She was still frightened, perhaps, but by the anticipation. By how much she wanted this. How much she wanted him. He had spoken to her more in the past few minutes than Atholl had their entire marriage.

"I should think it would be like any other night," she said, trying to hide her amusement. "But if you like, we can wait—"

It was the wrong thing to say. Or perhaps the right thing. He crossed the room in three strides and lifted her from the chair to her feet. His arms wrapped around her. "Not a chance, my lady wife. You won't get out of it that easily."

Get out of it. As he took her in his arms, and that delicious warmth spread over her, she was certain that was what she *should* want to do. Should.

Seventeen

The anticipation had been building inside him all day. By the time Kenneth walked into the room, he was ready to pick her up, toss her on the bed, and lose himself in mindless oblivion.

He hadn't had a woman in . . .

He didn't want to think about how long. Had he made love with another women since that night at Dunstaffnage? He couldn't remember. *Liar.*

He'd been angry at first and then too busy, damn it. He'd been focused on earning his way into the Guard.

There had been opportunities; he just hadn't much felt like acting on them. Even no effort had seemed like too much. Which sure as hell didn't explain all the effort he was going to for her.

Despite the deprived state of his cock, and that it didn't seem to take more than a glimpse of her to put him in a very pained state, he'd forced himself to take it slow. Wooing. Seducing. Putting her at ease.

Nothing that should have made him feel so damned *nervous.* Nervous? Hell, he hadn't ever been nervous with a woman. Ever. Even when he was young and inexperienced enough to warrant it.

But then again, he'd never made love to his wife before. He'd never cared about getting something so right. He wanted it to be perfect. For his mission, of course.

But the moment he wrapped her in his arms, the edginess seemed to disappear. He was back on solid ground. No more thinking. No more talking. Time to let instinct take over.

"I wasn't trying to get out of it," she whispered.

"You weren't?" His hand took a long, slow journey down her spine; he loved the way she shuddered against him.

She shook her head.

She looked so sweet he had to kiss her. His mouth covered hers with a groan. Hunger rose inside him like a maelstrom, but he forced himself to slow. Tasting the honey sweetness of her lips with a gentle caress. Letting his mouth move over hers in a smooth, sensual dance.

But damn, she felt good. He slid his tongue deeper and deeper in her mouth the way he wanted to make love to her. He started to tighten his arms to fit her more closely against him, when the swell of her stomach stopped him.

Hell, how could he have not considered the babe?

He lifted his head. "Perhaps this isn't a good idea."

Her expression changed in an instant, from soft and aroused to pale and crestfallen. And something else he couldn't quite identify—almost vulnerable.

She dropped her gaze and tried to pull away. "Of course. I see myself every day, so I don't realize how much I must have changed."

He frowned. What in Hades was she talking about? As the thought had never occurred to him, it took him a minute to realize what she meant. He caught her before she could slip away. "You *have* changed. You are even more beautiful than you were before."

"That isn't saying much," she said wryly.

He laughed. "I suspect that was your intent." She didn't deny it. "You were far too thin. Believe me, sweeting, your new curves have only added to your beauty, and my desire for you. If you like, you can feel for yourself." He was pleased to see a blush rise to her cheeks, but unfortunately, she didn't take him up on his offer. "My concern is for the child. Is this . . . I don't want to do anything to hurt . . . "

A shy smile returned to her face. "The baby will not be hurt. The church might not like it, but I believe it is quite common for a husband to share his wife's bed until near the end of the pregnancy."

"Are you sure?"

She nodded, and that was enough. He swept her up into his arms—or arm, as he could easily bear her weight on his good arm—and carried her to the bed.

Laying her gently atop the bed coverings, he proceeded to remove his boots, plaid, and shirt. Bared to the waist, he turned to see her studying him with a distressed look on her face.

"What's wrong?"

Troubled eyes lifted to his. "Your arm. Does it hurt very badly? I never thanked you for what you did for Davey." She shivered. "Had you not been there . . . "

He sat down on the edge of the bed and leaned toward her, putting his finger on her mouth to stop her from finishing the thought. "Don't think about it. But you're welcome." He moved his arm around. It was stiff and still a bit sore, but it felt surprisingly strong. Thanks to his sister. "The wound is healing well. I should be able to resume my duties on the battlefield soon enough."

Just not too soon.

"I wish there was something I could do."

His blood heated at the innocent offer. He could think of a lot of things she could do. But those would keep for later.

Stretched out on the bed before him, with her golden hair spilling out on the pillow behind her head, her lush form clad in a thin chemise and velvet robe tied loosely around the middle, adorably tiny feet peeking out from below, she was doing plenty. He drew in his breath and traced the lush curves and contours of her breasts with the back of one finger.

He heard her draw in her breath as well, and when he looked at her face, he watched as the flush of desire washed over her. Her lips parted. Her eyes drew heavy. Her cheeks pinkened. It was one of the most erotic things he'd ever seen.

With one touch he could arouse her passion, and it was just as hot and fiery as his.

Desire roared through his veins. His heart started to pound and his cock swelled hard, straining and throbbing against the ties of his breeches. He wanted to take her tiny hand and wrap it around him. He wanted to feel the wet heat of her mouth sucking him. But most of all he wanted to bury himself deep inside her until she couldn't deny this connection between them.

"There is something you can do," he rasped, the heat in his eyes leaving no question of his meaning.

She feigned shock. "Are you asking me to pay you back with my body, my lord?"

He grinned unrepentantly. "I am. And I intend for you to pay dearly. Starting right now." His finger found the nub of her nipple, and he started to draw tiny little circles around its tip until it hardened to a delicious point. It was everything he could do not to rip the robe and chemise apart and take it in his mouth. Her breasts were incredible. So full and ripe.

But this wasn't going to be about lust. He was going to seduce his bride if it killed him. He wanted her begging for him.

Mary couldn't move. Every nerve ending in her body was flared and straining in the direction of his finger. Sweet heaven, what was he doing to her? This wasn't going at all as she'd planned. She'd envisioned a quick and passionate coupling. Preferably in the dark. Not this intimacy. Not talking. Not teasing. Not slow, unhurried seduction.

Like a spider to the fly, he was luring her into his dangerous web. She could feel herself sliding, slipping into a place of confusing emotions. A place where she would be unprotected and vulnerable to emotions she didn't want to feel.

She had to get back on track. Open her eyes and harden her heart. Passion, not tenderness. Lust, not intimacy.

But the more she knew him, the harder it was to resist him. He wasn't just a handsome, wicked scoundrel who'd taunted her with a night of passion. He was still cocky and arrogant, and he still had far too many women throwing themselves at his feet, but behind the bold facade he was also kind, considerate, and at times surprisingly sweet. Looking at his fierce, imposing facade, you would never know it. But she did.

If only he would stop looking at her like that. If only he would stop touching her like that. He'd taken command of her body with one deft finger.

"Do you like that, sweeting?" he said softly.

She wanted to tell him no. She didn't want to draw this out any longer than was necessary, but her breasts were so heavy. Her nipple throbbed, ached for something more.

She was trying so hard to resist. But finally the sensation built until she couldn't hold it any longer. The restless, impatient feeling was coming over her again. She let out a soft cry, arching into his hand. "Please."

Finally, he cupped her in his palms, rubbing her nipple between his finger and forefinger with just the right amount of pressure. She remembered the heat of his mouth through her gown the last time . . .

She cried out again, a rush of heat pooling between her thighs.

His slow seduction slipped. He let out a growl and covered her mouth with his, cupping and squeezing her breast with all the frenzy she could have asked for.

His incredible chest was leaning over her, naked and warm. She didn't have to tell herself to reach up and put her hands on him; it was instinctive. A shock of heat reverberated through her at the contact. His skin was so smooth, which seemed incongruous with the hard granite of his muscles below. Muscles that flexed and flared at her touch as her hands roamed over the broad spans of his shoulders and back.

His kiss was growing more passionate by the second, more aggressive, his tongue plunging into her mouth with wild, carnal abandon.

She could feel the hard press of his erection against her thigh. Feel his hands sliding between her robe to push it apart.

Yes, she thought. This was exactly the way she wanted it. Hurried and frenzied. Hot and passionate.

She moaned her encouragement, her hands slipping down his back to settle at his waist, pulling him more urgently against her.

But he had more control than she. Just when she thought he was going to loosen his breeches, toss up her skirts, and plunge inside, he drew back with a harsh grunt. "Not so fast, little one. We have all night, and I intend to use every minute of it."

Kenneth saw her eyes widen with something that almost looked like fear.

"Is th-that . . . necessary?" His gaze narrowed, and she explained hastily. "It's just that I've had a long day, as I'm sure you have. I'm rather tired."

Tired? When a few seconds ago she'd been writhing in his arms, her body a lit keg of black powder getting ready to explode?

His mouth fell in a hard line, suspecting what this was about. Apparently, she still wanted only one thing from him. But he had no intention of letting her dictate the terms of their marriage bed. Unwittingly, his bride had just set down a challenge to a man who couldn't resist one.

He hid his irritation behind a complacent smile. "Of course. I understand. We can go as fast or as slow as you like."

Her brow furrowed skeptically. "Really?"

"Really."

He was just going to make sure she never wanted it to end. She eyed him warily.

Smart lass.

Without preamble, he started to loosen the sash at her waist. She caught his hand. "Wh-what are you d-doing?"

"We can't very well get this over with, with you wearing all these clothes."

Her eyes widened again, and she clenched the edges of her robe against her chest protectively. "I like these clothes."

He shrugged. "Suit yourself. You can leave on your chemise, but take off the robe." He gave her a taunting smile. "It will go faster if it doesn't get in the way."

Her eyes narrowed, guessing that he was up to something. Surprisingly, for once, she did as he asked. Sitting up, she loosened the sash, shrugged the robe from her shoulders, and tossed it on the trunk at the foot of the bed.

He drew in his breath, momentarily distracted by the body revealed by the thin, achingly translucent piece of linen. Her breasts strained against the fabric, having obviously grown larger than the garment was originally designed to fit. The pleasant handful that he recalled from before had swelled into two firm, round mounds as big and ripe as peaches. Her pearl-sized nipples were taut and straining against the fabric.

He felt his cock do the same.

He glanced sharply away, smothering a pained groan, before he got distracted. Hell, he was already distracted. But his wee wife had drawn the battle lines, and he was going to do whatever it took to win.

He stood and began to work the ties of his breeches, which given the state of his arousal wasn't easy.

She made what sounded suspiciously like a squeak. "What are you doing?"

He smiled, having finally managed to free himself. "I sleep naked."

"You d-do?"

"Every night."

Her eyes met his. He could see the frown start, almost as if she'd guessed his plan. But before she could say anything, he slid his pants down.

She made a strangled sound in her throat and he tried not to laugh. Stepping out of the legs, he kicked the breeches aside. Naked as one of those Greek statues he'd seen pictures of once, he stood proudly before her. If she liked his body, well then, she was going to see a whole hell of a lot of it.

He glanced to the bed, pleased to see his actions had elicited the appropriate response. She was staring at him as if she were trying to commit every inch of his flesh to memory.

But she was more stubborn than he'd anticipated. Her eyes flew to his. She licked her lips. "Would you mind blowing out the candles. I'm afraid I'm feeling quite shy."

His mouth tightened. The little vixen! She didn't have a shy bone in her passionate little body. He was about to refuse when she said, "Unless you find it difficult to perform in the dark."

He nearly choked. Him have difficulty performing? God, didn't she see the size of his erection? But he clenched his jaw, hearing her challenge. Without a word, he stalked over to the candelabra on the sideboard and blew them out. The lamp at the bedside table as well.

The room went dark for a moment, but when his eyes adjusted, he realized there was still a soft glow of light coming from the coal in the fireplace.

More than enough for what he intended. His eyes fixed on the woman in his bed. He gave her a predatory smile. "If you don't have any more directions, what's say we begin?"

Mary knew she'd made a mistake. Somehow he'd guessed what she was about. Worse, he'd taken it as a challenge and turned it into some kind of contest.

Her heart pounded erratically as she heard his footsteps approach the bed. Unfortunately, it wasn't nearly dark enough, and she could still see far too much of him.

He was incredible. Could a man so fiercely masculine be beautiful? If so, then he was. His body was like a statue. A massive, perfectly chiseled statue. It had been hard to know where to look, from his broad shoulders and thickly muscled arms, to his sculpted chest with band after band of ripped muscle, to his heavy, powerfully built thighs. And then there was that other part of him. The uniquely male part of him she shouldn't notice but had looked at with far too much and very unmaidenly curiosity. The thick column of flesh with the plump hood that strained past his belly button. Hard and red, she'd ached to touch it. To feel him in her hands.

The bed shifted with his weight when he slid in next to her. For a moment, he simply lay beside her in the darkness. She was so highly aroused, so painfully aware of him, however, that it only increased her anxiousness.

Did he have to be so blasted hot? His body seemed to radiate heat, and her skin felt flushed and uncomfortable—as if it were too small for her body.

He's naked.

Try not to think about it.

But she couldn't help it. She kept thinking about how it would feel to have all that hot skin pressed against her.

He was torturing her. And he knew it.

"Still tired, Mary?"

The blighter. "A little," she said stubbornly, as her body screamed for him to touch her. She squirmed.

"Bed not comfortable?" he asked innocently.

"The bed is fine," she snapped.

"I just heard you moving around—"

"I wasn't moving around!"

He rolled to his side and began his infernally slow game of tracing every inch of her with his finger, when she ached—yes, ached—to have the full pressure of his hands. She was more aroused than she'd ever been in her life.

"Any more instructions, Mary? Or are you going to let me proceed?"

Something about him brought out her fight. She wasn't going to let him run over her. She lifted her chin. "Nothing that I can think of right now, but I will let you know if something comes up."

"Something has come up, all right," he mumbled irritably.

Mary smiled, glad to know she wasn't the only one suffering. "What's that?" she asked innocently.

His reply was a kiss. A very slow, very expert, very thorough kiss. A kiss that radiated down to her toes. A kiss that made her limbs heavy and her bones dissolve. A kiss that made her *want* with all her heart.

He was seducing her, and if Mary didn't do something, she knew she'd be lost. She was halfway there already. She had to find a way to take control.

He was on his side, leaning half on her. She could feel the thick imprint of his manhood on her stomach. The image of him holding himself in his hand sprang to mind. The fact that it aligned with her previous thoughts of wanting to touch him made the possibility even more intriguing.

If he'd pleasured himself that way, would he like it if she did the same?

Testing her theory, she moved her hand from his arm to his chest, lightly trailing her fingers down the rigid bands of his stomach muscles.

She knew she was on to something when he stilled, pausing in his kiss, stomach muscles clenching. He hissed when the heel of her hand met the plump tip. "What are you doing?"

She wrapped her fingers around him, and he groaned, instinctively thrusting himself deeper in her hand. She wondered at the sensations. At the feel of him. His skin was so hot. A velvety-thin glove over steel.

"I should think that was obvious," she said. "I want to touch you." She looked up at him in the darkness, holding his gaze. Slowly, she began to move her hand the way he'd done. He groaned again, closing his eyes as if the pleasure was too much to take. "I hope that is all right?"

"Oh God," he said, covering her hand with his, showing her how to find his rhythm. "God, that feels so good. I've dreamed of this."

"You have?"

But he seemed incapable of speech. She watched the pleasure build inside him. Saw as his face drew clenched and tight as he strained against the release that she knew was only moments away. He was throbbing, beating under her hand.

His hand found the edge of her chemise and dipped underneath. His fingers brushed between her legs, and the wave of pleasure was so intense she almost forgot to keep moving her hand.

His fingers dipped inside. No teasing now. He stroked and thrust, readying her for him.

She heard his breath quicken. Felt his body clenching. When he pulled his hand from her, rolled over, and positioned himself between her legs, she knew she'd won.

Lust. She could feel it crackling in the air between them. He was out of his mind with lust for her, just as she was for him.

Check . . . mate.

Kenneth knew he should have stopped her, but the feel of her soft, small hand wrapped around him, stroking him, was more than he could resist.

All he could think about was being inside her. He wanted so badly to come that it hurt.

But when he held himself over her and looked into her eyes, he knew he had to find a way to pull himself back from the edge.

If she knew how easy it was to control him, he would never be able to break down the wall she'd erected between them.

So he countered her attack with one of his own. Before she realized what he intended, he slid down her body, positioning his face between her legs.

"What are you—"

He brushed his lips over her.

"Oh!"

She bucked, and he took the opportunity to slide his hands under the soft curve of her bottom to hold her steady. He kissed her again, rubbing his jaw against her mound as his tongue slid inside with long, languid strokes. She tasted so good, so soft and silky smooth, he couldn't seem to get enough of her. He made love to her with his mouth and tongue, her back arching and her hips rising to meet the wicked onslaught of his kiss.

She was breathing hard, frantic little moans echoing in his ears. He knew he could make her come, but he purposefully drew it out until she was writhing in agony.

He lifted his head, looking up at her. The subtle curve of her belly made his chest swell with a strange emotion. His voice was oddly rough when he spoke. "Look at me, Mary."

Her eyes were soft and unfocused, so heavy with lust it made his cock clench. Holding her gaze, he flicked her with his tongue. She shuddered. She was his. He held his mouth against her, giving her the pressure she yearned for, and sent her flying over the edge.

Mary had never felt so close to anyone in her life. Looking into his eyes as he'd kissed her like that . . .

She'd never imagined sharing that kind of intimacy with anyone.

When he'd finally given her the release that she'd craved, she was so tired, she forgot to fight back.

Barely had the ebb of pleasure started to slip away when he was pushing inside her. Filling her. Becoming a part of her.

He forced her gaze to his as he took the final thrust of possession. At least that's what she told herself. It wasn't that she couldn't look way.

He moved inside her slowly at first. But then the battle became too much for both of them. He surged once. Twice. And then his body stiffened and jerked as the spasms of his own release hit.

When it was over, they were both too tired to speak. He rolled to the side and tucked her against him. Strangely, she didn't fight it.

The battle had been won, but by whom?

Eighteen

Mary woke to the warmth of sunshine on her face and the scent of flowers in her nose. She stretched like a lazy cat in the sun. Surely it must be a sin to feel this good? Opening her eyes, she discovered the source of the smell. A small sprig of lavender lay on the pillow beside her. She smiled, bringing it to her nose to inhale the delicate fragrance.

Aware that the source of her gift was watching her from across the room, where he stood by the basin with a razor in his hand, she lifted a brow. "Flowers today?"

The first morning, he'd surprised her with a warm bath. The second, with a pretty ribbon (she didn't have the heart to tell him it was one of her own). The third, with a batch of her favorite sugared buns that she'd mentioned the day before. And today it was flowers.

As if his seductive passion at night wasn't hard enough to resist, now she had to contend with his courtship during the day. But even knowing it was only a contest to him, and that the attention wouldn't last, she couldn't help but be amused—and touched. More than she wanted to admit. She'd never put much store in romantic gestures before, but she could not deny the spur in her heart. The gestures might be speciously motivated, but they were not without thought.

"Do you like them?" He frowned. "I know you mentioned pink roses were your favorite, but given my recent allegiance I wasn't sure that would be wise."

"I should think not." The pink rose had become a subversive symbol of Bruce sympathizers after Isabella MacDuff, the Countess of Buchan, had worn one in her cloak on her way to be imprisoned in a cage. Unwittingly, Mary shivered and pushed the image away. She knew how close she'd come to sharing such a fate. But that was all behind her now. "They're perfect," she said, inhaling the small bouquet again. "Don't tell me you picked them yourself?"

He lowered the blade from where it had been scraping against his jaw—a very hard, very masculine jaw—and grimaced. "I wish I had. I sent my squire to find them. My squire who has yet to learn to keep his mouth shut."

She tried to bite back her smile. "Damaged your fierce reputation, did he?"

"More than you can imagine," he said dryly.

Mary sobered. "You don't have to do this, you know—whatever it is you're doing."

Their eyes met and held. For longer every time. Just as it was becoming harder to drag her gaze away.

Had he taken her words as a challenge to give up? It wasn't how they were meant.

"Aye, I do," he said softly, and then more lightly, "Don't worry, I've had my share of needling; I can take it."

"You? What do you have to be teased about? From where I sit, you're infuriatingly perfect."

A cocky grin spread across his face. "Do you think so? I wondered if you were ever going to notice."

"Nauseatingly, I meant." She tossed the pillow at him.

He laughed, catching it in the air and tossing it right back at her.

She rolled on her back, staring up at the ceiling as he finished getting ready. As they did every morning, she pre-

tended not to watch him, and he pretended not to notice
her doing so.

How long could this game go on? That was all it was, a
game . . . wasn't it? But it didn't feel like a game; it felt real.

At night it was easy to pretend she was in control of her
feelings. She could lose herself in passion, go to sleep, and
not have to think about it—not have to face how every
time he held her in his arms, every time he touched her
with heartwrenching tenderness, every time he looked into
her eyes as he entered her, it was getting harder and harder
to tell herself it meant nothing.

She was running out of ways to fight back. She was a
novice competing with a master in the art of passion. How
many more ways could she find to distract him? To bring
it back to lust?

In the daylight it was worse. In the daylight there was
nowhere for those feelings to hide.

He rubbed his hand over his jaw, feeling for any places
that he'd missed, and then wiped his face with a damp
towel. When he was finished, he came to stand beside the
bed, looking down at her. "Your water is getting cold."

She shot him a glare. Though his expression was blank,
she knew he was laughing at her. "I don't mind. A cool
bath can be . . . uh, invigorating, don't you think?"

"I think I deserve to watch after arranging to have a bath
brought up to you every morning without waking you." He
shook his head. "You sleep the sleep of the dead."

She hadn't until recently, but she decided not to mention
that. "I'm shy, remember?"

But he knew what it was really about. She was embarrassed.

"I want to see you, Mary. *All* of you."

She looked away. "There is *much* to see."

He laughed, sat down on the edge of the bed, and tilted
her chin to him. "You're beautiful."

"Men always say that when they want something."

He chuckled. "Maybe you are right. Take your bath in privacy, then. For now. But you won't hide from me forever. I will see you—soon." He stood. "What are you doing later today?"

She sighed, anticipating the long hours until she saw—

She stopped. Sweet heaven, how had it happened so fast? Could she already be measuring the day by the hours until she saw him next?

Her chest squeezed. It was true. During the day he was busy with his duties. She would see him in the yard sometimes, when she was able to watch Davey, and at meals, of course, but it wasn't until they were alone at night that he belonged to her.

Except that he didn't belong to her. *Eyes open.*

"The usual," she said. "Between prayers and meals, I will work on some embroidery with the other women and listen to the castle gossip, attend to some correspondence with the clerk, and if Davey isn't away from the castle today, watch him practice in the yard."

"Ah, that's too bad. I was hoping you might have some time."

She perked up, hoping she didn't look as eager as she felt. "Time?"

"Aye, to go on a ride with me. I'm getting tired of looking at these same stone walls."

"But can you?" She blushed. "I mean, have they granted you permission to leave the castle alone?"

His mouth curved. "Aye, I guess Percy has determined I'm not a threat."

Mary scoffed. The man was nothing but a threat.

"What's that?" His eyes glinted with amusement.

She scowled at him, realizing she must have spoken her thoughts aloud.

"But if you're too busy—"

"I'm not," she interrupted, far too quickly. But she couldn't hide her excitement. She, too, was feeling cooped up. "I should love to go on a ride with you." She frowned, her hands instinctively going to her stomach. "Though I'm not sure I should."

He seemed to understand her fears. "Don't worry. You'll be perfectly safe. I won't let anything happen to you."

He said it with a look that made her wonder what he was up to. Knowing him, she suspected it was something calculated to wear her down. If she'd learned anything about her fiery husband, it was that he did not give up.

Kenneth was running out of ideas. Having never gone to this much trouble to win a woman's heart before, he didn't exactly have a repertoire of romantic gestures to work from. He'd operated on instinct (which sounded better than accident), which thus far seemed to be working well. She'd delighted over the bath—even if she wouldn't delight him by using it in front of him—as well as the ribbon and the sugary buns.

But the woman was stubborn—and too damned suspicious of his motives. Which made her too damned smart.

This wasn't turning out to be as easy as he'd expected.

Although he had to admit there was one place he wasn't minding her challenges. He almost looked forward to finding out what she would do next to make his control slip at night.

But while she might win a few battles, he knew he would win the war. His lust wouldn't be roused like this for long, and he would be back in control. Eventually, he knew the novelty would wear off and his interest would wane as it always had before.

He frowned. Wouldn't it? It sure as hell hadn't waned yet. He had an unsettling thought: what if it never did?

Of course it would. Just because Mary wasn't like any woman he'd met before didn't mean his life—his entire way of thinking—would change.

He liked variety. And simplicity, for that matter.

At least he used to. But sparring with his very *un*simple and-not-so-eager-to-please wife was proving interesting.

He frowned, pushing the disturbing thought away as he opened the door.

He was glad to see her alone. Some of the ladies were less than subtle in their interest in him, which made him uncomfortable—and angry. They were her friends; they should try to act like it. Having learned of the pain of her first marriage, the last thing he wanted to do was remind her of Atholl.

He took in her hooded cloak, gloves, and sturdy boots. "Are you ready?" He grinned, suspecting she'd been ready for some time.

She nodded and he took her hand, leading her out of the chamber, down the stairs, and out into the yard.

She waited outside while he went to retrieve his destrier. He was only gone a few minutes, but it was long enough for Felton to find her.

Kenneth felt his temper prick hot. If he'd hoped the marriage would put an end to Felton's interest in his wife, he was to be disappointed. The bastard was furious, but he hid it well, aiming his venom toward Kenneth. To Mary, he was the soul of English chivalry, as charming and solicitous as he could be.

Kenneth, on the other hand, was feeling every ounce of his barbarian blood. When he saw Felton's hand on his wife's arm, his first instinct was to reach for his axe. The surge of possessiveness that hit him was both primitive and undeniable.

He was jealous, he realized. Deeply and pathetically jealous, and he couldn't do a damned thing about it.

If Felton had chosen that moment to press him, Kenneth didn't think he would have been able to back down.

Mary must have sensed something and carefully extracted her arm. Only then did the red haze begin to recede.

"Where do you think you are going?" Felton demanded.

Obviously, anger was still clouding Kenneth's judgment a bit, because he couldn't resist snapping back sarcastically but all too truthfully, "To leave a message for Bruce with all the English secrets. Where the hell does it look like I'm going, on a ride with *my wife*."

He knew he'd put too much emphasis on the last two words when Mary's eyes widened.

Felton's, however, narrowed. "You don't have permission to leave—"

"I sure as hell do. Check with Percy. Not that it's any of your damned business." Only because he knew it would antagonize the bastard, he couldn't resist pointing out, "You might be champion for now, but I don't take orders from you."

As the heir to the earldom, Kenneth outranked him.

Felton's face turned florid. "For now? I thought you might have tired of losing—having done so many times at the point of my spurs, but when you are done hiding behind that injury, I'll be happy to oblige you again. We'll see if the barbarians have taught you anything."

Kenneth lunged, ready to show him exactly how much the barbarians had taught him. He would have thrown his fist right through Felton's sneering grin if he hadn't felt the press of a hand on his arm.

His wife's hand.

The idea that something so small could hold him back was patently absurd. Except that when he looked down and saw her tiny gloved hand on his arm, he knew it wasn't so absurd at all.

How the hell had she done that? When he lost his temper, nothing penetrated. He didn't think, didn't hear reason, just reacted. That was what made it so difficult to control. But with one gentle press of her hand, she'd restrained him. He was so stunned he couldn't speak.

"I'm sure my husband is looking forward to meeting you

on the practice yard, Sir John. But surely it would be a Pyrrhic victory, at best, if he is not fully healed."

Had she just used "Pyrrhic victory"? She had, he realized. His wife had also succeeded in shaming Sir John.

The knight stiffened. "Of course. I only meant—"

"I know what you meant," she said sweetly. Felton held her gaze for moment, then gave her a curt nod and moved off as if he had a pike up his arse.

Kenneth's blood was still pounding when she turned to him. "You shouldn't antagonize him. Sir John is not a man you should wish for an enemy."

He stiffened. "Felton doesn't concern me."

"He should. He is Percy's best knight, reputed to be one of the best in England."

He felt a stab of something like disappointment, except that it was harder and more acute. "You think he would best me?"

Her brow furrowed. Something in his voice must have alerted her. "I wasn't thinking about it that way. Who wins is immaterial. I simply don't think it's wise to make an enemy of a powerful man. Nor would I wish to see you hurt."

Her answer mollified him somewhat, but it still stung of a lack of faith. "Who wins always matters."

She looked up at him, studying his face, perhaps seeing more than he wanted her to see. "So you've said. Shall we go?"

Kenneth motioned over the stable lad to bring the horse forward.

Mary looked around. "Where's my mount?"

He smiled. "Right here."

"You can't expect me to ride that beast!"

He patted the big black destrier fondly on the rump. "Oh, he's as gentle as a lamb."

She looked at him as if he were mad.

He laughed. "Besides, I'll be riding with you."

Immediately grasping his intent, she narrowed her gaze. "Perhaps it's not the horse I should be worried about."

As he'd said before, smart lass.

Alas, Kenneth's plan to take advantage of having her in his arms while they rode was not to be. No sooner had he settled her before him and snuggled her up against his chest than she promptly fell asleep.

Instead of teasing her with the gentle motion of her bottom rocking against his cock, instead of "accidental" brushes of his hands over her breasts and thighs until they both were squirming with need, he had to make himself content with the warmth of her back against his chest and the soft floral scent of her silky hair under his nose.

Surprisingly, it wasn't difficult. He was content—very content. In her sleep she forgot to be wary. There was something inherently trusting about her position curled up against him, her cheek nuzzled into the leather of his *cotun* like a child rather than a woman of six and twenty. She was so small, her pregnant stomach making her seem that much more vulnerable, that he felt a fierce wave of protectiveness swell inside him.

He would die a hundred times over before he let anything happen to her.

The intensity of his reaction took him aback. What was she doing to him?

They rode for about an hour, traveling southeast over the gently rolling hills of the Northumberland moorlands. The Cheviot Hills, the range that straddled the border, dominated the not-so-distant landscape. They passed a few villages, and a number of farms, but otherwise the road was blissfully peaceful. Though he would not have brought her had he not thought it safe, this close to the border it was always wise to take care, so he kept a cautious watch on their surroundings.

As they drew nearer their destination, the countryside

became even more desolate. The English—like the Scots—were a superstitious lot. They kept a distance from the ancient stones that peppered the landscape, believing they held magic.

For Kenneth, the stones were a means of communication. He would leave a message here for the Guard. As the son of an earl, he'd had some formal education—at least enough for a rudimentary note about his wedding and his plan to bring Mary with him and the young earl. He'd also written the name of every lord and knight and the number of men-at-arms who'd gathered at the castle so far. It wasn't much, but it was something.

The lack of additional supplies heading north still bothered him, as did Clifford's continued comings and goings, but recalling MacKay's warnings, he kept his thoughts to himself. He also didn't mention volunteering to go with Clifford on a recent journey to Roxburgh. A mission that had turned up nothing.

Kenneth stopped when they reached the circle of five stones known locally as the Duddo Stones. He glanced down at the woman still sleeping in his arms and felt something inside his chest shift. Something that ached as he took in the fair hair glistening in the sun like gold; the soft, creamy skin; the tiny, pointed chin; the lush, pink mouth, and the long flutter of dark lashes against her rosy cheeks. Her features were delicate, just like her beauty. Classic and understated rather than bold and flashy. It was the type of beauty that would last for years, beyond the fresh dewiness of youth. She had a face that a man could be content to look at for the rest of his life.

God, he sounded like an idiot! This wooing and acting like a lovesick knight was turning him into one. He could almost hear MacKay laughing at him.

She opened her eyes. He watched her blink as she took a moment to realize where she was. He felt like a ray of sunlight hit him when she smiled and looked up at him. "We're here?"

He smiled back at her. "Aye. I thought you might sleep the day away."

Her cheeks flushed adorably. "I seem to be taking a lot of naps lately. I think it has something to do with the babe."

Her hands covered her stomach, as he'd noticed her instinctively do many times before. She jumped a little and said, "Oh!"

"What is it?" he said, instantly concerned. "Is it the child?"

She nodded. "She's kicking me." At his obviously dumbfounded expression, she laughed and said, "Would you like to feel?"

He wasn't sure, but he nodded.

She took his hand and placed it on her stomach, and a moment later he startled when something indeed kicked him.

She laughed at his horrified expression. "It's all right. It's perfectly normal. Although this baby seems to be much more active than David was. I think she's anxious to get out."

It stunned him how little he knew about any of this. "When will that be?"

"I should think around Ascension Day."

Kenneth felt his breath relax. The end of May. He had time, then. He wanted to make sure she was safely away well before the child was born. His child. That wave of protectiveness grew even stronger.

"Where have you brought me?"

"See for yourself."

He helped her down so that she could look around. She gasped when she saw the five ancient stones standing in a small circle on the flat top of a hill. "Druid stones? They're magnificent." But then she noticed the much larger range of hills in the distance. "Isn't that the border?"

"Aye."

She shivered. "Is it safe to be so close without a guard?"

"I won't let anything happen to you, Mary. You have nothing to fear."

She held his gaze. He could tell she didn't believe him, and it struck something cold in his heart. A wry smile turned her mouth. "I've heard that promise before."

His mouth hardened, and he tried not to feel the prick of jealousy. *Atholl.* "But not by me. I'm not your first husband, Mary."

She looked up at him, blinking in the sunlight. "No, no you're not."

"What did he do to make you so cynical?"

"Cynical?" she repeated, as if she'd never made the connection. "I suppose you are right. Atholl swore to protect us, but he gave no thought to what would happen to us when he rebelled. He cared more about glory and being a hero than he did about a wife and son. Aye, he protected us as long as it didn't interfere with what he wanted to do. I asked him to take us with him, but he refused. He said we would be safe. That he would come back for us if something went wrong. I trusted him. But of course, he never did. He abandoned us to Edward's mercy, and I was left to pick up the pieces of his decisions. Decisions that took everything from me—my son, my home, my family—but which I never had a say in."

Kenneth felt a prickle—nay, a stab—of unease. "That's why you wanted me to give you that promise?"

She gazed up at him. "Aye. I swore I'd never let a man put me in that kind of position again."

Ah hell. It wasn't the same, he told himself. He *would* protect her. He didn't just care about the glory. That wasn't why he was so intent on joining the Highland Guard. At least not all of it. He wasn't making choices for her. She would want to go when the time came.

But all the rationalizing in the world couldn't erase the flicker of unease that had crept over the day like a dark shadow. "Come," he said, taking a bag from the horse. "I've a surprise for you."

The wariness was back. "I don't need any more surprises."

"Perhaps not, but you'll like it all the same."

He was right. A few minutes later, after he'd led her over to the circle of stones, spread out a plaid for her to sit on, and handed her the bundle, she moaned with delight at the scent of cinnamon and caramel that wafted from beneath the piece of linen. "More sugar buns? I'm going to be as fat as that old cat that hangs around the barn, if you keep having the cook bake these for me."

"I like you curvy."

She didn't respond; she was too busy biting into the crusty sugarcoated round of bread. The sounds she made went right to his cock—as did the look of rapture on her face.

Jesus. He adjusted his breeches. A woman shouldn't look like that unless she was naked and under him.

She finished chewing and looked up at him, realizing he was watching her. "Don't you want any?"

He shook his head. "I'd rather watch you." He reached over, running the pad of his finger over her upper lip.

She sucked in her breath, wide-eyed.

He lowered his mouth to hers. "You have a little bit of sugar right here."

He wanted to lick it off, but instead he swiped it with his finger and brought it to his mouth. "Hmmm. Very sweet."

Mary pulled back. "Why are you doing this? Why are you going to all this effort? What do you want from me?"

It almost sounded like fear in her voice. "I want *you*." He was surprised to realize it was the truth. It wasn't just about stung pride and proving she wasn't immune; it wasn't just about winning her heart for his mission. He wanted her for himself.

"We're already married. You have me."

"Do I?" He smiled. "I very much doubt that." He leaned back, eyeing her speculatively. "What is it exactly that you object to?"

She rolled her eyes. "You'll not hear a recitation of your finer points from me, my lord. I'm sure you've heard them well enough from others."

Perhaps she was right, but he was surprised how much he wanted to hear it from her. Not her admiration but her respect. The thought made him frown. "I've never met a woman like you."

"One who doesn't fall at your feet?"

She was teasing him, he realized. He shook his head. "You sound like my sister."

"The one who was married at Dunstaffnage?"

"Aye, I only have one sister. Her name is Helen."

A frown gathered between her brows. "I wish I'd had a chance to meet her. Whom did she marry?"

"The son of the MacKay chief."

Her eyes widened. Obviously she knew something of the feuding history between the MacKays and the Sutherlands. "I remember meeting him. That must have been an interesting wedding feast."

He laughed. "It was. You should have seen Will trying to keep the peace. You'd have to know my brother, but he's one of the fiercest warriors I know and always ready to fight. He's not a peacemaker. I think he spent the better part of three days trying to *prevent* fights by threatening to beat the men senseless if they did."

"That sounds familiar," she said with a smile. "I'm sure there must have been a lot of fights between you when you were young."

"Drubbings, you mean. One-sided, for the most part."

"It's hard to think of you being on the losing end."

He shrugged as if it meant nothing to him. "It made me work harder. My brother made me the warrior I am today."

"You are close?"

Suddenly, he realized his mistake. Damn it. He'd been jabbering on as if he hadn't just broken from his family. "*Were* close," he corrected.

But from the way she was looking at him, he feared she'd picked up on the mistake as well. "Why did you change your allegiance?"

Damn. "It's complicated," he hedged, and then turned the question back to her. "Did you ever consider returning to Scotland?"

A sharp look of pain crossed her face. She nodded. "Aye. Once."

"What happened?"

For a moment, he didn't think she was going to answer. She reached over and picked a piece of grass, making tiny knots over and over. "I lost my sister."

She gave a brief rendition of what had happened. How her sister had appeared one night at Ponteland to bring her home after Atholl's arrest, how Sir Adam had arrived ahead of the king's men, how they'd raced across the countryside only to be caught in the middle of the battle. "I'll never forget that moment. One minute I was looking at her and the next, the bridge exploded into flames. It must have been lightning, though I didn't recall hearing any before. There was a loud boom—the strangest thunder I've ever heard— and then everything went black. I woke up, and my sister was gone."

Something about the story niggled at his consciousness. "Sir Adam was there?"

She nodded. "I heard his voice right before I fell. He was a godsend. Were it not for him, I'm sure David and I would have been imprisoned. He had his men look for Janet for hours, but it was as if she'd vanished."

All his instincts were hammering now. Could it be possible? God, if it were true, it could be just what he needed.

"Do you remember anything about the smell?"

She gave him a puzzled look. "How strange that you should ask. I remember it smelled like rotting eggs."

Damn. It was true. Sir Adam Gordon shared the same knowledge his nephew had. He knew how to make black powder.

Mary knew she had said too much. She was supposed to be guarding her heart, and here she was spilling all her secrets to him. But for such an outwardly hard and imposing man, he was surprisingly easy to talk to. He listened, and actually seemed interested in what she had to say, which was a novelty among men of his station. At least it was in her experience. But she was beginning to realize that her experience wasn't the *only* experience. Kenneth was right; he wasn't Atholl.

But eventually his interest in her—in this game—would wane, and when it did, she wasn't going to let him break her heart.

She was going to have to be careful, very careful. She could see how easy it would be to slip and let herself believe in faerie tales and happy endings.

He had married her, given their child a name, and promised not to do anything reckless that would put them in danger without telling her. It was enough. She would be content with what she had.

And the passion. Aye, he'd given her that. She was going to savor every minute of it, knowing that it wouldn't last.

He was strangely contemplative after she'd told him about her sister. She finished eating the bun, forcing herself not to eat the second, and accepted the wine he offered her from a leather pouch to wash it down.

When she was finished, she handed the pouch back to him and reclined against one of the large stones where he'd set the plaid.

It was still warm, and the sun felt so good on her face, she felt her eyes fluttering.

"You aren't going to fall asleep again, are you?"

She blinked. How had he moved so close without her realizing it? "Are you ready to leave?" Her heart was fluttering so fast, her words came out high-pitched and nervous.

One corner of his mouth curved in a very wicked smile. "Not quite yet."

She thought about scooting away but knew it would be useless. He'd only catch her. And kiss her. And make her dissolve into a mindless bundle of sensation.

She tried to sound unaffected. "What else did you have planned?"

He leaned closer, his mouth achingly close. She could smell the wine on his breath and it was intoxicating. *He* was intoxicating. "Oh, I'm sure we can think of something."

His mouth fell on hers with a groan that tore through her heart. It was only for a moment, but long enough to make her breathless and hungry for more. His mouth slid over her jaw, down her throat, to the bodice of her dress. He started to tug at it, when she stopped him. "We can't. Not here."

"Why not?"

Wasn't it obvious? "It's the middle of the day. Anyone could see."

He grinned. "There isn't anyone around. I won't undress you."

She eyed him skeptically, not trusting him. "I thought you offered to take me on a ride, not seduce me."

A wicked glint appeared in his eye. He lifted her as if she weighed nothing and put her on his lap so that she was facing and straddling him. She gasped, feeling the hard swell of his erection against the intimate juncture between her thighs. "You'll have your ride, Mary."

He lifted her over him and showed her exactly what he

meant. She muttered a protest, but only halfheartedly. She was hot and achy, her body already melting for him.

With a quick fumble of his breeches, he released himself, and then a frantic heartbeat later he surged inside her, impaling her on the long sword full hilt.

She cried out in pleasure. Wave after wave of delicious pleasure, as he showed her how to ride him. How to find the perfect rhythm. How to take him in deep circular strokes. How to take her pleasure.

In the warm afternoon sun, she took her pleasure over and over. She just had to remember that was all she should take.

Nineteen

Mary kept her eyes closed and tried to ignore the slight slam of the door as Kenneth left their chamber. She told herself she had nothing to feel guilty about, but she couldn't quite convince herself of the fact.

The way he'd been making love to her had been so poignant—so sweet—she'd reacted in fear, attempting the whore's trick she'd overheard some women talking about once.

It had worked. Mary knew she should be happy. She'd won. Yet it hadn't felt like a victory. Increasingly, her attempt to keep herself at a distance, to not let an emotional entanglement complicate the passion they shared, felt wrong. No, she corrected—it always felt wrong.

The past weeks had been some of the happiest of her life. She was spending time with her son, enjoying every moment of the baby growing inside her, and experiencing passion that she'd never thought could be hers. But she knew that wasn't all of it. It was her marriage—or, more specifically, her husband. He'd eased some of the burden she hadn't even realized she'd been carrying. With him she felt safe for the first time in a very long time. It didn't seem to matter that the war was coming, that he would be riding off in some not-too-distant future to fight against their countrymen; he made her feel safe and protected.

Slowly but surely, he was chipping away at her defenses. The passion they shared at night had spilled over into the day—and not just because of the romantic gestures like the bath, flowers, sweets, and ribbons. It was hard to stay distant with a man who knew every part of her body, who could make her weep with pleasure, and who slept beside her every night. Even watching him dress in the morning had taken on a new fascination. All these little things that she'd never shared with a man—with anyone—before were drawing them closer. It was so different from her first marriage. She had never shared a bed with Atholl. Never shared a washbasin in the morning. Never helped him with his shirt and surcote. Never jested with him. Never talked with him. She'd never known him. Not in the way she was coming to know Kenneth.

She liked challenging him. Liked the combat of wills that had risen between them. He made her feel bold and strong. Nothing like she'd felt with Atholl; with him she'd been timid and accepting. Kenneth not only listened to her, he seemed interested in what she had to say.

More and more, she could see that her new husband was nothing like her first.

He was funny and smart, wicked and passionate, and the fierce attraction was wearing her down.

She liked him. And it terrified her.

Had she misjudged him?

He'd given her no cause to doubt him. Indeed, he was attentive almost to the point of doting. It was clear he was trying to win her heart, but why? Was it just some kind of game, or was it something more?

Could she dare to hope?

But she knew it was too late to ask that question. Hope had been lit that first night and had been stoked hotter every day since.

She didn't know how much longer she could keep her defenses up. Perhaps . . . perhaps tonight, she wouldn't.

A slow smile curled her mouth. Buoyed by the thought, she tossed off the covers and called for her maid. She had a busy day ahead of her and wanted to make sure she was back in plenty of time to get ready for the massive feast planned for later today.

With tomorrow being Ash Wednesday and the beginning of Lent, this would be the last celebration until Easter. Anticipating the deprivations of the next forty days, the castle inhabitants would be celebrating to great excess. Given Cornwall's lavish taste for entertainment, it felt more like a long celebration than a preparation for war.

Though Kenneth had grumbled, she'd extracted a promise from him to dance with her. She knew it was silly, yet she felt like a young lass at her first dance being picked by the most handsome knight at the feast, and she was looking forward to it.

Dressing quickly, she hastened downstairs to break her fast and nearly ran into her son. He was clutching a sword and muttering to himself, and didn't see her right away.

She clutched his shoulders before he plowed into her. "Davey, where are you going in such a rush?" He glanced up, and she caught a look at the dark expression on his face. "What's wrong?"

He twisted out of her hold, refusing to meet her gaze. "Nothing."

But it was obvious something was wrong. She'd thought he'd seemed preoccupied the past week but had attributed it to his duties. Now, she wondered if it was something more. "Is there something I can do? Does it have to do with your duties? Shall I talk to Sir John?"

He drew back in horror. "God's blood, no! That will make it worse."

"What worse?"

His face twisted with an emotion she couldn't read, except that he was in turmoil. She wanted to reach for him and comfort him, but instinctively she knew that was the last thing he wanted right now.

"I have to go," he said, pulling away even more as if he

sensed her impulse. "I need to get this done." It sounded like he muttered "again," before he hurried out of the Hall.

Mary watched him go with the familiar sense of helplessness rising up inside her. Being the mother of a thirteen-year-old lad was like walking through a thick forest. At night. In the snow. Without a guidepost. Just when she thought she found the path out, another obstacle blocked her path.

She startled, an idea taking hold. Maybe what she needed was another set of eyes.

That was it! Who better to have insight into the mindset of a young lad than someone who'd been there? Perhaps Kenneth would be able to help?

Feeling as if a weight suddenly had been lifted from her shoulders, Mary hurried about her tasks. For more reasons than one, she was looking forward to the night ahead.

Kenneth stormed out of the tower after breaking his fast and headed across the yard to the armory. For a man who had spent the morning being pleasured in the way every man dreams of being pleasured, he was in a foul mood. His body might be well sated from more than three weeks of increasingly passionate lovemaking, but the rest of him was teeming with frustration.

Nothing about this mission was going well. Bruce was furious that he'd married Mary without his permission; Kenneth hadn't been able to offset his anger with any information of value; they were annoyed at him for straying from his task (apparently, someone was watching him and had informed them of his little journey to Roxburgh with Clifford); each day without practice he felt his battle skills withering like a grape in the sun, Felton lost no opportunity to give slight and offense, making MacKay look subtle by comparison; and to top it all off, his wee wife was proving infuriatingly resistant to his attempts to woo her.

He didn't understand it. He—one of the most elite warriors in Scotland only months away from what might be the biggest battle of his life—had been dancing attendance on her for more than two weeks like some lovesick swain from one of the troubadours' songs. The worst part was that he didn't even mind. He *liked* spending time with her. Which was odd, as he could hardly characterize her as uncomplicated and eager to please. Complicated and constantly challenging was more like it.

"Maybe they would hold your attention longer if they had something more interesting to talk about?" Her words came back to him. Well, she sure as hell had his interest.

Women weren't supposed to be this difficult, damn it. But every time he thought he was getting close to breaking through the wall she'd erected around her heart, she countered with a bold, sensual attack guaranteed to make him lose control.

Like this morning. He'd woken to see the sun streaming across her sleeping form and felt an unexpected wave of tenderness strike him. She looked so young and sweet. So peaceful and uncomplicated. Unable to resist, he'd started to make love to her while she was still half asleep. Slow and lazy, he stroked her with his hands, with his mouth, with his tongue. He'd felt her resistance slipping away, damn it. He'd seen it in her eyes. She was falling for him.

But then she turned the tables on him.

She'd kissed his chest before, so at first he didn't realize what she meant to do. It was only when her mouth slid to his stomach that he had the first inkling, and by then it was too late.

His mind shut off and base instinct set in. With her mouth hovering inches from the tip of him, she could have had anything she wanted from him. He didn't think he was the type of man who could be led around by his cock, but she'd proved him wrong.

The feel of her lips brushing him, her tongue darting out to lick him, and then—God help him!—lips wrapping around him and taking him deep into her mouth was more than any hot-blooded man could withstand. He'd been so out of his mind with lust—as no doubt was intended—his slow, tender lovemaking went to hell.

It was obvious that the skill was a new one to her, but she'd taken to the task with such enthusiasm that he had no doubt she'd be a master in no time.

Wonderful.

He should be counting his blessings, damn it. A wife who took to the marriage bed with all the passion of a harlot was every man's dream, wasn't it?

But he didn't want just her passion; he wanted her heart. For his mission, damn it.

God was sure as hell having a good laugh at his expense. The first woman he'd ever set out to woo wanted only one thing from him. And blast it, it grated. *Stud.*

His mouth tightened. It was a good thing he had no intention of letting emotion interfere with his marriage. He wasn't like his sister and brother. He was different.

Except he didn't feel so different right now.

He was so irritated, he barely noticed the other soldiers gathered in the yard readying for practice. But when he caught sight of Felton and David near the door to the armory, his irritation turned to full-fledged anger.

The bastard was berating the lad again.

Though he hid it well around Mary and the others, Felton was taking out his anger at their marriage on the lad. But Kenneth knew it would only be worse if he interfered. Until he was awarded David's wardship—which could take some time—Percy, and through him, Felton, was David's lord and master. Still, he couldn't stand to see the strong prey on the weak. Kenneth already bore the bulk of Felton's ire, but he wanted all of it directed toward him.

With a few more harsh words, Felton stormed off. Shoulders slumped, David slipped dejectedly into the armory.

Kenneth would have gone in after him, but Percy intercepted him. "Ah, Sutherland. 'Tis good to see you in armor again. I'd begun to fear your arm would never heal. Or perhaps you just have a hard time tearing yourself away from your pretty new wife?" He laughed heartily and slapped him on the back. Kenneth tried not to frown, realizing there was more truth in his words than he wanted to admit. He needed to focus on his entire mission, not just turning his wife and her son. "We need you, lad," Percy added, still smiling, "if we're ever to get this campaign moving."

Kenneth showed no reaction, but his senses pricked. "Has a date been set, then?"

Percy hedged. Kenneth knew his former compatriot was beginning to trust him—but only beginning. "More than one. The king was supposed to arrive after Easter, but now there is word he may be delayed." His mouth hardened. "Cornwall is eager to show off his military prowess and has written to Edward asking to let him proceed without him. I have urged the opposite. We need a king to rally the men, not a pretentious peacock."

It appeared that the chasm between Cornwall and the other barons was deepening. Percy could barely hide his disdain for the king's favorite. Kenneth filed the information away for the next time he could manage to get a message to Bruce and the Guard. Division in the ranks was good for the Scots. As long as the English were fighting each other, they would not be able to unite their strength against them. Perhaps they could even find a way to take advantage of it?

"I assume Clifford agrees with you? I haven't seen him around as much of late."

Percy gave him a look that was hard to characterize. It wasn't suspicious, but he'd taken more note of the question than Kenneth would have liked. "There has been trouble with the rebels in Douglasdale again. But he agrees with me, of course."

It was a logical explanation. There was always trouble in Douglasdale. But was that all? "Has the king given an indication of how long he will be delayed?"

"Not long, I hope." Percy slapped him on the back again. "Time enough to get your strength back. I know Felton is looking forward to meeting you on the lists again. I'm afraid my champion has not forgotten the last time you nearly bested him."

Kenneth was anxious to ask him more about Edward's plans, but it was clear Percy was finished with the subject. Was he purposefully avoiding discussing it with him? He didn't know. But the fact that Percy was keeping the battle plans so secret alone suggested that they were up to something. The English didn't typically rely on stealth, but on strength in numbers and weaponry. Perhaps they were taking lessons from Bruce.

"I look forward to the challenge," he lied. Though he would like nothing more than to silence Felton, he knew he couldn't, and the idea of having to lose to the bastard rankled. But he couldn't put it off much longer. Felton had already accused him of delaying his recovery. "But it may take a few weeks yet to get back my strength. The ligament was nearly severed."

"Aye; Welford is surprised by how well the injury has healed."

Not surprising, since it hadn't been the physician's skills that had healed it. "I feel fortunate indeed."

"I will see you on the practice yard?"

Kenneth nodded. "If I can track down my squire. I sent him to sharpen my sword some time ago. I fear it has grown dull with disuse."

Much like his battle skills. Kenneth had been in the peak of physical condition and battle readiness when he'd arrived. He intended to be ready when the time came both

for war and for another chance at MacKay. But how the
hell was he going to do that if he was sluggish from holding back?

Stepping away from Percy, Kenneth started back toward
the armory.

Upon entering, he found his squire speaking to a very
irate young Earl of Atholl. David's voice was raised, and it
was obvious he was complaining about Felton to a sympathetic ear. Despite the circumstances, Kenneth was actually relieved to see some emotion on the lad's face. For his
age, David had an unnaturally blank expression most of
the time, making it difficult to guess his thoughts.

Kenneth's status as hero and rescuer had taken a blow
since the wedding. It was clear young Atholl didn't know
what to make of the sudden marriage, and his behavior
had been watchful and wary.

The two squires fell immediately silent upon seeing him.

Willy jumped up guiltily. "My lord, I was just coming to
find you. I've finished your sword."

Kenneth gave him a look that told him he knew better.
But he'd deal with his squire later. He took the sword from
him—one of the shorter arming swords—and after giving
it a brief inspection, fastened it in a scabbard around his
waist. "Wait for me outside. I should like to speak to David
for a moment."

Willy jumped to do his bidding, shooting a glance of
apology to David on the way. But it wasn't necessary.
Kenneth had no intention of adding to the lad's woes.

When they were alone, Kenneth sat on the bench beside
David that had been recently vacated by his squire. The
wariness had returned to the boy's face as he resumed
sharpening the blade of Felton's sword.

"May I see that?" Kenneth asked.

David frowned, but after a moment handed it to him.
Kenneth held it up to the light streaming through the
wooden slats of the building, inspecting the edge, and then

ran his gauntleted finger over the blade. "'Tis fine work. Though I take it Sir John does not agree?"

David's mouth fell in a belligerent line. He knew better than to speak against his lord.

"I'm afraid this is my fault," Kenneth said.

David shot him a look of surprise. "It is?"

He nodded. "Aye. Sir John hoped to marry your mother. He's angry at me for doing so, and since he can't take it out on me," he lifted his arm, "I'm afraid you are an easy scapegrace."

"I thought he was going to marry my mother, too."

"Are you upset that he didn't?"

The boy eyed him with far too much composure and maturity. It was hard to believe he was only three and ten. He shrugged noncommittally. "It was a surprise, that's all."

He bowed his head and resumed working on the blade. Kenneth debated what to say. David was obviously confused. The lad deserved an explanation. "If I tell you something, will you promise to keep it a secret?"

Puzzled, David nodded.

"We *needed* to marry quickly," he said meaningfully. But it was clear the lad didn't understand. "Your mother is carrying my child."

Shocked, David's hand slipped. He would have sliced his finger had he not been wearing gloves. Once he'd composed himself, he turned to Kenneth. "Why didn't she tell me?"

"I suspect she's embarrassed and was waiting for the right time." Belatedly, Kenneth realized that she might not appreciate him telling her son.

"That's why she's seemed so happy lately," David said, almost to himself. He thought for a minute, appearing to try to sort out his own feelings. "I'm glad for her. My mother has had a difficult time."

Once again, Kenneth was struck by how unnaturally

composed and mature David seemed. Because of his long captivity? "As have you," Kenneth said quietly.

David met his gaze and shrugged.

"You don't have to worry about her anymore, David. I will protect your mother—and you, if you'll let me."

David gave him a look as if he wanted to believe him, but his long-held wariness held him back. Given what the lad had been through, it was understandable. *Like his mother*, Kenneth realized. Mary, too, was wary because of her past. Earning her trust was the key to unlocking her heart. But how the hell was he going to do that when he wasn't telling her the truth about his allegiance and purpose for being here?

The lad stood. "I need to return this to Sir John or he'll have me spending the rest of the day mucking stalls and cleaning garderobes like a serf."

Kenneth chuckled. "There's no shame in hard work, lad. I've had to muck a few stalls and dig in a few cesspits myself."

He might as well have announced he'd grown wings and flown to the moon.

"You have?"

"Aye. Name any unpleasant task, and I assure you I've done it."

David eyed him skeptically. "When you were a squire?"

"Nay, when I was a knight. In war, you do what needs to be done, no matter how unpleasant or menial. I'll let you in on a little secret: I actually find 'menial' labor relaxing."

David laughed as if he knew he must be jesting now. "I'll know who to come to then the next time I'm punished."

Kenneth smiled and watched the boy hustle away. A few minutes later he followed. Reluctantly. David wasn't the only one not looking forward to Felton's punishment. Kenneth knew it was going to take everything he had to keep his temper under control.

* * *

It was late morning by the time Mary finished her transaction with the merchant recommended by Master Bureford in the village. But if she hurried, she should have time for one more errand before returning to the castle.

There was a small church and nunnery nearby, and she couldn't pass by either without inquiring about her sister. She gazed up at the sun, already high in the sky. She bit her lip, knowing that the feast would be underway soon. But this wouldn't take long.

Collecting the two soldiers who'd accompanied her from the place where she'd asked them to wait while she went about her business—not wanting them to see that she wasn't shopping, but selling, she mounted the old horse that she'd borrowed from Sir Adam and informed them of their next destination. Assuming that she meant to pray or give a donation, the men didn't protest the change in the instructions given to them by Sir Adam to see her to the market and back. Though the horse was docile and it was still safe for her to ride, she had to admit she wouldn't have minded Kenneth's protective arms around her.

Mary felt a stab of guilt at not telling Kenneth where she was going. But she knew he would question her, and she didn't want to lie to him. She would not be caught in the position of helplessness and dependency that she was in before. The money she earned from her embroidery work was her protection against that. It belonged to her, no matter that the law would see it otherwise. She had nothing to feel guilty about.

Yet she did. And not just about hiding the money from him, but also for this morning. I'll make it up to him, she vowed, but still couldn't completely assuage the niggle of disquiet.

The small church and nunnery were located just on a hill above the bustling Berwick-upon-Tweed market. It took only a few minutes to reach the gate. Walls protected most of the churches in Berwick and other border towns, not that they seemed very efficient in keeping out raiders.

Leaving the soldiers with the horses, she approached the church first, and then when her inquiries proved fruitless, the nunnery.

"I'm sorry, my lady," the abbess said. "I was here three years ago, and I don't recall a woman as you describe seeking refuge." She studied Mary a little closer. "You say she was your twin?"

Mary nodded. "We look very much alike." Even more so now that Mary no longer looked like a "half-starved sparrow." She glanced down at the gown she wore. For her journey into the city, she'd donned one of her old veils and gowns. She was surprised how much she disliked doing so. She'd grown used to pretty things again. But it had seemed wiser not to draw attention to herself at the market. Her mouth quirked. "Although she would have been far more colorfully dressed than I am. With long golden hair—"

The nun shook her head. "I'm sorry, my lady. She was not here."

Mary tried to smile. But no matter how many times she asked, she couldn't hide her disappointment. "Thank you." She handed her a coin. "Please, take this, and remember her in your prayers tonight."

The woman nodded but seemed to avoid meeting her gaze. Mary was almost out the door when the nun called after her. "I hope you find her, my lady. Someday."

Mary smiled for real this time, tears glistening in her eyes. "So do I."

Lost in thought, she wasn't watching where she was going and nearly collided with a monk outside. He dropped a book he'd been holding—obviously, he hadn't been looking either—and bent down to pick it up. "I'm sorry, sister—" He startled when he saw her face. Mary saw the flicker of recognition before he smiled. "You're back!"

A buzz ran up her spine and spread over her skin. Her

entire body froze with excitement. "Do you know me, brother?"

He looked surprised again, taking in the details of her face and clothing that he hadn't before. "You aren't a nun."

"But have you seen me before?"

His expression grew troubled. "I thought so, but now I can see that I made a mistake. You look a great deal like a young nun who traveled through here before."

Mary felt every nerve ending in her body flare with excitement. This was it. This was the break she'd been waiting for. She tried to control the frantic pounding of her heart, but it was blaring in her ears. "When?" she breathed.

He stroked his chin. "About a year ago, I think."

"What do you know about her? Whom was she with?"

Without realizing it, Mary had grabbed onto the monk's arm. He was looking at her as if she were a madwoman. "No one, my lady. She stopped for the night to take a meal, that is all."

"Where was she going?"

Obviously wishing he hadn't said anything, the young churchman carefully extracted his arm. "I don't know, my lady. Do you know her?"

"I think she is my sister. She's been missing for over three years."

His eyes filled with sympathy, and something else. Pity, she realized.

"I'm sorry, my lady. It couldn't have been your sister. The young woman I spoke of was Italian."

Mary felt her heart sink. "Are you certain?"

He nodded. "She didn't speak a word of English and very little French."

The disappointment was even more crushing than before. Despite the monk's certainty, Mary wondered if maybe he was mistaken. But why would her sister be pretending to be Italian? Janet had been horrible with languages.

Mary apologized to the monk for her zealous questioning and quickly took her leave. But she could think of nothing else on the ride back to the castle.

It was later than she'd realized by time she passed through the gates. The feast had already been going on for nearly an hour by the time she'd changed and started toward the Great Hall.

She'd half hoped Kenneth would be waiting for her. Not only was she eager to speak to him about Davey, she also wanted to get his impression about what had occurred at the church. Usually she would have gone straight to Sir Adam, but her first instinct was to find Kenneth.

She had to apologize for what had happened this morning. A blush stained her cheeks. Well, maybe an apology wasn't necessary in light of how much he'd enjoyed it, but she knew things could not go on as they had been. She wanted to give him—them—a chance.

The Hall was a flurry of sound and color as she entered. Obviously, the ale and wine had been flowing freely for some time. People were swarming about the room. She stood on her tiptoes, trying to see where Kenneth was seated but was unable to see over all the heads.

Finally, after fighting her way through the crowd near the door she saw him. The smile that had become reflexive in such a short time rose and then fell. The blood drained from her face, as everything inside her body seemed to curl inwardly. Her heart. Her stomach. Her hope.

The sear of white-hot pain across her chest was nearly unimaginable.

He was surrounded by women and basking in the glow of their adoring light, like some Greek god at a temple. The women on either side of him were leaning so close their bodies were pressing against his. He wasn't doing anything to encourage them. Yet. But it was only a matter of time. He'd made her no promises. The picture before her was brutally familiar and a reminder that she could not forget that. No matter how much she wanted to. If she'd wanted her eyes opened, they were now.

Oh God. I can't do this again.

"Are you all right, my lady?"

In a daze, Mary turned, seeing that Sir John had come up beside her. "You look quite pale."

"I'm not feeling too well. I-I think I shall return to my room."

She could see the concern in his face. "I will escort you."

Mary nodded, too numb to object.

Twenty

It had been bad enough to learn that his wife had left the castle without telling him and sought out Sir Adam's assistance rather than his for her errand. Kenneth was irritated, and yes, maybe even a little jealous. But it was nothing compared to the dangerous emotion that surged through him when he heard who'd escorted her back to her room.

"Felton? You are sure?"

Lady Eleanor gazed up at him in surprise. "Yes, perhaps an hour ago. I thought that you knew."

He'd been trying to have a good time. Trying to bury his irritation with his wife in the celebratory atmosphere around him. But as the hours dragged on, and she still had not appeared, irritation had turned to worry, and finally he'd sought out one of her attendants.

Kenneth tried to hide his reaction, but he suspected he wasn't all that successful. "I did not."

"She was standing right there." Lady Eleanor pointed to a place a few tables away. "It was fortunate Sir John was there, my lord. I thought she was going to faint for a minute. She did not look well."

Kenneth felt his stomach drop. Dear God, was it the babe?

Sensing his reaction, Lady Eleanor hastened to explain. "I'm sure it's nothing for you to worry about. A stomach upset, Sir John said. That is all."

But Kenneth wasn't listening; he was already making his way from the Hall.

Had something happened? His mind raced with all the mishaps that could occur to a woman with child. Damn it, why hadn't she told him? He would never have let her go to town on her own.

By the time he reached the tower chamber, he was nearly out of his mind with an emotion he didn't recognize. Panic? Fear? The way his heart was racing, it could very well be both.

He threw open the door, "Are you all ri—"

He stopped, seeing her standing by the window, her figure backlit by the setting sun. She turned as he entered, her face a mask of serene composure. Serenity and composure that made his own panic and fear fall flat on the floor.

He didn't need to finish his question. It was clear that his distress had been for naught; she was perfectly fine.

"You are back early."

There was something in her voice—a hint of sarcasm— that didn't sit well with him.

"And you are not. What were you thinking to leave the castle without telling me?"

She arched a delicate brow. "I did not realize I needed your permission."

The cold challenge in her eyes was back. But he was too angry himself to heed the warning. "Well, you do. You will not leave this castle again—you will not go anywhere— without telling me." He crossed the room in a few strides. Wanting to ruffle that composure of hers, he took her arm and brought her up to him. "Do you hear me, Mary?"

But she would not be rattled. None of his heat could melt the ice that seemed to have formed a shell around her. "I hear you perfectly well, since you are shouting in my ear."

Her very calmness infuriated him. It was everything he was not. He wanted to make her as angry as he was. It was nearly inconceivable that he could be this passionate about a woman and she could be so . . . not. "And stay away from Felton. Need I remind you that you are a married woman?"

Her eyes snapped to his, the first crack in her composure. "And you are a married man. But we all know how little that means to you."

"What are you talking about? I've done nothing—"

"I saw you at the feast. It must have been interesting—whatever you were talking about—you had quite an audience and seemed enthralled."

He'd been worried about her, but hell if he'd tell her that. Not when she thought him so . . . shallow. But he felt a surprising twinge of guilt. His pride had been stinging. He hadn't gone to the feast with the intention of seeking out more appreciative company, but he hadn't exactly pushed the women away, either. It was effortless. *They* were effortless.

And she wasn't.

It had been a mistake. He could see that now. He knew how sensitive she was about Atholl, but damn it, she had unrealistic expectations. What man in his right mind would want to bind himself to one woman for life?

He thought of MacLeod. MacSorley. Campbell. MacKay. His brother. Hell, even Lachlan MacRuairi. All men he respected and were sure as hell in their right mind.

But he wasn't like them. He didn't confuse duty with emotion. She was just his wife, damn it.

It had to be anger making his chest feel so damned tight.

But any apology he might have made was silenced by her next words. "Is the game over, my lord? Is that it? Have you grown weary of playing the doting husband? Or perhaps I am not adoring enough or whispering enough platitudes in your ear?"

His mouth thinned. "Not all women are as hard to impress as you, my lady."

"I think you confuse flattery with respect."

He stiffened. It was clear he didn't have hers. Why the hell did it bother him? He shouldn't care. "I thought you didn't care what I do."

She stiffened, pulling her arm away as if his touch scalded. "I don't."

Heat was pounding through his bones. "Then stop acting as if you want more."

She lifted her chin. "I wasn't aware I had a choice."

He heard her challenge but was too angry to take it up—or make promises he wasn't sure he could keep. All he could do was stare at her, seething, his jaw clenching as tightly as his fist. "What the hell *do* you want, Mary?"

Their eyes held. He felt something tighten, almost as if a winch was drawing them together. He thought she felt it too, but then she looked stiffly away. "Nothing more than you promised," she said. "Of course, your 'duties' will not be required for some time."

His eyes narrowed. "What are you talking about? I warned you I would not be kept from my wife's bed."

"Have you forgotten? Tomorrow is Ash Wednesday and the beginning of Lent. It is a sin to copulate during Lent."

Kenneth saw red. He knew what she was doing. He knew it wasn't piety but merely an excuse to keep him from her bed. Hell, the church considered it a sin to enjoy pleasure or passion in the marital bed at all!

But he was too damned angry to care. If that was the way she wanted it, he would do this her way. God knows, he hadn't been able to win her heart in her bed; perhaps it would grow fonder in his absence.

But he wasn't going to let her win without a fight. Not without leaving her something to think about. He would give her *exactly* what she wanted, damn it. If she thought he was nothing more than a stud for hire, that was exactly what she would get. "As you wish."

He took her in his arms and flipped her around, pushing her gently against the wall.

"What are you d-doing? I thought you said—"

He buried his face in her hair and neck, ravishing the soft skin with all the fury of the emotions surging through his blood. "It isn't Lent yet."

Mary saw the anger flashing in his eyes and knew she'd pushed her hot-tempered husband too far. She should have known better than to try to provoke him, but she'd half hoped—perhaps more than half—that he might give her the answer she wanted to hear. That he might make promises she had no right to expect from him.

Would she ever learn?

Heat washed over her as he took her in his arms, molding her back to his chest and hips. His mouth and jaw tore across the soft skin of her neck. The pain and hurt that had been simmering so close to the surface erupted into a different emotion. Into lust, need, and a desperate attempt to hold on to him.

He was kissing her with a punishing hunger and a frenzy he'd never shown before, and she responded with a desperation of her own. She melted against him in complete surrender, letting him take whatever he wanted. He was gripping her breasts, cupping and squeezing as his mouth devoured every sensitive inch of her neck and shoulder.

Carefully, he planted her hands on the wall in front of her. "This is what you want, isn't it?"

There was an edge to his voice she'd never heard before. But she was so hot, her skin on fire. He tipped her hips back to meet the bulge of his erection, moving it against her suggestively.

Images of the stable returned.

She knew what he was going to do. And for a moment,

she thought about stopping him. But whether it was shock or lust, she was powerless to escape the sensual web he'd spun around them both.

She moaned, pressing her hips back against him and arching her back to give him even more access to her neck.

He groaned and swore, one hand caressing her breast as the other fumbled with his breeches. She could feel the cold air hitting her legs and backside as he tossed up her skirts.

She was already wet when his fingers slipped inside her. "Should I give it to you, Mary?" That edge to his voice should have alerted her, but she was too lost in the haze of lust to exercise caution.

He nudged the blunt head of his erection between her legs, teasing her with long strokes over her dampness. He was so big and thick between her thighs, the wicked sensations he was arousing drove her to the very peak of need.

She could hear her own frantic moans in her ears, feel her body begging him to ease the restlessness he'd built inside her.

He held her hips, positioning himself at her entry. "You want to come, don't you?"

The crude words made her shiver, touching the dark, wanton part of her that responded to the wickedness. Not with revulsion but with desire. This was wrong. She knew it was wrong. But she was too far gone. He'd stoked the fires too hot. And there was something about this fierce, aggressive side of him that made her feel reckless. That tricked her emotions, making her think that this mattered. That if he was this out of control he must care.

She could feel the hot, steely flesh against her, the thick club nudging at her entry. Her legs were shaking, her body throbbing with need. She rocked back against him, wanting him inside her so badly she could weep.

He circled himself against her, and she rocked her hips back to meet him.

But he wouldn't give her what she wanted. He was teasing her. Dragging it out. Forcing her to face the depths of her desire for him.

"Tell me," he whispered in her ear.

"Yes!" she cried. "Please, yes."

He held her hips steady and drove inside, possessing her in one hard stroke that shook her to her core. He slid her hips back against him, leaning her against the wall until she was at the perfect angle, and then he thrust again, sinking into her even deeper.

He held her there until she moaned. Until she thought her body would come apart just from the sheer force of him inside her. He filled her completely. Deeply. And then he sent her flying. Pounding into her with long, deep strokes that were every bit as frantic and hard as the cries of pleasure he tore from her.

It was rough. It was frenzied. It was lust in its most raw and primitive form. Her body was still spasming when she heard the hard grunt of his own pleasure a moment before a rush of heat pulsed through her.

But like a violent storm, when it was over, there was only destruction in its desolate wake. The room was painfully quiet. He pulled out of her and a blast of cold swept over her exposed skin. She was still bent over and supporting herself on the wall; otherwise she would have stumbled.

She stood, immediately grasping the front of her dress, which she'd just realized had been ripped apart at the bodice. Her skirts dropped back over her bare bottom, but the damp chill between her legs was a brutal reminder of what had just happened.

Shame washed over her. How could she have let him do that to her? And worse, how could she have liked it?

She wobbled, and he reached out to catch hold of her arm. "Jesus, Mary, I'm—"

"Thank you," she said, forcing her eyes to his, when all she wanted to do was collapse in a ball and cry. *Protect yourself.* "That was exactly what I wanted. The woman in the barn was right. You are every bit as good as they say."

She thought he flinched. But perhaps it was only the flicker of firelight. His eyes burned into hers with something raw. Something that made her throat hurt and chest burn.

She wanted to take the words back, but it was too late. He turned on his heel and left, the door slamming definitively behind him.

He never looked back.

If he had, he would have seen her slide to the floor in a pool of horror and despair. If he had, he might have guessed the truth. He'd given her exactly what she wanted—lust without a hint of tenderness—but it wasn't what she wanted at all.

What have I done?

Kenneth stayed away for as long as he could. He volunteered for anything and everything that would take him from the castle. Scouting missions, escort duties—hell, even helping to repair a wall at a nearby castle that had been damaged in an attack by Bruce's raiders.

But if he thought that absenting himself from the castle would take an edge off the dangerous emotions clamoring inside him, he was wrong. No mission, no task, no amount of physical labor could make him forget what had happened. Nothing could penetrate the black rage that hovered around him like a dark, forbidding cloud. He was a man on the edge, and he knew it.

He'd lost his temper. He'd wanted to force her to acknowledge there was something between them, but all he'd succeeded in doing was proving her right.

Maybe MacKay was right. Maybe he wasn't cut out for this. How much longer before he did something rash? The mission that he'd hoped would establish his place in the Guard wasn't turning out as he'd planned. He wasn't impressing anyone. Sticking close to Percy had yielded little information of value, he hadn't been able to confirm the castles the English would use on their campaign, his hopes of turning his wife and her son voluntarily to Bruce were dwindling, he hadn't lifted a weapon in combat in weeks, and the steely control he'd fought so hard for was deserting him.

Sangfroid! Hell, he'd settle for anything below boiling right now.

It wasn't until a week had passed that he trusted himself to return. It turned out a week was not long enough.

He'd barely had a chance to wash the dust and grime from him when he walked across the yard from the seagate (a cold swim in the River Tweed had seemed preferable to a warm bath in his chamber) and saw something that set off every instinct in his body to fight—and he had a hell of a lot of them.

Felton was in the yard practicing with some of his men. "Again!" he shouted.

Percy's champion knight appeared to be demonstrating some swordsmanship techniques, but the unfortunate target of this lesson was David Strathbogie.

The young Earl of Atholl was on his knees, apparently having been knocked down. From the amount of dirt on the lad's armor and the difficulty he seemed to be having in dragging himself to his feet, it probably hadn't been the first time.

Perhaps it was because Kenneth had been the one to drag himself out of the dirt more times than he wanted to remember, but seeing Felton humiliate the lad struck every raw nerve, going against every ingrained sense of fairness in his body.

David managed to get himself upright, but Felton came at him again, shouting orders at him to get his sword up, to defend himself like a man, before knocking him back down with a complicated and highly skilled set of swings of his sword. Moves that no green squire could hope to defend against.

Kenneth's blood boiled. He clenched his fists again and again at his sides. This was a lesson all right. A lesson in humiliation. Felton was purposefully making the lad look bad in front of the other men.

"Get up and fight," Felton said, with a nudge of his sword in the boy's side. "We aren't finished."

Red swam before his eyes. Kenneth could almost taste the lad's humiliation and feel the sharp sting of his young pride. Before he could stop himself, he pulled his sword from his scabbard—in a moment of sanity using his left hand, as he was still claiming his injury prevented him from fighting full force—and strode forward, bursting through the circle of men. All he could see was Felton's sword, pointed at the lad. With one sharp flick of his blade, Kenneth sent the knight's sword sailing from his hand.

The shattering clash of metal seemed to echo through the shocked silence.

Beneath the steel helm, Kenneth saw Felton's face explode in anger. "What the hell do you think you are doing?"

"A sword is not a toy. I was merely showing the lads that you should not hold it as such. You might remind yourself of that when you go pick it up."

"How dare you interfere—"

"Perhaps your men might like to see you practice your techniques on someone your own size."

Felton didn't miss the slur and his face burned hotter than before. One of his men had retrieved his sword and stepped forward to hand it to him.

Felton's eyes gleamed with anticipation as he took it. "I thought your arm was still healing?"

"It is. I will use my left." He wasn't as good with the left, but he'd be good enough. He was going to humiliate the bastard. Pay him back for everything he'd done to the lad tenfold. And he was going to enjoy every bloody minute of it.

"Wait!"

Kenneth turned at the sound of the familiar voice. Looking over his shoulder, he saw Mary rushing toward them. Something lurched in his chest, but he refused to acknowledge it. She wore a hooded cloak that swallowed her up in its heavy folds, as much to hide her pregnancy, he suspected, as for the cool weather.

"There you are," she said breathlessly. "I've been waiting for you."

Her words might have had a different effect on him if he didn't see the worry behind the overly bright smile.

His jaw clenched, guessing what this was about. Her next words confirmed it.

She feigned as if she had just become aware of the crowd around them. Her eyes widened, and a delicate blush rose to her cheeks. "I'm sorry, did I interrupt something?"

She knew perfectly well what she'd interrupted. She'd done it on purpose. She didn't want him to fight Felton because she thought he would lose.

Suddenly, she noticed David, still on the ground covered in dirt. Kenneth anticipated her instinctive move forward, and before she could embarrass the lad further by showering him with motherly distress, he caught her by the arm to stop her. He shot her a warning glance. "Nothing that can't be resumed later. Was there something you needed?"

She glanced over at David again. She may have picked up on his warning, but it was clear she didn't want to heed it. "Uh, yes." She forced her gaze from her son and turned a beaming smile to Felton. "I hope you don't mind, Sir John. But there is a matter with one of my dower estates that needs to be attended to as soon as possible."

Felton gave her a gallant bow. "Of course, my lady." But it was clear from the taunting look that he directed toward

Kenneth that he, too, had guessed the cause for the interruption. They both knew that his wife thought Felton the better knight. "I can finish this anytime."

Kenneth gritted his teeth at the boast, fighting a fresh surge of heat through his blood. He didn't need to prove anything to anyone, but he wanted to, damn it. His muscles clenched.

"Kenneth," Mary said, putting her hand on his arm.

The soft entreaty broke through the haze. No matter how tempting, he couldn't do this. The personal satisfaction he would get in besting Felton wasn't worth the risk. His wife was right—albeit for the wrong reasons—but antagonizing Felton wasn't wise. It had been a mistake to make an enemy of Felton, and she'd saved him from making an even bigger one. Kenneth would have humiliated the other knight, and Felton would have made it his sole purpose to discredit him. Felton was already watching him too closely. But although Kenneth might appreciate her interruption later, right now it stung. He never wanted to be second best in her eyes.

With a look that told Felton this wasn't over, Kenneth led his wife away from the fray.

They walked in silence back to the tower chamber that they'd shared since their wedding. Once in the room, she untied her cloak and tossed it on the trunk before the bed. He could tell that she was nervous by the way her hands shook and how she fluttered around the room for a few minutes rather than meet his gaze.

He stood stone-still by the door, waiting.

She filled a goblet of wine from the pitcher at the side table. "Would you like some?"

"No."

She turned to the side, and he could just make out the soft swell of her stomach beneath the wool folds of her gown. She'd changed in only a week. She wouldn't be able to hide the pregnancy for much longer beneath heavy gowns and cloaks. He should send her away . . .

He cleared his throat. "The babe . . . You are well?"

She glanced up at him, surprised. "I'm fine."

There was another uncomfortable silence, in sharp contrast to how it had been between them before. The walls of the small chamber seemed to be closing in on him. She was too close. He wanted to touch her. He wanted to hold her. He wanted to take her in his arms and make love to her until she admitted that she cared for him.

He had to get out of here. "I believe you mentioned an estate matter."

She flushed, biting her lip. "There isn't an estate matter. I was on my way to the Hall when I saw you and Sir John. The way he was looking at you . . . " She shivered. "Whatever is between you, I wish you would put it aside."

He gave her a long look. "That isn't possible."

She was what was between them. But she didn't see it. "Why not?" Her face fell. "Sweet mercy, I thought he was going to kill you."

"You should have more faith in me."

She frowned, picking up on something in his voice. "I do, but . . . " She looked away. "Your arm is still injured."

But. They both knew it wasn't just his arm. He stiffened. "You've nothing to worry about. I have no intention of locking swords with Felton."

She looked at him quizzically. "You don't?"

He forced a smile to his face that he didn't feel. "I'll not make you a widow so easily."

She frowned. "That isn't what I meant."

"Isn't it?" He shrugged as if it didn't matter to him, although it did. Very much. He was surprised how much he wanted her to believe in him. He didn't know when it had become important, but it had. Damn it, he thought he was done with this. He'd been proving himself his whole life; he'd just never thought he'd have to do so with his own wife.

"Did your argument have something to do with Davey? I've wanted to speak with you, I've been worried—"

"Leave the boy alone, Mary. He needs to work this out himself."

Her eyes widened in alarm. "Work what out? I knew something was wrong. He's been so quiet lately. Even more quiet than normal. Is it Sir John? One of the other boys? You must tell me if you know something."

She was fierce in her defense of her son, if only she could feel the same intensity of emotion about him. She would be a good mother to their child, but mothering wasn't what Davey needed from her. Not now at least. "He's too old for coddling, Mary."

Her eyes shimmered with dampness. "I know that."

"He will need you again. Just give him time."

He turned to leave.

"Wait, where are you going? Are you leaving again?"

"I'm afraid not. Percy is waiting for my report." He held her gaze. "Was there something more you needed?"

She flushed and looked away. "No."

He held her gaze. What had he thought? "I may be back late. Don't wait up for me."

"Oh," she said, a strange look on her face. Disappointment? He didn't know. He was too full of his own emotions to try to decipher hers.

As Kenneth escaped from the room that was beginning to feel like a torture chamber to him, he knew he was going to have to do something. He wasn't going to last another four days, let alone the thirty-three that remained of Lent, if he didn't find a way to rid himself of the frustration teeming inside him.

Twenty-one

Mary had made a mistake, and she knew it. The stiff, awkward conversation a week after her husband had taken her against the wall in an explosion of lust—and nothing else—had been a precursor of what was to come.

In the nearly forty days since she'd sent him from her bed, there had been no more ribbons, flowers, or buns, no more rides, and no more long conversations. She arranged her own bath, she couldn't think of an excuse for riding, and their conversations were brief and impersonal.

It was as if she were married to Atholl all over again. The only difference was that Kenneth collapsed beside her at night when he finally returned from whatever it was that kept him away from the castle so late, reeking of whisky and damp from a dunking in the river.

Her heart stabbed. At least he had the decency to wash the scent of his liaisons from him before coming to her bed. But she couldn't be grateful for his discretion, when the very idea of him with another woman made the misery she'd felt with Atholl seem like a pittance in comparison.

Despite her best efforts to approach this marriage with open eyes and a hardened heart, she'd failed. Miserably. She'd fallen in love with her husband. Not the starry-eyed young girl's infatuation based on a myth, but the mature love of a woman who appreciated the flawed man as much as she admired the hero.

She loved the young boy who'd always had to fight to

prove himself and had the confidence and belief in himself to become the best. She loved knowing that beneath the seemingly impervious shell of the fierce warrior was a man of surprising depth and—yes, Sir Adam was right—sensitivity. She loved his passion. Envied it. Was drawn to it. Even when he lost his temper. She loved going toe-to-toe with him—challenging him. He brought out her fight and made her feel bolder and stronger than she ever had before. He'd never treated her as an afterthought or as chattel, but as an equal. He listened to her. Cared about her thoughts.

Ironically, by trying to protect herself from having another marriage like her first, she'd all but ensured the second turned out the same way. She'd sent him from her bed; why was she surprised that he'd found another?

She regretted so many things. She'd been a fool to think it had only been passion. The hollowness in her heart when he'd left her that night told her that. She shouldn't have let her pride and jealousy prevent him from telling him she cared. And she shouldn't have interfered in his argument with Sir John. Although Davey refused to discuss what had happened, she suspected Kenneth had been protecting her son.

He was also right to urge her patience. Her son wasn't used to having a mother around to love him. It was no wonder that Davey was uncomfortable and defensive. Knocking down those barriers would take time—especially when his attention was focused on trying to become a knight. She needed to think of him as the man he would become, not the boy she never had a chance to know.

But it was more than that.

"You should have more faith in me." He was right. She'd seen him fight. She knew what he could do; it was just that he wasn't fully healed. But his admonition was about more than his fighting skills. Yet how could she believe in him when he wouldn't make her any promises?

Of course, she'd never asked him for any. She'd just tried to accept what she *thought* was her fate. She'd tried to make do with what life had doled out, the way she always did.

But that wasn't good enough. Not this time. She wasn't content to be grateful for what she had. She wanted more. She wanted his heart.

But how was she going to breach the seemingly impenetrable wall that had been erected between them?

Every time she inquired about his day or activities, he cut her off. Even her attempt to tend the wound on his jaw he'd received in a tavern brawl the week before was refused. Though he'd yet to resume full activity in the practice yard, he had suffered an inordinate number of scrapes and bruises lately. But every time she expressed concern, he bristled as if she were questioning his skill, so she'd stopped mentioning it.

Lent was nearly over, but she dared not wait for him to return to her bed. What if he did, and it was merely a repeat of the last time? Or worse, what if he didn't return at all?

The answer of what to do came to her a few days before Easter when a missive arrived for her from Brother Thomas, the monk who had confused her with the Italian nun. She'd considered enlisting her husband's help or Sir Adam's in her search for more information about the nun, but as Kenneth wouldn't give her the opportunity and Sir Adam had returned to Huntlywood Castle in preparation for his journey to France, she'd sent one of the stable lads with a sizable donation to the church for Easter, and a note asking him to send for her should he hear any more about the nun who looked so much like her.

To her shock and barely contained excitement, the castle priest found her after the midday meal and passed on a message from Brother Thomas that the nun in question had returned.

She raced back to the Hall, hoping to find her husband still lingering with his men. She'd been wanting to ask him for help with her sister and now she had a chance. Surely, he would accompany her?

She found his squire, Willy, and to her surprise learned that Kenneth had returned to their chamber. She hastened across the courtyard and up the stairs.

But once she pushed open the door, the excitement fell from her face. He'd changed from the fine surcote he'd worn to the evening meal into a worn dark leather *cotun* and chausses. Despair shot through her like a flame, scorching the insides of her chest and throat. She knew what those clothes meant.

"You're leaving?"

He stiffened, as if bracing himself for something unpleasant. "Aye, I have business in town."

"At another tavern?"

Perhaps he heard the unspoken accusation in her tone. One corner of his mouth curled. "I thought you didn't care."

She swallowed, burying her pride and taking, if not a leap, at least the first step. "What if I do?" she said softly, her heart drumming in her throat. Their eyes locked, and for a moment she thought he wanted to say something, but then he turned away. He didn't want her to care.

"I may be back late."

He was back late every night. She swallowed again, the second attempt to break through even harder than the first. Her pride and her heart were raw and ragged. It was like the time she'd asked Atholl to take her and their son with him. "May I come with you? There is something I need to do in town. I've had some exciting news, and I would be grateful for your help."

"I'm afraid it will have to wait."

"It can't—"

"Not today, Mary."

She flinched at his curt tone. Maybe it was too late.

Maybe he'd lost interest in her. Maybe it really had only been a game.

"All right." She tried to hide her disappointment, but she feared she looked just as wounded as she sounded.

"It's not like that." He took a step toward her before he stopped himself. "Ah hell." He muttered another oath, dragging his fingers through his hair. "There is a lot happening right now. I have many things on my mind."

Things he wasn't going to talk to her about. "I understand," she said, even though she didn't. "You are busy preparing for war." And women.

"Aye."

But that wasn't all of it. She was sure of it. Something was bothering him. What was he keeping from her?

"Edward will be coming north soon. I've spoken with Sir Adam, and I think it is time."

"Time?" she echoed.

"For you to leave the castle."

Mary froze, her senses struck numb. "You are sending me away?" Her voice sounded as ragged and dry as it felt.

He wouldn't meet her stricken gaze. "The child," he said. "You won't be able to hide the babe much longer. There will be less talk this way."

She didn't say anything. Tears were burning at the back of her throat, and she feared they would escape if she opened her mouth. He was right—her attendants had guessed her secret weeks ago—but she knew it was also an excuse.

"This was always the plan, Mary." She met his gaze. "I'm trying to protect you."

"When?" she said dully.

"After the Easter celebration. It won't be for long, and you will be only a few miles away. Sir Adam has given us the use of Huntlywood Castle while he is in France. You can bring your attendants. It has all been arranged."

But no matter what he said, they both knew he was sending her away.

"How considerate of you both. Did you even contemplate taking my wishes into consideration?"

Why should he? She was his to do with as he pleased.

He didn't answer, but moved to the door. "I know you don't understand right now, but it will be for the best."

The best? Mary no longer knew what that was. But that didn't mean she didn't want a chance to decide for herself. "How thoughtful of you to decide that for me."

If he heard her sarcasm, she didn't know. She wasn't looking at him. She thought he hesitated as he passed her on the way to the door, but whatever he felt, it wasn't enough to stop him.

Not long after he left, Mary donned her cloak and headed for the stables. Her heart might be breaking, lying in pieces and stomped on, but she wasn't going to allow the first possible lead on her sister slip by.

She'd planned to arrange for a few of Percy's men to accompany her, but Sir John happened to see her as she was leaving and insisted on escorting her into town himself. Perhaps because she knew how much it would anger her husband, she didn't try to dissuade him.

She quickly regretted the moment of pique. By his manner, Sir John made it clear that he did not see her marriage as an impediment to his courtship. He implied a number of times—too many for her to be mistaken—that if something were to happen to Kenneth or if things "did not proceed as she expected," he would be there for her. *And* her son. Needless to say, her pregnancy had little to do with the uncomfortable ride.

Then, when they arrived at the church and she learned that neither the monk nor the nun could be found—indeed, the abbess told her they'd had no visitors the past few days other than the Bishop of St. Andrews and that the monk must have been mistaken—her disappointment had been such that she would have welcomed the quiet and peace of her own thoughts.

Darkness had fallen while she was in the church, and as they rode down the hill into town Mary started to pay more attention to their surroundings. She'd never been in town this late at night, and there was an unsavory element that seemed to have replaced the merchants and tradesmen of the day.

Sir John must have sensed her unease. "You have nothing to fear. You are safe with me. No one would dare attack the king's men."

Mary wasn't so sure. Many of the rough-looking men they passed looked as if they would dare quite a lot. But she was somewhat relieved to see a number of women in the crowd as well.

The crowds were getting thicker on the high street. It was almost as if something big were about to happen. A performance, perhaps? Some kind of festivity?

Her suspicions were confirmed when she heard a large cry go up, the roar of a crowd exploding in applause. "What is that?" she asked.

Sir John's eyes narrowed as he held his hand up for his men to stop. He scanned the row of tall buildings and narrow wynds. It wasn't hard to see where the noise was coming from. There was a large pool of light shining from down one of the wynds. "I don't know, but we are going to find out." He held his hand out. When she hesitated, he added, "This won't take long."

Somewhat curious and bolstered by the presence of Felton's half-dozen armed and mailed men-at-arms, Mary allowed herself to be helped down, careful to protect her stomach to keep anyone from learning her secret. As with her first child, Mary had put on a relatively small amount of weight. In her heavy gowns, she looked more plump than pregnant. Although with the child due in less than two month's time, she was much more uncomfortable of late and easily tired.

Another cry went up as they entered the wynd. It was dark between the two buildings, but there was enough light coming from ahead of them to enable them to see.

As they drew near, she could see Sir John's mouth harden.

"What is it? Is something wrong?"

He shook his head. "It's as I expected."

It didn't take her long to figure out what he meant. By the time they reached the source of the light, everything was perfectly clear. The narrow wynd opened up before them into the space of a small square courtyard. A building had once stood there, she realized, and in the bowels of that building two men were fighting.

Like a circle of fire, torches had been hung on the structures around the makeshift pit, casting the entire area in blazing light. The crowd was dispersed around the pit on a haphazard mix of old walls, stones, and planks of wood set out like stands. People were also watching from the tops and windows of the adjoining buildings.

"A clandestine tourney?" she asked.

Sir John nodded. "The king will be very pleased to hear what we've discovered. He's been trying to put an end to all the unsanctioned combat tourneys in the Borders—if you can call the crude brawling of common ruffians a tourney."

She'd heard of the illegal brawls before but had never seen one. They were essentially a melee of two. A no-holds-barred, no-rules fight that was supposed to end when one person uttered "craven," but often ended in death.

The crowd was chanting something. It sounded like "ice." Curious, she edged forward a few feet, trying to get a better look at the contestants.

She gasped in horror. Both men were helmed but stripped

to the chest, wearing only their braies and chausses. Sweat and blood stained their broad, muscled chests as they attacked each other with a ferocity she'd never witnessed before. There was nothing elegant, nothing noble. It was a contest of raw strength and brutality. Each man wielded one crude weapon in addition to his fists. The taller and more leanly muscled of the two had a crude-looking hammer; the heavier-set man, with a neck as thick as his head, held a stave with a mace. Unlike in regular tournaments, the weapons were not blunted.

The sight of such brutality alone would have made her knees go weak. But that wasn't what made her stomach lurch to the ground and her legs turn to jelly. Despite the steel helms they wore to mask their identities, Mary instantly recognized the taller of the two men as her husband. She would know those arms and chest anywhere.

Any relief she might have felt from discovering that he wasn't in some tawdry tavern with a woman was overwhelmed by the more immediate concern of the danger he was in both from the man trying to kill him and from Sir John, were it discovered that he was fighting in an illegal tournament.

The question of why he was fighting here and not with the other English soldiers floated to the back of her mind to be answered later. She had to get Sir John and his men out of here.

She spun around on her heel to insist that they leave, accidentally bumping into the man next to her. Under normal circumstances it wouldn't have been of any circumstance, but at that moment something happened in the pit that caused everyone to lurch forward. Unbalanced, as much from the movement as from her pregnant stomach, Mary cried out and started to fall.

She would have fallen backward into the pit a dozen feet below if Sir John hadn't caught her.

She was still leaning toward the pit, her arms latched around his neck, when their eyes met.

His were stunned. "You're pregnant!"

Something was off tonight. For nearly a month Kenneth had fought twice—sometimes three times—a week in the Pits of Hell, as the secret combat tourney was called. He knew it was risky to fight in the illegal tournaments, but Felton's taunts had only worsened as the weeks passed, and his control where his wife was concerned was stretched to the breaking point. The fighting had provided both the outlet he needed to take the edge off his anger and a means of preparing himself for the upcoming war and his place in the Guard. Ironically, it was MacKay's hidden-identity appearance in the Highland Games that had inspired him.

He was undefeated. A champion and a crowd favorite. Normally, the shouts of Ice—the war name he'd jestingly given himself as a reminder of why he was here— invigorated him. Got his blood rushing and made his muscles flare with anticipation.

But not tonight. Tonight he felt none of his usual excitement and bloodlust. He exchanged punishing blow after blow with his opponent, more with an eye to ending the fight as soon as possible than to savoring victory.

His thoughts weren't on the fight but on the conversation earlier with Mary. She'd been trying to tell him something, but he'd been too focused on what he needed to do to listen. Time was running out, and he had to get her to safety. Removing her from the castle would be the first step. But of course, she hadn't understood. How could she, when she didn't know the truth?

Distracted, his head snapped back when his opponent's meaty fist connected with his jaw. A swing of his mace followed. Narrowly evading the sharp points in his ribs,

Kenneth realized he'd better focus on the thick-necked brute doing his best to kill him.

He'd just landed a rib-crushing blow of his hammer on his opponent's side and followed it with a leaping kick that sent him careening to the ground, when a cry pricked his senses. A woman's cry.

His gaze shot in the direction of the sound. He saw a flash of movement—a woman lurched toward the pit before being pulled back by a man.

Not just any woman. He tried to tell himself it wasn't possible. But every flared nerve ending in his body told him it was *his* woman.

He didn't know whether it was the delayed panic of almost seeing her tumble into the pit, knowing that he wouldn't have been able to do anything to stop it, that made him snap or the fact that the man who *did* stop it— and who now held her in his bloody arms too tightly and for too long—was Felton.

He looked as if he were about to kiss her, damn it.

Catapulting out of the pit by stepping on a piece of the broken wall, he launched himself at Felton. "Get your hands off her!"

Felton looked up at him in shocked recognition.

"Kenneth, no!" Mary cried, extracting herself from the other man's embrace.

But he was too far gone to heed her plea. His frustration. His heart-knotting confusion of feelings for his wife. His fear that he might lose her. Seeing the man who'd been taunting him for weeks with his hands on her. All came together in one mind-numbing rage.

The bastard was going to have the fight he'd begged for. One fist connected with the steel of Felton's helm, the other with his mail-clad gut.

Felton's men would have rushed forward to the knight's aid, but someone in the crowd shouted "soldiers" and the crowd surged toward the wynd. Thinking they meant to attack, Felton's men drew their swords, and then did find themselves under attack as the crowd reacted to the threat.

Felton tried to grab his sword as well, but Kenneth anticipated his movement and knocked it from his hand.

Felton was fully armored in chain mail and Kenneth was naked to the waist, protected only by the steel of his helm. But it didn't matter. There was nothing knightly about the way Kenneth fought. He used his fists, elbows, legs, feet—whatever he need to win. Felton used his shield—until Kenneth wrenched it from his hands—his dirk, whatever he could get his hands on, but his weapons were no match for Kenneth's fierce skill and brutish strength. He'd been hit so many times the past few weeks that his body had become almost immune to pain. In less than a minute, Kenneth had the victory he'd been craving for months. He had Felton on his back, pinning him to the ground with his foot pressed against his throat.

"Put your hands on my wife again and I'll kill you."

Felton's eyes burned hatred through the steel of his helm. He wanted to say something, but Kenneth's foot prevented it.

The crowd had given them a wide circle, but he was aware of only one gaze on him. Mary stared at him in wide-eyed shock, looking at him as if seeing him for the first time.

"Please," she said, her soft voice soothing him like a balm. "I'm fine. It's over. He was helping me."

Kenneth clenched his jaw, primitive instincts warring with honor. He wanted to kill Felton, but just enough rationality penetrated the haze. The bastard might have been holding her too long and too close, but he'd saved her. Kenneth had plenty of reasons for killing the man, but this wasn't one of them.

He lifted his foot off Felton's neck and stepped back. Heedless of the blood and grime, Mary raced into his arms, burying her face against his chest. His arms automatically closed around her. It felt so perfect, so right, that at that moment he recognized the truth.

Concentrating on soothing his sobbing wife, he watched while Felton struggled to his feet.

"I'll see you thrown in the pit prison for this," Felton seethed, rubbing his neck.

Kenneth's gaze narrowed. "If you value your place as Percy's champion, you won't say a bloody thing."

"Clandestine combat is illegal."

"With war coming, do you think Edward will imprison one of his best knights for long? Especially after it becomes known that I bested Percy's champion? Perhaps I shall choose to have my trial by challenging you to a wager of battle and we can let the entire castle witness your dethroning."

Felton's face was livid with rage. "You bastard! What happened to your arm injury? Why are you fighting here but not at practice? What are you hiding?"

Kenneth swore inwardly but appeared nonchalant. "This is part of my recovery. I was ensuring that I was back to full strength before we met in the yard." He smiled. "But I guess we've established that I'm ready. This is a different type of fighting experience, one you can't get on the lists with knights."

Felton swore again, but Kenneth was finished with him. They both knew he would keep what happened to himself. "Find your men and return to the castle."

Mary had lifted her head from his chest and was blinking back tears as she watched the verbal duel between the two men.

Felton held out his hand. "Lady Mary."

Kenneth stiffened, but before he could reply, she shook her head and tightened her hold around his waist.

His chest swelled. "I will see my wife safely returned."

With a look hard enough to cut steel, Felton turned on his heel and left.

Kenneth knew he'd made a mistake. His loss of temper had given Felton even more reason to want to discredit him. But he didn't care. Mary had chosen him.

Twenty-two

Kenneth would have been content to hold her here forever, but the crowd was too unruly. He cupped her chin, tipping her face to his. "Are you all right?"

She nodded, and the emotion swimming in her big greenish-blue eyes made his chest squeeze.

It seemed to take an interminable amount of time to fetch his belongings, change his clothes, and locate his horse, which he'd given a coin to a lad to watch. But eventually, he and Mary rode in silence back to the castle, her safely seated before him. When he thought about how close she'd come to falling . . .

What the hell was she doing there? And why was she with Felton? The questions kept pounding through his head on the ride back to the castle.

Not surprisingly, there wasn't a guard to greet them as they rode through the gate. Felton prized his place as champion too much to risk losing it when he couldn't be certain of the outcome. But Kenneth knew like a cornered dog that Felton would be looking and waiting for his chance to strike back.

Despite his victory, Kenneth did not delude himself; by losing his temper, he'd given Felton an axe to hang over his head.

But it was the questions about Mary's role that ate at him. By the time they reached the solitude of their chamber, he was fighting an ugly bout of jealousy and suspicion.

The door had barely closed behind them when he took her by the shoulders and turned her to face him. His heart clenched to see her tear-ravaged face, but he steeled himself. "Why, Mary? Why were you in town with him?"

She drew back in shock. "You can't be accusing me of something?"

His mouth fell in a hard line, the muscle below his jaw ticking. "Do I not have a right to be suspicious when I find my wife with another man in the middle of a damned melee, where she could have fallen to her death? Were you following me, or is there another reason you and Felton traveled to town together?"

The spark returned to her eye. "*Your* suspicions? What of mine? You knew what I thought you were doing every night in town. But you let me believe you were with other women, when instead you were fighting in an illegal tourney that could get you killed or imprisoned."

His eyes burned into hers. "I thought you didn't care."

She pursed her mouth. "Well, I do. I care very much, and I'm afraid you are going to have to accept that."

He was so surprised by her admission that it took him a moment to reply. What did she mean? He was slightly dumfounded. "You do?"

She nodded. "I wasn't following you, and it is your fault I was with Sir John in the first place."

"My fault? I believe my instructions were for you never to leave the castle without my permission."

She gave him a look that told him just how seriously she'd taken that particular order. "I assumed you didn't mean that, of course. You spoke in anger."

He'd meant every bloody word of it. If he had his way, he'd lock her in a high tower on some remote western isle until this war was over.

But he listened as she explained how she'd received a note from the monk about the nun who had looked like her. She'd come to him to accompany her, but when he turned her down, she'd accepted Sir John's offer instead.

Ah hell. He hadn't realized. Guilt pricked him. For the first time, she'd come to him for help, and he'd turned her away.

"On the way back," she continued, "we heard the commotion, and Sir John decided to investigate."

"He should never have taken you with him." When he thought of what could have happened to her—what had almost happened—that sick, helpless feeling knifed through him again. "My God, you could have been killed!"

She studied his face as if trying to discern the sentiment behind the words. "It was an accident. In my effort to leave before Sir John recognized you, I stumbled. I know you might not like to hear it, but Sir John did me a service."

She was right on both counts. He gritted his teeth. "I may have overreacted—"

"May have?"

Kenneth continued as if she hadn't interrupted. "But don't tell me he didn't take advantage of the situation. He was holding you too damned long. He looked like he was going to kiss you."

The fact that she looked like she was fighting a smile didn't help his rationality any. "I think he was shocked more than anything." She put her hand on her stomach, smoothing the fabric over the swell. His chest swelled, seeing how much she'd changed in the past month. "He realized I was with child."

Kenneth felt the urge to smile himself. "Good. Maybe that will make him see that you aren't going to change your mind."

Their eyes held. "There was never a danger of that." Before he could ponder what she meant, she added, "Why were you there, Kenneth? Why are you fighting like a common ruffian in an illegal combat tourney and not in the yard with the other knights?"

"It's as I told Felton, I've been trying to build my strength back up in preparation for giving him the challenge that he's been clamoring for."

It was a poor excuse, and he could see that she didn't fully believe him, but what else could he say? His mission wasn't over. He couldn't tell her the truth. Not until she was safely in Scotland. He couldn't risk it. Not when he'd begun to realize just how much of a betrayal this was going to seem to her.

But this was nothing like what Atholl had done to her. At least that was what he kept telling himself. Aye, he was making decisions for her—decisions that would put her in danger—but he'd had no choice. His course was already set when he'd discovered that she was carrying his child. And unlike Atholl, he would protect her. Though he was no longer confident she would see the difference.

"I'm sorry I didn't take you to the church. Did you discover anything about your sister?"

She shook her head, her eyes filling with sadness. She repeated what the abbess had told her. "It doesn't make sense. How could Brother Thomas have made such a mistake? I only hope he will return soon so that I may ask him. He went somewhere with the Bishop of St. Andrews."

Lamberton? Kenneth hid his reaction to the mention of Bruce's former ally, but his senses pricked. Agreeing that it was odd, he said, "If you'd like, I can make some inquiries."

Her expression stopped his breath. For the first time, he knew what it would feel like to have her admiration. It was as if he'd just plucked a star from the sky and handed it to her. He'd been the recipient of such looks countless times before, but all of them together had never meant as much as this one did. It felt earned.

"You would do that for me?"

He suspected there was very little he wouldn't do for her. "I still have some contacts in Scotland that may prove helpful." Contacts was an understatement.

He watched her reaction, but saw only concern, not suspicion.

"You won't do anything that would put you in danger?"

One corner of his mouth lifted. Every day he stayed here he was in danger. "I will be careful."

"Then thank you, I would be very grateful if you would try."

Her eyes shone, and something tightened in his chest. He felt a nearly overwhelming urge to take her in his arms. But he doubted his ability to touch her and not give in to the urges that had been plaguing him for thirty-seven blasted days. Though who was counting?

He nodded, breaking the connection. "You must be tired and wish to ready for bed."

Her face fell. "You are leaving? But I thought . . . "

The disappointment in her voice tugged at him. Damn it, didn't she know how hard this was? His fists clenched at his sides, fighting the primitive instincts that seemed to take over every inch of his body when he was in the same room with her. After a fight, it was even worse. His blood was pumping even hotter. "You thought what, damn it? The last thirty-seven days to the contrary, I am not a bloody monk, Mary. I want you so badly, I can't see straight."

Her eyes widened. She gasped. "You do?"

"What did you think? That I would lie beside you every night and not want to make love to you?"

"You know exactly what I thought. I thought you were exhausted from being with another woman."

"I don't want another woman."

It was the truth. And tonight after seeing her almost fall, he would finally admit what had been staring him in the face but his pride wouldn't let him acknowledge: he loved her. She was going to hate him when she learned the truth, but he loved her in a way that he'd never thought possible. Apparently, he was just as susceptible to emotion as everyone else. It had only taken the right woman.

She'd been different from the start. It wasn't just because she hadn't fallen at his feet—although he could admit that might have been part of it initially—but she challenged him, intrigued him, didn't seem to be interested in his accomplishments but in him.

He didn't even mind when they argued. Actually, he kind of liked it. He could lose his temper around her and not feel like a bully—she just gave it right back to him. It was strangely freeing—invigorating even.

For the first time in his life, he didn't feel the need to impress, the need to be the best. But he wanted her to believe in him. He wanted her trust, even if he didn't deserve it.

If he weren't so tormented, he might have enjoyed the look of disbelief on her face.

"You don't?"

He shook his head. "I haven't been with another woman since I met you."

It was clear she didn't believe him. "What about the woman in the stables?"

He wanted to tell her it was his sister, but how could he explain? He couldn't. "It wasn't how it looked." Unable to resist, he reached down and smoothed the back of his finger along her cheek. Her skin was so soft it made his chest squeeze. Hell, everything about her made his chest squeeze. One look at those big blue-green eyes, those delicate features, the lush pink lips and baby-soft skin, and he was so filled with emotion there wasn't enough air left in his lungs to breathe. "I only want you, Mary."

Mary's heart was pounding so hard and loud she could barely hear. Had she really heard him correctly? Part of her said to leave it, that "I only want you" was enough for now. To take the morsel that he'd given her and be happy. The other part—the cautious part—knew it wasn't. "For how long?"

He was holding himself so still, only the burning intensity in his eyes as he looked at her betrayed the fierceness of the emotions battling inside him. He knew what she was asking him. She wanted commitment. Fidelity. A promise.

He didn't hesitate. "For as long as you want me."

She stilled, everything inside her coming to a sudden stop. Her heart seemed to be hanging on the edge of a precipice, ready to tumble over at the barest nudge. "What if that is forever?"

He gave her a wry smile that tugged at every string in her heart. "Then you'll make me a very happy man." He tipped her chin so she would meet his gaze. "If you haven't guessed, I'm in love with you."

Mary's breath caught high in her throat, hearing the words she thought would never be meant for her. She was stunned, awed, and full of disbelief at the same time. It seemed impossible that this could be happening. She'd thought her chance for happiness was behind her. That any hope of the love she'd once dreamed of as a girl was gone. But here was this incredible man telling her he loved her.

If she listened to the voice of experience, she had every reason not to believe him. He was every bit as handsome, every bit as magnificent, every bit as popular with the women as Atholl had been. But he wasn't Atholl. And this wasn't the past. If she listened to her heart, and judged him on himself, she knew it was true. From the first, he'd always treated her differently. She'd recognized it, but hadn't wanted to believe it.

She slid her hands around his neck and raised up on her tiptoes, pressing a soft kiss on his mouth. Their eyes met, and what she saw there gave her courage. She spoke the words that fear had kept at bay. "I love you, too."

It was as if a dam had burst and all the emotion, all the feelings, that had been held back between them came rushing out in a torrential wave.

He groaned, wrapped his arms around her, and covered her mouth with his.

He kissed her. God, did he kiss her! He kissed her until her knees were weak and her heart wanted to weep with joy. The warm slide of his tongue sent ripples of emotion fluttering through her heart.

But perhaps "kiss" was far too ordinary a way to describe the perfection of his mouth moving over hers, of the gentle stroke of his tongue, of the aching tenderness of emotion he elicited with each deft caress. He didn't just kiss, he devastated.

It was incredible. The warm, soft heat of his mouth on hers. The dark, spicy taste of him. The smooth stroke of his tongue, delving . . . coaxing . . . entreating.

There had never been any doubt of her husband's expertise in matters of lovemaking. He knew just what to do to make a woman weak with pleasure. The skilled movements of his lips and tongue could rouse her passion in an instant.

But this was different. This wasn't just about passion. The soft caress of his mouth over hers, the heart-tugging strokes of his tongue, were gentle and sweet, tender and inquisitive. Not a plunder but a promise. A bond. A vow.

This wasn't just a kiss intended to make her body hot and needy; he seduced her heart and soul as well. It was everything she'd fought against. Everything she'd struggled to deny but had been between them from the first. Not just passion but emotion. A deeper connection. A joining not just of bodies but of souls. Finally, she let herself accept all the tenderness he'd been trying to give her that she'd tried for so long not to want.

It was hard to believe the same man who'd fought so brutally hours before, who'd seemed hard, unyielding, and merciless, whose big, muscled body could be used as such a deadly weapon could be touching her so gently. Nor could she have imagined that the cocky, arrogant warrior she'd first seen in the barn, who'd exuded passion and virility, would be capable of such tender emotions.

Cradled against the big shield of his chest, Mary felt as if she were the most precious woman in the world. She felt cherished and protected. And most of all, she felt loved.

It was so heartwrenchingly perfect, so achingly poignant, it almost hurt—which it did, when he stopped. He lifted his head, and she cried out in protest at the loss.

He smiled, gazing down at her as he held her tightly in his arms. The warmth of his body around her was something she would never get used to. It made her feel as if nothing in the world could hurt her.

"You know what this means, don't you?"

Seeing the challenging glint in his eye, she hesitated to ask. "I'm afraid I don't."

"No more chemises, Mary. No more hiding. I intend to see every gorgeous, naked inch of you."

Heat rose to her cheeks, but she didn't argue. He was right. She didn't want anything between them, even embarrassment.

He grinned at her silent acquiescence, and in a smooth motion, swept her up into his arms. Looping her hands around his neck, she buried her face in the fuzzy warmth of the plaid he wore around his shoulders as he carried her to the bed. Depositing her atop the covers, he proceeded to remove his clothing.

It was clear the man didn't have a lick of shame. Nor should he, she was forced to admit. His body was incredible—as he very well knew. And after nearly two months of sharing a room, he also knew exactly how much she admired it.

He removed the arsenal of weapons he wore strapped to various parts of his body. Then, piece by piece, he tossed his clothing on one of the chairs before the fire. Plaid. *Cotun*. Chausses. Boots. Shirt. And then finally, his braies.

He stood proudly before her in all his masculine glory. And sweet heaven, his body was glorious. She drew in her breath as a warm, melting heat spread over her skin. Not even the cocky grin on his face could make her turn away. The man was arrogant beyond belief. She should knock him down a few pegs, but she feared it was impossible. When it came to his body there was nothing to fault. Unless you didn't like lots—and lots—of perfectly defined, granite-hard muscle. Shallow female that she was, she, unfortunately, did.

His body was a sharply honed weapon of war, every bit as hard and impenetrable as the armor he wore. From the breadth of his shoulders, to the thick, powerfully built arms, to the narrow, lean planes of his waist, to the bands of muscle crossing his stomach, it was hard to know where to look. Of course, there was also that other part of him that drew the eye, demanding attention. The long, thick column of flesh that bobbed against his stomach, hard proof of just how much he wanted her.

"See something you might be interested in?"

She shot him a glare. "Would you believe me, if I told you no?"

He laughed. "With the way you are looking at me, I don't think so." He dropped down on the bed beside her and lay back, crossing his arms behind his head. "Your turn."

She balked. "I hope you don't expect a performance like the one you just gave."

"Not tonight."

A big, strapping warrior shouldn't look so mischievous. She slid her hand over the hard ridges of his stomach,

letting her wrist brush over the heavy head of his erection. "Are you sure you can wait? You appear to be ready
right now."

He groaned into her hand as she circled him, letting her
draw it up and down a few times before catching her wrist
to stop her. "I won't let you distract me, Mary. I've been
waiting too long for this. Take it off—all of it."

She bit her lip, her heart fluttering nervously. "Perhaps
we could blow out a few of the candles?"

"Not a chance."

She frowned. "I can see you are going to be difficult
about this."

"I'm waiting, love. Make me wait much longer and we'll
save this for morning. With the clear skies tonight, I suspect it will be a bright and sunny day."

She gave him a sharp scowl that promised retribution,
sat up, and began to remove her robes. He had to help her,
and it didn't surprise her to discover that her husband was
far more efficient than any lady's maid. "Had practice at
this, have you?"

"Some," he said blandly, not rising to the bait.

When she was down to the last layer of linen, she clung
to her chemise like a lifeline. Perhaps she should prepare
him? "I'm much bigger—"

"You are carrying my child, Mary. I doubt there is a way
you could look any more beautiful to me."

What could she say to that? He killed her objections
with sweetness.

Taking a deep breath, she lifted the last veil between
them over her head and tossed the fine linen chemise atop
the other items of clothing. Instinctively she crossed her
hands in front of her, but there was no hiding the big bump
of her stomach or the heaviness of her breasts.

She couldn't look at him, feeling far too vulnerable.
She'd never been naked before a man. Heat rose to her
cheeks. Why was he being so quiet? Was she so horribly

unattractive to him? Eventually, she couldn't stand the silence any longer and ventured a peek from under her lashes.

The expression on his face made all of her insecurities slip away. He looked moved. Humbled. Overcome by an emotion she didn't recognize.

"You are so beautiful," he whispered. He reached out and skimmed the back of his finger over the curve of her breast. "Your breasts are incredible." He cupped her in his warm, callused hand, circling his thumb over her nipple until it hardened to a taut peak.

"You don't think they are too large?"

That made him laugh. "Sweetheart, I don't think there is a man alive who would think that. They're perfect."

He bent down and took the nipple he'd hardened into his mouth.

She gasped as heat and dampness enfolded her sensitive flesh, as his tongue circled, as his teeth nibbled, as he sucked. She buried her fingers in his thick, dark hair, holding him tightly to her. Sharp needles of pleasure shot from her breasts to between her legs. She was gasping with pleasure, her already heavy breasts growing fuller, her nipples throbbing.

But he had only just begun. He took his time exploring every inch of the naked flesh that she'd hidden from him. He caressed her with his hands, tasted her with his mouth, and devoured her with his eyes, until there was no part of her left untouched and she was weak with wanting.

Finally, when he'd brought her to a fever pitch, when every inch of her skin was burning from his kiss, when her body was damp and writhing with restless desire, his mouth found hers again.

She moaned, reaching for him. She held him tight, her hands gripping the hard slabs of his back and shoulders.

He was stretched out beside her, leaning over her, and the heat of his naked skin against hers felt so good, she wanted more. She tried to pull his chest toward hers, seeking the solid heaviness of him on top of her, but he held himself away.

He put his hand over her stomach. "The babe."

She didn't think there was a reason to worry, but decided not to argue. Instead, she succumbed to the power of his kiss, letting the warmth spread through her limbs like molten lava, dissolving everything in its wake.

But eventually, it wasn't enough—for either of them.

The slow, lazy seduction and the gentle exploration had reached its limit.

His kiss turned harder, more determined. Each powerful thrust of his tongue, each possessive stroke, taking her deeper and deeper. His groans echoed hers as their passion built together. She could feel the beat of his heart against hers, pounding faster and faster.

The hot column of his manhood pressed against her hip and instinctively she turned toward him, needing to feel the hardness. The thickness. The sweet pressure. Her heart dropped at the sensation. Right there.

She rubbed up against him like a cat. A warm, sensual cat. She'd never felt so free, so open. For the first time in her life, she wasn't holding anything back. With every touch, every kiss, every long, slow slide of her body against his, she showed him exactly how much she loved him.

Kenneth had never felt anything like this. The primitive attraction that had sprung between them, the raw unbridled lust that he'd thought couldn't get any better, paled beneath the force of the sensations surging through him right now. Everything felt deeper. Stronger. More meaningful. The heat didn't just surge through his blood, it burned in his heart. Hell, it went deeper than that—it burned in his soul.

Her beauty humbled him. From the top of her golden, silky head to the tips of her tiny pink toes, she was beautiful. A dainty package of lush femininity. The long, softly curved limbs, the ripe swell of her stomach, the bouncy pink-tipped plumpness of her breasts, the velvety smooth-ness of her skin . . .

His throat had gone dry just looking at her. But then when he'd touched her, when he'd slid his mouth over every inch of her skin and marked her with the scrape of his beard, he thought he'd died and glimpsed the peaks of Olympus. She was a goddess who brought him to his knees.

He smiled. Who would have guessed his too-skinny gray nun would turn out to be the source of such divine inspiration?

He never wanted this to end. But unfortunately, when she started to rub against him, his body rather powerfully disagreed.

Breaking the kiss, he lifted his head. When he started to roll off the bed, she blinked as if suddenly coming back to earth—he knew the feeling.

"Where are you going?"

He moved to the edge of the bed. "Right here." Taking her legs, he guided her around and positioned her at the edge of the mattress—which happened to be the perfect height for what he had in mind. He looped his arms under her knees and held her legs apart, probing her gently with the tip of his cock.

"I don't want to lie on top of you, so we're going to need to be a little creative until the babe comes."

She made a sharp sound, her back arching as he probed her a little harder. He rocked his hips, readying her with little nudges.

He liked to make her moan. Liked to make her head fall back and her lips part as she begged him to ease her agony. But that wasn't what he wanted right now. He didn't want to tease her, her wanted to love her. He wanted to hold her gaze as he entered her, as she took him into her body. As she took him into her heart.

"Look at me, Mary."

Their eyes locked. Then slowly—agonizingly slowly—he pushed inside her. Inch by inch, he buried himself in the wet, velvety heat of her body.

It felt so damned good, sensation roared through him like a lightning rod. He could have groaned. But he didn't. He was too focused on the woman before him. He would remember this moment forever. He would never forget how it felt to look into her eyes as he entered her and see the overwhelming emotion squeezing his chest mirrored in deep aquamarine. They were bound together, and just for right now he could believe nothing could ever break them apart.

When he'd gone as far as he could go, when he was buried to the hilt in the tight grip of her body, he stilled, held her gaze, and nudged a little deeper, bringing a startled gasp to her lips.

"Kenneth . . . !"

"I love you," he said. "Let me show you."

And then he began to move. Slowly and gently, in long, languid strokes. For the first time in his life, Kenneth made love to a woman. He told her with his body how much she meant to him.

Mary was in heaven. Her husband had roused her passion, taken her to higher peaks of pleasure than she'd every imagined, but she had never expected anything like this.

The raging firestorm of lust had given way to a slow, deep burn that proved just as hot and even more devastating. There was not a part of her that he left untouched, or unclaimed. He possessed her body, her soul, with each long stroke.

He gave no quarter, holding her gaze to his. It was impossible to look away from the emotion she saw burning there. She devoured it like a greedy child, burying it deep in her heart where it would always be safe. Where no one could ever take it away.

She didn't want it to end. But the feel of him, so big and full inside her, was too good. And it had been too long. Her body responded.

She lifted her hips to meet the gentle rhythm of his thrusts, increasing the speed as the sensations built inside her.

She gasped, moaned, cried as his thrusts grew longer, deeper, harder. He circled his hips, stirring her into a passionate frenzy.

She wrapped her legs around his waist, bringing him closer, wanting to increase the friction and the pressure. He moved his free hands to her bottom, gripping her harder, steadying her as the force of his thrusting intensified.

Everything moved, jarred by the fierce pounding of his body into hers.

It felt so good she couldn't stand it. She arched her back, feeling her body clenching, gripping him harder and harder.

His face was a mask of strain, every muscle bunched and coiled. His arms flexed and the muscles lining his stomach stood out in stark relief.

"God, I'm going to come," he grit out from between clenched teeth.

The knot of tightly wound muscles unwound as she spiraled into an abyss of pleasure so intense it stole her breath.

He stilled and cried out. She felt the flood of heat fill her as his release mixed with the spasming wave of her own.

Her legs fell from his waist. He bent over her, drained, as if he'd just run a long race. Collapsing on the bed, he dragged her up alongside him and held her in the circle of his arm. In a tangle of damp naked limbs, with her cheek pressed to his chest, their baby nestled between them, and her palm resting on his heart, she knew she'd finally found it. It had taken six and twenty years, but Mary had the love she'd been searching for her whole life.

Twenty-three

❧

"When will you be back?"

Kenneth glanced back over his shoulder at the naked woman lying on the bed tangled in bedsheets. With her mussed hair and pouty bruised lips, Mary looked as though she'd just been very thoroughly ravished—which she had been. But it didn't stop him from wanting to climb right back into bed and make love to her again.

It seemed he could think of nothing else. He had an almost desperate need to bind her to him. It was as if the more he made love to her, the stronger their love would be to weather the storm that was hovering on the not-so-distant horizon.

But if anything, it was making him more anxious about all that he had to lose. What if she never forgave him? He knew it was better to wait until she was somewhere safe to explain, but every instinct told him to tell her now. That every day he waited made his betrayal worse.

Unable to help himself, he set his knee on the bed, bent over her, and slowly kissed the pout from her lips. When she responded, threading her fingers through his hair and drawing his mouth closer to entwine her tongue with his, a shaft of heat ignited inside him and threatened to drag him under.

He had to tear his mouth away. "A couple of days. You won't even have time to notice I'm gone." He smiled, unable to resist teasing her. She'd been moving furiously around here the past few days since they'd arrived at Huntlywood Castle, like a bird building a nest. "Though perhaps you will have crenelated the tower house by then, and I won't recognize the place."

"Wretch." She tossed a pillow at him. "Sir Adam said I was free to make the place as comfortable as I like for my stay here. It's been some time since anyone has stayed in these upper chambers."

"And you've taken to the task with enthusiasm."

"Since it seems I will have much time on my own, what else is there for me to do?"

He felt a stab of guilt and instantly sobered. "I'll come as often as I can. I know it's not the same as being at the castle, but it won't be for long."

If she only knew just how short her stay would be. He hoped that in a matter of days—a week, no longer—he would have her safely ensconced in Scotland. Mary could stay with Helen and Campbell's wife at Dunstaffnage. Close enough for him to reach her when the babe came. Later, he would send her north to Skelbo, the castle he kept for his brother.

She sat up, dragging the sheet along with her. Untangling a few strands of golden-blond hair from her lashes, she tucked it behind her ear. "I shouldn't complain. I know it could be far worse. I'm fortunate to be this close to the castle. At Ponteland I would see you far less."

"Sir Adam will be here to keep you company for a few more days." He knew the answer, but he thought he'd try anyway. "Are you sure you don't wish to reconsider? France . . ." He paused. "It might be a good idea. It will be safer for you there."

Her expression fell, her eyes instantly growing large and round. "I don't want to go to France, I want to stay here with you and Davey. I thought you wanted that, too."

"I do," he assured her. "It's just that I worry about your safety while I am away. When war breaks out—"

"We have plenty of time for that. The king hasn't even arrived yet. When you leave for Scotland, I will go farther south. To my dower estate in Kent if need be. But don't send me away now—it's too soon."

He understood only too well what she meant. It *was* too soon. Their love was too new, too fragile. It needed time to strengthen before it was tested by distance—or deception, damn it. But it was time he didn't have.

He leaned over and gave her a light peck on the cheek so he wouldn't be tempted to linger. But the soft, velvety skin and faint floral scent worked its own magic. He wanted to sink into her. To inhale her sweet femininity.

He had to drag himself away. "Very well. You win. But only because I'm selfish and want you near me for as long as possible."

A wide smile spread over her face, causing his chest to expand. "Are you sure you must go? Is there no one else who can take a missive to Edinburgh?"

"Aye, I'm sure." The rare opportunity to read Percy's correspondence couldn't be missed. Moreover, he'd had a message from his contact in the village that his friends were anxious to see him. This was the first chance he'd had to arrange a meeting with the Highland Guard at a safe distance from the castle—and Felton.

As he'd anticipated, Felton was watching him closer than before. Kenneth had half expected him to insist on joining him on the journey to Edinburgh. That he hadn't asked bothered him.

He didn't realize he was frowning until she said, "Is there something wrong? You've seemed distracted the past few days."

His wife had learned to read his moods too well. "You mean other than that I will be spending the night in the cold rain with a half-dozen men rather than in bed with my wife?"

But she would not be so easily placated. She eyed him intently. "I know something is wrong." She bit her lips, her eyes looming large in her face. "Does it have something to do with my sister? Have you had news?"

His chest squeezed, wishing there were some way to ease her sadness. He'd hoped to soften the sting of his betrayal with news of her sister, but so far he'd run headlong into a stone wall. His inquiries to Lamberton had been met with sharp resistance. Lamberton had instructed him in no uncertain terms to not disturb ghosts that had been laid to rest. Whether that was meant as a warning or a confirmation of her death, he didn't know.

"I'm afraid not," he said. "I've learned nothing more than you already know. The abbess insists no such nun has ever been there, and Brother Thomas has yet to return."

"When he does—"

"When he does, I will talk to him."

She relaxed back against the wooden headboard with a sigh. "Thank you."

"I will return as soon as I am able."

She nodded, and he turned to leave.

"Kenneth."

He looked back at her.

"I love you."

She seemed to be trying to tell him something. Almost as if she were trying to ease the turmoil she sensed wrestling inside him.

He smiled. "I know."

He only prayed that when this was all over, she felt the same way.

They were pulling him out. Damn it, it was too soon. "I'm not ready," Kenneth said. "I need more time."

MacKay gave him a glance sharp enough to see in the moonlit darkness. "From what I hear, *Ice*, you are plenty ready."

Ah hell. They must have heard about his fighting.

Kenneth clenched his jaw, ready for the arse-chewing that he knew he was about to get.

MacKay didn't disappoint. He never did when it came to that. "What the hell were you thinking? What if someone from the castle discovered what you were doing? You would have a lot of explaining to do."

The fact that someone *had* discovered him made MacKay's anger even more justified. But he sure as hell wasn't going to tell him about Felton. "It was the only way I could think of to keep my skills sharp. I won't be much good to Bruce if I'm not ready when he needs me."

"What he needs you to do is stay close to Percy and find out all you can about what Edward is planning. He doesn't need you fighting in secret tourneys and ending up in a dungeon. Nor does he need you to worry about Clifford's absences—or inquire about missing nuns, for that matter."

Kenneth stilled. If MacKay knew about his inquiries, that meant Lamberton had told Bruce. It didn't take Campbell-like senses to know they were hiding something. Which meant he'd just found the source of his stone wall, and worse, he suspected why it had been put there: they knew something. And he couldn't tell Mary. He'd wanted to find a way to soften the blow for his deception; instead he was compounding the secrets between them.

"Leave him alone, Saint," Ewen Lamont said from his place in the shadows. They stood in the forest just east of the Pentland Hills, a short distance from Edinburgh. Kenneth had managed to slip away from the rest of the men on his ride north to scout the road ahead, when he'd spotted them. But they didn't have much time. "From what I hear, the recruit did us proud. No harm has come of it. And he's brought us more than we could have expected."

Kenneth didn't know what surprised him more: that the acclaimed tracker had jumped to his defense or the length of the speech by which he'd done so. He didn't think he'd heard Lamont string more than two or three words together at a time the entire duration of his training. Lamont, war name Hunter, was the polar opposite of MacSorley in social skills. Blunt was a nice way of putting it. Inept was another. The man said what he thought, when he wanted to, in as few words as possible.

Which made his partnership with Eoin MacLean easily the most muted of any of the pairings, as the famed battle strategist possessed a silent, grim intensity and also tended to keep his words to a minimum.

It was MacLean who spoke next. "This letter is just the confirmation we need. Now that we know Edward is sending supplies to Edinburgh Castle—and probably Stirling as well—in preparation for his campaign, it means we can guess the route he will take, which will make it easier to prepare our attacks. It's time to put the plan for your exit in motion. From what we hear, one of Percy's men has been asking a lot of questions about you. Edward's ship is leaving from London any day. Why wait and risk something going wrong? Part of waging a successful mission is knowing when you should get out. You've done well—better than we could have hoped. But now you are needed with us. Bruce wants us with Douglas in the forest, gathering support and readying the troops."

Kenneth shook his head. "It's too easy." He held up the letter that he'd been entrusted to deliver to the constable at Edinburgh. "Percy just happens to send me ahead with a message about an impending delivery? It doesn't feel right." The moment he'd read it, he'd known it was too good to be true. "Give me a little more time. As soon as Sir Adam leaves, I can get Mary away without anyone knowing; then we'll see. We need to wait for Hawk anyway."

With Mary's pregnancy, he'd decided it would be easier to get her to safety by ship.

"And the young earl?" MacKay asked.

"Once we have him, I think he can be convinced." He hoped. But Davey was hard to read and good at keeping his thoughts to himself. He was counting on the boy's admiration for him, and Mary's persuasion.

The three men looked at each other. After a moment, MacKay said, "Don't take any chances. If something doesn't feel right, get out of there. With three thousand English soldiers garrisoned nearby, we won't be able to get you out of Berwick's pit prison anytime soon. And as MacRuairi can tell you, it's not a place you would wish to stay for long."

Kenneth remembered. His brief stay had been long enough. "And if something does go wrong?"

His brother-in-law held his gaze. "We'll take care of her."

Kenneth nodded. Strange, but there was no man he would trust more with his wife than his former enemy. MacKay would take care of her. Whatever else happened, Mary would be safe. He could take solace in the knowledge that he'd kept one promise.

He just hoped it didn't come to that.

Mary tugged on the leather handle, but the blasted thing wouldn't budge. She plopped down atop the trunk and with a deep sigh blew a strand of hair from her face. She'd thought she might be able to move it by herself, but it had to be stuffed with rocks.

She had enlisted a few of the serving girls to help her clean the room in preparation for the baby, but they'd gone to ready the midday meal and she'd decided to continue without them.

The hard work seemed to keep her mind from inventing reasons to worry. Her husband was preoccupied with his duty, that was all. God knew Percy was keeping him busy. She'd seen so little of him since she'd left Berwick Castle.

Already, it had been three days since he'd left for Edinburgh. There was no reason to worry. He would come when he could.

But she couldn't shake the feeling that there was more to it than that. There had been an almost frantic, desperate edge to his lovemaking the last time he'd been here. She'd never felt closer to him, yet at times she felt him going somewhere in his mind that he would not take her.

She wanted his trust. She thought she had it. But what was bothering him and why wouldn't he confide in her?

With another sigh, she stood. A billow of dust rose from her skirts as she shook them off, wiping her hands on her already filthy apron. For a small room, it had held an inordinate amount of dust—and spiderwebs, she thought with a shiver. Thankfully, the worst of it was gone. By the time they finished, this room would be spotless.

Returning to the problem of the trunk, she knelt down and lifted back the lid. She coughed as another blanket of dust was disturbed and the dank scent of mold and stale air filled her nose. It must have been years since someone had opened this.

She glanced inside. No wonder it had been so difficult to move. It wasn't loaded with stones, but books. A veritable treasure trove of leather-bound portfolios, wrapped in exotic-looking fabrics that she recognized as having come from Outremer. There were also a few large potted jars, but as they were sealed with wax, she did not try to open them. Curious, she removed one of the books and flipped through the thick parchment pages.

It appeared to be a journal of some kind. Though she had some education, and could make out a few words, many of the entries appeared to have been written quickly, and the lettering was difficult to make out. But the drawings were beautiful. Flowers. Plants. Vistas. A veiled woman. And some of the strangest-looking animals she'd ever seen, including one that looked like a big, gangly horse with a long neck and hump on its back.

The book was magnificent. She would have opened another, but she heard a sound that made her jump to her feet.

She glanced out the small window and let out a yelp of excitement. He was back! Kenneth and a few of his men had just ridden into the yard.

Putting the book aside, Mary rushed down the stairs to meet him. She was winded and glowing with exertion by the time she reached the bottom of the third level. She entered the hall at the same time he did from the opposite side. With a cry that told her exactly how worried she'd been about him, she raced into his arms.

She could hear the reverberation of his laugh in his chest as he lifted her up and spun her in his arms. Still in his embrace, he set her feet back on the ground and pressed a quick kiss on her lips, the brevity of which she suspected was due to their audience. His voice was low and husky. "Miss me?"

An unexpected threat of tears rose behind her eyes. She seemed to cry at the drop of a pin lately. "Very much. I'm glad you're back."

His face clouded ever so slightly. "Not for long, I'm afraid. I have to return to the castle, but as Huntlywood was on the way, I couldn't resist a brief stop to check on you."

She smiled, trying to hide her disappointment. "As you can see, I'm fine."

"I'm glad to hear it." He dropped a kiss on her nose and released her.

Suddenly conscious of the men standing behind him, and remembering her duties, Mary blushed and immediately arranged for food and drink to be brought out.

They were seated at the trestle table and halfway through the meal when Kenneth glanced around with a frown. "Where is Sir Adam?"

"He was called to the castle."

"I thought he was leaving tomorrow."

"He was. His journey has been delayed a few days."

"Why?"

She wrinkled her nose. "I don't know."

"He didn't say anything? Did something happen?"

She frowned at the intensity of his questioning. "You'll have to ask him."

"If it's anything important, I will find out soon." He tried to dismiss it as if it didn't matter, but she sensed it did. He was edgy again.

"Is there something wrong?"

He lifted his goblet, taking a long drink of wine. "Why do you ask?"

She shrugged. She couldn't put her finger on it herself. "You seem preoccupied. As if something is bothering you."

"Tired, that is all. And regretting that I cannot delay my return to the castle any longer."

Mary held his gaze, wishing she could believe him. "Must you go already?"

He nodded. "I will return as soon as I am able. What do you have planned—other than cleaning?"

How did he . . .

Suddenly, she blushed, glancing down at her skirts. She'd forgotten all the dust. Her hands went to her hair. "I must look a fright."

"You look beautiful."

The look in his eyes made her blush deepen for a different reason. "I was cleaning out one of the rooms in the garret for the baby." She knew she was smiling like an excited child, but she couldn't help it. "It's going to be perfect. There's a nice window where I can put a chair, and a small antechamber for the nursemaid to sleep. I wish that I'd had time to make something myself, but Sir Adam said he has some tapestries I can use for the walls. I can't wait for you to see it."

A shadow crossed his face. "Mary, you know this is only temporary."

The gentle reminder made her flush with embarrassment. "I know. It's just hard not to get carried away a little when I'm so happy." She thought he would be, too. But he didn't look happy. He looked a little pained. "I thought you would understand."

"Of course I do. I'm sorry. You're right. I must be more preoccupied than I realized. I should love to see the room, when I return."

He seemed so genuinely contrite that she smiled. "I shall put you to work. You can help me move the trunk. It's the most wonderful thing. I think it must have belonged to Sir Adam's father."

He seemed to go very still beside her. "What makes you say that?"

"It is filled with the most wonderful treasures from the east. Sir Adam's father went on crusade many years ago with King Edward."

"And my grandfather," he said carefully.

"That's right, I'd forgotten. You must see the journals, then."

The cup slid from his hand, but he steadied it before it tipped over. "Journals?" he said hoarsely.

She nodded, wondering at his strange reaction. "Aye, a whole trunk of them."

Kenneth couldn't believe it. Was it possible the recipe for black powder was hidden in one of those journals? Anxious to investigate, he'd hoped to return later that night. But it wasn't until the following night that he crept up the staircase of Huntlywood tower.

With King Edward's departure from London imminent, the preparations for war had intensified, and Percy was keeping them all busy. Moreover, knowing his time was running out, Kenneth was taking every opportunity to discover what information he could before he had to leave. He couldn't shake the feeling that the English were planning something secretive and that Clifford was at the center of it.

Perhaps it was Striker's warning, but Kenneth also couldn't shake the feeling that they were watching him. The letter conveniently falling into his hands bothered him. As did Percy's seemingly innocuous comment that he should have more care the next missive he carried did not get damaged before he arrived. There had been a small crack in the seal after he'd broken it open. It should have gone without notice, but apparently the constable thought it significant enough to report back to him via one of the other men.

Could Felton have said something to Percy? It wouldn't surprise him.

All this added up to one incontrovertible fact: it was time to take Mary to Scotland. Only when she was safe could he extricate himself and the young earl. Her presence had become a liability. It made him vulnerable. If something went wrong, he wanted her far away from here.

The unexpected delay in Sir Adam's journey had complicated matters, but the older knight was supposed to depart for France the day after tomorrow. As soon as he did, Kenneth would make his move.

Kenneth passed the tower chamber where Mary slept on his way to the garret. He knew it must be after midnight. He intended to surprise his wife, but *after* he searched the trunk.

There were two doors at the top of the stairs. He chose the one on the right and pushed it open as quietly as he could in case someone was sleeping inside. Fortunately, the room appeared empty. With the shutters closed, it was dark—and cold. The candle he'd brought with him didn't shed much light, but it would be enough.

As there were only a few items in the room, he saw the

trunk right away, heaving a sigh of relief that it hadn't been removed.

It was clear Mary had been busy. The room was spotless: wooden floors swept clean, plastered walls cleaned and brushed with a fresh coat of lime. Even the low angled ceiling looked clean.

He had to duck as he crossed the room to the trunk. Lifting the lid, he knew at once Mary had been right about the identity of the owner. He recognized the same leather covers of the journal his friend William Gordon had that had burned in the fire all those years ago. A buzz of excitement ran over his skin, crackling like lightning when he saw the sealed pottery jars. Suspecting what they contained, he put one aside to examine later and started in on the journals. He flipped through page after page, looking for anything that might be a recipe or formula. With every minute that passed, his disappointment grew. He'd been so certain, damn it. He was on the third volume when he heard the door behind him open.

"What are you doing?"

Damn, it was Mary. He slammed the volume closed and placed it back in the trunk. "I didn't mean to wake you."

"My room is just below this one. I thought I heard something. But what are you doing up here?"

He smiled. "I thought I would move your trunk."

"In the middle of the night?"

"I was curious."

She immediately brightened. "To see the baby's room? You should have woken me. What do you think?"

He felt a stab of guilt. Her happiness and excitement ate at him. He hadn't been thinking about the child's room because he *knew* it wasn't going to be the child's room at all. He looked around the small chamber. "It's nice."

She rolled her eyes, walking toward him. "Nice? It's perfect. I'm going to put a chair over here," she pointed to a place before the window, "the cradle will be against the far wall, and the nurse will sleep in the antechamber."

Kenneth felt ill. "You have it all planned out."

She gave him a funny look. "It won't be long now. Davey came a few weeks early. Perhaps this baby will do the same."

Kenneth hoped the sudden lack of blood in his face wasn't visible in the candlelight. "I didn't realize . . . "

He'd just assumed. Ah hell, he really had to get her out of here.

She laughed. "Babies have their own time. They come when they want to, and I just want to be ready."

And he was just realizing how unready he was.

"Is something wrong, Kenneth? Is something bothering you?"

Something was bothering him all right. She was so damned happy. What he was doing was wrong. He'd created a world of illusions for a woman who'd already had them shattered once before.

But how was he going to tell her the truth? "I've been a bit preoccupied with my duties, that's all. With the king leaving London, everyone is anxious."

"Are you sure that is all?"

"What else could there be?"

"I thought it might have something to do with me. Have I done something to displease you?"

He smiled, caressing her cheek with his hand. "You please me very much."

But she wouldn't be distracted by sensual teasing. She turned her face from his hand. "That isn't what I was talking about. Have I done something to make you not wish to confide in me? I had hoped you would trust me to share your confidences."

"I do trust you." At least he wanted to. But it was all so new to him. Now that he had her love, he didn't want to lose it.

"And I you. I'm sorry I ever doubted you." She put her palm on his chest and looked up at him, the trust shining in her eyes making his chest knife. "You are nothing like Atholl. I know that now."

Kenneth flinched. He wasn't like Atholl, he was worse. Atholl hadn't loved her. Atholl hadn't deceived her.

He needed to tell her. He probably should have done so before. He thought it was wiser to wait until she was safely in Scotland, as by then it would be too late for her to refuse to go. But if he told her now, he could still keep part of his vow to her. He had to have faith in her. In them. She would be angry at first, but he had to trust that she would understand.

"If Atholl had given you a choice, Mary, what would you have had him do? Would you have told him to fight with Bruce or with Edward?"

She blinked up at him in the candlelight, obviously taken aback by his question. "I would have had him protect us."

"Aye, but after that. If things were different, what side would you have picked?"

Her brows furrowed. "What does that matter anymore? The decision was made for me many years ago."

"What if it did matter? What if you could go back? What if you and David could be in Scotland with your former brother-in-law right now, would you do it?"

Her face shadowed. He could tell she was beginning to get annoyed with his questions. "What difference does it make? It's hypothetical. We are here, making the best out of the situation that we can."

"Don't you want to go home Mary?"

"Of course I do," she snapped, finally losing her temper. "I miss my home, as I'm sure you do. But it does me no good to wish for things that aren't possible."

He held her gaze intently. "What if they were?"

She stilled, her voice lowered to a whisper—as if the

walls had ears. "You should not speak that way. It's dangerous."

"I would never let anything happen to you, Mary. You know that, don't you?"

Her eyes raked his face. "Why are you talking to me like this? What are you trying to tell me?"

"That it's time to go home."

Twenty-four

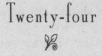

Mary stared at him, at first not understanding what he was saying. But a dark shadow of premonition had begun to creep its way up her consciousness. "I can't go home. King Edward would never allow it."

"Edward won't know. Not until it's too late, anyway."

Fear washed over her. She shook her head. "No. I lost my sister the last time I tried to flee. Why are you talking this way? Has something happened? Is Sir John making it difficult for you? Surely, it couldn't be so bad as to make you question your loyalty?"

He didn't say anything, and all of a sudden the truth hit her. *Loyalty*.

She drew back in horror, understanding sinking like a stone in her gut. She knew why he'd been asking her all those strange questions earlier. Why his sudden shift of allegiance hadn't made sense. Why he'd talked so fondly about a brother he was supposed to hate.

"Oh God." She covered her mouth, feeling sick. Betrayal ripped inside her like a jagged knife. "You never changed allegiance, did you? You are working for Robert."

She inched back, but he reached out to catch her arm. "Mary, wait. Let me explain."

Heat choked her throat, hurt and disbelief filled her eyes with tears. "Explain what? That you deceived me?"

"I had no choice. I probably shouldn't even be telling you this, but I made you a vow."

Anger helped to forestall the tears. She made a harsh sound of disbelief. "It's rather late to remember that, isn't it? You promised not to embroil me or my children in anything dangerous, but you did that the moment you forced me to marry you."

From the glint in his eyes, she could tell he took exception to her choice of words. "I couldn't tell you then. Not when I wasn't sure of your feelings for me."

A second wave of understanding hit, this one even harder than the first—if that were possible. "And now you are," she said numbly. "I see. Was that why you went to such an effort to seduce me? So that I would follow you willingly like one of your starry-eyed admirers when the time came?"

Had he ever loved her?

Thin white lines appeared around his mouth. "I will not deny that I wanted you to come with me, and I thought it would be easier if you cared for me, but that doesn't change how I feel about you. I love you, Mary. I've never said those words to another woman in my life. Hell, I never even thought it possible for me to feel this way about a woman."

Bile rose to the back of her throat. God, it was true. He had set out to make her fall in love with him. She'd thought it was a game, but it was an even bigger one than she imagined. The stakes weren't just her heart, but her life and the lives of her children. Her heart curled like a piece of burning parchment.

How could he have made love to her all those times, knowing what he was going to do?

"Is that supposed to make me feel better?" she said hoarsely, her voice raw with emotion. " 'I betrayed you. I lied to you. I used you. But I love you, so it's all right?' "

A muscle in his jaw pulsed. "I deserve your anger but not your scorn. What choice did I have?"

"You could have told me the truth."

"And what would you have done with that knowledge? Could I be sure you wouldn't run to Sir Adam or someone else and tell them the truth? You made your opinion of me quite clear many times. People are counting on me; I couldn't take the chance."

She turned away. "Then you should have left me alone."

"I couldn't do that. I wanted you. And you were pregnant with my child."

"And what about my other child? Where does Davey fit in all this? I assume it would be quite a coup for you to bring the Earl of Atholl back into the Scottish fold."

He stiffened, not flinching from the truth. "Once I get you to safety, I will follow with David."

Terror struck her heart. She shook her head frantically. "No. It's too dangerous. They are watching him too closely. They will not let you slip out of Berwick Castle with the Earl of Atholl."

"I have a plan. Trust me."

She had, and look where that had gotten her. Was she doomed to have her life destroyed by thoughtless husbands reaching for glory? He'd thrust her right back into a nightmare and never considered her at all. She'd put her fate in a man's hands again and he'd betrayed her.

She squared her shoulders. "You ask for too much. Davey won't go, and neither will I."

His mouth drew even tighter, and Mary knew he was fighting to keep a rein on his temper. "Your son is a Scottish earl, Mary. He belongs in Scotland. Yet sounds as bloody English as Edward."

She prickled, perhaps because she knew there was more than a grain of truth in what he said. Had she not thought the same thing many times? But it didn't matter. She would rather have David in England alive than in prison or with his head hanging in the same place as his father's. "It is for me to decide what is best for myself and my son, not you."

His eyes flashed. "Wrong. You gave me that power when

you married me. I vowed to protect you, and I will. You will just have to trust me."

"And if I refuse to go, what then, Kenneth? Will you take me against my will? Abduct your own wife?"

His mouth fell in a hard line. "I will do what I have to to keep you safe. Don't you see? There is no other way. When the truth is discovered I will be a hunted man, and you will be the wife of a traitor."

"A position I've been in before, if you'll recall. I weathered one traitor well enough, why should I not weather another?"

His gaze burned into hers. "You don't mean that."

"Don't I?" It was the same nightmare all over again. How could he do this to her? How could he have put her—them—in this position? She couldn't go through it again, she couldn't.

"You love me. When your anger cools you will see that this is for the best."

She wanted to hurt him, as he'd hurt her. "Are you so sure of that? I've survived a broken heart before; what makes you think I can't do it again?"

His eyes flashed. He grabbed her arm and pulled her close to him. "This is different, and you know it. This isn't some girlish fantasy; this is real."

She sagged against him, not bothering to struggle. If he wanted a fight, he wasn't going to get it from her. "Is that right? Nothing feels very real to me right now. It all feels like a lie."

He released her, dragging his hand through his hair, clearly trying to cool his temper. "Let's go downstairs. We can talk about this—"

"Do you honestly think I intend to share a bed with you? I can't bear to look at you right now." She gave him a hard look. "I want you to leave."

"Mary . . ."

He reached for her, but she shrugged away. The tears at

last caught up with her, choking her voice. "God, can you not even give me this? Or do you intend to throw me over your shoulder and carry me out of here right now?"

If she weren't so angry, the turmoil of the emotions crossing his face might have softened her heart. "The day after tomorrow," he said. "As soon as Sir Adam leaves."

She stared at him in horror. "So you gave me two days to decide."

"I gave you two days to prepare."

She stared at him mutely, understanding. He wasn't giving her a choice. He'd stuck the last blade through her heart. "It seems you've decided everything, then."

"It's not like that." He reached for her, but she flinched from his touch. The look of hurt in his eyes was mildly satisfying. She wanted him to feel as bleak and horrible as she did now. If he could only know an ounce of the pain he'd just inflicted on her. "I love you, Mary."

"Don't! Don't you dare say that to me! If you loved me, you wouldn't have done this to me."

He dropped his gaze, looking away from the challenge in her eyes. "Very well, I'll go. I need to be back at the castle by morning as it is." He took her chin and forced her gaze to his. "I know you are angry and scared, but we have our whole lives for me to make it up to you. I'm asking you to have faith in me, Mary."

She turned away coldly, the sting of betrayal still reverberating through her. He asked for more than she could give.

It was still a few hours before dawn when Kenneth arrived outside the walls of Berwick Castle. With the gate closed for the night, he dismounted and found a rock to sit on while he waited.

It had been worse than he expected. He'd known Mary would be upset, but the look of betrayal in her eyes had cut him to the quick. She'd looked shattered. Disillusioned.

Hurt. She'd looked at him as if she didn't know him. As if he'd let her down beyond repair.

But that wasn't possible. He wouldn't allow himself to consider the possibility that she wouldn't forgive him. She was hurt now, but she'd come around eventually.

Wouldn't she?

A knot of uncertainty lodged in his chest. What if she didn't? What if he'd wounded her so deeply and shattered her illusions so thoroughly that he'd lost her love forever?

Jesus. His stomach turned, and he felt the sudden urge to retch.

Nay, he couldn't let himself think like that. She would forgive him. Once she had time to think, she would see that he'd had no choice. That he'd done the best he could under the circumstances.

He only hoped she thought quickly. He didn't know what the hell he was going to do if he showed up to take her away and she refused to go. Recalling her taunt, he didn't relish the idea of abducting his own wife.

What a bloody mess.

Knowing there was nothing he could do about it for now, he exchanged his rock for a tree to lean back on, closed his eyes, and tried to sneak in a few hours of sleep.

But given the events of the night, the cold morning mist, and the general discomfort of using a tree for a bed, it was a fitful sleep—which proved fortunate. About an hour before dawn, when the blackness of the evening sky had just started to soften to gray, he heard the faint sounds of grinding metal.

Jolted fully awake, he peered through the cold, shadowy mist to the castle, where the metal portcullis was being raised. It was the sounds of the chain being winched and the gate sliding through the grooves that he'd heard.

He came immediately to attention, thinking it odd that the gate was being opened so early. Peering through the mist, he watched as a team of a half-dozen men rode out.

He recognized the "Chequy Or and Azure, a Fess Gules" of Clifford's arms. That pricked his senses immediately. English knights much preferred to travel in large war parties. Where was Clifford going so early in the morning without a score of men to protect him?

It had all the vestiges of a secret or clandestine mission.

Every instinct urged to follow them. But Percy was expecting him. How would he explain his absence?

He debated for all of ten seconds. He would think of a way. This was just the opportunity he'd been awaiting.

"*Let us worry about Clifford.*" He pushed aside MacKay's voice. Kenneth's mission might be to stay close to Percy, but part of his skill was his versatility. Adapting. Fitting in where they needed him. And every instinct clamored that this was important.

Mounting his horse, he set off after them. He might not be as ghostlike as Campbell or MacRuairi, or as good a tracker as Lamont, but for second best he was damned good.

"Are you sure there is nothing wrong, my dear? You look a little pale."

Mary gazed over her bowl of stew to the concerned visage of her old friend. Everything was wrong. She'd given her heart to a man only to have him betray her in the worst way possible. He was a traitor. A rebel. She wanted to sink her face into her hands and weep. But she'd already done that for most of the night, and it hadn't helped.

She forced a wan smile to her face. "I did not sleep very well." It was the truth, albeit only a small portion of what was making her such poor company for the midday meal.

Sir Adam gave her a wry smile. "I remember the last month or two was always the most difficult for my wife. She often slept poorly. Are you very uncomfortable?"

"It's not so bad yet."

He studied her, as if he suspected there was more.

"Perhaps I should have told you I was bringing David. I wanted to surprise you, but I should have realized—"

"Nay!" she protested. "It is a wonderful surprise. I've missed him terribly since I left the castle. I'm just fortunate that Huntlywood is so close. I can't thank you enough for allowing us to stay here."

He waved off her thanks. "It pleases me to know someone will be livening up these old stone walls while I'm away."

A dark shadow crossed over her. Would she be here? What choice did she have? Despite her brave words, she didn't know if she could weather another storm of being declared the wife of a traitor. She felt a stab of anger, hating her husband for putting her in this position—not only of having her choices taken from her, but also of having to deceive a man who'd never been anything but wonderful to her. "I will miss you."

Something in her voice must have betrayed her. A furrow appeared between her brows; he studied her carefully before he replied. "It will not be for long. Besides, I think you will be so well occupied, you will not know I'm gone."

They spoke for a few minutes on other subjects before Sir Adam asked, "Where is Sutherland? I expected to find him here."

Mary hoped she hadn't flinched at the mention of her husband. She fought to keep her expression neutral. "He returned to the castle last night."

Sir Adam frowned. "That's strange. I did not see him this morning. Percy was looking for him. He was supposed to attend him this morning for some meetings with Cornwall."

Her heart, which had come to a standstill after last night, flickered to life. It started to beat rapidly. *There is no reason to be concerned.*

"It was late when he left. Perhaps he overslept?" Realizing how that sounded, she hastened to explain. "He was helping me clean out the garret. I found an old trunk of your father's."

Sir Adam stiffened almost imperceptibly, but she noticed.

"I'd forgotten that was up there. It's been many years since I looked through it."

"He kept the most wonderful journals." Heat rose to her cheeks. "I hope you don't mind that I took a peek inside?"

"Of course not." He returned his attention to his food, making an effort to appear unconcerned. But it was an effort, she realized. "And your husband, did he admire the journals as well?"

She recalled the intensity with which she'd observed Kenneth poring over the journals. She'd been so surprised to see him, she hadn't thought about it at the time. "I believe so, although we did not speak of it." She paused. "Perhaps . . . Would you mind if I showed Davey? I think he would find some of the pictures interesting."

"Not at all. And then when you are finished, I will move that old trunk out of your way."

A short while later, Mary was in the garret chamber with her son. As she'd suspected, Davey had enjoyed looking over the drawings of the exotic locales. But she had another reason for bringing him up here. She'd been delaying telling him about the baby, not sure how he would react. Given the date of her marriage and the impending arrival of his brother or sister, she didn't want him to think badly of her.

Without any furniture to sit on, she closed the lid of the trunk and invited him to take a seat beside her. "There is something I should like to tell you, and I hope you will be as excited about it as I am," she said.

The handsome youth on the cusp of manhood looked at her oddly. "About the baby?"

Her mouth dropped open. "How did you know?"

"Sir Kenneth told me some time ago. He thought I was upset by the suddenness of your wedding."

Kenneth's perception took her aback. "And were you upset?"

He shrugged.

She bit her lip. How had she not realized? It must have been confusing for him. "I'm sorry, I should have told you."

She raked his face with her eyes, trying to penetrate the enigmatic mask. More than anything, she would have liked to see some real emotion on her son's face. Even anger would have been preferable to bland acceptance. It seemed to be the way he reacted to everything.

God, what had the years of imprisonment done to him?

"I am glad to see you happy, Mother. Sir Kenneth is a fine knight."

"Are *you* happy, David?"

He considered the question as if he'd never thought of it before. "I make do."

His answer took her aback. Her son was more like her than she'd realized. But it sounded different coming from him. Was "making do" enough for her son?

Was it enough for her? Didn't they both deserve more?

"I know it has been difficult for you since your father was killed."

His mouth tightened, and his eyes flashed with surprising venom. "You mean executed for treason. My father was a traitor who suffered the punishment he deserved. His dishonor has nothing to do with me."

She'd wanted emotion, but not like this. Mary hoped her horror didn't show. "Your father fought for what he believed in, Davey. He wasn't a traitor to his people. To your people."

It was strange to defend Atholl after so many years. But no matter what he'd done to her—to them—he had been a great patriot. She wanted Davey to see that. Time and her marriage to Kenneth had erased some of the bitterness and given her perspective.

He sniffed his nose as if at something unpleasant. The so thoroughly English mannerism took her aback even further. "My people are under the influence of a usurper. Once Bruce is defeated, they will see the truth."

Kenneth had been right, at least in this. There was nothing Scottish in her son. My God, how she'd failed him! She'd made a vow to fight for his heritage, fight for his patrimony, but she'd ignored the most important part: his identity. He was a Scot. His father had been executed fighting for Scottish independence, and Davey was "Dear cousin Davey" to the men who'd done so.

Suddenly, Kenneth's question last night came back to her. What would she have done, had she been asked? Listening to her son, she knew the answer. She would have stood behind Bruce. She'd believed in Robert as much as Atholl had. That belief was buried under years of fear and making do, but it was still there. Atholl should have protected them better, he should have given her a say in her future, but she could not fault him for his allegiance to Bruce.

"My sister was married to that 'usurper,' David. Robert is a great man—one of the greatest knights in Christendom," she added, knowing what was likely to impress him. "I should like you to meet him. I think you would like him."

"I will meet him. Across a battlefield."

"He would like to have you back in Scotland."

He frowned. "How do you know this?"

"He told me when I was there."

"I will be. When we win."

Mary knew she had to tread carefully. But it was his life at stake; he deserved some say in it. "You aren't English, you know that, don't you, Davey? You are a Scottish earl. You belong in Scotland. Wouldn't you like to go home? To see the lands of your ancestors?"

He looked at her as if she'd just uttered treason, which perhaps she had. "Why are you saying this, Mother?"

She paused, debating how much to tell him. In the end, she decided she'd said enough. Why was she pressing her son for an answer, when she didn't even know her own?

She smiled. "Don't pay me any mind. I'm in a maudlin mood."

He stared at her for a long moment and nodded. Standing, he walked over to the window. "That's strange."

"What?"

"Sir John is approaching with at least two dozen men."

Mary's heart dropped. *It's probably nothing*, she told herself. But every instinct told her otherwise.

Twenty-five

Kenneth followed Clifford's party for hours. He'd expected them to take the road southwest along the border to Jedburgh, but instead they took a path due west toward the town of Biggar, skirting the dangerous Selkirk Forest, which was controlled by Bruce's men under the command of Sir James Douglas.

Where the hell were they going? Continuing on this road up the Clydesdale would take them to Bothwell Castle, just south of Glasgow. He stilled. Bothwell Castle, where the English garrison could easily be supplied by Clifford's border castles of Carlisle and Caerlaverock.

His senses hummed. He was on to something; he knew it. What if the reason there didn't seem to be enough supplies going north to Edinburgh was because that wasn't the path they were going to take? What if *this* was the path? What if Bothwell, Rutherglen, and Renfrew were the English-held castles that would keep the English army supplied and protected on their Scottish campaign?

It felt right, but how was he going to prove it? All he had was his gut to go on.

But Clifford wasn't accommodating enough to hand him conclusive proof today. When the small party turned around near midday to return to the castle, Kenneth followed. The ride to seemingly nowhere only served to further convince him that it had been a scouting mission in advance of the army.

But he needed proof, damn it. Was it too much to ask for a nice, colorfully drawn map to fall into his hands? If only spying were that easy.

It was nearing dusk by the time Clifford's party rode through the gate of Berwick Castle. Kenneth waited a short while before following.

He was expecting to have to do some explaining for his absence, but as he neared the gate, he wondered if it was going to take a lot more than that.

He heard the call go up when the men who were keeping watch from the battlements above sighted him. Was it his imagination, or had the air suddenly become more charged? Were the men at the gate nervous? They seemed to purposefully not meet his gaze, and more than one hand was gripping the hilt of a sword. He was beginning to get a bad feeling—a very bad feeling—about this.

Had Mary betrayed him? For one horrible moment, he wondered. But he quickly pushed the thought aside. She wouldn't. No matter how angry, he refused to believe she'd condemn him to the same fate as Atholl.

But it was clear something was wrong. The moment he rode through the gate, he could feel the men moving into position behind him.

He swore. Catching sight of Percy coming down the stairs of the Great Hall, he knew from the cold fury on the knight's face that he was in trouble. Whether it was his unexplained absence, Felton giving him up for illegal fighting, or something else, he wasn't going to stay and find out.

His time in the English camp was over, and he liked his chances of getting out now with only a handful of men behind him better than he did from a pit prison.

He could be completely wrong, but if he'd learned anything in this long war, it was that when in doubt, trust your senses. Sometimes they were the only things that kept you alive.

He didn't hesitate. Swinging his mount around, he plunged through the men who'd come around to block his exit. The sudden move caught them by surprise, but one man managed to get his sword up in time to take a good swing at him. Kenneth yanked the sword from the scabbard at his back and managed to save his leg—and more importantly, his horse—from the soldier's blade.

With a fierce cry, he landed another blow at one of the men guarding the portcullis to his right. Reacting quickly, he fended off a blow from the man at his left. He could hear the shouts behind him to lower the gate, to not let him escape, but it was too late. Lowering his head to the neck of his mount, he tore out the gate. He tried not to think about the arrows that were going to start raining on him from above—

He flinched as an arrow found its mark right in his back. But he felt more the impact than pain, and suspected it had only found the steel of his mail. A second arrow grazed his arm as he started to weave, the quick changes of direction making it harder for them to hold a target.

An arrow hit the flank of his horse, but it, too, found armor. The heavily armored warhorses the English favored might not be as maneuverable and quick as the smaller mounts used by the Scots, but at times they had their advantages.

He focused on his destination—the tree line about a hundred yards ahead—and rode as fast as his already tired horse could carry him. He knew he should be out of arrow range soon. The shots didn't seem to be falling as often or as close. Gritting his teeth he held on, praying that his fortune held out for a few more minutes . . .

It did. He plunged through the trees and heaved a sigh of relief. He'd made it. But he wasn't safe yet. They would be hunting him.

His mouth fell in a grim line. This sure as hell wasn't the exit he had planned from England. His mission had just exploded in his face. He'd lost his chance to find proof for his suspicions, and worse, extracting Mary had just become much more dangerous. Her son would have to wait.

But he didn't have time to dwell on his failure. All he could think of was Mary. A cold chill permeated his blood. They would come for her, too. He had to reach her first.

Instead of taking the road to Huntlywood, he steered his mount on the more direct route through the treacherous terrain of the countryside. He needed all the extra time he could make. The English might guess where he was headed, but he had no intention of being there when they arrived.

Mary had thought there could be no worse moment than learning that her husband had deceived her, that he was actually aligned with Bruce and intended to take her back to Scotland.

But that wasn't the worst moment at all. The worst moment was seeing the ill-concealed smugness on Sir John's face when he announced that a warrant had been issued for Kenneth's arrest.

She'd nearly fainted and might have fallen to the ground had Sir Adam not caught her.

"You'd better have a damned good explanation for this, Felton," Sir Adam demanded, after seeing her safely to a bench.

Mary listened in horror as Sir John explained. The purported charge was for illegal fighting, but Kenneth was also suspected of treason. According to Sir John, Kenneth had failed a test of his loyalty when he'd delivered a missive with a cracked seal. His desertion today only made his situation worse. Where was he?

Mary smothered a sob. The thought of her husband imprisoned and possibly executed . . .

Her stomach knifed. Every fiber of her being recoiled in absolute horror.

But once the shock faded, Mary knew Sir John had brought a clarity of mind that she might not have reached so quickly on her own. When faced with her husband's arrest, the truth in her heart could not be denied. She was furious at him for deceiving her, but she still loved him.

"Find him," Sir John ordered his men.

"I already told you he isn't here," Sir Adam said, his normally even temperament giving way to icy fury. "Are you questioning my word?"

Sir John smiled. "I just don't want there to be any confusion. You have known Sutherland and his wife for many years, haven't you?"

Sir Adam's face turned florid. "Have care, Felton. Think carefully before you impugn my loyalty. When you are proved wrong, it will go badly for you. I will make sure of it."

Felton was instantly contrite. Sir Adam was a powerful man, one of the most influential Scots on the English side, and making an enemy of him could prove costly. "I meant no offense. I was ordered to return the Earl of Atholl to the castle immediately, and to search for Sutherland. I am merely following orders."

"Then be quick about it," Sir Adam bit out. "And then get the hell out of here."

While Sir John oversaw the search, Sir Adam tried to comfort Mary.

"Try not to upset yourself," he said. "I'm sure it will all be cleared up soon."

Mary nodded unconvincingly, knowing better.

"Is there truth to the charge of illegal fighting? Felton said you were there."

She nodded again. "I'm afraid so."

"The king will be displeased, but if Kenneth has a good explanation, it shouldn't be too difficult to dismiss. It's the other charges that worry me. Is it possible . . . could there be truth to what Felton says? Is there any chance Sutherland is deceiving us?"

Mary was torn. She wanted to protect her husband, but she couldn't bear the thought of lying to her old friend. She dropped her gaze. "Anything is possible."

What Sir Adam made of her nonanswer she didn't know. Out of the corner of her eye she noticed Felton talking to Davey on the other side of the Hall, and something about the way Davey's eyes kept shifting toward her made her take notice.

Following the direction of her gaze, Sir Adam asked, "Could David know something?"

Mary thought back through their previous conversation. Could her son have pieced something together about leaving from what she'd said? "I don't think so."

But her hands twisted in her lap, seeing the guilty flush spread over David's face, when their eyes met for an instant, before he quickly looked away.

David wouldn't betray her. Her heart squeezed. Would he? Whatever filial devotion he had to her was new and unproven. Could he say something to make it look bad for Kenneth?

She should never have spoken to him of his father and Bruce. The decision whether to return to Scotland was too complex for a boy of thirteen.

For a time, it seemed her fears might have been for nothing. Davey ran off, presumably to gather his belongings, and Sir John returned to overseeing his men. But a short while later, when the search had come to an end, Sir John strode toward her with a look on his face that did not bode well.

His gaze was harder and colder than it had ever been before. "Gather your things. We will be returning to the castle soon."

Mary blanched.

"What are you talking about, Felton?" Sir Adam said. "Lady Mary is staying here."

Sir John shot him a glare. "Not anymore. It seems Lady Mary has been contemplating a return to Scotland."

Sir Adam didn't look to her for confirmation or denial. "And what proof do you have of this?"

"She's been having some interesting conversations with her son."

Mary's heart squeezed. *Oh Davey, what have you done?*

"I said nothing about leaving for Scotland," she said.

It was true. But Sir John appeared unmoved. "Under the circumstances, I think it is better to exercise an abundance of caution, don't you agree, Sir Adam? For her safety, of course."

"Are you arresting me?"

"Not if I don't have to." But his men had gathered around him. She could feel Sir Adam's men behind her. They would defend her if she asked them to. But what purpose would it serve, other than to put Sir Adam in an even worse position if the truth were discovered?

At that moment Davey burst into the room. Looking back and forth between the two groups of soldiers, he quickly appraised the situation.

"What are you doing?" he asked Sir John, betrayal stark on every inch of his handsome young features.

"Your mother will be coming with us, isn't that right, Lady Mary?"

"But I didn't mean . . . You aren't supposed to . . . "

Mary looked at her son's pale, horror-stricken face and knew he'd misjudged the effect his words to Sir John would have. He hadn't intended to harm her.

She put her hand on his arm, telling him silently that it was all right. "I will go and gather my things."

Sir Adam started to argue, but she stopped him. "Please. I don't want there to be any trouble." She put her hand on her stomach meaningfully. Anything could happen if violence broke out. "We will straighten this out at Berwick."

Kenneth would do something. She had to trust him. But the idea of entering one of the most heavily defended castles in the Borders took every ounce of her faith.

Sir Adam held her eyes and nodded.

"I will leave some of my men, just in case Sutherland attempts to return here," Sir John said.

They understood his meaning: if Sir Adam thought to warn Kenneth, he wasn't going to be able to do so.

But wherever he was, Mary knew Kenneth would find a way to get them out of this. He would not leave her to face danger alone. She only wished it hadn't taken this to make her realize it.

Despite the urge to race through the gate to reach Mary, Kenneth forced himself to watch the appropriately named Huntlywood Castle from the safety of the surrounding forest. His atypical caution was rewarded when he saw the increased guard at the gate. Closer inspection of the arms identified at least one of the men as Felton's.

Damn. He knew Felton couldn't have beat him here from Berwick, so he must have already been here—which meant Kenneth had just lost whatever advantage he'd had in time.

He thought quickly. Not knowing what awaited him inside, he would have to sneak his way past the guard. He decided to employ one of the Highland Guard's favorite tactics: diversion and speed.

After removing anything he might need from the bags tied to his saddle, he gave the trusty steed a fond stroke on his muzzle and thanked him for his faithful service. Even though he knew the stallion was spent and would be of no further help to him tonight, it was with much regret that he gave him a smack on the flank and urged him to the castle.

The horse shot off through the trees, heading for the gate. Kenneth circled around to the opposite side of the castle on foot, waiting for the cry to go up when the horse was sighted before making his move.

He had just reached his position when he heard, "Rider approaching."

He hoped it would cause just long enough of a distraction for him to climb over the palisade wall. He was more than a little grateful for all the times MacLeod had forced him to lift himself up from a dead hang. Still, without a good grip and laden down with weapons and mail, it wasn't easy to propel himself over in one smooth—and silent—move. He was just fortunate that Sir Adam had yet to build the much higher stone wall that he had planned.

He'd chosen a place in the wall opposite the gate, in a dark corner between the stables and armory. Slipping into the shadows, he drew his sword and waited to see whether anyone had noticed him.

But his ruse had worked. He could still hear the commotion at the gate where the riderless horse had arrived. As he slid around the armory, he could tell that something indeed was wrong. There were too many people around. Too many soldiers. He counted at least a half-dozen of Felton's men. But interestingly, they weren't interacting with Sir Adam's men. Indeed, it seemed as if the two groups were eyeing one another suspiciously.

With his fear for his wife intensifying, he didn't hesitate a minute longer. As soon as he had an opening he took it, crossing the yard and climbing the stairs to the tower.

Once inside, he took a quick scan of the Hall. Noting Mary's absence, he headed up the stairwell in front of him. His heart pounded as he raced up the two flights. It was almost as if he sensed even before he opened the door that she wasn't there. Still, he felt a hard jarring in his chest when only dark silence greeted him.

Where the hell was she?

Perhaps the babe's room?

Holding out hope, he raced up the next flight of stairs, opened the door, and felt an even harder jarring than the first when he found only emptiness.

His heart was pounding even faster now, panic slipping in.

She had to be here. He would find her if he had to tear apart every inch of this castle—Felton's men or not. The entire English army wouldn't be enough to keep him from her.

But it would be easier with help. Those pottery jars he'd seen earlier in the trunk would work, but the trunk was gone. Which left Sir Adam. The older knight cared for Mary; Kenneth just hoped he was right about how much.

Retracing his steps down the stairs, Kenneth stopped at the level below Mary's room. Not bothering to announce himself, he pushed open the door.

Sir Adam stood by the small window staring out into the yard below. Glancing over his shoulder toward the door, his gaze met Kenneth's. "I wondered how long it would take you to arrive. The horse was a clever distraction."

Kenneth strode into the room. "Where is she?"

"Felton took her a short while ago."

Kenneth's heart dropped. "Took her? Where?"

"To Berwick Castle." Sir Adam's eyes narrowed. "He came here looking for you. He has a warrant for your arrest."

Kenneth swore.

"Aren't you going to ask the charges?"

"Do they matter?"

Sir Adam shook his head. "I suppose not."

Kenneth tried to steel himself against the disappointment he saw in the other man's eyes, but it didn't work. Betrayal was never easy, and this one was particularly difficult. He hoped one day they would meet again as true allies.

"How long ago did they leave?" he asked.

"Not long. Twenty, maybe thirty minutes."

"Then I still have time to catch them."

"What makes you think I won't have you arrested right now?"

Kenneth stilled, eyeing the other man carefully. "Because I know you love her and want her to be happy."

"And you think you can make her happy?"

"I know I can." He paused. "I also don't think you are as opposed to Bruce as it appears."

The other man bristled. "My fealty is to King John."

"Balliol is deposed and living in France. You know he will never be accepted again as king."

Sir Adam didn't argue.

"I suspect that is why you have not told the English of your knowledge of the Saracen powder."

The older knight stiffened. Kenneth could see he was going to deny it and cut him off. "I know about the explosion on the bridge when Mary lost her sister. It was you, wasn't it?"

Sir Adam paled. "My nephew shared our family secret, it seems. I suspected as much. It was an accident. Does she know?"

Kenneth shook his head. "Not yet."

"But you will tell her."

"Aye. But you can make it up to her. I need your help."

Sir Adam considered him for a long moment. Kenneth could see the warring going on inside him between the fealty he owed his deposed king and the love he had for Mary. Eventually, his shoulders sagged, as if the battle had proved too much. "Tell me what you need."

The ride to the castle could be done in as little as an hour, but due to Mary's condition and the darkness, the journey was progressing at a much slower pace.

She could claim to be slowing them down purposefully,

but she was genuinely uncomfortable. Her back had started to hurt, and she felt an occasional cramp.

Despite his anger toward her, Sir John was a chivalrous knight, and when quietly reminded of her condition, he slowed the pace considerably.

Her heart jumped at every little sound. She scanned the darkness, half expecting her husband to jump out of the blackness like some avenging apparition. She knew it was silly to think he could take on nearly twenty English soldiers by himself, but part of her knew he would try if he could. The other part feared he would do exactly that.

Where was he?

A short while later, she had her answer. They were a couple of miles from the castle when they neared the bridge over the Tweed.

Riding near the back of the procession, at first all she heard was a shout, followed immediately by a burst of action in the men around her. Sir John shouted orders, and a dozen of his men circled around her and David. "What is it?" she asked. "What's happening?"

No one answered. She managed to catch a glimpse through the line of mailed soldiers in front of her of a solitary torchlight about twenty yards ahead. A man stood holding it. She didn't need to see the yellow shield with three red stars to recognize her husband.

Her pulse jumped and a soft cry tore from her throat. Tears sprang to her eyes. She didn't know whether it was happiness at seeing him alive or fear that he might not be so much longer. It was Kenneth. But what was he doing?

"Release my wife," his voice rang out clear and strong, cracking the darkness like a whip.

Sir John moved forward a few feet to address him. "You are in no position to be giving orders. You are under arrest."

"Very well, but Lady Mary has nothing to do with this.

My men are on the other side of this bridge. Let her go, and I will put down my sword and come to you."

Sir John laughed. "Why would I do that?"

She could almost hear her husband's shrug. "Would you prefer to try to catch me?" He paused. Mary was sure they were both thinking about the last time they'd done battle. "Look," Kenneth continued. "Your fight is not with Mary. I know you do not wish to see her hurt. Let my men take her, and you will have what you want: me. This could be over quickly—you decide. But don't take too long; my men are growing restless."

And just like that, a smattering of torches appeared out of the darkness on the other side of the bridge.

If Sir John thought Kenneth was bluffing about support, he quickly reconsidered. "Fine. Throw down your weapons and surrender."

"I have your word as a knight that you will let her go?"

Sir John stiffened. "You do."

"I'll put down my weapons and walk to that tree. Just in case you are tempted to reconsider before she is across the bridge."

"Very well," Sir John spit out, obviously irritated by the slight at his honor.

She heard a few thumps of weapons being tossed to the ground, and then after a few minutes, Sir John motioned for her to come forward. "Go," he said.

Mary turned to David. They both knew Sir John would never let him go. "I'm sorry, Mother."

"I am, too." Not knowing how long it would be before she saw him again, she leaned over and threw her arms around him. "Don't forget what I told you," she whispered.

Drawing back, she saw him nod. The venomous glance he cast in Sir John's direction told her that her son's admiration of the English knight had taken a beating from which it might not recover. Perhaps, Sir John had done them a favor by taking her. His actions might help sway her son when the time came.

Maneuvering her horse through the wall of English soldiers, she passed by Sir John without a glance. Catching sight of Kenneth, their eyes met for the first time. Her heart lurched. She had to fight the urge to run to him. "Go," he said. "Don't worry about me. I'll be fine."

Their eyes held. He seemed to be asking her to trust him. She did. But she dearly hoped his plan included more than surrendering himself for her.

Nodding, she gave him one long last look and steered her horse toward the bridge. The sound of hooves clopping over the wooden planks brought back memories of the last time she'd tried to flee England.

Her heart squeezed. *Please let this turn out differently.*

She was surprised to be surrounded not by Kenneth's men, but by Sir Adam's.

"Come," Sir Adam said. "We don't have much time."

"Wait," Mary said. "We can't just leave him. Where are we going?"

"To the coast. Don't worry. He will catch up with us."

It took every ounce of her faith in him to force herself to agree. "Thank you," she said. "Thank you for helping us."

Her old friend nodded. "I hope this time turns out better than the last."

So did she.

They took off at a much faster pace, her discomfort temporarily pushed aside. The bridge was not yet out of view behind them when Mary heard a sound that shook her to her core: a loud boom, followed by a crack of lightning. The memories came back to her. It was just like before, except this time there was no storm to explain the strange sounds.

She glanced around behind her and cried out when she saw a burst of flames in the distance. The bridge was burning. "Wait! We have to go back. We have to help him."

Sir Adam reached over to grab her reins, preventing her from doing just that.

"That won't be necessary."

She stilled at the sound of the disembodied voice coming from the darkness ahead of them. She looked to Sir Adam, but he seemed just as confused as she did. The half-dozen men he'd brought with him fanned out around her.

She kept her gaze fixed in the direction of the voice. A few moments later, one of the most terrifying-looking warriors she'd ever seen stepped into a beam of moonlight. She shivered, instantly recoiling in fear.

Good God, he was even more heavily muscled than her husband! Four additional impressively tall and muscular warriors came out behind him. All wore blackened nasal helms, black war coats, and oddly fashioned plaids around their shoulders. Even their skin appeared to be darkened with something. They seemed to blend into the night like phantoms. *Bruce's phantoms!* she realized. Could these men be the phantom warriors who'd struck terror in the hearts of the English?

She was so scared, it took her a moment to recognize the smile beneath the helm. "My lady," he said with a bow. "We meet again."

His face half hidden beneath a ghastly looking steel nasal helm, Mary found herself staring into the eyes of the fearsome warrior Robert had introduced her to last summer: Magnus MacKay, Kenneth's brother by marriage.

Twenty-six

Sir Adam's torches were still visible when Felton spoke. "She's gone. Now you will surrender."

"I said I would come to you, and I shall," Kenneth responded. He hadn't said anything about surrendering. If Felton wanted him, he was going to have to take him.

But first, Kenneth was going to ensure Felton didn't change his mind and go after Mary.

Holding the torch in front of him so they could see him, Kenneth walked toward Felton. He stopped about ten feet away, making sure he was between Felton's men and the bridge. He glanced down, seeing the thin line of black powder between his feet—unnoticeable, unless you were looking for it.

He sure as hell hoped this worked. He wouldn't have long once he lit the fuse, so to speak.

"Toss down the torch," Felton ordered.

Kenneth did as he ordered, making sure the torch was close enough to his feet to maneuver toward the powder when he was ready.

"Seize him," Felton ordered the two men closest to him. Kenneth let them approach, then grab him from either side. "You five," he pointed to a group of men at his right, "go after the lady."

David gasped behind him. "But you gave your word to let her go."

Felton's gaze turned to the young earl's. "This man is under arrest; he is in no position to bargain."

Fortunately, Kenneth had expected Felton's breach, even if young Atholl had not. With a roar, he attempted to break free of his captors, lifting and wrenching his arms at the same time that he kicked the torch across the line of powder.

It didn't catch.

"Hold him!" Felton yelled. "Quick, get something to secure him with."

A few more men rushed forward to do his bidding.

Kenneth knew he was going to have to improvise. He needed to get that powder lit, but the two men holding him were strong and proving surprisingly capable. With his arms secured, he had to use his feet—and quickly, before the other men were able to restrain him with the chains.

He used the heel of his boot to kick one of the men's legs, and then immediately moved that foot behind the weakened leg to knock him completely off balance. The soldier went down, dragging Kenneth and the other soldier along with him. Taking advantage of their surprise, he wrenched his arms free before he hit the ground. His gauntleted fists wouldn't do much lasting injury to the mail-clad soldiers, but a few well-placed blows and kicks kept them out of his way for now.

He needed his sword. But first he reached for the torch, still near his feet, and set the flame directly to the line of powder. This time, it took.

A ball of bright yellowish-orange fire and billowing smoke started to race toward the bridge. He tried to follow it, but Felton's men anticipated him.

There were enough of them to slow him down, especially since he was unarmed. He dodged more than one deadly swing of a sword.

He wasn't able to reach his sword before the night exploded—or more accurately, the half-dozen bags of Sir

Adam's black powder that Kenneth had packed under the bridge exploded. The blast of the fire pushed them all back.

His plan had worked exactly as he'd hoped, except for one thing: he was supposed to be on the other side of the bridge. The powder had exploded too quickly.

Bloody hell, he couldn't have actually expected this to be easy!

It appeared he was going to have to fight his way out. Him against . . . he counted eighteen men. Unfortunately, his sword was now out of reach, engulfed in smoke. A problem he was able to rectify when one of Sir John's men came rushing toward him, sword high above his head. Kenneth kept his eye on the blade, waiting until the man was fully committed, before spinning out of the way at the last minute. The momentum of the soldier's blow swung him around and Kenneth took advantage of his unprotected side, pummeling him in the lower back, kicking his feet out from under him, and then stomping on the wrist that held the sword to free it.

Armed and better able to defend himself, he took position near the burning bridge and let Sir John's men come. At first, it was one at a time, but with one after another of the men ending up at his feet, they increased their numbers, sending two, three, and then four at once against him. Yet with smoke and fire at his back, they could not circle around him.

Kenneth fought like a man possessed. His sole focus was ridding himself of these men, getting on the other side of the river, and catching his wife before she sailed away without him.

He was well on his way to joining her. There were only a half-dozen men remaining, not including Felton and young David.

Felton was furious. Kenneth could hear him screaming at his men, ordering them to keep attacking, to take him, to kill him.

Felton must have saved his best men for last. The six came at him at once—as a unit. Kenneth tried to fight them off, but they were pushing him back. He was getting closer and closer to the edge of the river. He picked up a pike from one of the men who'd fallen at his feet, using it to keep the men far enough back. They weren't attacking, they were pressing. He waited for a hole, but they weren't giving him one.

Damn it. He swore, knowing he had to think of something fast. It was like a wall of steel coming toward him, and he had nowhere to go. He needed to break their formation. Choosing the second man from the left, he threw the pike at his head with enough force to knock him back. He feigned in the opposite direction, giving the attackers an irresistible opening. One took it. The moment he did, Kenneth reacted. He swung his sword in a deadly arc, cutting the man off at the knee—literally. With a big enough hole to slide through, Kenneth was able to maneuver out of trouble.

Suddenly, he heard the sound of clapping behind him. In the flickering glow of the fire he could make out three familiar forms watching from the opposite side of the riverbank: MacKay, Lamont, and MacLean. The thirty-foot span might be a barrier to most men, but Kenneth knew it would be nothing to stop the Highland Guard. In fact, he'd just caught site of his means of escape a few feet away. One of the men—probably Lamont, who was good with a bow—had shot a rope tied to the end of an arrow over a tree.

"Well done," he heard MacKay say with a laugh.

Kenneth swore, not seeing the humor. "I could use a little help!" he shouted over his shoulder while trying to fend off the four remaining soldiers.

"You seem to be doing fine on your own."

Proving MacKay's point, Kenneth cut down one of the

remaining men, who'd been foolish enough to make a move toward him.

There were still three soldiers left, but the one man Kenneth had eyes for was hanging back. "What's wrong, Felton? You wanted a chance to face me—here it is."

Felton hesitated, spitting every vile name and slur at him. But his hand was fixed firmly around the Earl of Atholl's wrist. He'd lost Mary, and Kenneth, too, but losing Atholl would make his shame unbearable. "Come, David," he said, backing away.

But David surprised them both. "Let go of me!" he shouted, jerking his arm away and scooting back a few feet. The lad looked back and forth between Kenneth and Felton, not looking as if he trusted either of them.

Felton lunged toward him, but that only sent the youth scurrying closer to Kenneth. Cognizant of the opportunity, his Highland Guard brethren had finally decided to intervene, shooting a few arrows toward the remaining soldiers to drive them back. Kenneth glanced at the rope a few feet away. He sure as hell hoped it was strong enough for two.

He held his hand out to David. "Now, lad. It's time to decide."

"Nay, David. I command you to stay. You are an English subject."

David's eyes narrowed on Felton. "But I'm a Scottish earl."

He ran toward Kenneth.

Felton raced after him. Kenneth would have liked nothing more than to put a decisive end to his battle with Felton, but with David's decision he couldn't take the chance. He had to protect the lad and get him to safety as soon as possible.

He reached for David and grabbed hold of him around the waist. Saying a prayer, he closed the distance to the rope, cut it from the arrow pinned in the ground, dropped his sword to grab the end, and held on tight as he swung David and himself over the wide span of river. As soon as he saw ground beneath his feet he let go. MacKay quickly cut the rope from the tree he'd secured it around.

Kenneth had hit the ground first and rolled to absorb most of the impact, but as soon as he extracted them from the rope, he looked at David. "Are you all right?"

"I th-think so." But the boy was eyeing the three warriors warily. "Who are they?"

"Friends," Kenneth answered simply, helping the young earl to his feet. The secret of the Highland Guard was not something which the earl needed to be privy to. He addressed MacKay. "Mary?"

"Safe," his brother-in-law said. "Probably waiting for us at the boat."

Kenneth shot him a dark glare. "I might have been faster if you'd made yourself known earlier."

"And miss all the fun?" MacKay said. "Not a chance. We thought they almost had you there for a while. Six against one, and you backed into a corner." He shook his head. "It was a bold move to give the one an opening like that."

"It worked," Kenneth challenged.

MacKay grinned. "Aye, it did. I'll have to remember it."

Not wasting any more time, they mounted their horses and raced toward the coast. They had a ship to catch.

Mary experienced the first pains not long after Sir Adam left. He parted from her reluctantly. Magnus MacKay (cutting her off before she could identify him) informed Sir Adam that they'd been sent by Kenneth to protect her and would see her safely to Scotland. Sir Adam had done enough, he'd said. It would do no good for his part in their escape to become known.

Sweet heaven! Bruce's phantoms! Her husband had sent Scotland's most famous band of warriors to protect her? She didn't know how he managed to do such a thing, but it did soften the sting of his deception somewhat. It was a bit awe-inspiring to realize she had the most elite group of soldiers in Scotland looking after her. But how was Kenneth connected to them?

Sir Adam seemed to realize who they were as well. Yet it was only after Mary assured him that she knew one of the men that he agreed to let her go.

But before he left, Sir Adam strode over to Magnus. "You knew my nephew. He was part of this . . . secret army."

Magnus appeared startled. "I did."

"He died well?"

Magnus clenched his jaw. "He did," he said solemnly. "Your nephew was one of the best men I've ever known."

The two men held gazes for a long time. Finally, Sir Adam nodded, seemingly satisfied. He removed something from his pocket and slid it into Mary's hands. "See that your husband gets this."

Mary frowned, puzzled, staring at the folded piece of parchment. "I will."

Her old friend seemed troubled, as if he were searching for the right words. "When he tells you . . . I hope one day you will forgive me. I was only trying to do what I thought best."

Her frown deepened, not understanding. He'd done so much for her. But there was no time to question him. Magnus sent Sir Adam on his way, ordered her to go with two men he called Hawk and Viper, and took the two other men he called Hunter and Striker with him to find Kenneth.

They'd been riding for a few minutes when the first pain struck with rather alarming intensity. She pulled up on the reins of her horse so sharply that she nearly fell off.

The marginally less terrifying of the two—the one who smiled—swore and managed to get her horse back under control. "What's wrong?"

Mary put her hand over her stomach. "I don't know." But she did know. "I think I might be . . . that is, I think the babe—"

It was too early. The baby wasn't due for at least another month.

The one Magnus had called Viper swore. "Bloody hell, don't tell me you're having the baby right now?"

If she wasn't wracked by another painful cramp, she might have laughed at the terrified expressions on the faces of the two men who themselves looked as if they were the bogeymen of children's nightmares.

"Not right now," she hedged.

"But the pains have started?" the man they called Hawk asked in a far gentler voice.

She nodded.

The man called Viper swore. He looked at the other man. "You take her. You've done it more than I have. I don't think I can handle it again."

"I thought you could handle anything, cousin. You actually sound scared."

"And you're not?"

Hawk grimaced. "Point taken. Damn, I wish Angel was here."

Mary was trying to prevent herself from crying out, but a small sound must have escaped.

The two men swore in unison, although the one called Viper used a far more vile word. She found herself lifted from her saddle and put in front of the man who used to be smiling—he wasn't smiling anymore.

She could feel the tension emanating from him in the seemingly interminable ride to the eastern seaboard, though it couldn't have been more than a few miles. Every time a pain wracked her—the pains were erratic, but seemed to be about twenty minutes apart—she could feel the anxiety building in him.

"Just hold on, lass," he said, trying to soothe her.

But the two men were clearly out of their element and their tension and anxiety increased her own. She wanted her husband. Where was he?

She must have spoken her question aloud.

"He'll be here soon, lass," Hawk said, leaving off the "I hope" that she heard unsaid.

One hard contraction later they reached the ship, which the men had hidden in a cove, somewhere north of Berwick. There were a dozen additional men waiting for them aboard the *birlinn*, the type of ship favored by the West Highlander seafarers. She shivered seeing the terrifying-looking hawk carved into the prow, which was all too reminiscent of their ancestor Viking longships.

At least she knew how one of the men had earned his name. She didn't think she wanted to know the other. "Viper" had all kinds of ominous connotations that seemed to fit the menacing-looking warrior. The captain—Hawk—helped her into the boat, trying to make her as comfortable as possible. She could see the wide-eyed look of fear spread over the crew as her situation became known, which didn't relax her any. Mary was scared and in considerable pain, but she did her best to hide it from the others, seeing their helplessness.

She tried to take long, deep breaths, thinking it would calm her. It didn't, but at least it kept her mind focused on something other than the prolonged absence of her husband. She could feel the men getting restless. Obviously, sitting in wait a few miles from three thousand English soldiers was making them uneasy.

Surely, Kenneth should be here by now? Her party had been forced to travel at a much slower pace; he should have caught up. What if he hadn't been able to get away? What if they'd taken him to the pit prison in Berwick Castle? How would three men—even Bruce's phantoms—be able to get him out?

She smothered a cry, holding her stomach in her hands and curling up in a ball as another pain struck.

"Count," one of the sailors said from beside her. He was a heavily bearded man with the rough, craggy face of someone who'd spent many years on a boat. "My wife has had ten babes, and she says it helps to count aloud. If you know how long they'll last it helps to bear the pain."

Mary wasn't sure about that, but at least it would give her something to do. She counted to twenty before the contraction started to release. "Men approaching, Captain!" someone shouted.

It seemed as if an enormous, silent cheer went up. Apparently, the men were eager to relinquish their responsibility: her. From her place in the curve of the hull, it wasn't easy to sit up, so she was forced to wait for him to find her.

"Where is she?"

The men cleared a path, and she caught her first glimpse of him. He was filthy, covered in dirt and blood, his face streaked with soot, dark hair matted with sweat from his helm, but he'd never looked more magnificent. She wanted to throw her arms around him and bury her head against his chest like a bairn. She tried to sit up, but felt a pinch that made her wince and sink back against the comfortable hull.

Kenneth swore, his furious gaze shooting to Hawk. "What's wrong with her? Is she hurt?"

"Nothing—"

Not waiting for the rest of Hawk's answer, Kenneth jumped from bench to bench (or more accurately, wooden trunk to wooden trunk), closing the distance between them. Mary sobbed with relief, finding herself enfolded in her husband's strong embrace.

It was going to be all right. He was here. She was safe. She wasn't going to have to do this alone. She let go of some of the fear she'd been holding, knowing he would take it for her.

"What's wrong?" he soothed gently. "Where are you hurt?"

"I'm not—"

"Mother?"

Mary pulled back in shock. She gazed to the rear of the boat, where her son had just boarded beside Magnus MacKay. "Davey?" she whispered.

Her heart swelled with joy.

She looked to Kenneth. "How?"

He smiled tenderly. "I will tell you everything later, but first tell me—"

He stopped when she cried out in pain again. Holding her stomach, she started to count. This time she counted to thirty.

Vaguely, she was aware of her frantic husband beside her. "What's wrong with her, damn it? Why is she counting? Do something to help her!"

Mary didn't know to whom he shouted the last order, but it was Magnus MacKay who responded.

"Congratulations, Recruit."

Kenneth answered, "What the hell are you talking about?"

"You're about to become a father."

Kenneth's gaze shot to hers for confirmation. The pain had relaxed enough for her to nod.

His eyes widened for a fraction of an instant, and she saw the same fear and helplessness she'd seen in the other men's faces. But then his expression changed into one of steely determination. "Not yet, I'm not. This babe is going to be born in Dunstaffnage, with my sister's help."

No one dared argue with him.

"How fast can you take us home, Hawk?" he asked.

Mary's heart caught. Home. To Scotland. With her husband and her son. She'd never dared to dream of this.

"By tomorrow night. Maybe a little sooner if the winds are with us."

"Tomorrow night!" she exclaimed. She couldn't do this for a whole day. How long had it taken with Davey? Nearly that long, she realized glumly. It wasn't something she liked to remember. "What if the baby comes before that?"

"He won't," Kenneth said with such conviction, she almost believed him.

He sat beside her and pulled her back against his chest into the protective circle of his arms, settling in for the long battle ahead. He held her like that for hours. Her volatile, hot-tempered, passionate husband had become her anchor in a stormy sea. He smoothed her hair, mopped her brow with a cool cloth, whispered gentle words of love in her ear, and helped her count as the contractions became more frequent, more intense, and longer. He calmed her with stories when the pain became too unbearable and she started to cry, telling him she couldn't do this any longer.

"Yes, you can," he said softly. "You can do this. You're strong. I have you."

His calm, steady voice kept the panic at bay. He told her of the life they would have together. The castle in the north of Scotland that he kept for his brother. The green of the grass, the white of the beaches, the impossible blue of the sea, the white foam of the waves crashing against the black rocks, the briny tang of the air. He told her of his family. Of the children they would have. He spoke of the quiet, peaceful years they would spend together.

It sounded like heaven. Even when she didn't think she could bear it a moment longer, those stories kept her going. She wanted to live that life with him.

Mary had almost forgotten about the other men on the ship until she heard a cry go out, "Castle ahead, Captain!"

The relief around her was almost palpable.

"You did it, love." The pains were only a minute apart, and another one hit. He held her, almost as if trying to absorb the pain for her. "Hold on just a little longer . . . "

But Mary couldn't hold back anything. She was too weak. She screamed as the pain took hold and the urge to push became overwhelming.

"He's coming," she gasped, her voice racked with panic.

Their eyes met. His steely determination, his absolute confidence, his unwavering certainty that everything was going to be all right eased her fear.

"Someone get me some light!" he shouted at one of the men. Day had turned to night again without her noticing. A torch was handed back, and he handed it to one of the men seated nearby. Most of the men had given her a wide berth. Though at the time she didn't care, she knew she would be glad later that her modesty was preserved when he moved her skirts up to see what was happening. She watched his face the entire time, but if he was concerned, he gave nothing away. "Hawk, you'd better make it quick."

Twenty-seven

❧

Kenneth had never been more scared in his life, seeing the top of his son's head between his wife's legs. But the brash confidence that had gotten him in trouble more than once proved a useful mask. The wife who calmed him needed him to calm her.

It had been the most harrowing twenty-four hours of his life. He felt as if he'd been chewed up by a great beast and spit out in ragged pieces. Every nerve ending in his body was raw and frayed. But this wasn't over yet. If he had to deliver his son on this damned boat, he would do it.

Fortunately, it didn't come to that. Hawk defied the laws of nature and sailed them into the small harbor in record time. Their ship had been sighted, and his sister was at the shore, waiting to greet them. Instead, she was rushed into service. As there wasn't time to move Mary, men were sent running for the things Helen would need.

A look of shock broke through the pain when Mary caught sight of Helen. "Your sister? The woman in the stables was your sister?"

Under the circumstances, the look of outrage on her face nearly made him laugh. "I told you it wasn't how it looked."

She glared at him until the next pain took hold. He held her hand, letting her squeeze his, her tiny nails digging into his skin as a spasm seemed to envelop her entire body.

He didn't know how she could bear it. He wanted to

shout out his frustration. To kill someone for doing this to her. To take her pain for himself. But he couldn't. So instead, he stayed by her side, calmly and soothingly trying to ease her suffering.

After all the hard work he'd endured during their long journey, it seemed unfair that Helen arrived in time for three long pushes and all the glory when a few moments later, the future Earl of Sutherland made his appearance. Tiny and wrinkled, the laddie nonetheless possessed a remarkable set of lungs, and his fierce wail had the makings of a formidable future battle cry.

Kenneth was so happy that both Mary and the child were all right that once he could pry his arms from his wife, he enfolded his sister in a fierce embrace. "Thank you."

A sheen of tears sparkled in her eyes as Helen hugged him back. "He's beautiful. But you look horrible. Let's get you all back to the castle."

He insisted on carrying Mary—who had fallen into an exhausted sleep—and Helen carried the babe as they walked up the beach and through the sea-gate of the royal castle of Dunstaffnage, Bruce's headquarters in the West Highlands. His fellow guardsman, Arthur Campbell, had been appointed keeper of the castle, and his wife, Anna, had already readied chambers for them.

He didn't remember much of the next twenty-four hours. Once he'd assured himself that Mary and his son were being well cared for, he'd collapsed in an adjoining chamber and slept most of the next day. He woke and would have gone to Mary, but his sister told him that she and the child were still sleeping. So he took a much needed bath, and recalling his duty, found his way down to the Hall to fill in the king on what he'd learned.

His mission hadn't been a complete failure. He'd returned the Earl of Atholl into the Scottish fold. But he'd wanted to give them more. "I'd hoped to find proof," he explained to the king about his theory of the route the

English planned to take. "But Felton used my illegal fighting to secure an arrest warrant. I had to leave."

"Aye, well, we'll talk about that, *Ice*." The king's mouth curved in a wry smile. "Although from what MacKay and the others say, you earned the name on that journey back. MacKay said it was the most nerve-wracking experience he could recall, but you were icy calm the entire time."

Kenneth's mouth twitched. "I did what the situation called for."

The king laughed. "You did indeed. That is what you are here for, is it not? Although not even I anticipated *that* much versatility. You did well, Sutherland. If you think there is something to this scouting foray of Clifford's, that's enough." Kenneth looked around the room filled with his fellow guardsmen, surprised to see the universal agreement in their expressions. They trusted his instincts—even without proof. "Once Edward marches from Berwick Castle, we'll have men ready all along this route. We'll hit him hard and fast, making sure his sojourn in Scotland is a short one."

They discussed the coming battle for a little while longer before Kenneth excused himself to check on Mary.

She was sitting up against the back of the bed, holding the baby, when he walked in. His sister was standing there, along with a few other women, but he didn't notice any of them. His eyes were only for his wife and son. His heart squeezed so tightly he couldn't breathe. He didn't think he'd ever seen anything more beautiful in his life.

But when he thought of what had happened to her, how she must blame him for putting her in danger, the squeezing knifed. Could she forgive him?

He crossed the room, feeling suddenly uncertain. In the turmoil of their escape and sea journey there hadn't been time for awkwardness and questions. Emotion had been stripped to the bone. Love, simple and unfettered by complication. But now, the hurt and pain hung in the air between them.

The babe was swaddled in a soft woolen blanket and tucked into her arm. "He looks so small," Kenneth said, overwhelmed.

"He is," Helen said. "But he's a fighter."

"Will he . . . " Kenneth's voice cracked; he couldn't even let himself say the words.

Helen smiled. "He seems a strong lad. He's breathing well, and already had a few meals while you slept the day away."

Kenneth scowled at his sister. "You should have woken me."

Helen laughed. "You needed your sleep. From what I hear from Magnus, you all had a long night. I don't think my husband has recovered yet. It will be some time before he wants to go through that again."

Kenneth wasn't looking forward to the battle of wills between his sister and MacKay when she became pregnant. Helen was enjoying her position in the Guard, and Kenneth didn't see her relinquishing it without a fight.

Mary watched the interplay between the siblings with a wistful expression on her face. He knew she was thinking of Janet. He was going to have a talk with Bruce about that very soon. If he knew anything about her sister, Kenneth intended to find out. Mary deserved an answer.

"How are you feeling?" he asked.

Their eyes held. "Much better." She held out the babe. "Would you like to hold him?"

Kenneth hoped the horror didn't show too plainly on his face. But when all the women in the chamber started to laugh, he knew it had.

Helen was still chuckling when she reached for the baby. "Here, I'll take him. You two will want some privacy. And once my brother gets over his irrational fear"—he didn't bother denying it—"I suspect I won't get a chance to hold him very often." Helen turned to him. "Have you decided on a name?"

Kenneth looked to Mary. "I thought William would be nice," she said. "In honor of your brother."

His chest swelled, touched by the gesture to a brother who would have no sons of his own. He could see that Helen was as well. He nodded, remembering another William, too.

Helen left the room, taking baby William and the other ladies with her.

Kenneth felt himself strangely at a loss for words. He sat down on the edge of her bed and took her hand in his. "I'm sorry, Mary. I'm sorry for getting you into this. I know you didn't want to come here—"

"But I did," she interrupted. "You were right. It was time to come home."

"I should have given you a choice."

"Aye," she agreed. "But I can see why you did not at first."

"I was scared of losing you," he said, trying to explain what kept him from telling her.

She nodded. "I can understand that, too. When I heard you were to be arrested—" She stopped, her face paling. "I knew nothing else mattered as long as you were safe. I was so scared that they'd taken you. What happened?"

He gave her a short explanation, piecing together what he knew as well as what Sir Adam had told him. "I knew that I had to reach you before they took you into the castle. It's not impenetrable, but it would have taken time and been much more dangerous to get you out."

"You convinced Sir Adam to help you?"

"It wasn't too difficult. He wanted to help."

"He said something strange before he left. He asked for my forgiveness."

Kenneth watched her eyes widen with surprise, and then fill with tears, as he told her the part Sir Adam had played in what had happened the last time she'd tried to escape.

"I don't believe it," she said. "He betrayed me?"

"He didn't think he was betraying you, he thought he was protecting you. The English were too close. He thought they'd catch up to you and you would be imprisoned. He made a deal with the English soldiers, giving them Lady Christina's men in exchange for the promise that you would be kept safe. But when the MacRuairis defeated the soldiers, everything went wrong. He tried to prevent you and your sister from being trampled on the bridge by destroying it, but then your servant fell and your sister ended up where she shouldn't have been. He blamed himself for what happened to her, even though he couldn't have known she would turn back."

Mary appeared stunned. "No wonder he became upset every time I asked him to help me find her." Her brows drew together. "That sound at the bridge last night—the boom and crack of lightning—it was just like that night with my sister. What was it?"

"Black powder. My foster brother William Gordon, Sir Adam's nephew, had knowledge of it as well. As do I, although not at the level of theirs. I was looking for the recipe in those journals when you found me in the baby's room. I didn't find anything, but I suspected after what you told me about that night that Sir Adam had similar knowledge. I knew that it would help our chances of getting away, and he agreed to give me what I needed to see you free." He smiled. "I wish I'd been able to carry more of it; it would come in handy the next few months."

Suddenly, Mary seemed to recall something. "If you'll hand me my bag, I think you will find that won't be necessary."

Puzzled, he handed it to her. She pulled out a folded piece of parchment and gave it to him. He scanned the page, his eyes widening when he saw the recipe he'd been searching for. "He gave this to you?"

She nodded. "To give to you."

He shook his head in amazement. Without realizing it, his wife had just handed him a place in the Guard.

Nay, he realized. He'd done that on his own—even without the powder. He'd brought Mary and Atholl back to Scotland. He'd uncovered key information about the castles for the upcoming war. Not to mention single-handedly defeating nearly a score of English soldiers. He'd proved himself more than equal to the task. He'd proved himself one of the best.

He'd achieved what he wanted—more than he wanted—so why wasn't he happy?

Because looking at his wife, he knew that none of it mattered if he didn't have her by his side. Kenneth had been fighting his whole life, but winning her was the only fight that counted.

He took her small hand in his, looking deep into her big, blue eyes. "Can you forgive me, Mary? I know I hurt you. I should have told you sooner, but I was scared to lose you. I love you. Just give me a chance to prove it."

Mary had never seen him like this. The cocky, too-handsome-for-his-own-good knight looked worried and unsure of himself. Didn't he know he'd proved himself many times over in the past few days? Not just during the long, horrible hours on the ship where he'd gotten her through some of the most difficult and terrifying hours of her life, but by giving himself up for her, seeing her and her son to safety, coming for her, protecting her.

She shook her head. "No."

His face fell. "No, you won't give me a chance?"

Her mouth curved at his crestfallen expression. "No, you don't need to prove yourself to me. I believe you. I believe *in* you. How can I not, after what we just went through? There is no other man I would have by my side."

His entire body seemed to relax. "Do you mean that?"

She nodded. Mary knew she could face the challenges

ahead of her on her own, but she didn't want to do that. She wanted to face them with someone else. She wanted to share her life with him.

Her mouth twitched. "But I will hold you to your vow to discuss your plans with me. If you are involved in anything dangerous in the future, please let me know."

She'd meant it as a jest, but his face shadowed. "Aye, well, about that."

She sat up a little higher in the bed. "Don't tell me there's something else?"

He winced. "I took a vow of silence before I met you."

She frowned, her nose wrinkling. "Does this have something to do with Bruce's phantoms?"

He looked at her in surprise. "How did you guess?"

She stared at him. Could he really not know? "You mean besides the fact that they are supposed to have virtually inhuman strength and skill, and I've seen you fight? There's also the fact that you are all uncommonly tall and built like siege engines. But most important, I saw you with them. Even in pain, I could see that you were one of them."

He looked stunned. "You could?"

It was obvious, apparently except to him. She nodded. "I must admit I was surprised to see that you are so close to your brother-in-law, given your clan history."

"MacKay?" He shook his head. "We hate each other."

She arched a brow. Men were so blind sometimes. "You act like brothers to me."

He frowned, as if he'd never considered it. She refrained from laughing and rolling her eyes. "Why did he call you Recruit?"

"That's what I am. I've been trying to win a place on the team since I met you last summer at Dunstaffnage."

He told her why the loss that day had meant so much to him. "I let my temper get to me," he explained, "and MacKay took advantage of it. Instead of winning a place outright on the team, I've been fighting ever since to earn my place."

Mary felt a pang, understanding probably more than he intended. It was always like that for him. Having to fight his way on. Having to prove himself. That was why winning was so important to him. "And have you?"

"Yes, I think I finally have."

"I'm happy for you."

He tipped her chin. "It's what I thought I always wanted. But it isn't. You and our son are the most important things in the world to me. I know what you've been through. I won't put you through this, if you don't think you can handle it. I won't lie to you—being part of the Guard is extremely dangerous. Not just for me. You could be in danger if my part in it is ever discovered. If you don't want to be a part of it, I'll understand."

"What are you saying?"

"I'll tell Bruce I can't do it, if you want me to. There are other ways I can fight for him."

Mary was stunned. She knew how much this meant to him. After a lifetime of proving himself, he'd finally done so, earning his way into the most vaunted team of warriors in Christendom, and now he would walk away from it for her? "You would do that for me?"

"I would do anything for you."

Her heart swelled until she thought it would burst. Tears glistened in her eyes. He would never know what that offer had meant to her. Just as she knew she could never ask it of him. "I don't know, I think I should like being married to a real-life hero." She smiled. "Besides, I don't think you want to see your brother-in-law get all the glory, do you?"

A wide grin spread across his face. "Hell no! He's bloody unbearable as it is."

"Then you must keep him in his place."

He reached down and cupped her face in his warm hand. "I love you."

The look of tenderness in his eyes brought a fresh lump of emotion to her throat. Tears filled her eyes. "And I love you."

He kissed her. Gently. Reverently. A soft brush of the lips that sent her heart slamming against her ribs. Too soon, he lifted his head and smiled. "I should let you get some rest."

She shook her head. "Don't go. I'm not tired." She'd just gotten him back; she didn't want him to leave again.

He seemed to understand. "Scoot over."

He moved onto the bed beside her, leaning against the headboard, so that she could snuggle against him. She sighed with contentment, resting her cheek against his steel-hard chest and feeling the protective strength of his big arms wrapped around her.

Warm and content, happier than she thought possible, she fell asleep. And for the first time in a long time, she let herself dream. For dreams did come true. She would never make do again.

Epilogue

Late summer 1310
Skelbo Castle, Sutherland, Scotland

Mary kissed her son on his downy-soft head and handed him to his nurse. He protested with a tiny whinge, but then settled into the woman's arms contentedly. "Good night, sweeting," she said, as the old woman took him away for his nap.

Her sister-in-law turned from her place by the window overlooking the yard. "I doubt he shall get any sleep with that racket going on down there."

Mary sighed. "Who's winning this time?"

Helen squinted into the bright sunshine. "I think your husband."

"What does that make it?"

Helen shrugged. "I lost count. Maybe five to five?"

"When do you think they'll stop?" Helen looked at her, and Mary laughed. "All right, you're right. They won't stop." She shook her head. "You would think they would have had enough fighting the past couple of months."

"Ah, but that is easy," Helen said with a grin. "That's against the English. This is fighting to prove who's the best Highlander."

Mary came to join her by the window. "I think you better fetch your bag, Angel. It looks like you have a few bruises and cuts to tend."

Helen's mouth pursed. "I don't know why I bother; they'll just do it all over again tomorrow."

If they were here tomorrow. Mary knew that her husband's brief, three-day respite from war could be over at any time. Edward had marched on Scotland nearly two months ago, and Bruce and the Highland Guard had been ready. Kenneth's instincts had proved correct. Edinburgh Castle had been an attempted diversion by the English. The troops had followed the same path Clifford and his men had taken that fateful scouting trip. Thanks to her husband, Bruce's men were waiting for them. The English had been hit hard and often on his progress north. Edward was currently taking shelter at Renfrew Castle southwest of Glasgow, but Bruce hoped to have the demoralized English king back in Berwick soon, licking his wounds.

Mary followed Helen out of the Hall, down the stairs, and into the courtyard. The two men were sitting on over-turned wooden crates, arguing. From the looks of them, it was hard to tell who won. They were both bruised, scraped, and looked like they'd been rolling in mud—which they had.

Helen didn't say anything. She just stomped up to her husband, put her hands on her hips, and glared at him until he dropped his head. "Aw, Helen, don't look at me like that. He had it coming."

"He always does. And did you prove anything?"

"Aye, that his neck looks good under my sword," Kenneth interjected gamely.

His sister shot him a look. "I'll deal with you later. Come," she said to Magnus, with a long-suffering sigh. "Let me see what I can do with that eye."

Mary shook her head and folded her arms, looking down at her gloating husband. "Well, Ice, what do you have to say for yourself?" She used the war name given to him by the Highland Guard when he and Helen had been given a ceremony a few months ago. "I thought the sword would be enough. But it seems this contest will never be over."

Since Kenneth had lost his sword saving her, Bruce had gifted him with a new one. On it was inscribed *Par omnibus operibus, secundum ad neminem.* Equal to every task, second to none.

"It was his fault."

"It always is. When are you two going to admit that you don't hate each other?"

He gave her that provoking smile that tended to make her knees weak. "Now why would we do that? He's the best sparring partner I have."

He'd also become his real partner in the Highland Guard. Hell indeed had frozen over.

Mary gave up. Her stubborn brother-in-law and hot-tempered husband would just have to figure it out on their own. She hoped without killing each other in the process.

Kenneth picked her up and spun her around. "Put me down." She wrinkled her nose, trying to swat his hands away. "You're filthy."

He kissed her anyway. Deeply and passionately in the bright sunshine until her heart was pounding, her breath was quickening, and her knees were turned to jelly.

His eyes were hot as they met hers. "Where's William?"

"With his nurse, taking a nap."

His grin deepened. "Sounds like an excellent idea."

She blushed. Helen had finally given her approval to resume her marital "duty," and Kenneth seemed intent on making up for lost time—not that she minded. "It seems you have been propositioning me for improper naps since the first time I met you."

Their eyes locked, remembering their first conversation at the Highland Games. "It was the best proposition I ever made," he said softly. "But I should have tossed you over my shoulder that day and carried you up the stairs. It would have been a lot easier."

She met his gaze, all the love in her heart shining in her eyes. "But not half as rewarding. What's victory without the battle?"

He laughed and shook his head. "Spoken like a true fighter."

"I learned from the best." And she had.

AUTHOR'S NOTE

As with the other books in this series, many of the characters in *The Recruit* are loosely based on historical figures, including the hero and heroine. Some time after 1307, Kenneth de Moravia, the younger brother of William, Earl of Sutherland, married Mary of Mar, the widow of John Strathbogie, Earl of Atholl (who made a brief appearance in *The Viper*).

Most historians believe it is the same Mary who married both Atholl and Sutherland, but there seems to be a possibility that they were two different women. She is alternatively referred to as Mary, Marjory, and Margaret. Moreover, the genealogical charts are all over the place on her date of birth. Some are highly implausible, i.e. having her well over forty when she married Kenneth, who was probably in his early twenties at the time—which, given that they had at least three children together, seems a stretch for medieval procreation. Most sources have Mary as the daughter of Donald, Earl of Mar, but others have her as the daughter of Gartnait (his son). I decided to go with the conventional wisdom of her being the same person, but adjusted her age to fit my story. The possibility of more than one Mary did, however, give me the idea for a fictional twin sister, "Janet."

If there is one thing I've learned in researching this series, it's that intermarriage between noble families seems to have made everyone related. I'm exaggerating, but not by much. The connections are numerous and at times extremely convoluted.

Case in point: Mary of Mar. Mary's sister Isabel was Robert the Bruce's first wife and the mother of his daughter Marjory, who at the time of this story is his heir and imprisoned in England with his second queen, Elizabeth, and Mary's nephew Donald, the current Earl of Mar. But Mary's brother Gartnait was also married to Bruce's sister, Christina (who later would marry Christopher Seton, Alex "Dragon" Seton's brother). Another of Mary's brothers (Duncan?) seems to have been the first husband of Christina of the Isles, the half-sister of Lachlan "Viper" MacRuairi.

Got all that straight? Those are just the connections I mentioned. I didn't mention that Mary's mother was Helen, daughter of Llewelyn the Great, Prince of Wales, and Joan, King John of England's natural daughter. In other words, Mary's maternal great-grandfather was King John of England, which makes her second cousins with Edward I of England and gives her more connections than I could possibly name. But that isn't all. Mary's paternal grandmother was Elizabeth Comyn of Buchan (the Comyns, of course, being Bruce's archenemies); thus her father's first cousin was John Buchan, Earl of Buchan (Bella MacDuff's first husband from *The Viper*). I can't imagine trying to put together a family tree of all this!

Kenneth became the fourth Earl of Sutherland on his brother's death in 1330. Kenneth and Mary's son William, who is born at the end of this book, later became the fifth Earl. Their second son, Nicholas, married a le Cheyne heiress, and was the progenitor of the Sutherland lairds of Duffus. They also had a daughter Eustachia and possibly another daughter.

Significantly, their son William married Margaret, the daughter of Robert the Bruce and his second wife, Elizabeth de Burgh, making Mary and Bruce in-laws three times over! For a brief time William and Margaret's son John (Kenneth and Mary's grandson) was named the royal heir, but unfortunately he died of the black plague in his teens.

As Bruce had only four children to reach adulthood (only three of whom were alive at the time of this marriage), the royal alliance certainly shows that the Sutherlands—who had fought with the Comyns and the English until 1308–09—had firmly established themselves in the Bruce fold. To my authorial mind, it also could show Kenneth's importance to Bruce and/or his fondness for Mary.

As is unfortunately common for most women of the era, information on Mary's whereabouts and what happened to her in the days after Atholl's execution did not seem to make it onto the historical record. The timing and circumstances of her marriage to Kenneth, therefore, were left up to my fictional imagination.

Much more, however, is known about her son. David Strathbogie, like his young cousin, Donald, Earl of Mar, was an English prisoner in his youth and spent time in the royal household of the Prince of Wales (later Edward II). David and Donald would be loyal to Edward of England for most of their lives.

So how do two Scottish earls end up loyal to an English king? The opponents in the Scottish Wars of Independence seem simple: the Scots versus the English. But of course, the reality is much more complex. One of the hardest things for me to wrap my head around was just how much the Bruce kingship divided the nation—this is the feuding that is glossed over in *Braveheart* and better explains Robert the Bruce's unheroic actions in that movie. The war was between the Scots and the English, yes, but it was also between the Scots loyal to Bruce and those loyal to the deposed King John Balliol (Comyn faction).

Men who had fought together against the English in the

early part of the war (like Atholl and Sir Adam Gordon) would take opposite sides when Bruce claimed the throne. Thus, you will see some of the early "patriots," who fought alongside Wallace, later fighting with the English. The old proverb "The enemy of my enemy is my friend" really holds here. There was a significant core of Scottish nobles who chose to fight with the English rather than join Bruce, even after it was clear he was making inroads (1307–08).

To my mind, as I allude to in the book, part of Bruce's greatness as a king was that he did not immediately disinherit many of these men, instead making a concerted effort to win over his detractors and unify his kingdom (with the notable exception of the Comyns and MacDougalls, his blood enemies who could never be forgiven). The Sutherlands and the Earl of Ross are good examples of this. The Earl of Ross was responsible for the imprisonment of Bruce's queen, his sister, and his daughter, but Bruce forgave him two years later and married one of his sisters to Ross's heir. Interestingly, one of the conditions for Ross to come over to Bruce was that he had to pay for mass to be said at St. Duthacs in memory of Atholl.

Some would take longer to be persuaded (such as Sir Adam Gordon), but others would never come over to Bruce's side. After Bannockburn, Bruce lost patience. The holdouts had their land and titles dispossessed and would become known as the "Disinherited."

David Strathbogie, Earl of Atholl (like his cousin Donald, Earl of Mar), was one of these Disinherited. Conveniently for my story, however, David does "switch" sides and come over to Bruce about this time (around 1311–12). He was part of the English truce party with Lamberton in 1311–12, which gave me the inspiration for Mary's role.

Alas, David's allegiance to Bruce was brief. He was back with the English by Bannockburn in 1314, and this time it was for good. The supposed reason for his defection?

Allegedly his sister Isabel (Mary and Atholl actually had two, possibly three, children) was seduced by Edward Bruce (Robert's only remaining brother) and he refused to marry her.

At the time of the novel, David was probably about twenty. Interestingly, he was also married to Joan Comyn, the daughter of The Red Comyn, whom Bruce killed in 1306. Their son David was born in early 1309 and baptized at St. Nicholas Church in Newcastle-upon-Tyne. Thus, I chose to put Mary in the area at the time, although Ponteland Castle doesn't come to the Earl of Atholl until slightly later.

So how does David Strathbogie, the son of a great Bruce patriot, end up married to a Comyn? I suppose it could have been arranged by King Edward to ally David with Bruce's enemy, but there is another explanation that goes back to my earlier point about former friends. Atholl (David's father) and The Red Comyn fought together at Dunbar for the patriot cause and were imprisoned in the Tower of London. Perhaps the betrothal was arranged when they were on the same side? Interestingly, when David temporarily switched sides, he left his Comyn wife behind in England. One can only imagine what that reunion was like.

As you can imagine, figuring out the possible motivations for why someone would have allied with Bruce or Comyn (and the English), given all these interrelations, can be a puzzle of its own. But there is another consequence of all these intermarriages that I really didn't "get" at first, which also complicated the decision for many of Scottish nobles. We think of Scotsmen or Englishmen as either/or. But the practical effect of all these marriages was a class of nobles who had significant land interests on *both* sides of the border.

Mary's first husband, John Strathbogie, Earl of Atholl, is an example of this, but it was also true for many others (including Robert the Bruce himself). John's mother was English, and in addition to his Scottish lands, he had holdings in Kent, England. Thus, choosing to fight for Bruce wasn't a simple patriotic decision. He was a Scottish earl, but he was also an English landholder (possibly a baron), and by rebelling he put his English holdings in jeopardy.

As I mention in the book, Atholl was captured with the ladies' party in Tain (1306), imprisoned, and executed— the first earl executed in more than two hundred years. He did attempt to sway Edward by reminding him of their familial relationship, but Edward's response was to simply hang him on a higher gallows as befitting his exalted status. Ah, that witty Plantagenet sense of humor. Atholl's head was placed on a stake beside that of Wallace and Simon Fraser. He was certainly a hero, but his profligacy is my invention.

Sir Adam Gordon is another example of the Scottish nobles who were put in a difficult position by the Bruce kingship. In the early years of the war, Sir Adam was considered a great patriot, fighting alongside Comyn and Atholl at Dunbar in 1296 (where his father fell). He seems to have escaped the capture and imprisonment that befell most of the other nobles, but was forced to surrender to Edward not long after the battle. Later, he fought alongside Wallace at Stirling Bridge (1297) and at Falkirk (1298).

His reasons for allying himself with the English until the relatively late date of 1313–14 are almost a checklist of the above tensions: his mother was English, he was loyal to the deposed King John Balliol (enemy of Bruce), and his lands were in the troublesome borders close to England. It wasn't until after King John died (1313) that Gordon came over to Bruce.

Ironically, King Robert granted Gordon the lands in Strathbogie and titles of the now dispossessed Earl of Atholl (David, Mary's son). Readers of *Highland Scoundrel* from my Campbell trilogy might recall these castles in the north. But the original Strathbogie and Huntly(wood) castles were located in the Borders.

Sir Adam also served as surety for the release of William Lamberton, Bishop of St. Andrews. Lamberton was part of the peace envoy sent to Scotland in 1309–10 and was given leave to stay there for a few months. Why Edward would allow Lamberton, who was thought to be one of the instigators behind Bruce's bid for the crown, to roam about Scotland is a mystery to me. One theory is that Edward trusted him because of the bishop's close relationship with Pembroke (Aymer de Valence).

This isn't the first time I've used the Highland Games in the series. Although there is a (apocryphal?) story on the origin of the Games from the time of Malcolm III (eleventh century), I would assume they weren't called that or organized to the extent I portrayed them. I decided to make them closer to tournaments—Highland style, of course—with the focus on sport and military prowess. Similarly, Highland "backhold" wrestling is thought to be very old, dating possibly from the sixth century. But for my Highland Games, I made the event more hand-to-hand combat than wrestling.

The Pits of Hell, the clandestine tourney in which Kenneth participates, is my invention (inspired by the TV show *Spartacus*). However, the 1292 Statute of Arms for Tournaments, promulgated by Edward I to regulate tourneys, suggests that it might not be that farfetched. There was a revived popularity of tournaments under Edward I, but they died out under Edward III. The last one was held in England in 1342.

I anticipated Henry Lord Percy's purchase of Alnwick Castle (better known today as the Harry Potter castle) by a few months. It was actually purchased on November 19, 1309 from the Bishop of Durham for what is said to be a comparatively small sum. Today, Alnwick is the second largest inhabited castle in England and has been home to the Percys for over seven hundred years. Those of you who follow Princess Kate's sister, Pippa, might recall her "friendship" with George Percy, one of Baron Percy's descendants. It was also home to the Harry "Hotspur" (reference to his hot temper) Percy made famous by Shakespeare.

Marriage in medieval Scotland and England is a very complex subject, which I've had to address many times in my novels. Clandestine marriages (those without banns and/or official ceremony) seem to have been common, but the church clearly didn't like them and sought to prohibit them. There were the inevitable problems of proof (he said/she said), but they also wanted to prevent secret marriages because they were concerned with consanguinity. Ironically, I did a paper in law school on the subject (I wish I could find it!). Basically, persons within a third degree were prohibited from marrying. If you've followed the family connections above, you can see how easily that could happen.

But note that even if the clandestine marriage was found to be "illegal," it was not necessarily invalid. Special licenses appear sometime in the fourteenth century, but I decided to use a dispensation. In the course of my research, I was surprised to discover that a widow was not permitted to have the mass inside the church after the vows were exchanged at the church door.

And finally, I adjusted the time of Edward's invasion by a couple of months. The English actually marched from Berwick in August/September 1310, and were back at Berwick by November. Bruce apparently had advance warning of the invasion, and the path taken by the English troops was the one that Kenneth "discovered."